DIRTY DESIRES

CRYSTAL KASWELL

Copyright

This is a work of fiction. Similarities to real people, places, or events are entirely coincidental.

Also by Crystal Kaswell

Dirty Rich

Dirty Deal - Blake

Dirty Boss - Nick

Dirty Husband - Shep

Dirty Desires - Ian

Sinful Serenade

Sing Your Heart Out - Miles

Strum Your Heart Out - Drew

Rock Your Heart Out - Tom

Play Your Heart Out - Pete

Sinful Ever After – series sequel

Just a Taste - Miles's POV

Dangerous Noise

Dangerous Kiss - Ethan

Dangerous Crush – Kit

Dangerous Rock – Joel

Dangerous Fling – Mal

Dangerous Encore - series sequel

Inked Hearts

Tempting - Brendon

Sign up for the Crystal Kaswell mailing list

About This Book

He'll do anything to have her...

Eve Miller is out of options. Between rent, and her sister's medical debts, she's drowning. She needs money, now, and she only has one card left to play.

Her virginity.

Ian Hunt has specific tastes. The feisty student is perfect. He has to have her.

His offer is simple. Six figures. Thirty days. Him introducing her to every kind of pleasure.

It's ridiculous. The British businessman is richer than sin and hotter than hell. He can have any woman he wants. Why her?

And why is she desperate to fulfill his every desire? There's something about his dark eyes, his deep voice, his firm touch… her body knows something she doesn't. It responds for her.

Yes. One month as his. Then they part.

But what happens when he decides he hasn't had enough?

Chapter One

EVE

"**I**s it really true?" A man with grey hair leans across the bar. Lowers his voice to a stage whisper. "Are you really a virgin?"

I press my lips together. No need to smile. As the owner put it, I'm not here for my charming personality. I'm here because the club is light on girls with a "punk bitch" aesthetic. "What was that? Appletini?" I pretend as if I can't hear the man. "Or was it chocolate martini?"

He looks me up and down. "You."

Is there a drink that sounds like *you?* Something bright pink. With a raunchy name. The kind of drink college girls order on spring break. I don't have a problem with grown men ordering a *blow job* but this guy—

No, that's only going to give him ideas.

Forget it. "Is the well vodka okay?"

He reaches for my hand. Wraps his greedy fingers around my wrist. "Eve, isn't it?"

"The apple martini—"

"Sure. Give me the best you've got."

I guess that answers that question. Is inappropriate

question guy embarrassed by a bright green drink? No. He wants the best. The very best vodka. The very best apple liqueur. The very best… shit, what else is in this drink?

The owner didn't hire me for my expertise. He hired me because a) I begged, b) a friend from high school vouched for me, and c) I could start work on my eighteenth birthday.

I guess there's also d) a lack of girls with teal hair and tattoos. I am the only "punk bitch" who works at Devil's Point.

It's a dive and the customers are assholes, but the tips are good. Besides, there's something satisfying about mixing drinks, learning formulas, perfecting recipes.

After six months, I know cocktails pretty well. But this is the first Appletini.

I improvise. Vodka, apple liqueur, lemon.

I shake the drink with ice, strain it into a martini glass, slide it across the bar.

To his credit, Drunk McHandsy offers his credit card without provocation.

I file the card. There's no space for Drunk McHandsy, but it's Tuesday evening. Quiet. Except for the bachelor party by the stage, the club is empty. I need to make this guy feel important if I want to go home with enough tip money to cover rent. "What did you say you do?"

"A doctor. I know the female anatomy well." He winks. Takes a long sip of his apple martini. "Shit, this is good." He turns to the stage for a moment. Watches a lean blond dancer undo the buttons of her blouse one at a time.

Yes, this isn't *just* a dive bar. It's a strip club. That's the other reason why the owner hired me. He was sure I'd "get dollar signs in my eyes as soon as I saw what the dancers were pulling in."

I understand his point.

Between rent, tuition, and Addie's medical expenses, I need money.

On a good night, I go home with a few hundred dollars.

On a good night, the woman working the stage—she goes by Britney—goes home with a few thousand.

Only she has to touch all these strange men. She has to let them touch her.

I see the way men reach for dancers. They think twenty dollars buys them carte blanche.

"Is that why you don't dance?" Drunk McHandsy turns to me with wide eyes. "Because you've never been with a man?"

"I like making drinks." I strain the extra liquor into a martini glass.

"Are you saving yourself for a good man?"

"Why? Do you know one?"

His laugh echoes around the room. "So it is true?"

"That I need a good man?" Let's face it, I need a man like I need another bill to pay. Eighteen years full of disappointing men. My father, my bosses, even the senior year English teacher who refused to let me pick Margaret Atwood for my final project.

"That you're a virgin?"

There's no way I'm getting out of this question with a good tip. Either I lie and say no. Claim an interest in women (if only). Or I tell him the truth.

Well, some of it.

"I am." I finish the green drink. Let it warm my cheeks and throat. Let it sweeten the music and soften the air.

"Really?"

"Really."

"You just..." He glances at Britney as the song shifts to *Hit Me Baby, One More Time*. Dancers work a three-song set.

Clothed, topless, nude. This is number three. Of course, she interprets nude in her way. The panties come off. The schoolgirl skirt stays on.

The frat bros celebrating a friend's wedding go wild.

It's an apt choice. Britney. Apparently, her virginity was *the* gossip of the day. Everyone was obsessed with the pop star maintaining her innocence.

This male obsession with virginity… I don't get it. Yes, I'm a virgin. Yes, I like men. Yes, I've had boyfriends. Two. In high school.

Yes, we did all the normal things.

We kissed, held hands, watched movies. Boyfriend number two even got to second base. His hands were too cold. His touch was too blunt. But I still enjoyed it. I still wanted more.

There was something stopping me. Fear. Nerves. An inability to trust him with my body. I'm not sure. I lost my chance.

Dad left and life got way too complicated for boyfriends.

"You don't look like a virgin." He studies my teal hair. My thick eyeliner. My black mini-dress. "You look like… a sex kitten."

Gross.

"Like you know how to please a strong man."

Even more gross. I reach for the drink, but it's empty. For the best. I need to stay focused. So I make rent. "It's the makeup."

Addie says I look like a punk rock princess.

I prefer to think of my attire as a shield. The eyeliner says *I don't give a fuck what you think.* The dark lipstick says *leave me alone.* The combat boots say *I will kick you in the head if you fuck with me.*

That's probably why this guy is asking. He can't see my

4

combat boots. He doesn't know I'm at the end of my rope. He doesn't know I'm completely out of patience.

He leans back to finish his Appletini. Then he sets the glass on the bar. Motions for another.

It's hard to keep a poker face with him watching me, but I manage.

There. I tap the order into the machine. Pour. Slide the glass to him.

"Guys must ask all the time." He holds up the drink as if to toast. "If you're a virgin."

"Word gets around."

His eyes fix on my breasts. He watches my chest rise and fall with my exhale. He watches like he's picturing me in his bed. Like he's sure he has me where he wants me. "Do you want them to stop asking?"

Why? Does he have a button that will change the culture. Swap gender roles, so we obsess over male virginity and shrug at the thought of women who sleep around. *Girls will be girls.*

"I have a solution." He holds up his drink. "A proposition, actually."

"Shoot."

"You don't work here for your health."

What gave that away?

"You must need money. I have money. A lot of it. But I don't have you. What do you say, Eve? What do you say we make a trade? Something I want for something you want."

Chapter Two

EVE

Britney saves me. She whisks Drunk McHandsy to the back room for a trio of lap dances. The bar picks up. Another bachelor party. A couple looking for a third. Men in suits doing business.

A normal Tuesday night.

I lose myself in the rhythm of fixing drinks, taking cards, making chitchat. Then it's cleaning, receipts, tips.

The sweet freedom of the June air.

It's still warm. That's one of the things I love about New York. The city holds onto the temperature.

Eighty and humid. Rare for June. With the sun down and the breeze light, it's comfortable.

Ten blocks in the warm air. A big silver moon. All the lights of Times Square.

Like any born and bred New Yorker, I prefer to avoid the tourist trap.

Most nights, I walk a few extra blocks, so I can take the Fifty-Seventh Street station.

Tonight, I'm exhausted. I descend the steps to the

massive subway station. Left, right, straight, left. All the way to my line.

At two thirty on a Tuesday night, the subway is quiet. A server lost in a book, a bartender listening to headphones, a drunk couple making out against a dirty post.

They grind and groan like they'll never get enough.

Even when the train arrives, they climb in. Take to one of the benches.

They stay hot and heavy. So in need of each other they don't care who sees.

Or maybe they want someone to see.

Or maybe it's the alcohol talking.

What is that like? Feeling that free? Wanting someone that much?

I close my eyes. Try to recall a make-out session with my high school boyfriend. The cute bassist with long bangs. For all his talk of skilled hands, he lacked a certain finesse.

Was that it? His lack of tenderness?

The question rattles through my brain as I get off at my stop. Walk the half a mile to our apartment.

Not the nicest part of Brooklyn. But with rent control, it's the best we can do. A third-floor walk-up with two bedrooms, a small den, big windows.

Quiet.

There isn't a sound in the place. Nothing from Addie's room. No lights, no music, no keys clacking.

She's asleep. At peace.

My shoulders ease. Even after all this time, I worry about her. More than anything.

She's only four minutes younger, but she's still my baby sister. And it's still my job to protect her.

Tonight, she's okay. Tonight, I have enough to pay the rent. Tonight, I sleep easy.

I count the money in my dresser. Stuff a stack of twenties in an envelope. Leave it on the kitchen table.

Then, it's my time. I shower, fix an almond butter and jelly sandwich for dinner, settle into my bedroom. The one place where I feel free.

I guess that's not accurate. My room is *mine*.

The ornate mirror, the shiny chandelier, the teal arm chair, the punk rock posters.

It's all cheap stuff—thrift finds and Ikea—but it's mine.

This room is proof I've survived the last two years. With all the baggage that comes with it.

I want to fall onto the cheap cotton sheets and soak up every ounce of breeze (not nearly enough). But every time my gaze hits the red mark on the wall, I remember sharing a room with Addie.

I remember Dad handing down his Black Flag poster.

I remember moving into my own space.

Finding Addie in her room—

Not going there tonight.

My happy place is more abstract. It sounds silly out loud. I'm almost embarrassed to admit it.

The place I feel free isn't a place at all. It's a website. An online diary.

I started it earlier this year. Because I didn't have anywhere to put my thoughts during lunches at the library.

After twenty minutes of spilling my guts, I felt better. The words were mine. For me and me alone.

Then I hit the publish button, not thinking it would make my post public.

When I logged in the next day, to a dozen views, I felt something. Exposed and freer for it.

I pour my ugliest thoughts onto the page.

People read them. They see them. Understand them. Accept them.

There's one guy in particular. He drops likes and comments.

Feel better.

Beautiful.

You have a way with words.

He never asks for more. Or offers anything of himself.

He's just there, watching me strip out of my defenses, taking in my naked pain and calling it beautiful.

Is he as much of a mess as I am?

I don't care. I don't have time to care.

Understanding, acceptance, love—those come after rent, food, tuition.

This is the one place where I don't have to hold it all together.

The place where I work through my messy thoughts.

And damn do I have a whopper today.

Chapter Three

EVE

Original Sin
Wednesday, June 3rd
Four a.m.

What's the difference between bravery and foolishness? How about fear and sensibility?

These are the kinds of questions most eighteen-year-old girls consider. Once upon a time, I saw them through a normal lens.

Crushing on the cute guy in English.

A "truth or dare" at a party.

A bottle of Manic Panic Atomic Turquoise and a box of bleach.

I answered the questions like a normal high school senior.

No, I can't ask out the cute boy. Not in the middle of our senior project. Not when he says "let's just watch the show. *The Handmaid's Tale* is boring, don't you think?"

Yes, I can say dare. Even if I need two shots before I'm

able to flash the less cute (but more pro-Margaret Atwood) boy from Chemistry my bra.

Of course, I'm ready to embrace my inner punk goddess. If Addie's willing to help with the back of my head.

I'm sure there's some joke in there about boys and the back of my head. Or the top of my head.

Why are all the boys so obsessed? Are blow jobs really that great?

More of society's shit. Men kick back and accept pleasure from women. Men kick back and watch women appeal to them. Men kick back and discuss whether or not women are hot enough for them.

I guess I'm burying the lead.

Yes, I'm brave enough to kiss the boy in Chemistry. I'm foolish enough to take that third shot at my best friend's birthday party. And the opportunity to rock blue-green hair?

That's good sense.

Only now, four weeks out of high school, six months into legal adulthood, I have a new lens.

What will I do to keep my sister safe? To keep us together? To keep this burden off her shoulders?

Look at me, still dancing around the question. Am I really that scared? Nervous? Ashamed?

I don't know what to say.

It's the logical thing to do.

A few hours ago, a customer made an offer. Five figures for one night. My virginity gone. My problems gone with it.

Okay, he didn't specify the amount. But a girl can dream. Not of his hands or his lips or his *ahem*.

He's a jerk who reeks of booze.

Who thinks his medical degree earns him the right to part my legs.

He's not the man of my dreams.

But my problems disappearing? Rent and tuition paid? Good tea in the kitchen?

Addie's medical bills, gone?

How can I say no?

It will take me three years to pay this debt on my own.

Even if I find a better job at a better place. And not one run by a guy who thinks an allusion to hell is the height of creativity.

Who laughs *ha ha, Eve, are you tempted by this forbidden fruit yet* as he points to the twenties in a dancer's g-string. (Yeah, it's the first time I've heard that).

Yes. I'm tempted. But it's not a moral opposition.

If I had the stomach to dance, I would.

I can barely handle fixing drinks at that place.

I certainly can't handle a year there. Much less three.

One night with one asshole?

It makes me sick, sure, but it's better than the alternative.

How can I say no?

Why do I want to?

- EVE

Chapter Four

IAN

F uck.

I lean back in my chair. Rub my eyes.

Her words stay the same.

How can I say no?

Some arsehole is offering to pay for her virginity.

No fucking way.

My fingers curl into fists reflexively. I need to hit something. To hurt someone.

To do whatever it takes to stop this from happening.

I need to breathe. Stay the fuck away from anger. Attachment. Anything that ends in a shattered heart.

Only Eve here…

Fuck.

It's eight a.m. Four hours since her post. She's probably asleep.

I've never tended bar at a strip club, but I've worked physical jobs. After six hours serving pissed arseholes, she's probably sleeping soundly.

Or tossing and turning over her lack of options.

I try to picture her.

A small room. A tiny twin bed. Sheets the color of her hair. But that's one of the only things I know about her.

Teal locks. Dark makeup. *Don't fuck with me* attire.

Not that I picture her in clothes.

Only those heeled combat boots.

Short hair in my hands. Dark lips parting with a groan. Soft body melting into me.

I've been good. Very good. Despite my skills—I'm paid handsomely to dig up people's dirt—I've practiced incredible restraint.

I haven't looked up her ISP address. I haven't found her name and ran a background check. I haven't accessed every single account she has.

I read her site. That's all.

Only that doesn't explain her place in my life.

It's more than that.

It's everything.

A few months ago, I was browsing a TV forum. I saw a woman tear down a man who dismissed her. She was sharp, articulate, insightful.

Of course, I clicked the link in the bottom of her profile.

Original Sin.

Her site. Half cultural criticism—she dissects a book a week. Half online journal. All public. All for my viewing pleasure.

Usually, I reserve that kind of language for a woman who's naked in front of me.

Usually, I keep strict rules about relationships. A set timeframe. Clear boundaries. No feelings.

I teach a woman everything she wants to learn.

Then we part with memories.

No one gets hurt.

No one sends divorce papers in the middle of a meeting.

No one tears through London in a bitter rage, sure he's going to find the other man and kill him.

It ripped my heart out. Now, the damn thing is quiet.

But Eve—

I don't know her real name. I've never seen her picture. Or heard her voice.

But I'm obsessed. Thoroughly and completely obsessed.

After I discovered her site, I made it a part of my normal routine. A break during my workday. The same way I visited Forbes or Slate, I visited Eve.

I get both sides of her. The analytical cultural critic. And the struggling girl offering every piece of her heart.

The rawness to her words captivates me.

The mystery—who is she and what does she want—is beautiful agony.

Or it was.

Until now.

I can't let this happen. I have to stop it. Whatever that requires.

I refresh the page.

The words are still there.

How can I say no?

Some arsehole trying to buy her. Offering money for her body.

I'm not letting that happen.

Even if it means breaking my rules. Looking into her life. Crossing a line I can't uncross.

Who gives a fuck about lines when some arsehole is trying to buy her?

Twenty minutes later, the post is still there. The office is still quiet.

Only the hiss of the espresso machine. The soft *drip drip drip*.

I should cover it with something. Music Eve likes. She often alludes to a love of thrashing guitars and emotional vocals. A taste for her father's favorite music. Green Day, Black Flag, the Ramones. Classic punk and a smattering of the pop that came after.

Fuck.

I'm too obsessed. I need to stop this. Now.

Before I'm storming through Manhattan in a rage.

Before I need another three thousand miles between me and my past.

I'm not moving to Los Angeles. New York needs to stay mine. Not tainted by a woman ripping my heart to shreds.

I put my computer in sleep mode and join my business partner in the kitchen.

Shepard looks up from the espresso machine. That *I am barely able to muster interest* glance of his.

What is it people say? Resting bitch face.

Whatever the male version is, he's got it. Shep always looks irritated by other people's inability to keep up.

Usually, he is. With a few exceptions.

His wife. His brother.

Me.

Somehow, I'm the prickly mogul's best friend. Somehow, I was the best man at his wedding.

I guess no one told him it's bad luck asking a divorced man to stand at the altar.

"Early today." I hold up my mug to toast. Cold English Breakfast. No longer worth drinking.

Shepard shakes his head. "You need some new material."

"Wait until I ask what your wife is doing with you."

"Besides coming on my face?"

My laugh is a welcome relief—that's blunt for Shep—but it's not enough. Tension returns to my shoulders. Words bounce around my brain. *How can I say no?* "Sneaking away to your mistress?" I nod to the espresso machine.

"I need help if my mistress makes coffee this shitty."

"Sounds like something to discuss with your therapist."

He laughs.

It used to be a rare sound for him. Since he reconnected with his ex-girlfriend—

It was a strange turn of events. Marriage by blackmail. A new one, even for me. Not Shepard, blackmailing his bride. A third party, blackmailing Shepard. Win her heart or else.

The bastard called it a game. I guess it is a game. There are rules, victory conditions, stakes.

But where the hell is the fun?

"Interested in other people's problems," he says. "You should discuss that."

"You have so many. I can't help myself."

His laugh is soft. It covers the *drip-drip* of the machine. "Here for tea or torture?"

"I have to choose?"

"Which is it today? Something about how Americans don't understand tea?"

"Well, you certainly understand torture."

He chuckles.

"Full of yourself too. As if the US is the only country in the Americas."

"Are you going to call me a Yank?" he asks.

"That's the nicest thing I'd call you."

He half-smiles. "And you can't talk about ego."

"Ego? What ego?"

He picks up the electric kettle. Fills it with water.

I raise a brow. "You're fixing tea?"

"I've learned from the best." He smiles at the allusion to his wife. Stares at the kettle like it's his beloved. Dreamy eyed and full of affection. Then he shakes it off. Sets the kettle to boil. "Why are you here so early?"

I shrug as if I don't understand the question. I'm always early.

Only I know what he's asking.

He's asking why I'm wearing my frustration all over my face.

"Weren't you out last night? I could swear Jasmine said something about your Instagram." He shudders *how awful, following you on social media.* "Where do you get the energy?"

"If you need a lesson in stamina—"

"Evasive."

I shrug like I don't care. Motion to the kettle.

Shep nods *sure,* grabs a mug, loose leaf tea, a plastic strainer.

"I have a business partner who treats me right and the best tea money can buy. How can I stay away from the office?"

He makes that *mm-hmm* noise that means *we both know you're full of shit.* "So it has nothing to do with your… what do you call her?"

"Temptation."

"I still don't understand the story there."

"Who said I wanted you to?"

He chuckles *you're not fooling anyone.* "Apparently, you and my wife were discussing it. She's smitten."

"I'm sorry, Shep. But you had to know she'd find a better man one day."

"With your love story." He scoops leaves into the

strainer. "You must have told her something I don't know. I can't imagine she'd care much about you fucking some naïve co-ed."

This time, I laugh. "She's not naïve."

"No, she's a wise teenager?" He rolls his eyes. "Is she even legal?"

"She's eighteen." I thought she was older when I found her site. A grad student. Or an artist in her thirties.

She doesn't usually discuss high school troubles. And she writes like a woman who's lived an entire life.

I guess she has. In a mere eighteen years.

The first time she dropped her age, I couldn't believe it. That someone so articulate was barely out of high school.

That someone so mature, driven, focused was only eighteen.

Or that I was obsessed with someone half my age.

I don't know any practical details. No name. No number. No career plans.

I don't know her eye color or her height or her body-type.

But I know Eve. Her hopes and dreams. Her obsession with *The Handmaid's Tale*, feminist literature, and what she calls "lesser dystopia."

I know she loves *The Hunger Games* because she'd volunteer as a tribute *like that* if her sister's name was called at the reaping.

I know she loves thrashing guitar music. Even though it's what her dad played. Even though it's full of immature suburban boys who don't know real problems.

I know she can't get into hip-hop, even though all her friends love Drake.

I know she loves chocolate, but not chocolate ice cream.

I know she dyes her hair teal, wears dramatic makeup,

adores the color black. "Even though it's not technically a color."

I know she doesn't feel like she can talk to any of her peers, because they aren't holding up the entire fucking world the way she is.

And I know she'd do anything for her sister.

Including accepting this arsehole's offer.

Or finding a higher bidder.

"So…" He pours steaming water into the plastic strainer. "What is it about her? Why did you make my wife swoon?"

"You realize I know Jasmine well."

"I do."

"You don't have to say *my wife* every time you mention her."

His gaze flits to the silver band on his left hand. "What is the story with your temptation?"

"There's no story. I stumbled on her website a few months ago." More like eight, but who's counting? "I follow her writing. That's all."

"And, what, she insulted your favorite TV show?" He takes a tiny sip of his espresso. Lets out a sigh. Half *this hits the spot*. Half *it could be so much better*. "You don't look happy in love."

"Not compared to you."

He shakes his head *you're not fooling me*. "I can hold this hostage." He taps the Starbucks *You Are Here* mug. London. Of course. A gift from a client.

A well-meaning gift I loathe.

During my stint in the Royal Air Force, I saw a lot of the world.

I always wanted to come home to London.

Until those papers landed in my lap.

Now, I need the Atlantic ocean between me and my painful memories.

"What? Does she think you're a handsome, rich man with a British accent?" Shep chuckles. "Women hate that."

It's true. I've always had an easy time attracting women. Even as a poor kid in baggy clothes. In the States, in a tailored suit, with a no-limit card and no fear of using it?

I'm drowning in opportunity.

"You are old," Shep says. He's nearly ten years my junior. Young for his position. He's always teasing me about my age. I'm always teasing him about not being able to keep up with a thirty-six-year-old. "Is that why you won't contact her?"

"What did your wife say?"

He smiles at the word wife. "Something about true love being blind."

"Understandable with your looks. She must be blind."

He chuckles *of course*. There's no mincing words. Shepard is an attractive man. Between the blue eyes and the athletic build, he looks like a Disney Prince.

A rich Disney Prince in a tailored suit.

He does well with women. Even with his prickly personality.

Not that he cares anymore. He's madly in love with his wife.

"I read her posts. That's all." Yes, I'm obsessed with Eve. I want to know everything about her. I want to possess her in every way I can. But, so far, I've resisted.

"Really? You read her posts and don't use your skills to find out every other thing about her."

It's better this way. Safer for both of us. Or it was. Until now. I try to shrug it off. Fail to project a casual attitude. "Too busy using them for med-vac missions."

"Rock climbing?"

I nod *of course*. "Surfing the North Shore."

He doesn't buy it. "How much do you know about her?"

"Enough."

"And…"

"She needs money."

"And you're planning to leverage that?" He turns to the tea. Strains it into the Starbucks mug.

"There's another man… A guy trying to buy her virginity."

"Your wheelhouse."

"I never pay."

"Is that the line you won't cross?"

"Usually, yes. Parting gifts are one thing. Money for sex is another."

He hands me the cup of tea. "Ready to cross it?"

"I'm not sure I have a choice."

"You do. You're just not willing to admit you've already made it."

Chapter Five

IAN

For two days, I resist digging into Eve's life.

Then she updates Original Sin with a short and simple post.

The doctor came in today. Made an actual offer.

One night.

Fifty grand.

The act itself. Nothing more. Nothing less.

One night for next year's rent and tuition.

Half of me wants to slap him.

The other half wants to counter. See if I can find a better offer. If one asshole is willing to drop fifty grand, is another willing to drop a hundred?

And there's this other part, that wants to say yes before he changes his mind.

I need that money. I can't afford to say no. No matter how much I want to.

Resistance is futile.

In five minutes, I find the club where she works. There are only so many strip clubs in Manhattan. Fewer with allusions to the devil or hell.

Another five minutes, and I work out her schedule. She posts later the nights she works. And she's consistent about it. Tuesday then Thursday, Friday, Saturday.

Half an hour to find her college applications. Good grades, especially in English and creative writing, but they slipped senior year. Still, she had options. Almost got into Oxford. Accepted at NYU, Princeton, and a few schools on the West Coast.

Chose Hunter over better schools. A public school in the city. Cheaper than others, but still five thousand a year.

Her sister is a straight-A student. Nearly perfect test scores. She's enrolled at Columbia. Starting in the fall.

Some aide—the Ivies are known for their generosity—but not enough.

There's no way Eve is covering the rest on a bartending salary.

How is she covering rent, much less some awful debt?

She needs help now. She needs help yesterday.

Shep is right. I've already decided.

I know what I have to do.

It's time to do it.

———

Like many Manhattan strip clubs, Devil's Point is just off Times Square.

The neon sign—a dancer on all fours, horns and devil tail in clear detail—is as bright as any billboard in the tourist trap.

All red and purple.

No subtlety.

It's Friday night. Busy.

The bouncer shoots me a curious look. The one I expect in the States.

People don't know what to make of a tall Black guy in a suit.

Then I flash my passport and British takes over. The bouncer nods *oh, of course, sir*. The look in his eyes changes.

Now, I'm class incarnate. The rest of the details are irrelevant.

I step through the velvet curtains. Past a group of college guys. A business meeting in a booth. A bachelor party by the stage.

The groom's friends toss bills on stage. A short dancer bends to gather them. Offers her leg. Taps the garter.

The groom slips a five into the lingerie.

He's shy. Embarrassed.

She goads him. Smiles that customer service smile. She has to convince him she likes him. Part of the job.

No doubt he believes it.

We are idiots. The lot of us.

After she pries tips from the men, she stands. Saunters to the pole. Slides her blue hot pants to her ankles.

She's wearing a bright blue thong and patent boots.

No lacing.

Brown hair.

A wig, maybe. It's possible that's Eve. Technically.

It's possible the details she offers are fabrications.

But I can tell.

There's something about the dancer. She's not Eve.

My gaze flits to the other stage. A blonde in a schoolgirl skirt.

She's too far away. I can't make out her features. Still, I know. There's something about her posture, her outfit, her aura.

Not Eve.

She must be at the bar.

It's against the leftmost wall. Crowded.

Mostly younger men. The type with something to prove. A few men alone. One in a full suit. Another in sweats. One in scrubs.

Maybe that's him. The doctor trying to buy her. Maybe he's smarter than he looks. Here with a six-figure check and a hotel key.

There's nothing remarkable about him. Grey hair. Light eyes. Wrinkles that say neither *shriveled geezer* nor *distinguished gentleman*. The scrubs are fine. They don't hide his beer belly. They don't make him worthy.

My fingers curl into fists. I see it—that arsehole falling to the ground from a solid punch.

Fuck. It's not him.

There are plenty of bastards in scrubs.

This arsehole probably wears a suit.

Or maybe he's some young man who wears jeans in his time off. Maybe he's handsome and worldly. Maybe he's going to make her come all fucking night.

The blond dancer greets the older man. After a short back and forth, she pulls him out of his stool. Leads him through red curtains. An hour in the Champagne Room? Or a semi-secluded lap dance?

Strip clubs aren't my thing. Too obvious. Not enough left to the imagination. And when the action starts—

I don't need a naked woman grinding in my lap if I'm not allowed to touch her.

I suppose it's an exercise in discipline. A skill I need to hone. There's a reason I'm no longer in the military. But right now—

"Can I get you something?" A loud voice cuts through the house music. I've never heard it before, but it's familiar all the same.

That's her.

Eve's berry lips part as she repeats her question. "A

drink? You can take it to the stage. Or stay." She motions to an empty spot on the bar.

There. On her forearm. *Nolite Te Bastards Carborundorum.*

Don't let the bastards grind you down. The quote from *The Handmaid's Tale.* Her favorite book.

My eyes stay on her tattoo. Crisp black letters on a ribbon. Surrounded by lush petals.

Beautiful.

Exactly what I expect of her.

"Sir? Something to drink?" Her voice stays soft.

"You have Fever Tree?" My eyes stay on her forearm.

It's bizarre. I've imagined this moment a million times.

Usually, it involves me ripping off her clothes and pinning her to the wall.

Never me standing slack-jawed, unable to take my eyes off her tattoo.

But, fuck, it's beautiful. Her. Another way she reveals herself to me.

I need that. All of it.

Her laugh fills the air. Draws my eyes to her lips. Shoulders. Tits.

My balls tighten. I force my gaze to her face, but that does nothing to help matters.

Deep teal hair that falls just past her chin. Dark makeup lining her grey-green eyes. Purple-red lipstick.

She's beautiful. And young. And she screams *stay away, arsehole.* Even in the sheer black frock.

"Fever Tree?" Her eyes find mine. Her dark lips curl into a smile that lights up her entire face. "The tonic water?"

"Is there another Fever Tree?"

Her laugh grows deeper. Fuller. "The premium tonic water? Here? Do we really look like that kind of place?"

"A man can dream."

Her eyes flare with something. An appreciation. "I'm afraid your dreams are staying that. We have—I'm not even sure. But it doesn't come in a glass bottle." She grabs a plastic cup. Fills it with a splash of something clear and sparkling. "I doubt it's up to your standards."

My fingers brush hers as I take the glass. It's electric. A pull I can't deny.

I've been with a lot of women since I moved to New York. But I haven't felt this.

My entire body buzzes.

My images of her snap into focus.

Her blue-green hair falling over her eyes. Her dark lips parting with a groan. Her soft body tangled in white sheets.

Her lips parting with a cry equal parts agony and ecstasy. That cry that means *I need you in a way I've never needed anyone.*

"Is it that bad?" She motions to the glass. "You can tell from there?"

I take a sip. It's shit. All sugar. No quinine. A waste of good gin. "You're right."

"I'll have to ask the boss if he'll stock Fever Tree. Something tells me—"

"He'll see the light? Realize he could attract every British businessman in the States?"

She laughs. "There's a girl who does an Austin Powers inspired routine. Wears a bikini with the British flag—"

"The Union Jack?"

"Yeah. I'm sure it's very offensive. Tossing aside your flag. Talking about shagging everyone. The groovy music is fun, but all night, guys ask *do I make you randy, baby* in that Austin Powers voice."

"You've seen *Austin Powers?*"

"I hadn't. Until that."

"How did you like it?"

"Funny. But I think I missed the point. I've never seen a Bond movie."

"Never?"

She shakes her head *never*. "Is that as offensive as Emma wearing the Union Jack?" She gives me a quick once-over. Sizing me up. Asking if I'm a good tipper. If she should waste her time talking to me. Or if I'll leave a quid and complain the dancers aren't attractive enough.

The women on stage are beautiful, yes. But they don't appeal.

Not with Eve right here.

Fuck, she's prettier than I imagined. Not because her face is perfectly symmetrical. Or because she's the picture of conventional beauty.

It's something about her. That tender heart wrapped in a *fuck off* package.

"Am I the expert on all things British?" I ask.

Her dark lips curl into a smile. "Tonic water. The flag. Bond… it's a trend." She motions to the glass. "Vodka or gin?"

I raise a brow *really*.

"The well is New Amsterdam. I'm guessing you prefer—"

"The Hendricks Reserve." It's the best bottle here.

She nods *of course*. Steps back to grab a bottle off the top shelf.

Fuck, she has dramatic hips. And that frock barely covers her arse. Her long legs are on display.

And those heeled combat boots—

I need her in those. And nothing else.

No, I need to get ahold of myself. I'm not here to get my rocks off. I'm here to—

God dammit, there's no subtle way to broach the topic.

I'm Ian. I hear you're a virgin. I'd like to be your first. Tell me what it will take.

She turns to the bar. Pours gin over ice. Passes the glass to me.

I pull my card from my wallet.

Again, my hand brushes her.

Again, my entire body buzzes.

I'm already losing control. I'm already losing interest in maintaining control.

"I've never been a Bond fan myself," I say.

"No?" She looks me over again. Slowly. Like she's trying to figure me out. "I… I guess I don't get the appeal."

"It's a little close to home."

"You're a spy?"

"I was in intelligence."

Her grey-green eyes go wide. "You're messing with me."

"No." My gaze flits to the empty glass. "I'll toast to it. What do you drink?"

"You'll toast to… your honesty?"

"My freedom."

"No longer a spy?"

I nod.

"Or is that what you want me to think?"

"Why? Are you harboring secrets?"

"Maybe."

"An undercover government operative?"

"Would I tell you if I was?" She fills a glass with ice. Holds up the bottle. "I have a policy. I drink what you're drinking."

"You don't have a preference?"

"I can't tell you. It might give me away."

"Smart."

She laughs. Pours a generous shot. Returns the bottle to its shelf. "Were you really in intelligence?"

"Aren't we toasting to that?" I hold up my glass.

She smiles as she holds up hers. "To your freedom." She taps her glass against mine. Brings the drink to her lips. Takes a long sip.

Her cheeks flush. Her throat quivers with her swallow.

It fills my head with too many ideas.

"Cheers." The gin fails to cool my temperature.

She sets her glass on the bar. Sinks into her heels. "Thank you—"

"Ian."

"Eve." She holds out her hand.

We shake.

Her gaze flits to a guy at the end of the bar. He's waving his hand. "Duty calls."

I nod. Watch her fix the guy a rum and Coke. She trades quips with the customer. Then she's refilling beers and mixed drinks.

It's a busy night. This isn't the best time to broach the subject.

This isn't the place.

But I need to move quickly.

I pull a business card from my wallet. Write my cell number on the back. Let her close my tab.

Trade her. A card for a card.

"I'm looking for someone like you." That's almost true. But it's not enough to sell a second meeting as casual. "To bartend a private party."

"Someone like me?" She motions to her short hair. The Latin quote on her forearm. An EKG on her wrist.

"Yes. A few hundred for a few hours. Plus tips. It's an ongoing meeting. Once a month. It's a poker game. Not strictly legal."

She nods, buying into the story. Or at least pleased by an explanation for the extra pay.

"Call me if you're interested. Or if you know someone who is."

Her eyes flit to my card. The banter is gone. Replaced by apprehension.

It's smart. I wish she was this careful online. I wish she was more careful.

But there's only so much I can do.

"Or you can stop by my office. Eight to eight, all week." I offer my hand.

This time, she shakes with a weak grip. "Sure. Thanks." She watches as I slide off the stool.

She watches me leave.

Then it's my turn to wait.

Chapter Six

EVE

Original Sin
Saturday, June 6th
Three a.m.

The question is still there. Am I brave or foolish? Am I cowardly or cautious?

Am I going to call Mr. Tall, Dark, and Handsome?

It's like the guy walked off the set of *Luther*.

British accent. Tailored suit. Six-foot something frame.

Broad shoulders. Coffee eyes. The most intense stare in the history of the world.

A presence that exudes power.

That demands every ounce of my attention.

There are cute customers all the time. Famous ones even. That guy who's rumored to star in the next Tarantino movie—

He's a regular. Not that I see the appeal (of the actor or the director. The characters banter. They're criminals. It's a race to drop as many f-bombs as possible. Okay, maybe the guy I dated sophomore year ruined the whole thing for me. He still had that *Pulp Fiction* poster in his room when he brought his lab partner to his bed. And I… well, I wish I still had these concerns).

The point is. There are cute customers all the time.

Only there's nothing cute about Mr. Tall, Dark, and Handsome. No boyish charm or youthful smile.

He's all man. Thirty-something. Designer suit. Dress shoes. Expensive watch.

Grown-up charm.

Devilish smile.

Eyes that scream *I'm picturing you naked*.

Only not the normal naked.

Mr. Tall, Dark, and Handsome barely blinked when Candy tossed away her thong.

Whereas he looked at me like he was undressing my soul.

Maybe I'm projecting. Maybe I'm the one who wants to undress his soul.

But that's silly. I don't have time for men. Especially not strangers with strange offers.

Or is that the excuse? The fear disguised as caution?

Would it really be so bad if I returned his call?

What am I risking?

What am I risking by ignoring his offer?

It's probably not five hundred dollars for three hours of bartending. It's probably a soft interview for stripping at a bachelor party.

Or something more illicit.

Lots of guys offer four-figure sums for dancers to go the, ahem, extra mile.

Hell. Maybe he's like the doctor. After my virginity.

What are the odds? Am I that popular?

I know this site gets visitors, but I'm not exactly The AVClub.

Only so many people want to hear my thoughts on *The Handmaid's Tale*… again. (The Tarantino comment is probably costing me a few dozen readers).

What are the odds he's reading right now?

It's probably the doctor.

Or a dancer with good intentions.

Britney is sweet. She knows I'm broke. If she knows a guy who's willing to pay for one night with a virgin…

God, I can't even say it.

How am I supposed to call Mr. Tall, Dark, and Handsome?

How can I resist?

What if he really is Prince Charming?

What if he really does want to erase all my problems?

―――――

As usual, I wake to the sound of Addie's music. A violin track. By this artist who considers herself a rock star.

If you ask me, it's still orchestra. Where are the drums and bass? Where are the screaming vocals?

I don't get the genre, but Addie loves it.

There is something about this song. A haunting pain that wants to find my weak point. Does Addie hear it too? Is that why she loves the song? Or is just her love of strings?

I'm not as punk rock as I look.

Sure, I love thrashing guitars and telling authority figures to fuck off. Yes, I feel more myself with colorful hair and thick eyeliner.

But I'm happiest in my bed, lost in a great book. Or a particularly binge-worthy TV show. Or a new entry.

Last night flits through my head. Rude customers, naked women, Cindy leaving me a sixty-dollar tip out with a *you deserve it kid. Thanks for taking care of me.*

She lets guys buy her drink after drink. They don't know her drinks are non-alcoholic. That's where I come in.

A fun game. More or less. I have a bottle of "well vodka" just for her. Okay, I occasionally use it on particularly rude customers. Like a barista who brews decaf for assholes.

All the normal business of work.

And Ian.

His name is enough to make my pulse race. It's too hot in here. I can't afford to warm the room further. It's already stuffy.

Usually, June is humid—thus the gloom—but this is August heat. Heat that demands cold showers and ice cream.

Not—

Shit, is that smoke?

I pull on a tank and shorts—it's too hot for pajamas—and I run into the main room.

The kitchen, I guess. It's all one room. Kitchen slash dining room slash den. Fridge, stove, counter, tiny table, TV.

Small by most people's standards. But a good size for New York. Even if we're practically in Long Island.

"They're not burning, I swear!" Addie flips a pancake. It's not burnt, exactly, but it's past golden brown.

"It's the chocolate chips." Mmm melting chocolate. Not mmm burnt chocolate. My nose is confused. "They burn faster."

I turn the heat to low. Push the window all the way open. Is it hotter in here or out there?

Either way, it's stuffy as hell.

She nods *right, of course*. "Sorry? Did I wake you? I can turn it down." She motions to the speaker in the corner. One of those wireless ones that connects to her computer. A present for her birthday. Well, our birthday, I guess. Since it's for me as much as it's for her.

"And ruin the mood? How else will I wake up to sadness?"

Her lips curl into a frown. That reminder neither one of us wants. The day, more than a year ago now, she almost died.

"It's not—"

"We can play Green Day instead."

Addie's face scrunches with displeasure. She has absolutely no interest in "suburban boys who want to pretend they're anarchists." Or "men who spend eight straight songs whining about their exes."

She has a point. If I had to critique swap one of these songs with a classmate, I'd have a different take.

But some things stick. Like the music Dad always played when we were younger. It should repel me—anything that man loved is bad news—but what is it they say?

The heart wants what it wants?

Not that I listen to mine. Not anymore.

My eyes flit to the clock on the wall—the cheap pink one from Target. For all her STEM nerdiness (she's a chemistry genius), Addie is a total girly girl. Pink and purple everywhere. Only it's pink leggings and t-shirts.

She rocks low-effort cute like it's her job. No makeup, ashy hair in a messy bun, pink tank top.

"You need help with those?" I motion to the pancakes. No longer smoking. Smelling a lot more like chocolate and vanilla and a lot less like burnt flour.

My stomach growls. I'm starving. And dead tired.

I need caffeine.

"I got it. I swear," she says.

I motion to the kettle on the counter. "Set it for me, please. I have to pee."

She nods *of course*. Calls out an apology for waking me as I run to the bathroom.

Another small space. With the world's smallest window.

Ah, the charms of the city. Really, I love New York. It's home.

When things were better, when Dad was working and sober, we visited Jersey, Florida, California, Iowa, Hawaii, Vegas. Sometimes family. Sometimes work. Sometimes fun.

Lots of places appealed. Constant sunshine and gorgeous beaches in California. Houses the size of a city block and fields of grass in Iowa. Bright lights and—

Okay, Vegas is like Times Square on New Year's Eve. All drunk people. No reason to visit.

New York is special. Unlike anywhere else. At least in the US.

Is Ian from London? Or is it that I can't name any UK cities outside of London?

Edinburgh. That's a place. There's the countryside. In that show *Broadchurch*. Or the other countryside in *Happy Valley*. God, I watch some depressing shit.

And I'm already in a bad situation.

Thinking about Ian as I pee, wash my hands, brush my teeth.

Even as I move into the kitchen and fix my chai. Extra strong tea, lots of almond milk (Addie is a vegetarian, but she's trying to go vegan).

A tiny sprinkle of cinnamon.

Another thought of Ian.

Is that his real name? Or is he really some sort of operative?

And why do I keep—

"You okay?" My sister shoots me a curious look.

"Tired." I try to avoid lying to her, but it's not always possible. I don't want her to know how much I'm struggling. I want to protect her from that.

"You sure?"

I nod *yeah*. Take a long sip of my chai. Sigh over the perfection that is cardamom. Or maybe the cloves are better. Hard to say.

Even with the sweltering weather, I need my morning tea.

The rest of the day, iced whatever, whenever. But first thing in the morning, chai. Always.

This isn't great tea. It's what I can buy off Amazon for fourteen cents a bag. The crushed leaves no one wants. It takes three bags to bring flavor, but with milk and extra cinnamon, I can barely tell.

"Maple syrup?" she asks.

It's not real maple syrup. We can't afford that. But why point out the artificial flavors? "I'm okay." I motion to the honey on the table. It's a little strange on pancakes, sure, but it doesn't taste like it was made in a lab.

She nods *okay*, brings pancakes and tea to the table, sits across from me.

I hold up my mug. "To your cooking."

"Taste it first."

"Even so."

She gives me that *you're ridiculous* look, but she still taps her mug against mine.

I smile as I take a sip. Cheap, oversteeped tea. Slightly burnt pancakes. Bulk honey. Discount chocolate.

It's not the finest breakfast in the world. But, here, with my sister across from me.

With Addie happy, healthy, alive—

This meal is priceless.

I'll do whatever it takes to keep things this way.

———

WHEN WE CAN NO LONGER TAKE THE HEAT OF THE apartment, we head to Central Park. The sweltering subway station. The frigid car. The wide open air of Columbus Circle.

Cold brews from Dunkin Donuts. (Not the best quality, but they're cheap and strong). Then we find a nice spot on the grass and we read.

The Bell Jar for me.

A non-fiction book for her. Something about physics. Something way over my head.

After a few hours, we part. Addie on her way to meet with a friend from Mathlympics. Me to a coffee shop with strong air-conditioning.

I reapply my makeup in the bathroom. Double-check my work clothes.

I have the entire afternoon, but it doesn't make sense to go back home. Even if I am craving the quiet privacy.

The very, very hot quiet privacy.

I find a seat upstairs. Don my headphones. Turn over his card.

Mr. Tall, Dark, and Handsome.

He wants something from me.

But what?

I should probably make him wait. That's what Britney always suggests. *Men want what they can't have. You can't be too available.*

I guess that's why she always keeps her plaid skirt on.

Or maybe she's only talking about men outside the club. Men worth her time.

Ian is a customer.

But it was so strange… like he was there just to see me. He barely looked at the stage.

He wants something from me.

Maybe it's a "punk bitch" bartender for his poker game.

Maybe it's more.

Whatever it is…

I have to know.

Chapter Seven

IAN

On Saturdays, I fly for a local hospital.

It's a long day. There isn't a lot of med-vac this close to the city. Mostly hospital to hospital organ transfers.

Lots of built up energy.

I finish equal parts wide-eyed and knackered.

After five kilometers on the treadmill and a long shower, I'm steady.

Then I check my phone.

See her text.

Lose my even keel.

My veins surge with adrenaline. Desire. Excitement.

Eve: Are you at the office today? It's a Saturday. I can wait until Monday, if that's easier. This is Eve, by the way.

Raw need. A need I don't recognize. A need I haven't felt in a long, long time.

I reply immediately.

Ian: I can be.

Eve: I assume it's downtown?

Ian: I can send a car to you.

Eve: No, I'm a subway girl. Besides, it's probably farther for you.

She's curious about my life. Where I live. What I'm doing.

Or am I imagining things?

I want her too much. It's clouding my thoughts.

Ian: A subtle way to ask where I live. You would make a good spy.

Eve: Or maybe I do make a good spy.

Ian: Then it's dangerous for me to accept.

Eve: Probably.

Ian: How about dinner?

Eve: How about it?

Ian: We meet at a restaurant. I buy you dinner. It's public. Safer.

Eve: You're afraid of me?

Ian: Shouldn't I be?

Is she smiling? Laughing? Does she realize how much power she already has over me?

Eve: There's this Margaret Atwood quote. Men are afraid women will laugh at them. Women are afraid men will kill them.

Ian: That's what I would say if I was a female assassin.

Eve: Would you admit the possibility you're out for blood?

Ian: Hide in plain sight.

Eve: It might work.

Fuck, is she always this adorable?

Ian: I'm happy to meet you at the office. But it will be the two of us. Alone.

Eve: I have work tonight.

She doesn't need to work tonight. But one thing at a time.

Ian: I stay up late. You can come after.

Eve: Nothing is open after.

Ian: Is that a test?

Eve: No, I'm sure you know someplace open at 3 a.m. But I prefer to crash after a long night.

My head fills with a beautiful image.

Eve, tangled in white sheets, her head falling back, her lips parting with a cry that's half pleasure, half pain, all need.

Ian: A private club then. Near your establishment.

Eve: That's the nicest thing anyone's ever called Devil's Point.

Ian: You know Brits. Always polite.

Eve: Are you?

Ian: No.

Eve: Six o'clock.

Ian: I can send a car.

Eve: Just the address.

Ian: And my bulletproof vest?

Eve: If you think that will stop me.

Chapter Eight

EVE

The man at the security desk shoots me a curious look. *What are you doing here?*

I flash him my best smile, but that does nothing to help matters. If anything, he's more suspicious.

This isn't my wisest idea. Not in this wardrobe.

Heeled combat boots. Short skirt. Sleeveless top with corset lacing.

All black, of course. It's easy. It looks badass. And it screams New York. Even on a hot day. New Yorkers don't break for weather. We don't admit weakness for snow, rain, or heat.

I ignore the guard as I move to the elevator. Hit the button for the thirty-second floor. The restaurant. In the middle of an office building.

But I guess that's New York too. No space to waste.

A man in a sleek suit gets in after me. A couple in dressy attire. Two guys talking business.

One of them shoots me that same look. *Clearly, you don't belong here.* The other's expression is more familiar. Something I see at the club all the time. *Sweet little girl, let me corrupt you.*

There are some men who don't take a hint. If I can be so generous as to call my style a hint. It's not exactly subtle. That's why it works.

Dark makeup, bright hair, black clothes—they're a shield. To keep my feelings in and the rest of the world out.

Probably not all that healthy. Probably more of Dad's influence.

But, hey, that's a concern for another day. A day when I've solved the whole money issue.

Bills take up all the space in my brain. There isn't room for anything else.

And this…

I'm meeting Mr. Tall, Dark, and Handsome. To discuss… something. There's no way it's a bartending gig. Who invites a potential bartender to an exclusive Manhattan restaurant?

The elevator stops at the restaurant floor. The couple gets out. Then the businessmen.

I move along the black and white tile. To the hostess table.

She recognizes me immediately. "Eve?"

"Do I know you?" My head is fuzzy lately. She doesn't look familiar, but she might be a former class-mate. Maybe she got her job the way I did. Maybe they run a brothel out of the back. Maybe that's why I'm here.

"Mr. Hunt is ready for you." She grabs a menu. Flashes a serene smile. The one that means *this customer is a good tipper.* "This way, please." She leads me through the inte-rior. To a wide open patio. Around a corner.

Holy shit. The buildings of Midtown come into view. Steel and glass in every direction. The Empire State

Building to the left. The skyscrapers of the Financial District to the right.

A sliver of the East River.

The clear blue sky. Still bright and vibrant.

I almost wish I called in sick. This place must be beautiful at sunset. And after. When the buildings light up the night sky.

"The one at the end." She hands me a menu. Another serene smile and she turns on her heels.

Okay…

Weird. But maybe that's what money is like.

People fawn over you. Help you arrange trysts with women you meet at strip clubs.

Is that what he expects? I don't know. This isn't the place. The restaurant is open and airy. Even by rooftop bar standards.

I trace the menu with my pointer finger. Okay. No problem. I can meet Mr. Tall, Dark, and Handsome.

I can hear his offer.

I can sit across from him without melting into a puddle of desire. Maybe he's not even that handsome. Maybe I had beer goggles. Uh, gin goggles. Whatever.

Deep breath. Steady exhale.

It's ten steps to the booth.

And there he is, on the bench against the wall, in a sleek black suit. Even sitting down, he's tall and broad.

Power incarnate.

It's something he exudes. I can't explain it. Plenty of rich, influential men come into the club. They all have a hint of his x-factor. But he's swimming in it.

No gin goggles.

He's still sexy as fuck.

Not pretty or beautiful.

Handsome. Masculine in every possible way.

"Eve." His deep voice flows into my ears. "I'm glad you made it." He offers his hand. Motions to the step to the booth. "Careful."

"Do you always help potential enemies into their seats?"

He nods. "Harder to kill sitting down."

I place my hand in his.

It's not in my imagination. His touch is electric. And there's something about the way his fingers close around my wrist.

Strong hands. Firm grip. Just the right amount of pressure.

God, he's so handsome. Coffee eyes. Dark skin. Short hair. And under that suit—

Ahem.

I force my eyes to the table. Step into the booth. Take a seat across from him.

There. I'm sitting. My knees can buckle all they want.

Why *are* my knees buckling? He's handsome, yes. Hotter than hell, yes. So what?

I see hot guys. I don't react like this. I don't have time to react like this.

If circumstances were different, sure. I could flirt all night. Go back to his place. Finally punch my v-card.

No concerns of following my heart (or my libido) instead of my head. No voice asking me *is he worth whatever the doctor will pay for my hymen?* No weight on my shoulders.

One night of bliss.

No strings.

The end.

It's a beautiful fantasy.

But it's just that. A fantasy.

I don't have time for trysts with strange men. Even strange, handsome, richer than sin, sexy as hell men.

His eyes meet mine. He stares at me with those soulful browns. Stares at something I try to keep hidden.

I reach for a reply. Come up with, "Aren't you hot in that?" Ugh. I bite my tongue. Talk about inability to banter.

He lets out a low chuckle. "I'm used to it."

There is a breeze up here. And the sun isn't quite as overpowering as it was this afternoon. But I'm sweating in my combat boots. "I'm not." I straighten my leg, showing off my shoes. "I'm dying in these."

"Take them off."

"Already asking me to strip?" Okay, that's a little better. Slightly less awkward. Pretty good, considering the circumstance.

"If it will make you more comfortable."

"And your suit jacket?"

"Are we trading?" His smile is wry. Barely there. Completely intoxicating.

I swallow hard. I want to say yes. To keep flirting. To follow this path all the way to his bed. I can't go that far… but I can have a little. "Two shoes and socks for one jacket. That doesn't seem fair."

He chuckles. Holds up his drink. "Is your policy the same outside of work?"

"My policy?"

"You drink what I'm drinking."

Oh. "I'm not twenty-one."

"I know."

Okay. He knows that. I don't really look older than my age. Maybe it's a guess. Or maybe he punched my phone number into Facebook. Does that still work?

"It's not a problem here."

"Do they have Fever Tree?"

His smile widens. "Three varieties."

"Then that. Whichever is the best."

"Best is a matter of opinion."

"Yours?"

"You prefer strong or light?"

What a question. With all sorts of implications. Words well up in my throat.

Whatever you're willing to give me. Light. Then strong. How do you like it?

I bite my tongue again. Find something more appropriate for the circumstance. "If you're going to get wet, you might as well go swimming."

He nods. "If I'm going to get wet?"

My knees buckle. Thank God for the seat. How is he… fuck. I'm in so far over my head. This isn't even a date, and I'm already thinking about our second.

Would it be so bad? If I relaxed, called in sick to work, let him whisk me back to his place for a night I can't forget?

For an hour, I want to believe in this fantasy.

But I need a lot more gin for that.

He turns to the walkway right as a waitress appears. "Two more."

"Of course." She drops off two glasses and a carafe of water. "And food?"

"Are you hungry?" he asks.

Yes. And nervous. But drinking on an empty stomach with him—bad idea. I glance at the menu.

No prices. It's that kind of place. So expensive they don't label.

I guess I might as well enjoy it. Something I like. That I don't usually afford.

Scallops.

He gets some sort of surf and turf. Hands the menus to the server. Pours two glasses of water.

I grab mine. Take a greedy sip.

It *is* hot today. I need the hydration. And the way to occupy my hands. Where do I put them?

Why is it so hard sitting still across from him?

Ian.

He's too handsome. In a way that's wrong. So wrong it's right.

"How much time do you have?" His voice is matter-of-fact. Like we're colleagues prepping for a meeting.

"I work at eight today."

"I'll keep it quick."

"Thank you."

Footsteps call my attention. Another waitress—a different one—drops off our drinks. Motions to Ian's melted glass of ice. *All finished?*

He nods. Says thank you. Holds up his fresh drink.

I take mine.

The glass is cool against my fingers. Real glass. Not the cheap plastic we use. Something breakable. Something valuable.

This restaurant is unconcerned with drunk idiots dropping drinks. If that's what comes with his offer—

It's already a compelling argument. Serving drinks in actual glass. With no concerns of drunk idiots. Or need to hear men debate how much they'd spend to fuck a dancer.

"Your freedom again?" I suck in a deep breath. "Isn't it bad luck to toast to the same thing twice in a row?"

"Is it?"

Maybe. I have no idea. "Is that what you—"

"What do you celebrate?"

That's an even better question. With Addie, I'm happy to toast to anything. She's alive. That's what matters. But I'm not sharing that with Ian. And there isn't anything else worth celebrating. I paid the rent on time. Hooray? "My hair looks great."

"It does."

"That's um… probably the highlight of my day."

"Eve, that hurts."

"So far." My cheeks flush. God, I already like him. How can I like him? I don't know him. "To the staying power of Special Effects Sonic Green."

"To Special Effects." He taps his glass against mine.

My fingers brush his. That same rush of desire. Heat against the cool glass.

I bring the drink to my lips. Let the ice try—and fail—to cool me.

This is the best gin and tonic I've ever had. Floral gin. The bite of lime. The strong taste of quinine.

Refreshing.

Balanced.

Unable to lower my temperature.

I swallow another sip. Suck on an ice cube.

It doesn't help. It gives me ideas. Which is ridiculous.

I'm not going to drop to my knees for some strange man. No matter how much I want to.

Why the fuck do I want to?

His gaze shifts to my lips. He watches me crush and swallow the ice cube. He watches like he has the same ideas.

Usually, that annoys me. Not on Ian. He's just so…

Sexy.

And vague about why I'm here.

But, right now, I don't really care. I want to watch him watch me.

I want to take in his deep eyes, his strong posture, his intense presence. For a minute. An hour. Forever.

Only I don't have forever.

I barely have an hour.

Ian takes another sip. Sets his cocktail on the table. Focuses every ounce of his attention on me. "I won't waste your time, Eve."

Okay…

"I do want you for something. I suppose you could call it a job. But not a traditional one."

I take another sip.

"I did work for British Intelligence. I'm still in information. And I came into information about you."

"About me?" What is there to know about me? I have teal hair and love *The Handmaid's Tale*. I live with my sister. I spend too much time watching TV and not enough soaking up air-conditioning.

"Your financial situation."

Oh. Of course. It hits me like a ton of bricks—

"You're a virgin."

"And?"

"A man made you an offer. Fifty thousand dollars. Am I right?"

How the hell does he know that? "Are you a cop?"

He shakes his head.

"A federal agent? Some international officer trying to break up sex-trafficking?" My head spins. "It was his offer. I didn't take it. I barely listened. And who do you think you are to try to stop me?"

"I do want to stop you."

"I'm not—"

"I'd like to outbid him." His eyes bore into mine. "So tell me, Eve. What will it take? A year of rent? Tuition paid in full? Give me a number and I'll make it happen."

Chapter Nine

EVE

What the actual fuck?

What will it take?

What number buys my virginity?

I...

He...

What?

I take another sip. Swallow hard.

The gin is just as refreshing. The drink is just as delicious.

I'm just as hot.

Ian's offer should repulse me. It should convince me he's a disgusting asshole. Some cretin with a virginity fixation. Someone totally unworthy of my time.

What kind of man tries to buy a woman's innocence?

I try to find rage.

I have a reserve of it. My deadbeat father. The jerk who runs the club. The high school boyfriend who slept with his lab partner.

The other one. Who dumped me because I was smarter than him.

He never used those words, but it was obvious. He didn't want to be with a "pretentious buzzkill." To him, that meant anyone who read books outside of school. Or for school. Why not use Spark Notes?

I hate all those asshats.

But I don't hate Ian. My simmering rage refuses to latch onto him.

I just…

Why? Why in the world does he want to pay me?

He's incredibly handsome. Powerful. Rich.

Every woman here wants him.

I want him.

A few more drinks, another date or two… there's a good chance I'd say yes. Very good.

Now…

"Eve? Are you all right?" His voice stays steady. Totally in control. It doesn't ruffle him at all, asking the price for my virginity.

No, I want to want to tell him to fuck off. But I don't.

Besides, I don't have that luxury.

I need the cash.

Badly.

"Why?" I take another sip. It's more refreshing than the last. But I'm still burning up.

"Does that matter?"

I don't know. Logically, it's a minor concern. But my heart… No, my heart is ice. It doesn't get a say until hell freezes over. "There must be a reason."

"Are you set on this?"

"On what?"

"Are you looking for higher bidders or looking to stop all offers?"

I'm not set on it, no. But I owe it to my future to consider it. What does that say about me?

No, I'm not letting other people's expectations define me.

Yes, some people will call me a whore or a slut for considering this. But they've never been where I am. They've never stared at a mountain of bills, wondering how they're going to pay them.

If they'll ever find someone, anyone who's willing to help.

This is my chance. This is my help. And it's practical. Entrepreneurial. Savvy.

My virginity is worthless to me. A little extra skin. An activity I haven't done yet.

My index finger traces the lines of my forearm tattoo.

Don't let the bastards grind you down. I needed it then. I need it now.

This is what makes sense.

But it's terrifying too.

"I, um…" Can't think with those dark eyes on me. It's impossible. "I should get to work." Figure out what the hell I'm doing.

He nods, still unruffled.

"I…" I swallow my last sip of gin and tonic. "I'll consider that." That keeps my options open. Sort of.

"I'll ask the waitress to wrap your dinner. Send it to your establishment."

"Thanks." I slide out of the booth. Offer my hand.

He shakes with a firm grip. "I'll see you soon, Eve." He says it with such confidence. He's sure I'll say yes. Or at least come back with a number.

It's ridiculous.

He's ridiculous.

I pry my eyes from his, spin on my heels, march away from the table. At least, I try to march. To project confidence.

To tell the world *no, I'm not for sale. Don't be silly. I considered the doctor's offer because it was so strange.*

I could never actually go through with it.

Even if I want to sleep with Mr. Tall, Dark, and Handsome.

Even if I'd happily jump into his bed for free.

If he earned my trust.

If I believed he'd be gentle with me.

Something tells me Ian Hunt isn't a gentle guy.

And something inside me aches at the thought of Ian Hunt rough with me. Something that needs to quiet.

It's Saturday night. I have to work. I have to exist in the real world and not in a fantasy one where a sexy British businessman wants to erase all my problems.

———

THE UNIVERSE IS AGAINST ME. OR FOR ME. IT DEPENDS ON the point of view.

Either way, it's determined to remind me how much I hate this job.

A group of drunk guys spend thirty minutes trying to convince me to take shots with them. Then they tip four dollars on their three-figure bill.

A bachelor party gets handsy with a dancer. Security throws out the groom. The best man stays at the bar. Offers me cash to come back to their hotel room and dance.

Why not, honey. We'll pay better than this gig. And we can wait until you're done with work. You won't believe how much my friend would pay for a night with someone like you.

A guy in a suit sits at the bar all night, friendly and courteous, ordering whiskey after whiskey. He smiles. Nods. Asks easy questions. Accepts simple answers.

I've worked here a few months. It's an all right job. I'd prefer a place with better music. But I have to say, I admire the athleticism of the moves. Look at Britney. She's upside down!

He leaves without paying his tab.

I finish later than usual. Spend half my tip money on cab fare.

Saturdays are always rowdy, but they're usually huge moneymakers too.

Saturdays are good for a few hundred dollars in tips. Most bachelor parties throw bills like they're candy spurting piñatas.

Here I am, at the kitchen table, counting twenties, asking myself if I'm on track to cover rent. Or do I need to scrimp on groceries tomorrow?

Is it another week of almond butter and jelly sandwiches? The goddamn almond butter is a fortune, but it's as cheap as dinner gets. I'm allergic to peanuts.

Four nights a week at that hellhole and I struggle nonstop.

I fight so hard. And for what?

I'm not on track to pay my tuition come August. Addie's?

Forget about it.

She thinks Dad's helping with that too.

And I…

Fuck, I'm so tired.

I shower. Wrap myself in a threadbare towel. Look for a snack in the fridge.

No seared scallops with butternut squash puree. No premium gin and tonic. No flourless chocolate cake.

Almond butter and Trader Joe's chocolate. In the fridge because we don't have air-conditioning. Because it's too hot for the cocoa.

It melts on the counter.

It can't take the heat.

Can I?

————

AGAIN, I WAKE TO ADDIE'S MUSIC. A DIFFERENT SONG FROM the violinist. Another that tugs at my heartstrings.

It's too early, but the room smells like cinnamon. And this is my Friday. Sort of. My last day of work before an entire day off.

After I move through my morning routine, I fix tea and oatmeal. With cinnamon, raisins, and a little vanilla extract, this is practically a cookie.

It's also cheap. Even if the vanilla extract is a bit of a stretch.

Addie steals a sip of my tea. Smiles as the album flows into the next.

"Something's up." I steal my tea back. "Something big."

"Marisol's planning a beach weekend." Her girlfriend. The very supportive girlfriend who is the rock she needs.

"And…"

"You're the one who goes on about how you're a goth mermaid."

"I do not go on."

"Don't make me load up your Instagram."

My laugh dissolves the tension in my shoulders. There is evidence on social media that argues against my point. "I may have said it once or twice." A long time ago. When things weren't so hard.

She shakes her head *okay*. Pulls out her cell.

A few taps of her finger and she's looking at my social media. My former glory.

All these posts of my hair, makeup, style.

A fierce black dress.

An epic crown braid.

The teal and purple bikini that screams *Ursula*.

Nothing recent. My recent life is far from Insta-worthy.

"Next weekend?" She looks at me with hope in her eyes. "Do you think you can come?" She presses her hands together. "Pretty please."

"I have work." I work four nights a week.

Addie works three days a week. An internship that pays double minimum wage and requires business casual attire.

It doesn't leave a lot of time for us to hang out.

But it's easier now that it's summer.

"At night. You can come out for the day. Her parents' place in Long Island," she says. "Not the boring part with all the freeways. A nice part, by the beach. And they have a pass."

"A nice part of Long Island?" I raise a brow *really?*

"I know you read *The Great Gatsby*."

"Are her parents in the Hamptons?"

"Uh…" She motions *a little*. "They're super rich."

A super rich girlfriend. Look at my baby sister. She's better at this than I am and she's not even trying. "You'll have more fun without me."

She shakes her head. "She's bringing her sister. And we haven't… I don't want it to be weird. Expectations. You know?"

I guess dating women comes with the same issues as dating men. Not that I've dated any *men*. Only boys. And not recently. "Won't you have the same issue if I leave at four?"

She bites her lip. "But maybe… you could get someone to cover for you?" Her blue eyes fill with concern. She needs me.

She needs me and I have to spend the weekend at a hellhole. A hellhole that doesn't pay enough to cover all our bills.

This is only the first no of the day. There are plenty more on the way:

The nice tea from that shop in Midtown.

The fancy cold brew.

Lunch at a sit-down restaurant.

Air-conditioning.

Boots that don't suffocate my feet.

A work dress that isn't threadbare.

Eyeliner that doesn't melt in the heat.

Or a night to myself. Where I don't need heeled boots and a skimpy dress.

A night walking around the city, taking in the wonder it has to offer.

I saw that once.

Now…

I owe it to her to consider this.

And to myself.

A weekend at a friend's beach house. A weekend without the weight of the world on my shoulders.

What does that even feel like?

"I'll see what I can do," I say.

She jumps out of her chair to hug me. "Thank you, thank you, thank you. You're a lifesaver, Eve. I'm so nervous about being alone with her. She doesn't know about last year and I just…"

"She loves you. That's what matters."

She nods *I guess so.* Launches into a discussion of their last date. Walking around the Natural History Museum (of course) then falafel in the Village. This kiss that screamed of more.

The kind of kiss that only exists in fairy tales.

I don't believe they exist. Not the Disney versions.

Twisted ones? A princess who will do anything to save herself? Prince Charming with illicit intentions?

I pull out my cell and text Ian.

Chapter Ten

IAN

E ve: *What are you offering?*

Thirteen hours.

Thirteen hours and she's considering it.

Nine a.m. on a Sunday and I'm still in the goddamn building. Sure, I'm halfway through a workout. But this isn't how I'm supposed to spend my weekend.

I don't wait by the phone.

I don't wait. Period.

Or I didn't. Until I started reading her site.

Until I started refreshing four times a day, waiting for another taste of her thoughts.

Nothing today.

She isn't sharing this with her readers. Only with me.

I finish another set. Wipe the sweat from my brow.

It's Sunday. A day of rest. Most Sundays, I take it easy. By my standards. A long workout, a longer shower, a late breakfast, some sort of social engagement.

A woman in my bed.

Who am I kidding? It's been months since I've invited a

woman into my bed. The second a woman touches my arm, I think of Eve. Of how much I'd prefer her.

She isn't how I imagined her. Younger. Taller. With the most gorgeous grey-green eyes. And all those tattoos that define her.

I have my own. Plenty. But nothing recent.

It's been a long, long time since I've felt the need to permanently mark my body.

And this… the way I want to trace every line of ink on her skin, commit them to memory—

That's new.

I need to understand her.

Everything about her.

Ian: What do you want?

Eve: Isn't it a disadvantage, being the first to quote a number?

Ian: Depends who you ask.

She's reading up on negotiation. Or smart enough to know it by heart.

That awful club, all those drunk arseholes—

She must negotiate nonstop.

My skin crawls at the thought of her in that place. Wearing nothing. That short skirt and low-cut blouse—

It's not enough.

There are too many pissed arseholes leering at her.

It's not like me to hate it—I'm not usually possessive— but I do. I want her in a parka at that place.

No, I want her away from that place forever.

Eve: Do you really know the doctor?

Not in the way she means. We certainly aren't friends. But I know enough.

A divorced man who lives in New Jersey. He frequents an escort service in the Financial District. He comes into the city on weekends, for a night at a hotel with a call girl.

I don't judge other people's choices. Not usually. I've made plenty of mistakes. But this man—

He's not worthy of her.

He's not touching her.

No one else is touching her.

Ian: I don't like him. I don't want him to do this.

Eve: Why?

Ian: Does that really matter?

Eve: I guess not. I just figure there has to be some kind of catch.

Ian: How is that?

Eve: I looked you up. Maybe Ian Hunt is an alias created by MI6. Maybe this is all an elaborate lie. But I'm not exactly a hacker. And I don't know any hackers.

Ian: I can recommend a few.

Eve: You?

Ian: I prefer operative.

Eve: Spy?

Ian: That's trying too hard.

Eve: International Man of Mystery?

Ian: Only if you're going to ask "do I make you randy, baby?"

Eve: Do people say randy?

Ian: Not anymore.

Eve: We should bring it back. It has a certain ring. Don't you think?

My smile widens. She's adorable. How can a badarse in combat boots—the smartest person I've ever met—be so goddamn adorable?

It's doing things to me. Things inappropriate for this venue.

Ian: I would recommend myself. But it's a conflict of interest.

Eve: How can I trust anyone you recommend? It could be a setup.

Ian: Possible.

Eve: If it is a fake identity, it's elaborate. There are plenty of news articles about you. A few mention your time in the military. You were a pilot.

Ian: Still am.

Eve: Really?

Ian: I can fly you somewhere.

Eve: Where?

Ian: Anywhere you need a good view. I fly helicopters.

Eve: What does a helicopter pilot do in New York City?

Ian: Very little. For its size, the city lacks helipads. But I volunteer with a local hospital once a week.

Eve: What do you do for them?

Ian: Mostly organ transfers. Some med-vac.

Eve: A philanthropist.

Ian: Do I need pure intentions for that?

Eve: What are your intentions?

Ian: I've been called an adrenaline junkie.

By my ex-wife. But no sense in bringing her up. It's not time to kill the mood.

Eve: What are your intentions with me?

Ian: I only send dirty texts if I'm sure a woman wants them.

Eve: You know what I mean.

Ian: I'm not sure I do.

Eve: Why are you offering to buy my virginity? You're a rich man. Clearly handsome. Very successful. And very tall. How tall are you anyway?

Ian: I suppose you want it in feet?

Eve: I can convert centimeters on my phone.

Ian: Other yanks have asked. Six three.

Eve: Yanks? Do you say that to make a point?

Ian: Usually. In other parts of the world, we don't see how you can claim the title America when you're in the middle of the Americas.

Eve: It's a bit myopic.

Ian: It is.

Eve: You like to rile people.

Ian: Maybe.

Eve: Is that it? You're trying to rile someone?

Ian: No. I don't joke about money. I made you an offer. I meant it.

Eve: But why? You don't seem to need help with women. You've been photographed with lots. Women more beautiful than I am. More successful.

Ian: I don't know any women more beautiful than you are.

Eve: That sounds like a line.

Ian: It's the truth.

Eve: It's not. I'm cute, sure. And, yes, I have a look. But I'm not beautiful. I'm not a New York ten.

Ian: That's an awfully conventional lens for you, Eve.

Eve: Because of the hair?

Ian: You have a large tattoo from The Handmaid's Tale on your arm.

Eve: And the hair?

Ian: I like your hair.

Eve: Got a thing for mermaids?

Ian: I can't make a mermaid come.

Eve: Oh.

Ian: That's my intention. To make you come.

Eve: That's it?

Ian: Eve, you're determined to hurt my feelings, aren't you?

Eve: Uh-huh.

Ian: What else is there?

Eve: Is that all you want from me?

Ian: Meet me somewhere. This will be easier in person.

Eve: I have work tonight.

Ian: You don't have to go.

Eve: I do. I have to fill the fridge somehow.

Ian: What are you doing right now?

Eve: It's barely nine.

Ian: And?

Eve: I'm drinking tea and eating oatmeal. Like a normal person. Are you between helicopter missions? Or maybe some sort of covert operation?

Ian: The gym in my building.

Eve: How normal. I can't see that.

Ian: Picture me naked. It might help.

Eve: That would be more fun somewhere else.

She's full on flirting with me. I don't know what to make of it. Of her.

Ian: Somewhere quiet. My office will be empty. Or my apartment.

Eve: Your apartment?

Ian: It's not wise to go to a stranger's apartment, I know. That's why I suggested the office.

Eve: Or you're afraid of me.

Ian: Terrified.

Eve: The office is downtown?

Ian: Yes.

Eve: Let me guess. You live on the Upper East Side?

Ian: I can't give away that information.

Eve: But you'll send me the address?

Ian: A driver.

Eve: I really am a subway girl.

Ian: Because you haven't been in the back of a limo.

Eve: Even so.

Ian: What if I insist?

Eve: I don't think you will.

She's right. I grew up in London without a penny. The Underground was a luxury. Cars aren't a big part of my life.

I don't have a car. Or a driver.

A service? Sure. I can hire a limo anytime, day or night.

I prefer to send women home in a car. Usually, they're too exhausted to remember their fucking subway stop.

Eve isn't there yet. She's smart to insist on riding herself.

She's careful.

I appreciate it. Even if it's making this harder.

Ian: The office then. One o'clock. Unless you want to call into work.

Eve: One it is.

Ian: I'll see you then.

I send her the address. Finish another set. Wipe my brow.

It's not the workout making me sweat. It's her.

In less than three hours, I need to convince Eve Miller to give up on finding a higher bidder.

No, I need more than that.

I need her to choose me.

Chapter Eleven

IAN

I check the floor one more time. No one is here. My office is clean. The kitchen is stocked.

Tea, tonic water, almond milk—whatever she wants, I have it.

Or I can find it.

I *will* find it.

It's an unfamiliar feeling. This need to take care of her. To make sure she's clothed, fed, rested, safe.

I need to keep her safe. Whatever it takes.

The ding of the lift steals my thoughts.

Its silver doors slide open.

Eve steps into the lobby. No combat boots today. Wedge sandals. They're soft against the carpet.

Ripped denim shorts. A tiny crop top. Sheer enough I can see her black bra.

I need to peel her out of those clothes. See if her knickers match her bra. Then do away with those.

Those gorgeous green eyes go wide as she takes in the view. Her defenses fall.

It's hard to explain the way she softens. Her shoulders then her jaw. Her brow. Her gaze.

She takes easy steps toward the window, the one that looks out on Battery Park. She moves close enough to press her palms to the glass.

Then her nose.

Fuck, those dramatic hips. That lush arse.

The things I want to do to her—

I can't let my head go there. Not yet.

I need to stay coherent. I need to stay patient. Not terrify her with my desire to tie her to my bed.

I take a step toward her. "Should I give you a minute?"

She jumps. Brings her hand to her heart. "You scared me." Her eyes fix on me for a moment, then they're on the other window. The one looking out on the Hudson. "It's beautiful here."

"When it's empty."

"It must be gorgeous at night. All lit up. Do you stay late enough to appreciate it? Or does it feel like work? God knows I'm sick of Times Square."

"No? You don't fill with excitement the second you see the *Coca-Cola* billboard? Think about your thrilling night at Devil's Point?"

"All the time," she deadpans. But the sarcasms is short-lived. Wonder spreads over her face as she moves toward the window. "Are you sick of it?"

"It's beautiful at night. I can show you sometime."

She looks back to me. *You would say that.* "Presumptuous."

"Or generous."

"Uh-huh."

"This is an office."

"So you've never?" She turns to me. Scans the room—

78

all glass and open hallways—trying to figure out which office is mine. "You've never had sex here?"

"Are you offering to christen my desk?"

She laughs *yeah, okay*. "You really haven't?"

"I don't mix business and pleasure."

"All those women at work events?"

"Were they naked?"

Her laugh is soft. Easy. "What's this then?"

I motion to the kitchen.

"That's where you bend women over the counter?" Her voice is strong. Bold. With this hint of vulnerability.

She's nervous. She's hiding it well, but it's there.

The perfect image fills my head. Eve's palms on the counter. Her black nails against the plastic. Her shorts at her thighs. Her cunt stretching to take me.

Fuck.

I clear my throat. "Something to drink?"

"Oh." Her gaze flits to the small space. "What are you offering?"

"I have Fever Tree."

"It's a little early."

"For tonic water?"

"Uh-huh."

I can't help but smile. She's adorable. And unbearably sexy.

It's impossible to keep my head straight. I want her too much. Want her enough to throw away every ounce of reason.

Do I have any left?

I'm ready to offer her six figures for thirty days of her life.

Yes, I have the paperwork set up to make everything legitimate. An NDA. A contract that explains I'm paying for her time, not her body. But the implication is clear.

A line I told myself I'd never cross.

A line I have to cross.

The only way to protect her.

"Just water. We can toast if we come to an agreement." She draws a circle in the air. *Which way to your office?*

"That one." I motion to the room in the corner. One window facing the Hudson. The other facing Battery Park.

Still, she follows me into the kitchen. Accepts a glass of water with a thank you. Takes a greedy sip.

"Hot today?" The weather report claims the heat wave is nearly over. But I don't believe it. Even with the air-conditioning on high, I'm on fire.

She nods. "Not as bad as yesterday." She takes another sip. "Is this your first summer in New York?"

I raise a brow.

"You're the one surprised it's hot."

"It's June."

"Okay, it's hot early. But if you've spent at least one summer in New York, you know it's going to be hot until late September."

"It is."

"Hot? Yeah." She makes a show of fanning herself with her hand. Then fanning her tight black crop top. "I'm wearing this for a reason."

"To drive me mad?"

"Besides that." She takes another sip. Swallows hard. "Does it really?"

"Does what really?"

"Does my top really drive you mad?" Her grey-green eyes fix on me. "You've been with other women. Seen them in far less."

"So?"

"So? Why does my crop top drive you mad?" She runs her finger over her bra strap. "Is this all it takes?"

"I don't understand the question."

"Will you drop to your knees and beg if I take off my top?"

"I don't beg." My eyes pass over her slowly. It's instinct. Uncontrollable.

She is fucking beautiful. Tall for a girl, though still a head shorter than I am.

Teal hair in a neat line. Dark eye makeup. Deep red lips.

Her breasts are a little small for her frame, maybe, but still fucking perfect. And that dramatic curve, from her waist over her hips. Those long legs—

I need them wrapped around my waist.

Now.

"I can't promise I'll control myself if you take off your top," I say.

Her pupils dilate. Her teeth sink into her lip. She shakes it off. Clears her throat. "I'll keep that in mind."

I lead her to my office. Motion to the couch. Black. Like her outfit.

"It suits me." She sits. Pulls her legs under her. Already comfortable. Or aware I want to see her comfortable. Aware her posture is driving me out of my fucking mind.

"Do you always wear black?"

"Mostly. Though I'm obviously partial to an accent color." She flips her blue-green hair. "Do you always wear a suit?" Her eyes pass over me slowly. They stop on my chest.

No tie today. Top button undone. The hint of the tattoo on my chest.

Can she see it in this light? Black on dark skin isn't a lot of contrast. Not in this lighting.

She can. From the way she's staring, it's clear. She wants more.

She wants to tear off my shirt and climb into my lap.

But I'm getting ahead of myself again.

"Usually." I motion to my unbuttoned collar. "Sometimes, I'm more casual."

"Is that casual?"

I nod.

"You wear that to the gym?"

"One way to find out."

"You're inviting me to the gym?"

"I'd like to see you sweaty and panting."

She shakes off her blush. "Do you wear it to sleep?"

"I don't wear anything when I sleep."

"Oh." Her eyes pass over me again. Fast this time. "I do that sometimes. When it's too hot. But I like a little something. It feels right." She takes a long sip of water. Sets the glass on the side table. "This, uh... I guess I don't know where to start."

"At the beginning."

"Okay." She folds her hands in her laps. "Well... before I can give you a number, I need more details."

I nod *of course*.

"Is it fifteen minutes in a hotel? The act itself? Virginity is an abstract concept, when you think about it. Sure, I've never done much with a guy. Never touched someone below the waist. Or had them touch me. I mean, I touch myself, but only outside. And would that even matter? If I had a sex toy? Some massive dildo? I don't, but if I did, would I still be a virgin? I use tampons and I—"

"Slow down."

She nods. Swallows hard. Looks me in the eyes. "What exactly do you want?"

Chapter Twelve

EVE

hat exactly do you want?

W The words echo around the room. They bounce off the big glass walls. Sink into my skin.

Despite the steady hum of the air-conditioning, it's warm in here. Hot even.

Or maybe that's the ache between my legs.

The emptiness that only he can fill.

It's ridiculous. Beyond ridiculous. I barely know him. And even then, I know I shouldn't take anything at face value.

The man is a former intelligence operative.

He's still in intelligence. Only now it's for businesses, not his country.

My brain refuses to care.

It fixes on his deep eyes, his broad shoulders, his tattooed chest.

Thin black lines. Words. A Latin quote maybe.

What suits him?

And why am I so eager to trace the lines?

Addie would say *duh, Evie, you have a type. Have you ever dated a guy who wasn't in a band?*

And I'd ask her not to use a nickname for a Pokémon. And we'd get into a whole thing about which Evie evolution is best. And why can't all problems feel this trivial?

I don't mind when she calls me Evie. Only that one time. When her voice was fading and her grip was weak.

Right now, the ugly memory is far away. Fuzzy.

Right now, the words echoing around the room are my entire world.

Ian holds that same poker face. He's infinitely collected. Impossibly collected.

His dark eyes stay fixed on me. Reading me. Seeing everything I keep secret.

I swallow hard.

"I want you." His voice is as even as his posture. "I want to be the first to have you. The rest of the specifics are negotiable."

"Okay." Where is my water? Where can I put my hands? I unfold and refold them. Try to project confidence. He's an ex-spy with more money than God. I'm a broke girl who haggles poorly at the flea market. I'm in over my head and I can't let it show.

"I make arrangements with a lot of women."

"You pay them?"

"No." His eyes pass over me again. Slowly. With a hunger that makes my thighs shake. "I told myself I never would."

"You never would—"

"Pay a woman for sex."

"Oh." Wheels in my brain turn. Rich, handsome, with all the information in the world… and usually unwilling to pay for sex. Either he's in dire need of a virgin. Or he truly wants to stop the doctor. Or it's something about me.

"I understand your predicament."

"What about it?"

"You looked into me." His voice shifts. A firmer tone. More business.

I nod. "I didn't hire a PI or anything, but I did some digging."

"It's amazing, how much information is easy to find. If you do hire an investigator, I'm sure you'll find things that unsettle you. There's plenty in my past." He folds one leg over the other. Leans back into the couch. "I won't mince words. I know you're broke. I know your sister spent time in an inpatient facility—"

"That's none of your business."

"Maybe. If you ask, I won't look further. But no crying over spilled milk."

Easy for him to say.

"You're a strong girl, Eve. I can tell. I don't want you to waste your potential serving pissed arseholes for the next decade."

"It's my potential."

"You're right. Your potential. None of my business. But I assume you're here to negotiate a price. Not lecture me on paternalism."

Damn, is he reading my mind? I have no comeback for that.

I want to lecture him for acting like my goddamn father... but I am here to negotiate. I can deal with a bossy know-it-all if he covers our expenses.

Deep breath. Slow exhale. Utmost confidence. "You still haven't told me what you want."

He reaches for his glass. "I want you. For one month." He takes a long sip. "For thirty days, you'll be mine. To use however I see fit. At the end, we say goodbye, we part, we never see each other again."

Okay… "What if I want to see you again?"

"Are you getting into tech?"

"Maybe."

"Then you will. I'm not going to banish you to another state."

"Thank God. I can't move to Jersey." The joke fails to lighten the mood.

He smiles anyway. "I won't ask you to leave the city. It's more that… once our arrangement ends, it ends. No friendship or booty calls or future help."

"Booty calls?"

"Do you have a new term for it? What were people saying? Netflix and chill?"

My laugh dissolves the tension in my chest. Ian Hunt saying *Netflix and chill*. It's absurd. And incredibly hot.

My body screams *yes, yes, yes. More, more, more.*

It overwhelms every thought in my brain. It's too hard to think around him. How am I supposed to negotiate intelligently?

"We still say booty calls," I say.

"I want to make that clear." His voice firms. "Once it's over, it's over."

"What if I don't want it to be over?"

"It's still over." His posture goes with his voice. Intense stare. Squared shoulders. All that presence.

I swallow hard. "What if you don't want it to be over?"

"That won't happen."

Okay… "What if it does?"

His brow furrows. His jaw cricks. For a second. Then he's back to the soft poker face. "It's never happened before."

"How many women have you… done this with?"

"Enough."

That's not really an answer. But I guess it doesn't

matter. What's the difference if he's done this with one woman or a hundred? It's not like I'm going to say *no, I won't take six figures because you're too big a slut*. As long as he's safe… that's all that matters. "Other virgins?"

"Yes."

"But you've never paid before?"

"Sometimes, I leave parting gifts," he says. "No, always. But sometimes they're small. A set of lingerie or a toy. Other times—" He sets his glass on the table. "A semester of tuition. A trip to Paris. It was mine. But I didn't feel right taking it when she was… inconsolable."

"You're that irresistible?" I bite my lip. That doesn't matter. And it's not a risk. My heart? Still ice. Ian Hunt isn't melting it. Even if he already sets me on fire.

"It happens."

"But you never have feelings?"

"Never enough to reconsider."

Okay. A firm time frame is good. An end point. Less chance of getting hurt. Emotionally. But why in the world am I worried about that? This isn't about feelings. It's about cold, hard cash. "How do I know I can trust you?"

"You haven't asked for an amount yet."

"You haven't made an offer."

He chuckles *fair point*. "After you accept my offer, I'll transfer ten percent into the account of your choice."

"Oh."

"Another ten percent after we sign the contract. The rest when the thirty days are up."

"So it starts… now?"

"After we sign," he says.

Seems reasonable. "And how is it staying legal?"

"I'm not paying you to fuck me." His tone shifts to something dirty and demanding.

My thighs press together reflexively. Fuck, that tone is

hot. I want him to use it again. Only with an entirely different implication.

"I want to fuck you, Eve. Very much. But I'm not paying for anything except your time."

"Isn't that what everyone says?" I'm not a lawyer, but I'm pretty sure that doesn't hold up in court.

"It's true. I'm paying for your time. Thirty days at my beck and call. You go where I ask you to go. Stay where I ask you to stay. Leave when I ask you to leave."

"So you ask me to go to your apartment at midnight and leave at two a.m.?"

He lets out a low chuckle. "That's not nearly enough time."

Ahem.

"Say I ask you to show up at my flat at midnight. And you do. I may ask for more."

"A blow job?"

His eyes pass over me slowly. With humor. Something I've said is funny. "I won't say it in a way that sounds like asking. It will sound more like…" His gaze meets mine. His voice drops to that dirty tone. "Get on your knees, vixen. I'm going to fuck that pretty red mouth."

Holy shit. I…

He…

Holy shit.

My cheeks flame. Then my chest. That's so incredibly dirty. And he's so casual about it.

And I…

I'm in so, so, so far over my head.

"Hopefully, you'll want to do whatever I've demanded," he says.

My body screams *yes. Everything. All the things. Let me fill every one of your dirty desires*.

He continues, "If you don't, you use a certain word."

"A safe word?"

He nods. "You can think about yours. Something easy to remember and hard to confuse. I won't push you to start. But I will eventually."

"You'll say something like that?"

"Yes."

"Oh." Words are impossible.

"I need to know you're ready to drop your safe word."

"So… it's on me to say no?"

"Partially. I'll read you the best I can. Try to stay within the bounds of what you can handle. But sometimes… people don't always know what they can take until they try it. I might push further than you can go. If that's not what you want…"

It is. But it's terrifying. Why do I want this stranger to order me onto my knees? "What if it isn't?"

"I can go slower."

"What if I keep using the safe word?" I ask.

"Then you keep using the safe word."

"You'll still pay me? If I never sleep with you? Or touch you? Or let you touch me?"

He nods.

"So you'll pay for my virginity… even if you don't actually get it?"

"On one condition," he says. "You agree not to sell it to anyone else."

More than fair. It's not like I want to go through this again. "You still haven't said a number."

His lips curl upward. A smile that should dissolve the sexual tension. Only it doesn't. At all. "For thirty days at my beck and call, playing by my terms?"

I nod.

He stands. Moves to his desk. Picks up a tiny blue notebook and an expensive pen.

In one quick motion, he writes a number. Then he returns to the couch and hands the notebook to me.

Almost half a million dollars.

Rent for the next decade.

Plus enough for mine and Addie's college and a trip to the Bahamas. A trip to the Bahamas every year. At a private resort. A luxury resort.

I trace the edges of the leather cover. I'm negotiating. I should counter. That's the rule.

"Can you do better?" I bite my tongue. Wait for the words to shatter glass. "Did I really say that?"

"Yes." He chuckles. "You did."

"Oh. Well… uh… I guess I stand by it."

"You guess?"

"I do."

His smile widens. He's charmed by me. For some reason. "I can."

I hand the notebook back to him.

He takes the pen. Scribbles a new figure on a new sheet of paper. Ten percent higher.

That's fifty grand in my bank account today.

A hundred grand after a contract.

Six-figures in my bank account.

"What's to stop me from running off with the cash?" I ask.

"That money is yours as soon as you have it." His eyes meet mine. "I like you, Eve. I want to enjoy this time with you. If you get scared, I'll understand. But if you're trying to play me…" His voice shifts to something low. A threat. "I'm not a man you want to cross."

That, I believe.

"I'll have the contract sent to your place. Take the week. Find a lawyer. Protect yourself."

"Is that… part of the contract?"

"Condoms?"

I nod. "I've never… I want to be safe."

"Are you on birth control?"

"Yes, but that doesn't protect against STDs."

"It's been a few months since I've been with someone."

Why? That doesn't fit anything I know about him. But maybe I don't know anything.

"I'll get tested again this week. Send you the results. If you still want to use condoms, we can. I'd rather not."

"Okay."

"Yes or okay?"

"Yes." My cheeks flame. My chest. My entire body. Is it possible to blush everywhere? "And the thirty days. That's fine. But I need next weekend free. I'm going to the beach with my sister."

"We'll meet the following Monday."

"I assume this is a secret?"

He nods *yes*. "I want you to quit that job right away."

I should argue. Insist he can't tell me what to do until I've actually signed. But I hate the job. The thought of not showing up tonight… hell yes. "Okay."

"Anything else?"

"I don't know what you have in mind for the thirty days. But I always go as me. I'll take nicer clothes. But I decide what I wear."

His eyes flit to my chest. He stares in a way that says *you won't wear much*. "Of course. I've picked you because I like you, Eve. Not because I want to turn you into someone else."

He must like me a lot. Half a million dollars for thirty days. It's insane.

And I…

Need to go. Before I talk my way out of this cash.

Before he starts confessing all his dirty desires.

And I start bending to fill them.

"I guess I should do that." I stand. Smooth my shorts. "The lawyer, I mean. And then… we can start."

He nods *of course.* "Next Monday. Here. Nine a.m."

"I'm not a morning person."

He smiles. "Seven p.m. then. We'll sign. Celebrate with dinner."

"Okay." I hold out my hand.

"Until then." He shakes.

"Until then."

Chapter Thirteen

EVE

There it is in big, blue letters.
Checking Account:
54,331.24

A year of rent, food, medical expenses.

No more almond butter and jelly sandwiches. No more bulk tea. No more cheap chocolate.

I roll onto my white sheets. With the breeze flowing through my window, the heat is bearable. But I don't have to settle for bearable anymore.

I can afford air-conditioning. A nice apartment. Soft sheets.

That ice cream place Addie loves. With that to-die-for non-dairy mint-chip.

I blast Bad Religion. Lie on my bed, staring at the ceiling, counting all the possibilities.

Yes, I need to be careful. To put aside money for tuition. To save for a rainy day. But that leaves plenty of splurge money.

Hundreds of scoops of ice cream.

Thousands of fancy iced coffees—from that place by NYU that charges a fortune for twelve ounces.

All the ten-dollar-a-bar chocolate I can eat.

A knock interrupts me. Addie.

"Come in," I call.

She does. She tugs at her coral tank top, fanning herself. "There's so much sweat between my boobs." She makes a show of wiping her chest with her top. "You're lucky you're more—"

"Flat?"

"Yeah. Sorry. But you are. They're nothing but trouble." She laughs. "Where have you been?"

"Out."

"Out…" She moves into the room. Presses the door closed. Steps in front of the fan. "With…"

"People."

"You don't talk to people."

"I do too."

"Which people?" She brushes a stray hair behind her ear. "Britney? From work?"

I only talk to Britney at work. I like a lot of the girls at the club, but I never want to think about that place. "I'm quitting."

"That's great, Evie! You're out way too late. And that place… it's not safe."

"You sound like… a grandma from Long Island. It's totally safe."

She adopts a grandma inflection. "Are you eating your veggies, little Evie? And drinking your milk? You're a growing girl, you know?"

"You push dairy as a grandma?"

"Almond milk. Of course. It's calcium fortified."

"Of course." I tease my sister about her love of almond

milk, but I love it just as much. "Is there tea? Or at least cookies?"

"Grandma ate all the cookies." She sits on the bed next to me. "You're in a good mood."

"The feeling of freedom."

She smiles. "How free are we talking?"

"Don't quit your internship."

She laughs. "I meant more—"

"It is uh…" I want her to know we'll be okay. That neither one of us has to worry about cash for a while. I want to tell her… but I'm not ready to tell her about Ian's offer.

She might not approve.

She might talk me out of it.

Still. I need to say something. To explain somehow. "I found a new gig. It's a little weird, but it pays really well." That is true.

She looks at me funny. Unsure what to make of my explanation.

"Enough we won't have to worry. Through the rest of the year."

She raises a brow, not really buying it.

No. I'm not giving that asshole credit. I need another explanation. Something. Anything.

Once upon a time, Dad was actually… a dad. He took us to the park; he made us dinner; he helped with homework.

At some point, his drug addiction took over. A little at first. Then all at once.

Sometimes he didn't show up for dinner. Or the weekend. Or an entire month.

But he worked. He helped. Yes, I took care of the actual bill paying, but it was the money he made. Addie cleaned, we both cooked. We were okay.

Two years ago, he stopped showing up.

He sends money sometimes. Sometimes enough to cover most of our expenses. Sometimes enough for a week of groceries. But I never know how much is coming. When it's coming. If it's coming.

Now... with this money from Ian...

I can tell my father to fuck off. To keep his bullshit apology cash. To swallow it along with his next drink.

I never have to take his help again.

That's worth so much.

My shoulders ease. "And my scholarship came through. So we don't have to worry about that."

"Oh my God, Eve, way to bury the lead! Let's celebrate." She jumps off the bed and holds out her hands *come here.*

I take them. Let her pull me up.

"Where do you want to go?"

"I heard something about cookies." My eyes flit to the window. Still afternoon. "Or maybe ice cream and coffee. A new dress from that place in the Village. And dinner. At that vegan restaurant by NYU."

"With the veggie meatballs?"

I nod.

"You sure? We can do Indian."

Mmm. Tantalizing options. But this place is Addie's favorite. And the meatball sandwich is surprisingly good. "Tomorrow. Tonight, veggie meatballs."

"You really are in a good mood."

"Life is good, kid." I motion to the makeup piled on my desk. "Just give me ten. Uh. Twenty. I'm going to savor the *I'm done* call."

"You don't want to do it in person?"

"I never want to see that place again." I pick up my lipstick. Cheap stuff. I can toss it now and replace it with something premium. The twenty-dollar-a-tube lipstick that lasts for hours.

"Okay." She moves to the door. Looks back at me with a smile. "When does your new gig start?"

"After the beach trip."

"You're coming?"

"Mm-hmm."

She bounces back into the room. Throws her arms around me. "Thank you."

"It's not for you. It's a free beach trip."

Addie beams.

It makes my heart warm. Ice, what ice? I'm a freaking puddle.

My sister is everything. The only family I have left. The only person in the world I trust. Seeing her happy and healthy... it's overwhelming.

Lying to her... not as much. But better than saying *guess what, my hymen is worth six figures. Who knew?* "I'll be busy once I start. The boss is very demanding."

"What are you doing for him?"

"Whatever he wants." Technically true.

"So you're like... his assistant?"

"Something like that." I don't want to come up with any more half-truths, so I motion to the door. "Give me twenty."

She hugs me again then she moves into the main room.

I press the door closed. Pick up my cell. Check the number one more time.

It's still there. Fifty grand in my checking account. The beginning of the end of all my problems.

Maybe fairy tales do come true.

Or maybe I'm about to find out Prince Charming is a very wicked man.

Chapter Fourteen

EVE

Original Sin
Thursday, June 11
Two p.m.

Have I answered the question? Brave or foolish? Careful or cowardly?

Is *yes* an answer?

Maybe all of the above.

It's right here. On my desk. A large manila envelope disguised as junk mail. Because Mr. Tall, Dark, and Handsome thinks of everything.

And I don't think anymore. I'm not sure how I'm writing this, because I'm no longer in touch with my brain.

Only the free fall in my chest.

I'm doing it. Taking the leap. Accepting an offer that promises to erase all my problems.

And in exchange…

I'm still a virgin.

In a month and change, that's unlikely to be the case.

Maybe I should say more. State it explicitly.

Normally, I'm not afraid of the harsh truth.

I don't mince words.

I don't beat around the bush.

But why do I need to make a big deal of this? It's my virginity. Why can't I make use of it instead of losing it at a hotel after prom?

Does that actually happen anymore? Or just in old TV shows?

It's a silly idea. The thought of saving it for someone special. If you asked me two months ago, I would have laughed at you.

Am I saving it? No. There's no "do not cross" line on my panties. No "only the worthy may enter" tattoo on my inner thigh. No "insert six-figures before you insert six inches."

Look at me, making jokes about dick size. As if I care. As if I'm another bro at school who needs to turn everything into a measuring contest.

Newsflash asshole: no one cares if you're five inches or six inches or seven inches or twelve inches.

And the more you discuss it, the more we think you're on the smaller side.

I guess I'm contradicting myself here. How can I consider it if I don't care? And how can I say "women don't care about dick size" when my only female confidant prefers pussy?

I really have no idea.

And no way to handle all the thoughts racing around my brain. The thoughts of him. How I'll handle him.

I don't believe in "big dick energy." Why am I sure he's *ample?* Besides the stereotypes from old TV shows?

I don't know.

But I do.

I guess, if I'm here, I want to contemplate something.

But it's still in soft focus. Distant. Blurred by the big, bright sky.

Life is good. No clouds. No drunk assholes. No bills to pay.

Just a new black bikini in a new purple suitcase. Because black suitcases are impossible to pick out of a lineup and I can't buy teal.

I can't take another person telling me my outfit matches my hair as if I don't own a mirror.

A weekend away from my problems. Lying in the sun. Splashing in the Atlantic.

Then I come back to the city and I dive into the deep end.

Which is scarier? Two and a half days in a ritzy suburb —with my sister's girlfriend's family—or thirty with Mr. Tall, Dark, and Handsome?

Both. In different ways.

Family is hard. The words Mom and Dad make me cringe. I lack the ability to smile and say *thank you, I so appreciate what you're doing for my sister.*

I'm too busy looking at the cracks. Wondering when shit is going to finally hit the fan.

Is it an affair? Drug addiction? Drug overdose? Suspicious circumstance surrounding a death?

I know it's something.

There's always something.

It must be true for him too. Mr. Tall, Dark, and Handsome is far too, well, handsome.

Too rich.

Too successful.

Too enticing.

The way he issues dirty demands—

There must be women everywhere ready to fall to their knees.

Fuck knows I am. Even though I have no idea what comes next. Yes, I know the general concept. I have a few articles with, ahem, tips. Instructions even. But there's nothing like practical experience.

And I'm lacking there.

But if that's what he really likes about me...

There's got to be a catch. Something wrong with him. Something behind the cool expression and the soulful eyes.

What is it?

What is he hiding?

And why am I so ready to throw the question away and jump into his bed?

I can give him my body. Even though I'm scared, I can handle that.

But what if that's not enough for him?

What if he wants my mind? My heart?

My everything?

- Eve

Chapter Fifteen

IAN

All day, I struggle to concentrate. Nothing helps. Not tea, running, diving into an enemy's secrets, re-reading Eve's last entry.

My body stays electric. My limbs stay light. My thoughts stay dirty.

How am I supposed to find the place this CEO has hidden his stolen money with images of Eve in my head?

They refuse to budge.

Her black nails against my back.

Her berry lips parting with a groan.

Her soft body splayed out over the bed.

And other images. Sweet, romantic ones.

Her eyes lighting up as she launches into a discussion of her favorite book.

Her lips curling into a smile.

Her laugh filling the room as she twirls on her heel, showing off some gorgeous black dress.

It's bad news. And, worse, I'm too far gone to care. This is it. Four hours until I sign the papers.

Four hours until she's mine.

For thirty days.

That's all I get.

Right now, it's unfathomable.

How can thirty days ever be enough? How can anything be enough?

I need everything.

Forever.

Which is why I need the strict end point. Thirty days isn't enough time to ruin me.

No open hearts or wedding rings or divorce papers.

No one gets hurt.

It's for the best. No matter how little I like it.

The day ticks by.

Three hours.

Two.

One.

Twenty minutes.

I shut down my computer. Ready my paperwork. Check the office.

It's emptying, but it's far from empty. Half a dozen assistants. Plus a few executives.

Shepard in the kitchen, chatting with a new associate.

Shep catches me watching. Shakes his head *sad to see a man who's fallen so far*. Dismisses the man he's talking to. Motions for me to come here.

He waits until the associate is out of earshot. "Someone put extra honey in your tea."

"Is that a metaphor?"

"I'm trying something new."

"It doesn't suit you."

"Neither does the attempt at playing cool." He takes a long sip of his coffee. Studies me with that Shep-like stare. *I'll find your weak point and exploit it.* "Is it today? Are you finally breaking your rule?"

"Nice to see you too."

Shep holds up his espresso cup. "Should I hand this straight to you so we can get it over with?"

"Absolutely."

He chuckles as he hands me the espresso.

I take a sip. "Rubbish. As always."

He shakes his head. Takes the cup. Places it in the sink. Starts fixing another. "What's the arrangement this time?"

"Thirty days."

"And her virginity?"

"Not technically."

"Of course. Not… technically." Shep fills the electric kettle. Turns it to boil. "Do you believe that?"

"What's to believe? Technically, I'm paying for her time. She can say no at any point. I'll still pay her."

"What if she does?"

"I'll be incredibly disappointed."

He half-smiles. "You're nervous."

I shrug like I don't know what he means.

"Should I grab the gin instead."

"Maybe. I'll need to toast soon."

He raises a brow. "What did it cost?"

"I would have paid more."

The espresso machine hisses. Then it's the *drip*, *drip*, *drip*. One of those pod machines. Not the best for the best. Mediocrity. Compromise. "Do I hear embarrassment in Ian Hunt's voice?"

"No."

"Apprehension?"

"Never."

"Then what is it? I've never known you to shy away from sharing a good deal."

"Since when do you want illicit details?" I ask. "You usually complain you're not interested in my dalliances."

"My wife is rooting for you."

"Call Jasmine. I'll tell her."

"She's at an acting class." He pulls out his cell. "But I can leave a message." He pretends as if he's leaving a voice mail for his wife. "Princess, you won't believe the gossip I have from Ian. The object of his obsession is about to be his for thirty days. The usual deal. Only this time, he's paying for the privilege." He looks to me and raises a brow.

"Less than you paid her to marry you."

"I paid for a year."

"Yes, and Jasmine is lovely. Far too beautiful and articulate for you."

"Ha ha." He rolls his eyes. *Heard that before*.

"But she's no Eve."

"I'm not sure you want to share that with my wife. Not in those words. Maybe focus on how you're obsessed with her and willing to pay anything."

"I'm not obsessed."

He raises a brow *really?*

Okay, I'm obsessed. Incredibly, painfully, unbearably obsessed. "It's the mystery. Once I have her, know her… it will be the same as it always is."

"A parting gift and nothing but memories?"

"Of course."

"Do you really believe that?"

"Yes," I lie.

He shakes his head *not buying it*. Turns to the steaming kettle. "Do you want that tea?"

The ding of the lift interrupts me.

It's her. I can feel it in the way the air changes.

Footsteps move closer. The soft thunk of her heeled boots. She moves down the hallway. Straight to my office.

Shepard follows my gaze. "You should pick your jaw up from the floor."

"I'm not—"

"You have that gin in your office?"

"Why? Ready to break your dry streak?" I don't usually refer to the man's alcoholism. He doesn't usually refer to my ex-wife. We taunt each other plenty, but it's playful, not blood-thirsty.

"Because you're going to need it."

"I don't."

"In thirty days, when she breaks your heart… I won't say I told you so."

"She won't." I say it without conviction.

He knows. But he doesn't call me on it.

Chapter Sixteen

EVE

After a quick hello, I pull the folder from my bag. A new bag. Filled with new things.

This folder. A nylon pen case. A dozen new pens in every color.

And a diary. An old school leather one. In case my thoughts start to jumble.

It's the only thing that helps. And something tells me I'm not going to have the patience to wait until I'm in front of my computer.

A mess is coming.

Ian is already sending me in every possible direction.

And this—

No second thoughts. Even if I'm scared.

This is a good thing. No matter how much the butterflies in my stomach want to argue otherwise.

They're not even saying *this is bad*. More *danger, danger, danger*.

My hand brushes Ian's as I give him the folder.

It's there. That same buzz. That same heat. That same need to feel his hands everywhere.

"All final. With the changes." All negotiated by lawyers over the last week. Nothing major.

A point demanding three days' notice before we leave the city. His counter: an ability to insist I sleep where he sleeps. Plus a credit card for assorted purchases. Makeup, clothes, lingerie, sex toys.

Anything I want. Within reason.

Does he do that with all the women he fucks?

Or just me?

It still makes no sense. Why would someone so rich, attractive, and powerful choose me over any other woman?

I push the question to the back of my mind. Sure, this is weird. But it's happening. And it's only thirty days. I might as well enjoy them.

"Thank you." He opens the folder. Peruses the pages. When he's satisfied, he sets the contract on the desk, grabs a fountain pen. "We need a witness."

"Right."

"Do you prefer someone in particular?" His eyes flit to the final page. The details there. That spell out the amount and the time frame.

"Someone discrete."

He motions *one moment*, steps out of the office, calls in a young woman in a pencil skirt. "Can you watch us sign, love?"

"Of course, Mr. Hunt." Her eyes flit to me. Curiosity spreads over her expression. *What in the world is she doing here?*

"Thank you, Ronnie." He picks up the pen. Signs. Turns and hands it to me.

I shake my head. Pull a gel roller from my bag.

I know it's a cliché, for writers to have strong opinions about pens, and it's true. I'm gel rollers all the way.

But I don't think of myself as a writer. Not usually.

I've certainly never called myself a writer. Or introduced myself as a writer. Or answered the question "what do you want to do when you grow up" with "write."

There's never enough room in my head for that question. But I guess that's changing. *How will I pay the rent* no longer gets space in my brain. Which leaves all this room. Room I don't know how to fill.

"I prefer mine. Thank you." I move to the desk. Skim the final page one last time.

Here it is.

My fate.

Thirty days at Ian Hunt's beck and call. Half a million dollars in my bank account. A month filled with his dirty desires.

I sign on the dotted line.

The witness does her part. Says a professional goodbye.

Ian pulls a bottle of amber liquor from his desk. Then two glasses. "Do you drink bourbon?"

"Not regularly." Or ever.

"You like chai?"

"I drink chai every morning."

"You'll like this one." He pours. Hands a glass to me. Holds his to toast. "To a beautiful future."

"To a beautiful future." I'm not sure we mean the same future, but, hey, I'm happy to drink to half a million dollars.

I tap my glass against his. Bring the drink to my lips. Take a small sip.

Sweet, spicy, expensive. I'm not sure how I can tell, but I can.

Expensive. And really fucking good.

I take another sip. Let the bourbon warm my cheeks, tongue, throat.

"You like it?" His eyes fix on me. My eyes. Then my lips. He watches as I swallow hard.

"I do. Thank you."

"I'll send you a bottle."

"That isn't necessary."

"Are you asking me not to?"

"No." I finish my drink. Set the glass on his desk. It's sturdy. Enormous. Expensive.

"You don't have to tiptoe with me. If you don't want something you can say it. You won't hurt my feelings."

"What if I say I don't want you? Or any time with you? Or any part of your body?"

"That would be a lie."

I swallow hard. "What if I did?"

"I'd say you're fucked, because you just agreed to thirty days on my terms."

"True. I guess they start now. According to the contract." Seven fifteen. It ends in thirty days at seven fifteen. Exactly thirty days.

"Are you already counting minutes?" His voice shifts to a playful tone. "Maybe you do despise me."

"No, I'm just…"

"Nervous?"

"Yeah." It's not like I'm hiding it. "I've never…" Signed away my freedom. Slept with a man. Seen a man naked in person. Kissed someone who set me on fire. The list is too long.

He gives me a slow once-over. "We are going to celebrate." He finishes his drink. Sets his glass next to mine. "Dinner at a private club."

"Let me guess? We're taking a limo." I try to lighten the mood, but it's not the mood that's tense. It's me. This is terrifying.

He half-smiles. "You object?"

"It's a nice day."

"It's—what is it kids say? Hot as balls."

"Am I a kid?"

"You're eighteen."

"And you're—"

"Thirty-six," he says.

And that only makes me crave him more. What does that say about me? And why don't I care? "What did they say? When you were a kid?"

"I stick with hot."

"It is. But it's still nice."

"You want to walk somewhere?"

I nod.

"I know a place nearby. Not as nice as the one uptown."

"No?"

"It will be harder to make you come." He offers his hand. "Still nice."

"Oh. Is that… the plan?"

Ian's laugh is soft. Easy. "No, vixen. You'll have to earn that."

Chapter Seventeen

EVE

As far as I know, the kids, meaning my peers, do not say hot as balls. Or amazeballs. Or holy shitballs.

Really, I don't know anyone using expressions about balls. Beyond the usual. *What balls. Look at the huevos on that guy. That takes cojones.*

The ball and dick centric slang of the teenage boy.

But holy shitballs, this place is crazy.

A restaurant on the top floor. Glass walls, high ceilings, balconies in every direction.

The hostess leads us straight to the balcony. One looking up to Midtown. A couch against the wall. A coffee table in front of it. Two armchairs on each side.

No way to see anything around the corner.

No way for someone around the corner to see anything. Not on the couch.

Better than a secluded booth.

Plenty of privacy for making me come. Not that I want Ian to make me come. I mean, I do. In an abstract way.

And a very visceral way.

I want to climb into his lap, tug at his tie, throw my head back as he slips his hand between my legs.

Ahem.

I take a seat on the soft couch. Press my legs together. Smooth my skirt. This is a new dress. Nicer than anything from H&M or Dolls Kill. But not in the same league as this place.

I swallow hard as I take a menu from the hostess.

She hands another to Ian. Smiles that serene customer service smile I know so well. "The usual, Mr. Hunt?"

He nods. "Thank you."

"I'll be back with your drinks in a few minutes." She says it with an implication.

Like she knows we might use our privacy for illicit activities. Or maybe like she wants to be the one engaging in illicit activities with him.

He takes a seat at the other end of the couch. It leaves the middle cushion between us.

To make me comfortable? Or for some reason I don't understand?

I don't like the space. I want to be next to him. To feel the warmth of his body against mine. But I'm not ready to admit that. It's too overwhelming.

I've never wanted someone this much. And certainly not someone with such murky intentions.

No, I'm overthinking it.

He wants to fuck me. It's not complicated. He's not Prince Charming. He's a rich man so interested in virginity he's willing to pay six figures for it.

That's the story that makes sense. Even if it fails to explain everything.

"I think she likes you." I skim the menu. Grass fed fillet mignon. Seared sea bass. Sea urchin sashimi. Expensive, fancy, hard to find. Enticing.

"She likes how well I tip." He sets his menu on the table.

"I know server friendly. It's more."

"Perhaps. I don't care one way or another."

"No. You aren't going to invite her to join us in a threesome?"

Ian chuckles. "Am I that bad at reading the room?"

It's a good point. I am clearly not at threesome point. "Maybe your desire is overtaking you."

He turns his body toward mine. "Is it?"

"Maybe."

"Maybe that's your desire."

"I want to have a threesome?"

He shakes his head. "No. You're not the type."

"How do you know that?"

"Am I wrong?"

No, but how does he know that? "You must say it for some reason."

"The way you look at me. Like I'm the only thing you've ever wanted."

Fuck. Is it that obvious? I clear my throat. "And you?"

"I'm not interested in a ménage à trois."

"Oh." I'm not all that articulate today.

It's him. Or maybe it's the high altitude. The thirty-seventh floor must be a high altitude.

It's so beautiful today. The very start of sunset. The pale blue sky. The hint of orange on the horizon.

"Oh?" he asks.

I turn toward him. Force myself to look into his dark eyes. I want to stare at them forever. And I'm terrified of losing myself in them. "Isn't that supposed to be every guy's fantasy?"

"Maybe. But it's not mine."

"Do you have one?"

His eyes meet mine. "More than one."

"Anything… specific?"

"Yes." He says it with confidence. Like he knows I'm going to ask for details. Like he's sure I want to know every one of his dirty desires.

I guess my poker face is terrible.

Or maybe I can let go of the poker face. Sure, Ian Hunt is a man with enough power to destroy me, with intentions I don't understand—

But we agree on one thing.

I want him and he wants me.

The waitress saves me from an embarrassing question. She drops off our drinks.

Two gin and tonics. Plus a carafe of water and glasses.

She sets everything on the table. "A few minutes to order?"

He nods *thank you*.

She smiles and disappears. A good server. Invisible.

He picks up his drink. "Would you prefer something else?"

"No. It's just… strange for you to order for me." And stranger, that I'm more relieved than annoyed.

"I'll drink it if you don't."

Not really an answer. I guess I didn't ask a question. I do want it. And I like that he knows that. Even if he's being so pushy about it.

I take a small sip. Mmm. Just as perfect as the last. In a different way. Sweeter. More herbaceous. Still incredibly refreshing. "What about food?"

"I don't know what food you like yet."

"But you know my drink preference?"

"Don't I?" His voice drips with that same steady confidence.

Does anything ruffle this guy? "And when you do know what food I like?"

"I won't order for you if it upsets you." He takes a long sip. "But I'd like to take care of your needs, Eve. All of them."

I sidestep the dirty implication. "You want to decide for me?"

"No. I want to know what you want before you do. So you have one less thing to consider."

It sounds reasonable like that. And... sexy, actually. Someone looking out for my needs first? Knowing what I want before I do and giving it to me?

That sounds like heaven.

For a while, at least.

"Okay. If you prove yourself, you can order for me," I say.

"If I prove myself?"

I nod *yes*. "I'll tell you a few dishes I like. You order something for me here. If I like it, I'll give you another shot."

"What if you don't like it?"

"We'll do best of three."

He laughs. "You're going easy on me."

"I'm picky."

"Are you?"

I shake my head. It's hard to be picky when broke.

"So this should be easy?"

"No, I need to love whatever you suggest. It needs to be the best thing I've ever had."

"High standards."

I nod.

"I appreciate that." He picks up the menu. "What do you like?" Intention slips into his voice. Just enough to hint at later.

That is what he wants. To anticipate my desires and give them to me.

"I like this." I hold up my drink. "But I guess you already know that."

"What about it?"

"The lime. The herbs. The balance. It's light and strong at the same time."

"You prefer subtle flavors?"

"I don't know. What makes something subtle? I like basil. And I like sriracha."

"Favorite cuisine?"

"Indian."

"Really?" He raises a brow.

"Why is that surprising?"

"It's better in London."

"How do you know? Have you tried every place in New York?" I ask.

"How can you doubt me if you've never been to London?"

"How do you know I've never been to London?"

"Educated guess." He takes another sip. Turns his attention to the menu. "What do you like about Indian food?"

"It's cheap. And veggie friendly. My sister is a vegetarian."

"What about the flavor?"

"The spices. And chai. I love chai. But my favorite dish is harder to find. Jalfrezi."

"It is hard to find here."

"Oh?"

He nods. "Popular in London. But not in the States."

"Oh." It's my new favorite word. How else can I respond to him? He's just... oh.

He continues, "What's your favorite food? Of all time?".

"Mint-chip ice cream."

He nods with understanding. "Savory food?"

"What's with the nod?"

"Mine too."

"Really?"

"Why is that surprising?"

"I don't know. It is the best flavor. But you don't seem like someone who orders something obvious."

He holds up his gin and tonic. "Who cares if it's obvious if it's the best?"

A good counter. I'm making too many assumptions. Sure, Ian is a rich British guy. But he's also bringing me to fancy restaurants.

He doesn't care if people judge him for a companion with teal hair and combat boots. Maybe he doesn't care about appearances.

"No one wants to feel average," I say.

"Not average. But a lot of people want to blend." His eyes flit from my dress to my hair. Then they're on my eyes. "You don't."

"Maybe this is another way I blend? The bitchy punk chick."

"Are you bitchy?"

"Only to assholes."

He chuckles. "Does it bother you? When people see you that way?"

"Sometimes."

"You must make an effort. The hair, the makeup, the outfits." His eyes pass over me slowly. Savoring every inch. "I suppose goth sexpot isn't exactly your aim."

"I happen to be pale. I was at the beach all weekend

and nothing." I pull my dress strap aside just enough to show off my hint of a tan line. Pale versus very pale.

He chuckles. "You look put together."

"Are you into goth sexpots?"

"Only if you'll start quoting Edgar Allan Poe."

I shake my head. Let my lips curl into a smile. He's funny. Really funny. And it's easy talking to him. Way too easy.

"I can't imagine you prefer 'punk rock sexpot.'"

"If I have to be some kind of sexpot, I prefer punk rock." My hands go to the edge of my skirt instinctively. "I guess… the sex appeal varies. It's necessary at a bar. For tips. And there were times when I wanted to play it up. Like a normal high school girl who wanted attention from boys. Now… I don't know."

"You want me to desire you?"

"Don't you?"

"Yes." His eyes pass over me slowly. "You can still want it."

"Do you?" I clear my throat. "Want me to desire you?"

"You do. But yes. Of course."

"It's not something guys talk about. Not to me, at least. Even now, with people more evolved, men think women should entice them. They think it's all about satisfying their desire."

"Are people more evolved?"

"I don't know. Maybe. I've only been alive so long."

"That's the second reminder of your age in a few minutes."

"Is it?"

He nods. "Does it bother you?"

"Maybe." Not as much as it should. I like it more than I should. I like that he's older. Worldly. Experienced.

"A part of you likes it?"

"If you say daddy issues, I'll throw this in your face."

His laugh is easy. "Do you have a strained relationship with your father?"

"That's very close." I hold up the drink. A playful threat. "I might do it anyway."

"Don't worry. I won't ask you to call me Daddy."

My cheeks flush.

"It's not my kink. But you can. If you want."

"If *I* want?"

He nods. "There's no shame in wanting someone to take care of you. Especially if you've never had that. Especially if you're usually taking care of the world."

It's like he's reading my mind. The information he got looking me up? Or something about my presence here? Maybe he just knows why women want him. Knows what role he wants to fill. "Am I that obvious?"

He doesn't answer. "Is that what you want?"

"Yes," I swallow hard.

"Good." He says it with pride. Pride I need. "I want to take care of you. In every way possible."

"You mean sex?"

"When you're ready."

"What if I am?"

"What did I tell you?"

"I have to earn that?"

He nods *exactly*.

"Have I?"

"Is that an offer?"

I bite my lip.

"I want to touch you, Eve. I want to pull you into my lap and stroke you until you come. But only if you're ready." His eyes meet mine. "Are you?"

Chapter Eighteen

EVE

N o.

Not yet.

I excuse myself. To the bathroom. I fix my makeup. Return to a fresh drink. And Ian ordering dinner.

The dish he orders is perfect.

Frutti di mare. With extra oregano.

A balance of chewy pasta, fresh tomato, seafood, herbs.

Everything I like. And expensive to boot. I didn't even know food could taste this expensive.

There are four kinds of shellfish. Enough, the dish is hands on. But there's something I like about that too. The crunch is satisfying. Primal.

The sun sinks into the horizon, turning the sky orange, then blue. Then that perfect indigo that only exists in New York.

The city lights up. Yellow bulbs against the dark sky. Moonlight. Steel and glass.

The totally and completely overwhelming presence of Ian Hunt.

He asks about my plans for the summer. During my thirty days—supposedly, he wants to give me plenty of latitude—and after.

The month of freedom before I start school.

It's hard to contemplate. I can't remember the last time I had a month to myself. With the spare cash to actually enjoy it.

There are so many options.

A hotel in Cambodia. A luxury resort in the Caribbean.

Or time to myself. Alone. With a pen and paper and plenty of space to unleash my thoughts.

I guess I can do that anywhere. But doing it in my room—a new room, with air-conditioning, and a queen bed, and one of those fancy adjustable height desks, and actual painted walls—

That's what I want.

A space that's mine.

Mine and Addie's. With no ugly memories. No deadbeat fathers on the lease. No assholes aware of the address.

After that... a week in the Caribbean. Or back to the Hamptons with Marisol's family. Their house is sweet and her sister is really nice. Even if I never, ever want to see my sister make out with her girlfriend again.

And that night...

Shudder. I love Addie more than anything, but I really don't need to hear her come.

Damn. I'm already thinking in terms of sex. Everything is straight to sex.

I contemplate the matter when I break in the bathroom. Rinse my mouth. Reapply my lipstick.

There. Perfect.

A punk rock sexpot. My snug dress is short enough it's

sexy. And the way Ian stares at my legs like he's thinking about diving between them.

I like it.

I like it way too much.

I like him way too much.

And maybe… Maybe I'm ready to answer his question.

Deep breath. Steady exhale. Utmost confidence. I compose myself, then I move back to the balcony.

It feels more private in the dark. With him in the middle of the couch, his eyes on me, his posture proud and in-control.

He motions *come here.*

I take a step toward him. Then another. Another.

My knees brush his slacks.

He offers his hand. For support.

I take it. Let him pull me into his lap.

My knees plant outside his thighs. His hands go to my hips. Slowly, he pulls me closer. Until I'm sitting on his thighs.

"Did you like it?" His hands curl around my hips. A soft pressure. Just enough to say *I've got you.*

"Dinner?"

He nods.

"It was perfect."

"I've earned another chance?"

My tongue slides over my lips. He's not asking about our next dinner. He's asking about this. Right now. Him… I don't know what he's going to do. Only that I want it. "Yes."

"Good." He traces the line of my body, over my hip, my waist, my shoulder. My jawline. It's soft. Gentle. Precise. "I want to know what you like."

I nod.

"Everything you like." His hand cups the back of my

head. His eyes flutter closed. He pulls me into a slow, steady kiss.

His lips against my lips.

The taste of gin and lime.

A tiny brush.

Then more. His hand knots in my hair. My legs spread. My pelvis shifts. Closer. But not close enough.

Nothing is close enough.

My hand curls around the back of his neck.

His tongue slips into my mouth. He explores my mouth with steady, patient movements. He pulls me closer. Closer.

Until I can feel him hard under me.

It's not the first time. I had boyfriends in high school. But this is different. Better.

So much better.

I rock my hips an inch. Just enough to feel his erection. That sensation of hardness and warmth between my legs.

It's good.

So fucking good.

I'm a writer. I should be more articulate. But I'm not in touch with fancy words. Only primal ones.

Yes. Now. More. Please.

He tugs at my hair. The sharp pull makes my sex clench. Yes. Now. More. A groan falls off my lips.

He places a kiss on my jaw. Then a line down my neck. Soft pressure. Then harder. Harder. Hard enough I yelp.

Ian releases me. He looks me up and down, settling on my chest. "I want to see you, vixen."

I don't need extra detail. Only the hunger in his eyes. I nod. Push my right strap off my shoulder. Then the left.

They fall down my arms, but my dress stays in place.

It's tight. Corset lacing. Tight enough I don't need a bra.

He brings his hands to the fabric. Peels it down my chest a quarter inch at a time.

My breath catches in my throat.

My fingers curl into my skirt.

My thighs shake.

This is a secluded balcony, but it's still a public place. I'm still exposed. To him. The server. Anyone who walks by.

Why is that so enticing?

He pulls my dress lower. Low enough my breasts spill from the fabric.

My sex clenches. The exhibition is thrilling. And the look in his eyes—like I'm the best thing he's ever seen—

Fuck. I need this. Him. Everything.

"Beautiful." He cups my breasts with his hands. A soft pressure. Then it's his thumb against my nipple.

A groan falls off my lips.

"Like this?" He drags his thumbs over my nipples again. Softly. Then a little harder. A little harder.

"Mmm."

"Harder?" He increases the pressure again and again. Until it's more rough than tender. Until it's all rough.

"The middle."

There. Less pressure. Then a little more. Just right.

He watches me with rapt attention as he draws circles.

Zigzags.

Figure eights.

"Fuck." My head falls to the side. My hair goes with it.

Long strands cover my eyes. Blur my surroundings.

His lips find my neck.

He kisses me as he toys with me. Perfect circles again and again. Winding the tension inside me tighter and tighter.

It feels too good. He feels too good.

Then his lips dip lower. The crook of my neck. My shoulder. My collarbone.

My chest.

He slips his hands under my dress. His fingers brush my thighs. Then his hands are on my ass.

Only a thin layer of cotton between his hands and my skin.

God, he's so close to where he needs to be. To where I need him.

How can I already need him so badly? It's wrong. And I don't give a fuck about being right.

He pulls me up onto my knees, bringing my chest to his mouth.

Then his lips are around my nipple. Soft pressure.

Harder.

The flick of his tongue.

That same circle, only so much wetter and warmer. Again and again.

Until I'm digging my nails into his neck. "Ian."

He responds with the soft scrape of his teeth.

Fuck. It sends a wave of pleasure through my body. Then he does it again. Again. Each scrape sends a shock wave through me.

To my fingers.

My toes.

My core.

He winds me tighter and tighter. When I'm sure I can't take more, he moves to my other breast. Tortures it just as mercilessly.

His hands find the waistband of my panties.

He slides them over my hips. Down my thighs. All the way to my knees.

The fabric binds my legs. Keeps me in place.

He holds my legs with a tight grip. But he doesn't touch

me properly. He just toys with my breasts as he digs his fingers into my thighs.

"Please." I'm ready to beg. Plead. Whatever it takes for him to touch me properly.

I'm not sure where the sane Eve is. Maybe the gin chased her away. Maybe the money. Maybe something about Ian.

But I don't care. I need this. Need him filling my desires.

Need to fill his desires.

"Not yet." He drags his hands an inch up my thighs. Moves to my other breast. Toys mercilessly.

"Mmm." My groans run together. Half agony. Half ecstasy.

I've never wanted this much. I've never felt this empty. I've never felt so desperate to be full.

I want it so much it hurts.

But a good hurt. The kind that makes me feel alive.

This is what it means to be alive. The freedom to want something more than food, sleep, shelter.

To want with my entire being.

"Please." My voice slips to a whine. It's a tone I've never heard before. A vulnerability that terrifies me.

And thrills me.

"Please, Ian." My nails curl into his skin. "Please."

"Please what, vixen?"

The pet name nearly pushes me over the edge. God, the way it sounds on his lips…

"Make me come." The words fall without a hint of friction. Inhibitions? What inhibitions? "Please. I need you."

He groans into my chest.

Something in his posture changes. More hungry and primal.

He drags his hands up my thighs. Closer, closer, closer.

His thumb brushes my clit. A slow circle. Then another. In that same steady rhythm.

He winds me tighter and tighter. Until I'm sure I might burst. Then tighter still.

With the next brush of his thumb, the dam breaks.

I go over the edge, groaning his name as I come.

Bliss spills through my senses. Turns the entire world into a place of pure pleasure.

Nothing but the pulsing in my sex.

More intense than anything I've ever felt.

Then I blink my eyes open and see him watching. And it's intense in a whole new way.

I need the wonder in his eyes. The desire. The fascination. The need.

He brings his hands to my knees. Tugs at my panties. "Stand up, vixen. I'm keeping these."

My cheeks flush. It's strange, feeling shy after that, but I do. "Help me."

He nods. Brings his hands to my hips. Helps me onto my feet.

Then he shifts off of the couch. Kneels next to me as he peels the panties off my feet.

He looks up at me like I'm a goddess.

Right now, I feel like one.

Right now, I'm terrified of how much I want Ian Hunt.

One night and I'm undressing in public.

Where will I be on night thirty?

Chapter Nineteen

IAN

Of course, Eve wants to take the subway home.

According to our terms, I can insist she take a car. A cab, an Uber, a limo I provide. According to our terms, I can demand she go to any place at any time. So long as I give her warning before we leave the city.

Part of me wants to insist. To send her home in a car under my control. So the driver will alert me the moment she's home. So I'll know she's safe.

Eve is independent. Stubborn. Headstrong.

She's also right. This is a safe station. The subway is practical. The city certainly needs the revenue.

I let the stubborn part of me win.

Call a car. Wait on the curb outside my building.

She rolls her eyes as a limo arrives. "The subway really is fine."

"Let someone take care of you for once."

Her eyes stay on mine for a moment. She studies my expression, trying to find my intent.

Is it obvious I'm saying that to get my way?

Yes, it's true. She needs to let someone else take care of her. She needs to learn to let her guard down. To let someone else shoulder that burden.

But where do I get off telling her that?

Trust isn't my strong suit.

I pull her into a slow kiss.

She's responsive. Eager. Hungry.

She groans as I slip my tongue into her mouth. Tugs at my suit as I claim her.

Sighs as I pull back.

She wants more.

But she isn't ready for it yet.

"Good night, Eve." I help her into the limo.

She looks up at me, that same curiosity in her grey-green eyes. Because she doesn't trust me? Or because she wants every thought in my head? "Good night, Ian."

I press the limo door closed. Issue instructions to the driver. Watch as the car pulls away.

It disappears around the corner.

My phone buzzes with an alert from the company. Fifteen minutes until she's home. Fifteen minutes until she's safe.

I walk to my flat. It's less than a dozen blocks and it's a nice night. Warm with a soft breeze. Clear. As clear as it gets in New York City.

No stars in the sky. There are never stars in the sky.

Today, I miss them. I want to take Eve to a cozy cabin in the mountains. Or a secluded beach miles from civilization. I want to hold her tightly as I watch the stars brighten the sky.

It's been so long since I've seen the sky like that. Since I've felt the thrill and possibility. The sense of wonder the universe has to offer.

Such a big, beautiful place. So much bigger than any of us.

Fuck, I'm already obsessed with her.

Now this.

I undress. Shower. Pour a glass of water. Check my phone. Then computer.

Work email. Private email. RSS feed.

Her site.

It's a reflex.

One that...

Fuck, I don't know. This *is* a public site. She puts everything here, knowing anyone can find it.

When I first stumbled on her site, I thought Eve was a pen name. A play on the title. Original Sin, Eve, the tree of knowledge.

I didn't think her name was actually Eve.

But it is.

And it's perfect.

If anyone would take fruit from the tree of knowledge, it's her.

This is a public site. Too public.

Even so...

A new entry draws my eyes.

A few minutes old. She just wrote it.

The Handmaid's Tale isn't a sexy book. But it's sexier than you'd think. How else can Margaret Atwood draw a clear line between state-sanctioned rape and a consensual affair?

Of course, she's dealing with her thoughts via her favorite book.

What is she saying? What is she thinking?

I need to know.

I need everything in her head and her heart. Every one of her secrets.

No walls. No hiding. No affair with her singing instructor.

Eve is offering these thoughts to anyone who reads.

But now that we've kissed, now that I've made her come—

It's different.

Wrong.

I can't keep reading her journal. No matter how public it is.

I know that. I know I can't cross this line.

But my body doesn't care. My heart doesn't care.

Everything inside me wants to read her words.

It's agony resisting.

Fuck.

I'm not going to make it out of this unscathed.

It's impossible.

I put the computer to sleep. Look for a distraction. Fail to think of anything but her.

Okay. I'm obsessed.

I might as well find a way to tease her.

That's just the thing.

I text Shepard to arrange everything. Then I set up the delivery. Early tomorrow morning. Early enough to wake her. But just barely.

Nine seems fair.

I'm sending tea.

Sure, it's all so I can savor the mental image of Eve naked, tangled in her sheets, rising to the sound of my delivery.

I check the size on her knickers. Then I spend an hour picking out the perfect extra for my delivery.

Plus a few more things.

Enough to make her jaw drop.

Chapter Twenty

EVE

"Wow." Addie's voice carries into my room. "That's... wow."

"Ms. Miller, was it?" A man with a British accent asks. Not Ian. Ian's voice is deeper. It has this edge to it, even when he's asking for a drink or mentioning the weather. Like he's a few seconds away from ordering me to take off my dress.

"No one calls me Ms. Miller," she says. "I kind of like it."

"Do you prefer Miss? Or perhaps Adelaide?"

"Usually Addie. But I kind of like Ms. Miller."

"Of course, Ms. Miller. I believe this gift is intended for the other Ms. Miller."

"Oh." I can hear her blush. "I'm not supposed to peek?"

"No. But seeing as you already have..."

She gasps. "Oh my God. That's... expensive. And pretty. How did you know Eve's size?"

"I know everything, Ms. Miller. Please, take a moment.

Read your invitation. Can I get you anything while you wait for the other Ms. Miller?"

"Can you get me anything? In my apartment?" she asks.

"Or outside your apartment. I'm here to help," he says.

"Uh… I'm good. But Eve will want that when she gets up. And I'm not waiting." Footsteps move toward my door. "Evie. Company. From…"

"Mr. Hunt," the man says.

"You didn't tell me you have a rich boyfriend," she says.

The man chuckles. Amused by their conversation. Or maybe Addie's expression. She's very expressive. And funny. In a different way than I am.

"He sent his… I'm sorry, Lock, right?" she asks.

"Yes, thank you, Ms. Miller."

"What should I call you?"

"Lock is perfect."

She laughs. "Are you an assistant or…"

"That's a close enough description," he says.

An assistant? With a British accent? I guess that makes sense.

According to the articles I browsed, Ian has only been in New York for a few years. He still does a lot of business in London. Though people speculate he avoids the city.

Because of his ex-wife.

He hasn't mentioned his marriage. I don't know if it's appropriate to ask. Sure, it's easy to find that information. It comes up on a Google search.

Ian Hunt. Spouse: Laura Howe. Siblings: Tyler Hunt. Children: none.

All that private information made public.

I don't feel right looking at it. And I want to dive into every detail. To understand him. Or at least his intentions.

He's lived an entire life. Long enough to have a company, a fortune, an ex-wife.

"Evie." Addie knocks again. "Get up. Or I'm drinking your tea."

"I can make more tea for you, Ms. Miller," the British man says. Though I'm not sure if he means me or my sister.

"This might get confusing," she says.

He chuckles. "If your sister prefers to go by a different name—"

"Just Eve." I throw off the covers. Pull on shorts.

It's cooler today. I don't need to sleep in the buff, but I'm not wearing a lot. A tank top and panties. I don't need to prance half-naked in front of a near stranger. Unless he's Ian.

My cheeks flush.

My fingers dig into my thighs. I already want more. A repeat of last night. Or an hour in his office. At his apartment.

Where does he live?

Is it a modest place or something huge?

Classic or modern?

Bare or decorated?

Are his walls white?

Are his sheets black?

Or maybe teal. New sheets that make him think of me.

How strange. Creepy even. What kind of person buys new sheets a few days after they meet someone?

But even as my head says *what the fuck*, my body screams *hell yes*.

I want him obsessed with me. Some part of me does. Some part of me that's been dormant for a long time.

"Ms. Miller?" The British man asks. "Do you need some assistance?"

"No. I'm good. Uh, who are you?" I check my hair—as messy as it gets—and adjust my shirt. Then I move into the main room.

Sure enough, there is a British man standing next to the dining table. An Indian man in a sleek suit. Like the one Ian wears but less expensive.

I'm not sure how I can tell. Maybe I can't. Maybe I'm imagining things.

This guy is still handsome and put-together. But without the presence Ian has. He doesn't seem like someone who knows he's rich and powerful.

I guess he's not. Not if he's Ian's assistant.

"It's lovely to meet you, Ms. Miller." He offers his hand. I shake. "Eve is fine."

"Of course, Eve. I'm Aalock. But I go by Lock. I work for one of Mr. Hunt's companies. Though I mostly work for a friend of his. Shepard Marlowe."

One of Ian's business partners. A finance guy. Also handsome. The spitting image of Prince Eric. With less smiling and more *I'm going to tie you up* vibes.

"I only mention Mr. Marlowe as he's part of your plans for Thursday evening," the British man says. Lock, I guess. "He's going to join you and Mr. Hunt at dinner. Along with his wife. Mr. Marlowe's wife. Not Mr. Hunt's. Mr. Hunt is no longer married."

"You're dating a rich, divorced guy?" Addie looks to Lock for information, but he keeps a perfect poker face.

"It's uh… complicated." My gaze flits to the giant gift on the table. A sleek black box with a deep teal ribbon. "Is that for me?"

"Yes, though your sister took a peek," he says.

"Hey! I thought that was our secret," she says.

"Ah, but you didn't ask me to pinkie promise." He winks at her.

She giggles. "It's… well, I won't ruin the surprise." She holds up an envelope with her full name written in gold script. "We're invited to an exclusive party. At the beach."

"We are?" I ask.

Lock nods.

"Apparently, Mr.—"

"Lock, please," he says. "I'm here to assist you in finding attire for the party. Mr. Hunt will be taking you to the Hamptons next weekend. This should be ample notice." He looks to me, checking if I understand. Not saying more in front of my sister.

"Yes, I appreciate that." My eyes flit to Addie.

She mouths *what the fuck?*

"You don't want to go?" I ask.

"I had to beg you to go to the beach last weekend."

"I'm converted."

She laughs *yeah, okay.* "Do we have a plus-one?"

"Ms. Miller, I believe that information is on your invitation. But I assure you, if you don't have a plus-one, I'll find a way." He winks at her again.

Is he flirting? Or just friendly?

It's weird. But I guess it's not a concern. She's not interested in men. Or anyone besides Marisol.

"Ms. Miller." He turns to me. "Whenever you're ready, we can leave."

"Leave?" I ask.

"A shopping expedition." He holds up another envelope. The kind that holds a credit card. "Mr. Hunt wants to make sure you're comfortable in your attire for dinner."

"Oh."

"He does have one request," he says.

"What is it?"

"That you wear your combat boots."

My cheeks flush.

"At dinner. And after," he says.

"After?" Realization spreads over Addie's face. "Oh. After."

My blush spreads to my chest.

"Oh my God. Are you actually getting laid? Evie, that's great."

"Sex is important," Lock says.

Oh my God, kill me now.

"Excuse me." I slink to the bathroom. Pee. Wash my hands. Wash my face. Brush my teeth.

Die of embarrassment.

———

THE PERFECTLY MIXED CHAI—PLENTY OF CINNAMON AND cardamom and almond milk—eases some of my awkwardness.

I'm still beet red. (The curse of paleness. A curse Addie did not inherit. She's a little darker than I am. With lighter hair and bluer eyes. She'd make a perfect California girl if she wanted to change coasts).

I just care less about the embarrassing situation with a chai latte in my hands.

Mmm.

How does Ian read my mind? Does he hack into my emails? Or is it just some power he has?

No, I told him I love chai last night. It's normal he knows. And I did mention something about almond milk. Maybe.

It's all a blur of city lights and anticipation.

His strong hands on my skin.

His soft lips on my—

"Are you thinking about sex right now?" Addie leans forward. "You're already obsessed."

"You're obsessed. You and Marisol were so loud. It was ridiculous." I hide behind my takeout cup.

Addie blushes. It's enough to change the subject.

For a few beautiful minutes she asks Lock about how he came to work for Ian's company.

Apparently, he worked for Ian in London. When Ian moved, he did. Though, now he primarily works for Ian's friend, Shepard. Or Shep, as he calls him.

He considers himself a bit of a cupid. Just look how happy Shep and his wife are. He assures me I'll see the results of his handiwork at dinner.

If I can take my eyes off Ian.

"Mr. Hunt is smitten." His voice beams with pride. "He's never asked to borrow me for help with a woman before."

"Are there a lot of women?" Addie asks.

"Men have needs. Some men aren't... discrete about filling them." Lock raises a brow. *Doesn't that answer everything?*

Uh, no, not at all. I need a lesson in British conversation.

Did he just tell her to fuck off? Or was that his way of saying *Ian is a slut, but it's no big deal?*

"Women have needs too," she says.

"Of course. They're usually more discrete though. I have to say... So many men have spilled details of our affairs. But never women," Lock says.

"Never?" Addie does not comment on his casual *yeah, I sleep with men and women, what's it to you* drop. But she does look impressed. Since she officially came out, she's struggled with when to bring up her sexuality.

It's not a secret. But it's not like she wants to go *hey, I'm Addie, I'm gay, what's up with you* either.

She's a lot of things. Gay is one of them. An important one. But only one.

"Mr. Hunt… I probably shouldn't say this." Lock's voice drops to a stage whisper. "But his divorce… his wife was seeing another man. For a long time. It became gossip amongst their circle. And it destroyed him. He overreacted to the hurt. Built all these walls around his heart." His eyes fix on me. "I never thought he'd offer a key to anyone. Until you."

"I barely know him," I say.

"Even so… I have a feeling about you two." He motions to the enormous gift. "Shall I place this in your room?"

"No. I will. Thanks." I finish my tea. Pick up the box. Move it into my room.

The sleek teal ribbon looks perfect against my sheets.

And the black box.

It's like he turned me into wrapping.

I peel off the top. Pull out the teal tissue paper. Let it flutter to the ground.

Silk lingerie on blue-green paper.

Soft black with tiny teal bows. Sweet, innocent, and illicit all at once.

Plus a note from Ian.

Buy whatever you'd like for the next few weeks. And the party. We'll be at a beach house all weekend, though I don't expect you'll need much in the way of attire.

Come as you.

Wear this underneath.

And the combat boots.

I want you in my bed in nothing but those boots.

- Ian

Chapter Twenty-One

EVE

We drive straight to an expensive department store in Brooklyn.

Lock motions to my credit card. Explains that Mr. Hunt wants me to have everything I need. For our weekend in the Hamptons. Dinners. Parties. Evenings we spend at home.

I focus on the beach attire. Breezy cover-up, black sandals, bikini. Black, ink purple, oxblood. Dark, saturated colors that feel like me.

Addie buys everything in pale shades of blue and pink. Similar but completely different.

When we're finished with the first round of shopping, we climb back into the car, and drive to a boutique in the Village.

Somehow, Lock finds parking right away.

He helps Addie out of the car. Then me. "When Mr. Hunt told me about your style, I was worried I wouldn't find a place that meets your needs. I don't want to put you in a box, Eve. I can already tell that wouldn't work."

Uh... sure.

He takes in my outfit—a black crop top, ripped high waist shorts, combat boots. "Even if I put you in some simple black sheath and pearls." He chuckles knowingly. "I once bought pearls for a companion of Mr. Marlowe's and I never heard the end of it."

Huh? I look to Addie but she's equally stumped.

"A crude slang. I'm afraid I can't bring myself to explain it. I'm sure…" He stifles a laugh. "Mr. Hunt will be more than happy to go into detail. He's a very… enthusiastic man."

I seriously need these lessons in British conversation. I can tell he means something by the way he emphasizes the word enthusiastic. But I have no idea what it is.

"You were saying?" I have Google. I can look up necklaces and pearls. But I'm not sure I want to know. "About the clothes?"

"Yes, Eve. Thank you." He motions to the boutique on our right.

A bright, open shop with three mannequins in the window. One in a fabulous red dress. Another in a more elegant black number. The third in a jumpsuit. All very trendy and cool. Dressed up enough to blend without looking stuffy.

"I'd hate to dress you like Audrey Hepburn in *Breakfast at Tiffany's*," he says. "Not that I dress anyone. I facilitate. The women here will help outfit you in exactly what you need."

"What do I need?" I ask.

"Are they going to a gala or something?" Addie asks. "It was just dinner with his friend, no?"

"Yes, Thursday it's dinner with Mr. And Mrs. Marlowe. But there are other events. Other dinners. Galas even. Mr. Hunt has a busy social calendar and he'd like Ms. Miller…

Eve to be prepared, should he request her company," Lock says.

He wants me around. If he decides he wants me around later.

Is the hesitation Lock's lack of information? Or is Ian just… playing things by ear? Is he going to toss me aside the second he fucks me?

The thought shouldn't bother me—four-hundred grand is four-hundred grand—but it does.

Addie looks to me with concern in her eyes. "How old is he?"

I clear my throat. "That's not important."

Her blue eyes go wide. "Now, I know it is."

"Marisol is twenty." I'm not helping my case.

Glare fills her eyes. For a second. Then it's gone. Replaced with disappointment. Addie doesn't get angry. She jumps straight to disappointed. And right now—

Lock saves me. "Ms. Miller, I'm happy to discuss Mr. Hunt with you—this information is all very easy to find—but after we help your sister find a few gowns. She's welcome to wear something from her closet. But Mr. Hunt would like her to feel comfortable. And some of the people in his social circle… certain styles read as bold. Others as clueless."

"And her current clothes are clueless?" Addie asks.

"It's okay, Addie." I follow Lock into the shop. "I felt it when I met him for dinner. Like I'd worn shorts to prom."

Curiosity streaks her expression. "You want to fit in?"

"Not exactly. More…"

"Sparkle," Lock offers. "Stand out for your luster, beauty, unique style. Not for your…"

"Cheap clothes?" I offer.

He chuckles. "New Yorkers are so blunt. It's charming."

"How long have you been in New York?" I ask.

"Enough I know you're typically more blunt. New Yorkers, that is. All you Yanks are so matter-of-fact. So I'll be matter-of-fact with you."

Something tells me his idea of matter-of-fact is not the same as mine.

Lock continues, "Mr. Hunt has never shown an interest in 'alternative' women before. But he's rather fixated on your punk rock style. He wants you to dress as you. At all times."

Addie shoots me an *I know he means sex* look.

I hide behind my purse.

"I'm here to help you blend… as much as you want. He'd happily bring you to dinner in this outfit." Lock chuckles knowingly. "Quite happily. Those shorts are cut rather high."

Addie's laugh melts the tension in her brow. "She does dress a bit provocatively."

"You're seriously a grandma," I say.

"I wish. I could sit with my cats and listen to orchestra all night. Teach my grandkids violin all day. It would be so relaxing," she says.

Lock smiles, charmed or pretending. He motions to the shop. "Take a moment to look around. I'm sure—"

A woman interrupts him. "Lock, is that you?" She steps into the main room. Turns to me. "I'm Cynthia. You must be Eve."

Everyone knows me. I'm kind of used to it. It comes with the unicorn hair color. It was the same at school last year. When I had time to go to parties, everyone knew me as the girl with teal hair. People I'd never met knew who I was.

I offer her my hand. "Yes."

She shakes with a steady grip. Cynthia looks like a

former model. Tall, thin, with dramatic features and fashionable attire. Black pumps. Grey slacks. Ivory blouse. Measuring tape draped over her shoulders.

Dyed hair, yes, but a soft shade of blond.

She's dressed more like Addie (jean skirt, lilac blouse, white sandals). Not me.

Though this place—

I don't know what to make of it.

At a glance, it's a normal place in the Village. A small rack of designer jeans and blouses. Ordinary basics on the table in front.

Then racks of dresses in every color, fabric, shape imaginable.

All sorts of shoes. Heels like the ones Cynthia is wearing. And taller, shinier, sexier pairs that scream *wear only these in bed*.

Or maybe that's me again.

Maybe I'm a sex-obsessed lunatic.

"Is Mr. Hunt sticking with his edict?" Cynthia takes a long, slow look at me, assessing me like I'm a doll she's about to dress.

"The combat boots?" Lock asks.

She nods, utterly matter-of-fact.

"Yes. I believe he is. But you know Mr. Hunt…"

"I do." She laughs softly. An inside joke for them to share. "A man of eclectic tastes."

In women.

He's sent other women here.

It bothers me more than it should.

Her attention turns to me. Then Addie. "Are you a friend of Eve's?"

"Her sister. Addie." She offers her hand.

"So nice to meet you." Cynthia motions to a small red armchair. "Feel free to take a seat. Or look around. There's a fabulous blouse in cream if you need something for work." She looks to Lock. "Will Addie need attire too?"

Lock shakes his head.

She nods and dismisses him. "If you prefer, there's a lovely coffee shop around the corner. We might be a little while."

Addie shoots me a look. Asking if I want her to stay.

I nod yes. For now. This is bizarre. I need the familiarity.

"Maybe in a bit," she says. "I'm going to look around first."

Cynthia nods *of course* and moves closer to me. She grabs the measuring tape. Holds it up to my shoulder. "Do you mind, sweetheart?"

"No." It should speed the process.

She nods and pulls the tape over my shoulders. She checks the number. Calls the measurement out to Lock, who marks it on a notepad, repeats the process.

Bust, underbust, waist, upper hip, lower hip, inseam, height.

When she's finished, she takes the notepad from Lock, takes my hand, leads me to the dressing room in the corner.

"You're welcome to look around yourself, Eve. But will you allow me to pull a few things for you first?" Her voice takes on a significance. As if she's discussing the technique for an art project. "I have an idea."

"Sure." I nod.

She motions *one moment*, turns on her heel, buzzes around the store. Straight to one rack. Then another. Another.

She knows exactly what she wants and exactly where to get it.

What's that feel like? That mastery?

I'm an expert when it comes to dying my hair. Everything else? Not so much.

Yeah, I'm pretty good at mixing drinks. Finding cheap food. Picking out music for a party.

Styling my limited clothing selection.

Writing.

I'm not sure *good* fits. Not yet.

I love the feeling of a pen in my hands, my thoughts pouring on the paper. That relief. That ease. That state of deep concentration.

But love isn't skill.

Even if I am good…

It's been a long time since I've looked further than next week.

I don't know what I want to study in college. Or do after.

I love writing, yes, but it's not practical. And I'm not working as a bartender for the next twenty years.

Only, after this month, I don't have to work as a bartender. I can't fund my entire life. But I have a pretty solid launching pad.

I can do anything. Take two years to travel. Start my own business. Pursue an impractical passion.

I have no idea what I want to do next month.

But right now, I know exactly what I want.

Him. Here. Watching me.

Touching me.

Holding me.

Fucking me.

Chapter Twenty-Two

EVE

Somehow, I push my dirty thoughts aside. Focus on the dresses Cynthia picks for me.

The first is a rich, heavy velvet. Beautiful, soft, way too hot.

I look like I'm dressing as a witch for Halloween. Not ready to attend a fancy dinner.

I take it off without showing her. Try the next.

A long, black dress in layers of chiffon.

It's a lot. Too much even. But I suppose that's what makes something fancy.

High heels were originally worn by noble men. They were pure status symbol. *Look at these impractical heels. I can wear them because I spend the day on my ass. No need to walk, stand, work.*

Hundreds of years and now women are expected to wear heels at work and play. Pumps at the office, stilettos at dinner, wedges at the park.

I live in my heeled combat boots. And I'm not exactly Miss Low-effort when it comes to style.

I touch up my roots every eight weeks. Refresh my

color twice a month. Spend twenty minutes on my makeup.

Sure, I'm not trying to look flawless. I'm not applying makeup to look prettier, exactly.

But I'm still painting my features, changing my look, molding myself into something different.

I study the gown. Backless. Thin straps that crisscross. No good with a bra.

I shimmy out of mine. Pull the zipper on the skirt. Adjust the top.

Plunging neckline. Open back. Long, dramatic skirt.

It's undeniably sexy.

And undeniably me.

Cynthia lights up as I step into the main room. Addie gasps. Lock whispers something to her.

The dress is popular.

It's gorgeous. And sleek. The fabric is so smooth it rolls off my skin. Like fingertips skimming my thigh.

Like Ian—

Ahem.

I swallow my fantasy. Focus on my reflection. On pleasing my limited crowd.

When I spin, Addie gasps.

"You look amazing," she says. "So pretty and grown-up too."

Cynthia isn't as sold. "It's lovely. For the weekend. For dinner—" Her eyes light up with an epiphany. "I know just the thing."

She rushes me into the dressing room. Buzzes to the rack. Grabs another dress.

At a glance, it's the same. A long black number made of chiffon.

But I'm not arguing over a free dress.

I undo the zipper. Push the straps off my shoulders. Watch the black fabric fall off my chest.

It collects at my waist. A stark contrast against my light skin.

So clearly half-off. So clearly rushed.

I'm so clearly exposed.

My sex clenches.

My thighs shake.

My fingers dig into the chiffon.

Already, I want him here. Behind me.

His lips on my neck, his hands on my skin, his voice in my ears.

I want to feel him hard against me.

Inside me.

The thought overwhelms me. What is it like?

I've read books that mention fullness. Satisfaction. Pain. Pressure. Pleasure.

I don't like asking friends. They laugh at my inexperience even when they mean well. And Addie—who I trust not to laugh—has no idea.

Though—

Nope. Not thinking about whether or not my sister uses dildos with her girlfriend. Or by herself.

That's mood killing.

Until my gaze returns to the mirror. The thought of him overwhelms the awkwardness.

I want to be exposed for him.

On display for him.

My breath catches in my throat.

My hands move for me. My phone. The camera.

A picture of the mirror. From my lips to my hips. My bare shoulders and chest, the tips of my teal hair, the dress at my waist.

The sparrow on my left shoulder.

It's clearly me.

And I—

I'm going crazy. I put my cell away. Slide out of the dress. Into the other.

As soon as my gaze hits my reflection, my body goes into overdrive.

I want to take a million pictures. Send them to Ian. Ask for his in return.

It's too dangerous. Too risky. Those pictures could end up anywhere.

But maybe if he starts…

No. I really am going crazy.

I need to pick out this dress, get lunch, find more caffeine.

Okay, I need to pick out the dress, get lunch, go home, and touch myself to thoughts of him.

But still, I need to pick out the dress.

Ahem.

This one is sexier than the last. Another deep plunge. The same open back. A slit in the skirt. Cut all the way to my hip.

High enough to show the edge of my cotton panties.

High enough I should skip the panties.

I take a deep breath. Will it to lower my temperature. Step into the main room.

My eyes go straight to the three-panel mirror. My thoughts go straight to the gutter. Him, behind me, ordering me to strip for his viewing pleasure.

Ordering me to touch myself.

To touch him.

To watch as I come.

To watch as he comes.

"Perfect." Cynthia marvels at her handiwork. Fails to

notice the blush spreading to my chest. Or decides not to call me on it. "Don't you think?"

"Yes. It is. And I, uh… is that all?" I ask. "Because I…"

"You're blushing," Addie says.

"I am not." The lie does not help matters.

"She likes that one," Addie says. "You should get it. And while you're here… a few more things. People will notice if you wear that dress twice in a week."

"It is going to make an impression." Lock nods.

"Okay. A few more things." I move into the dressing room. Turn my back to the mirror as I strip. It helps keep my dirty thoughts at bay.

But not enough.

It stays in my head, even after an iced tea, and far too many wardrobe changes.

Finally, I place my last garment on the hanger. A dozen new items. Worth…

God knows what.

I change into my street clothes, finish my last sip of iced tea, step into the main room.

And there he is. Like something out of a dream.

The door swings shut behind Ian.

He stands there in his sleek black suit, his eyes fixed on me, his expression bright with interest.

Addie's jaw drops. She looks to me and mouths *holy shit*.

"Hi." She stands. Wipes her palm on her skirt—she's also drinking something iced, though it looks like coffee. "You must be Ian."

"I must be." He crosses the room to her. Shakes her hand. "You must be Eve's sister."

She nods. "I am. Addie. And you… are very tall." Her cheeks flush. "Sorry. I've never met one of Eve's boyfriend's before."

He looks to me and raises a brow. Asking if he's okay to run with the term.

No. Maybe. I don't know. What can I say? I'm not explaining the whole arrangement to her. Boyfriend is close. Ish.

I shrug. It's not a lie. Just… not accurate.

"Do you mind if I borrow Eve?" he asks.

"Don't you have a meeting, Mr. Hunt?" Lock asks.

"It ended early." Ian holds out his hand, beckoning me. "If you're still shopping, I won't interrupt. Or if I can't negotiate your permission, Addie."

She giggles, but she still sends me one of those *oh my God are we talking about this* looks. "How late will you have her out?"

"Not late. I have another meeting. But I might need her tonight." Intention drops into his voice.

Mmm. Yes. Now. Please.

"Will you be coming to the party this weekend?" He turns his attention to her. All his attention. The way he looks at her… he's completely and totally present. "I'm sure Eve would appreciate it."

"Of course. I never miss the chance to swim. I hope it's not one of those pool parties where no one goes in the pool," she says.

"You'll have to tear me away from the water," he says.

Really? I know the UK is an island, but I don't hear much about swimming, surfing, water sports. And he was in the air force, not the navy. But who knows? Maybe Ian swims a mile a day.

Maybe he has plans to fuck me in the pool after everyone leaves.

"As long as you bring her home fed and caffeinated," Addie says. "And not too much to drink if you go out late. She gets hangovers."

"Addie!" My voice drops to a tone I've only heard on friends. That *oh my God, Mom, you're embarrassing me.*

She smiles. "What? You do. He should know. If he's going to tend to your needs."

Ian returns her smile with something a lot more wicked. "Of course. I wouldn't dream of sending you home wanting."

Chapter Twenty-Three

EVE

Addie texts the second I'm out of the store.

Not the *oh my God, what the heck are you doing* I expect from her.

Not even *be careful* or *rich guys make good husbands, make sure he puts a ring on it.*

Despite her grandma like worry, she's not practical when it comes to interpersonal affairs. She's a dreamer.

She believes in love and hope and other fairy tales. Like our father shaking off his drug addiction and helping out.

Addie: Are you going to explain why you suddenly have a rich boyfriend who's twice your age?

"Would you rather talk to her?" Ian presses his palm into my lower back. That soft pressure. Just enough my crop top skims my skin. Makes me aware of the warm air.

No more heat wave. Normal June. A grey sky holding in the humidity.

It's sticky and warm, but it's not hot. With a light breeze, the air is more comforting than stuffy.

Then his fingers skim the waistband of my shorts and the entire universe is hot.

I forget what I mean to say to Addie. Why I'm holding my phone. Why I'm standing on a street in the Village in front of a sleek limo.

There's really a limo.

Does that mean he…

We…

Ahem.

"You can." His voice is that same even, calm tone. He's not bothered by my desire to talk to my sister. "She's right there." He motions to the store. "If you don't want to be here…" He shrugs *your loss*, but there's something in his eyes.

He needs me too.

Not a conventional need like food, water, oxygen. Something deeper and baser. Not what I need to live, but what I need to feel alive.

Usually, I try to skirt those concerns. I do the best I can with what I have. But now I have everything and I can do anything.

And the only thing I want is his hands on my skin.

"You should have warned me." I step forward, breaking our touch, bringing my thoughts into focus. "I didn't explain our situation."

He opens the limo door for me. Motions *after you*.

I take another look at my sister—she's watching us from her spot on the armchair, pretending as if she's invested in her conversation with Lock and Cynthia—and motion to my phone.

Eve: Yes.

Addie: He's really handsome. And so tall. And the accent! Like the detective on that TV show. Tell me he doesn't have the same temper.

Eve: I don't think so. He's always in control.

Addie: Is that a British thing?

Eve: The show is British.

Addie: But it's a TV show. They have to do something to make it exciting.

Ian chuckles as he slides in next to me. He pulls the door closed, shutting out the soft light.

It's only a little smaller than my bedroom. But with Ian here, the space feels too big and too small at once.

He's too far away.

And he's too close.

I'm too afraid of how much I want him.

His knee brushes mine. His slacks against my bare skin.

He's wearing a suit again. A full suit, with a tie and a tie-clip and everything.

"What are you going to explain?" His voice stays even. Calm. Like he has all the time in the world.

His posture is just as strong and patient.

He sits tall, legs barely spread, hands at his sides, eyes on me.

"That's why you should have told me," I say. "I don't know. I told her I got a new gig that would keep me busy. But she won't like the idea of me sleeping with my boss."

He nods, pleased with my answer. "Would you tell her the truth?"

"That I sold my v-card? Uh, no."

"It's enterprising."

"Still."

"You don't want her to think you're a whore?"

The word makes my stomach twist. It's not like me. I'm not squeamish about labels. I'm an empowered woman. I believe it's any woman's right to do what she wants with her body. Including putting a price tag on sexual services. "Why? Do you?"

"Wouldn't that make me a john?"

"You wouldn't be the first john to look down on his... service provider."

His laugh deepens. His eyes light up. Not the heat of desire. Something else. Something in his heart.

God, his eyes are so gorgeous. Intense. Sexy.

Everything about him is sexy.

It's not fair.

Fuck. What am I telling my sister? How am I supposed to concentrate with those eyes on me?

I rack my brain for something, anything, but my thoughts are too far away. Ian is so close. And so tall and broad and sexy. I already want to climb into his lap.

"I, uh... can you uh... stop being so sexy for a minute?" I ask.

"Can I stop being sexy?"

"Yeah, I really can't concentrate."

He chuckles, at least. "I'll do my best."

"Thanks." I ignore the absurdity of my request. "I really do need to explain this. Addie is my best friend. My only true friend." I scoot to the other side of the bench. It helps. Not enough to clear my head. But enough to free my fingers.

Eve: I'll explain later. I promise. And I promise I'm safe.

I shouldn't be able to promise that. When is a woman really safe from a man? How can I trust this guy I barely know?

But I do.

Addie: He's way too old for you. I have to say that, as your sister. It's my duty. But he's also incredibly handsome. And, according to Google, incredibly rich. Even more than I would have guessed with the whole assistant bringing lingerie thing. So have fun. Make him buy lunch. Use a condom. I don't want to spend three hours waiting at Planned Parenthood.

Oh my God. My blush deepens.

I turn my phone on silent. Slide it into my pocket. Let my gaze shift to Ian. "Thanks."

"For?"

Uh... He isn't less sexy. And it's his fault I have to explain this. I mean, it's kind of cute he surprised me. Or it would be. If this was a normal relationship and not... whatever it is. "Not interrupting."

He smiles. "You're right. I didn't know your sister would be here. I should have asked."

"Oh."

Is that... an apology? I don't know many men who apologize. Even over little things. It calms the butterflies in my stomach. Until my eyes meet his.

The intensity in his soulful browns sends a flutter through my entire body.

His eyes trace a line down my body. He takes his time. Focuses on every inch. "You're wearing your boots today."

"How else would I know if they looked good with my dress?"

"Sharp." His smile is wicked. Somehow, it says *I'm picturing you naked*. It stokes the fire inside me.

Yes. Now. Please.

I'm losing words again.

And losing interest in holding onto him.

But how do I follow his lead?

I try to match his stare, but I don't have the intensity he does. I can't undress him with his eyes.

I can move closer. Or stay here. Or say something.

One of the dirty things he says.

Yes, pull me into your lap. Peel my shorts to my ankles. Remove everything that isn't my boots.

I do want that. But when I try to find the words, they tangle.

It's too much. I'm not there.

He sits back, watching me with interest. Waiting.

"I'm usually more articulate," I say. "I, uh, I don't know how to handle it."

"How much you want me?"

"Yes. But I meant more... being tongue tied. But maybe they're the same thing. I, uh, I've had boyfriends. And we've kissed. Fooled around a little. But never like last night."

He understands my meaning immediately. "You enjoyed it?"

"Wasn't it obvious?"

"Yes, but I want to hear your take anyway."

"My take?"

He nods. "What exactly did you like?"

"Everything."

"Specifically."

My blush betrays me. I'm not shy. I'm not a shy person. Not even about sex.

I spent the last six months working at a strip club, for fuck's sake.

But the way Ian stares makes me feel so naked. Physically, emotionally, spiritually.

It terrifies me. Thrills me. Sets me on fire.

I'm an exhibitionist.

But that doesn't make sense. The idea of dancing at the club terrifies me. All those strange men, staring, reaching, touching.

If it was just him, sitting in a booth, watching me move, beckoning me into his lap—

"You're thinking something." His eyes fix on mine.

"About the club. I thought about dancing. To make more money. The dancers made four, five times what I did. But I didn't have the stomach for it. The thought of strange men watching me... touching me... it made me sick. But last night… I liked that. Being on display. The way you looked at me when I peeled off my dress. Knowing we might get caught."

"You would dance if it was for me?"

That's a good way of putting it. I nod.

"Do you want that?"

"Maybe."

He studies my expression. Nods with understanding. "What else?"

"The way you touched me. And that tone of your voice." The rough parts. And the soft parts too.

His gaze travels down my body. Slowly. Carefully. "Take off your top."

I don't ask for more instruction. I turn toward him. Look into his eyes as I pull my crop top over my head.

He studies my bra—the plain black thing I bought on sale. I thought it was sexy, at the time.

Now, it feels cheap and worn. Not something that fits into his expensive world.

Even so, he looks at me like I'm a sex goddess. "You didn't like the lingerie?"

"It's for dinner, isn't it?"

He nods *true*. "You did like it?"

"Yes." My blush deepens. "A lot."

"I'll send more. Wear that under your clothes. At all times."

The imposition should annoy me. But it doesn't. I love that he's sending fancy lingerie. And not because it's more for my collection.

Because it's our secret.

His voice drops to that demanding tone. "Take off the bra."

I undo the clasp. Let it fall off my shoulders.

"Fuck." His pupils dilate. "You drive me out of mind, Eve."

"Already?"

"Since the first time I saw you."

"What about me?"

"Everything." He motions *come here*.

I scoot closer.

The leather of the bench seat is cool against my thighs. The air-conditioning is on full blast.

I can feel the pressure against my stomach, chest, nipples.

But I'm not cold.

I'm on fire.

There. My knee brushes his thigh. The smooth fabric of his slacks. There's something about the way it falls over his limbs.

Like a tattoo or bright hair or combat boots, the suit defines him.

What is that like? How does he feel when it comes off?

I need it to come off.

Now.

The ache in my sex is overwhelming. I need him in every way I can.

My lack of experience is a distant concern.

It doesn't matter that I have no idea what I'm doing. That I'm scared of embarrassing myself in front of someone so smooth and collected.

Only that I touch him. Feel him. Taste him.

He brings his hand to my cheek. "What do you want? Right now."

"You."

"Specifically." He runs his thumb over my temple. Brings his other hand to the curve of my waist. "Tell me exactly what you want."

Chapter Twenty-Four

EVE

W hat exactly do I want?

It's impossible to answer.

I want everything.

His hands, his mouth, his cock.

I want to strip and tease him. And I want him to throw me on the bench and fuck me immediately.

I'm not ready for that.

So I…

That's it. "I want you in control."

He nods with understanding. "Did you pick a word?"

"Austin Powers."

He half-smiles. "I suppose I can't ask if you feel randy then."

"I might slip. Say it by accident." My laughs melts the tension in my shoulders.

I'm nervous.

No, I'm terrified.

My entire life, I've clawed for every ounce of control.

Now, I'm offering it to a man I barely know. A man

pulling me out of debt. Paying for my future. Proving he has the resources to destroy me.

The thought only winds me tighter.

He can bend me, break me, destroy me.

Or make me come until I pass out.

"Come here, vixen." He pulls me into his lap.

I stare into his dark eyes for a moment, then my lids flutter closed. My lips find his.

He tastes so good. Like mint. Like Ian.

One hand goes to my lower back. The other goes to my chest.

He cups my breast with his palm. Runs his thumb over my nipple with slow, perfect circles.

His kiss is hard. Hungry. No patience. All need. Like he's going to die if he doesn't consume me.

He tugs at my hair, pulling me back. Then his lips are on my chin, neck, chest.

He sucks on my nipple until I groan. Moves to the other. Teases it mercilessly.

His suit covers too much. I can't touch him properly. Only his neck.

My hands go to his tie. I fumble over the knot—I've never used a tie before.

He breaks the kiss. "Like this." He places his hand over mine. Shows me how to unfold the fabric. How to peel it from his neck.

He's more wild without the tie. Or maybe it's the look in his eyes. Like he's a predator and I'm his prey.

It should scare me.

Instead, it makes my sex clench.

"Give me your hands." His voice stays firm.

I stare back as I place my hands in my lap.

"Behind you. Like this." His hands go to my hips. He

unbuttons my shorts then he turns me ninety degrees, so my back is to him. "On your belly."

Huh?

He takes my hands. Places them on the bench seat on front of me. Helps me onto my belly.

My forehead on the leather seat. My chest against his thigh. My stomach against his crotch.

I can feel him, hard against my belly. But still slow and patient.

He brings his arms behind my back. "Palms together."

I press my hands together.

He loops the tie around my wrist. Cinches a loose knot and pulls it tighter. Tight enough to restrict my movement.

Silk around my wrists.

His expensive tie binding me. Leaving me splayed over him, utterly at his mercy.

Slowly, he rolls my jeans over my ass and hips. All the way to my knees.

So my shorts are binding my legs.

He runs his fingers over my panties, pressing the soft fabric into my tender skin.

The friction is divine. Too much and not enough.

He does it again. So softly I can barely feel it.

Then again.

Again.

Until a groan falls off my lips. Then too many groans to count.

Fuck, that feels good. Too good.

He strokes me again and again.

Until I'm wound so tight I can't take it.

I need his hands on my skin.

Still, he strokes me with his first two fingers.

His other hand goes to my lower back. He presses me

down, just enough I feel his hard-on against my stomach. Just enough my entire body fills with need.

"Say my name when you come, vixen." He knows exactly where I am. Exactly how he's working me.

Exactly what I need.

I'm splayed over his lap in nothing but my panties, my wrists bound by his tie, my legs bound by my shorts.

I'm utterly at his mercy.

And it thrills me.

He winds me tight and tighter. Pushing me closer and closer.

My eyes close.

My world floods with soft, white light. Not the dim mood lighting of the limo, but pure, perfect pleasure.

It washes over me like a wave. Sends bliss through every single molecule inside me.

My sex pulses as I come.

I groan his name, arching my back, reaching for his hand.

He doesn't release me when I'm finished. Instead, he rolls my panties over my ass, hips, thighs.

They fall down my legs, joining my shorts.

"Spread your legs." He presses his palm between my shoulder blades. Telling me he's in control. Holding me steady.

It's enough I can part my thighs.

"You're perfect, Eve." He runs his fingertips over the flesh of my ass. "Has anyone told you that?"

"Only you."

"I haven't told you enough." His fingers brush the curve of my ass. The crook of my thigh. Then closer and closer and closer—

Then back up my thigh, ass, lower back.

He traces a line up my spine. Over my shoulder, chin, cheeks.

He catches my bottom lip with the pad of his thumb.

Then the digit slips into my mouth.

I suck hard. It's not enough. I want more. But this is what I have and I want every drop.

He pulls his thumb back. Slips his first two fingers into my lips.

The strangeness of the gesture fades quickly. I need him in my mouth. Whatever I can get.

"Good girl," he growls as I suck at his fingers.

I've never wanted that before. Never thought about taking a man into my mouth. Teasing him, tasting him, drawing out his bliss.

I groan against his fingers until he pulls them from my mouth.

There's no teasing this time. He brings his hand to my sex. Slips both fingers inside me.

A gasp falls off my lips. "Fuck."

It's not pain. More pressure.

Too much. So much I can barely breathe.

He's inside me.

It's his hand, not his cock, but it's still a part of his body in mine.

It soothes the ache. Fills the emptiness.

"Breathe, vixen." His voice softens. "Slowly."

I suck a breath through my teeth. Push it through my nose.

Then a little slower. Easier.

The pressure fades to something bearable.

Then he pushes his fingers deeper.

Deeper.

"Fuck." I reach for something to steady myself.

My wrists catch on his tie. I'm bound. Powerless. At his mercy.

It makes my thighs shake. My breath catch. My toes curl.

I turn my head. Let my eyes flutter closed. Let words fall from my lips. "More."

He pulls his fingers back and drives them into me again.

Slowly at first. Then faster. Faster.

At a perfect, steady rhythm.

He drives his fingers into me again and again.

Until the pain fades to pressure. And the pressure fades to pleasure. And it hurts in the best possible way.

He fucks me with his fingers.

When I'm sure I can't take it anymore, he brings his thumb to my clit. Draws slow circles exactly where I need him.

I come fast this time. It's harder, quicker, so hard it hurts.

I pulse against his fingers.

Everything inside me unravels.

Pleasure rocks through my body. That same wave, only this time it's not soft, easy light. It's hard and fast and intense enough to steal my breath.

Everything releases.

I melt into his body. A puddle. His to bend or break.

He pulls his hand back. Helps me into my panties and shorts. Out of his tie. Onto the bench.

Into my crop top.

No bra. He leaves that on the floor.

I understand immediately.

He likes taking trophies.

Maybe that should scare me, but it doesn't. The

thought of him opening some drawer filled with my under-wear, thinking of me, fucking himself to me—

It thrills me.

"Do you need to get home to your sister?" His eyes meet mine. "Or can I claim the rest of your afternoon?"

Chapter Twenty-Five

IAN

Eve places her napkin in her lap. Plays with the red edges.

Her eyes fix on me. The same look she had when she was seconds from coming.

She wants everything I have to give.

It fills an emptiness inside me.

It terrifies me, how badly I want to give her everything.

Sex, I understand.

The rest?

I haven't got a fucking clue.

Maybe that's bullshit.

What's the confusion here? We're sitting at an Italian restaurant in Midtown, surrounded by business lunches, propriety, air-conditioning.

Because I want to make sure she's eating. Because I want to hear every one of her thoughts. Because I want to soak up that look in her eyes—

Like I'm the most fascinating subject she's ever found.

"We were next to Little Italy." She takes a sip of her ice water. Swallows hard. "Is this place that good?"

No. It's the atmosphere I need. A busy restaurant with no private spaces.

She's too tempting. I don't trust myself with her.

Already, I want all of her. Her body, her bliss, her attention.

The curiosity in her grey-green eyes. The proud lift of her chest. The soft blush on her cheeks.

She's fascinating. I want to stay here with her forever. Until I understand her completely.

I make an excuse. "Little Italy is a tourist trap." It's true, even if it's not my reason. There are gems, sure, but most of the places are far too expensive and crowded for the quality.

"It's a little much sometimes." She looks around the restaurant, taking in every detail with care.

Square tables—close together, but not as close as the average Manhattan restaurant. White tablecloths. Red napkins.

Oak. Soft lighting. Exposed bright.

"I never eat there. Well, not pasta. Addie and I go to this really cute matcha place that's just… really extra. And this ice cream place with good non-dairy flavors. She's trying to go vegan, but I think that's just an excuse to eat more ice cream."

"Good mint chip?"

Her smile is soft. "The best."

I bite my tongue so I won't offer to take her. That's a statement of intent. An entirely different kind of intent.

She doesn't notice. "You're kind of like the matcha place. In a totally different way. Very extra."

"Extra?"

"Yeah… extra. Someone who's more than normal in some way. Like I am, with my hair and style. Or you, with your suit."

"People still say extra?"

She laughs. "*You* are doubting *my* slang?"

I nod.

"Well… I guess I don't know. I haven't seen anyone from school since I graduated. And I'm still working on bringing back randy."

"I hope it catches on."

"Me too." Her expression softens. "You are extra. You always look like James Bond." She motions to my silver tie-clip. "Not a thread out of place."

"Not anymore."

Her blush deepens. She fights her shyness.

It's adorable. And sexy as hell.

Eve isn't a shy woman. I know how to push her buttons.

I want to push them all day, every day.

When was the last time I felt like this?

I live a full life. Enjoy the company of friends, colleagues, lovers.

Never someone who fascinates me like she does.

No one fascinates me like she does.

"You fly helicopters, right?" she asks.

I nod.

"Do you wear that?"

"Sometimes."

"Really?" Her eyes fill with surprise. "You're messing with me."

"Maybe."

"Teasing." Her smile widens. "Is that what this was? The dress thing? You're teasing."

I shrug like I don't know.

She catches on immediately. "Or did you want to imagine me in the tiny space, undressing for you?"

My balls tighten. "Of course."

"I thought about it too." She brushes a hair behind her ear. "I took a picture. I almost sent it to you."

"Why didn't you?"

"It's too risky. You could do anything with it."

"I wouldn't."

She stares into my eyes, deciding whether or not she believes me. "How do I know if I can trust that?"

"You don't. It's smart to be careful."

"You're not asking?" Her voice drips with disappointment. She wants me to ask. Wants me to demand it even.

I want any and every picture of her. But I want her to be careful too. "Yes. I'm asking. Send me a picture. Once you trust me with it. I'll fuck myself to it."

Her cheeks flush. "Oh."

"Oh?"

"Yeah. Sticking with oh." She notices a passing couple. Sits up straight in her seat. Mimes zipping her lips.

She's nervous discussing sex in public.

Which is a good thing. I'm ready to take her right now.

I need to control myself.

Eve clears her throat. Switches to a more innocent topic. "I was thinking earlier… your suit. It's like my hair. This thing that defines you. Visually."

"It does?"

She nods. "Imagine you were a character in a movie."

"Is it a sexy movie?"

"Very sexy." She smiles. "There's a spy running around who makes everyone randy."

"It sounds groovy."

"Very." Her gaze goes fuzzy as she drifts into a mental image. "The costume designer would find a way to describe each character visually. I have my hair. My tattoos. My black clothes. They say *this girl is a free-thinker. A rebel. A young person who rejects the establishment*."

"Is it accurate?"

"Mostly. And you, with this perfect suit, not a thread out of place." She looks me up and down slowly. "It says *this guy is rich. Powerful. Someone who knows how to demand all the attention in a room. Someone who gets what he wants. He's cool and collected. Put-together.*"

"Does it describe me?"

"What I know." She picks up her fork. Presses the tong into the white tablecloth. Plays with the handle. "But no one is really like that."

"No? This groovy spy isn't cool and collected?"

"Sometimes, maybe. But… well, that's why I've never watched a Bond movie. He seems so cool and aloof, like nothing could ever bother him. There's no conflict."

"What about the villain capturing him? Forcing him to listen to a boring monologue?"

She laughs. "Sure, there are obstacles. But none of them ruffle him. It's not human. So you… either you're a robot. Or you're really good at hiding the things that ruffle you."

"Damn, you've found me out. I'm Sexbot Eight Thousand. Programmed to fill every one of your needs."

Her laugh gets louder. Heavier. Enough her tits shake.

Fuck, why did I take her bra?

There's barely any fabric covering her.

It would be easy to pull her to the corner, slip my hands under her top, toy with her until she's begging to come.

"Very lifelike." She runs her index finger over the edge of the spoon. "I'm convinced."

"Wait until you see my add-on."

This time, she laughs loud enough people turn toward our table.

A few look at us curiously. *What is that unusual young girl doing with that older man?*

It's not like I can pass for her father.

But it's not like I'm the only man here with a younger woman.

Maybe it's wrong. Maybe I'm taking advantage of her inexperience. Maybe it's completely fucked up.

I don't care.

I'm careful with her heart. I can't say the same for anyone else.

"The latest technology?" She plays along, despite her blush.

"Of course."

"When, um… am I going to experience that." Her blush deepens. She tries to say something. Stays tongue-tied.

"When I decide you're ready." The playfulness drops from my voice. It's all need. Demand.

"Oh."

"It's only been two days."

"It's only a question."

"You're eager?"

She swallows hard. "I've never… I don't know what I'm doing."

"I'll show you."

"Oh. Okay. I, uh… but what if I don't catch on?"

"You will."

"How do you know?"

"How long have you been bartending?"

"Six months. Give or take."

"Did you know how to mix drinks when you started?" I ask.

She shakes her head. "Not even the ratio for a rum and coke."

"And now?"

"Oh, am I finally going to hear about that bartending job?"

Yes, how about you pour bourbon over your tits and I lick off every drop. "I suppose I should make a joke about a sex on the beach."

"It would make sense. With the plans for the party." That curiosity fills her expression. "Do you really have a beach house?"

"It's a rental."

"Could you buy one?"

"Of course."

Her eyes flare with surprise. She tries to blink it off, but she doesn't. "How rich are you?"

"Don't you know it's rude to ask a man how rich he is?"

"What about a woman?"

"Still rude."

"I'm a New Yorker. I can't help it."

My laugh is easy. "Rich enough. Why? Do you want a house in The Hamptons?"

"No, reading *The Great Gatsby* the one time was enough."

"Somewhere more exotic? Hawaii? Or an island in the Caribbean?"

"I'll think about it."

"I'll include a bar. So you can mix all the drinks you want."

"I knew there was a catch. A beach house where I'm a servant." Her eyes meet mine. "Probably in some embarrassing outfit too."

"You can keep your boots."

"Oh?"

"They're all you'll wear."

Her blush spreads to her chest. "Do you really… is it a thing for you?"

"A thing?"

"Like… the guy who manages Devil's Point. When he first saw me, he went 'we don't have any punk bitch dancers. Show me what you can do and you're hired, honey.' I guess… he'll hire almost any pretty girl to dance. So many try for a night or two and give up, once they realize what it means."

"What's that?"

"It's not the dancing, really. It's the men touching them. Thinking a lap dance buys them carte blanche."

"That's what stopped you?"

She nods.

My head fills with ideas. Eve strutting around stage in knee-high lace-up boots. Tossing aside black lingerie. Climbing into my lap and begging me to touch her.

"I had to talk him into the bartending thing. I begged. It was pathetic, really. But that's what did it." She flips her teal hair. "The punk bitch look."

"Was I a teenager during the punk movement?"

"Kinda."

"I'm not that old."

"So it's not like… there was this one girl at your high school who always wore combat boots?"

"No. I don't like you because of your hair or tattoos. I like your hair and tattoos because I like you."

"You have them too."

"I was in the military."

"They're all from that time?"

"Most of them."

Her eyes flit to my chest. The only tattoo she's seen, though it's not visible at the moment. "Will you show me? Later?"

"Are you asking me to strip, Miss Miller?"

184

"Not here. But later. You are programmed for my pleasure, aren't you?"

I hold out my arm, as if I'm asking for her hand. "I live to serve, Miss Miller."

"Somehow, I have a hard time believing that."

"But it's true. All I want is your pleasure. It's just I go about obtaining it in a way that's—"

The server cuts me off. He clears his throat. "Ready to order?" His voice drips with equal parts discomfort and interest.

Eve's blush deepens.

Fuck, that blush is driving me out of my goddamn mind. I need her in my bed immediately.

Eve picks up her menu for the first time. She runs her finger over the edge.

"You trust me?" I ask.

She catches on nods. "If you're ready to use your second chance."

The server stares with impatience. "If you need a minute…"

She nods *I trust you*.

I order for the two of us. Only the entrees. No drinks. It's early and we're pressed for time.

As much as I want to cancel my entire day, I can't.

No, I can. It's a possibility. It's worth it. Beyond worth it.

But I can't let myself do that. I can't let myself give in to my obsession. I need every thought in her brain. Every wish in her heart.

Starting with mint-chip ice cream. Ending some place more terrifying than any war zone.

The server takes our menus. Leaves with a huff of impatience.

"He's in a rush," I say.

"You were being rude. Wasting his time undecided."

"I was undecided?"

She nods *yeah* with a smile. "How long *have* you been in New York?"

"Four years."

"You're not used to it?"

"Depends on the day. People in London are busy, but it's not like here. We know we've been around for hundreds of years. We've survived wars, fires, famines. We know we'll get there."

"I was going to say we're rude in New York."

"You're matter-of-fact. Not polite, but not rude. Usually." My eyes find hers. "You've always lived here?"

She nods. "I've visited other places. Though, not recently. Besides the trip to the beach. The people there were still… not polite, but in a different way. Less impatient, more *what are you doing here?*"

"Because of your look?"

"Maybe. Or maybe they're like that."

"How long have you had teal hair?"

"A year and a half. I do get a lot of attention. Sometimes, I like it. Sometimes I want to disappear. But I can't."

"I know the feeling."

"Right. I chose my hair. It's not like… it's just hair. But it feels like me. When I see it in the mirror, I see myself." Her eyes pass over me again. "Is it the same for you? With your suit?"

"Not exactly."

"Do you try to look unruffled?"

"Yes."

She swallows her surprise. Expecting a non-answer, I guess. "But things do ruffle you?"

"Of course."

"What?"

"How much I want to cancel my day and take you back to my flat."

Her eyes go wide. For a second, her blush overwhelms her, then she works through it. "You're trying to dodge the question."

"It's the truth."

"But not what I asked."

"It is."

It's not that I want to take her to my flat to fuck her senseless, though I do.

It's that I want to spend the night on the balcony, listening to her talk about costume designers and character and literature.

"Ian?" Her voice softens. "You don't have to answer. Maybe that is an answer. You're scared of people knowing what you're scared of."

"Isn't everyone?"

"I guess so." She runs her fingers over her fork. "I think… I guess that's what relationships are. Letting people know what scares you. Telling them how to hurt you." She lets out a soft sigh. "God, I sound like Addie. Pretend I didn't say that."

"It's insightful."

"Yeah, but so… ugh. She's a romantic, my sister. She believes in fairy tales."

"You don't?"

She shakes her head. "Do you?"

"No."

"Did you ever?"

"For a while."

"When you were married?"

My stomach drops.

My calm vanishes. My ease disappears. The world is someplace ugly and tense.

Eve notices right away. "Oh." She studies my expression. "I guess that's… oh."

"It was a long time ago."

"Is that why you moved to New York?"

"Yes."

"And now… you're still…"

"It's complicated."

"Do you love her?" she asks.

"No."

She nods, believing me. "But you're… heartbroken?"

"Not exactly."

Her eyes stay soft. Curious. "Is that what this is? Rules. So you don't have to risk falling in love again?"

Chapter Twenty-Six

IAN

I don't answer.

She changes the subject. Costumes in movies. The difference between the way people dress on British TV and American TV.

Everything is glamour on American TV. Even the police detectives wear false eyelashes and heeled boots. Everyone is beautiful. Everything is glossy.

Even the ugliness.

I try to listen.

She tries to talk.

But it lingers in the air. I have a past she knows nothing about. An entire life she knows nothing about.

It's how I like things.

Usually.

Right now, watching her green eyes light up as she discusses some New York set TV show. Watching her dark lips move with excitement. Watching her dig into her pesto, taste every drop, sigh with pleasure—

I want to tell her more.

I want to tell her about how quickly I fell in love with

Laura. About how she brightened the darkness. Wiped away my cynical impulses.

And about how quickly the darkness returned.

Or maybe it wasn't quickly. Work had been busy. She'd been distant. We'd been growing apart.

Still, I thought we were okay. That I still knew her. Still tended to her needs.

Then those fucking papers landed in my lap.

And all of a sudden, the voice in the back of my head, the one that whispered questions about late nights and extra singing lessons and new lingerie—

All of a sudden, it was a yell, and I knew she was fucking someone else. In love with someone else. Leaving me for someone else.

There's no dramatic twist to the story.

Only the one person who truly knew me deciding I wasn't enough.

It wasn't long hours or work conflicts or even my particular tastes.

No, it was much more simple and much more complicated.

She didn't love me anymore.

She didn't understand me anymore.

She didn't need me anymore.

Even with three thousand miles between us, I feel it. The heaviness in my chest, the emptiness in my heart, the lead weight in my stomach.

The sight of her hand in his. His lips on hers. Her nails in his back.

I don't think about Laura anymore.

I don't imagine her afternoons at the office. Her evenings at yoga classes. Her nights in his bed.

I don't think about their new home. Or their marital bed. Or the way she looks truly at ease in his arms.

But I still feel the ache of it. That knowledge that goes all the way to my core.

The one person who knew me decided I wasn't enough.

What the hell does that say about me?

So I ignore that other voice. The one begging me to cancel my afternoon and spend it with Eve. The one begging me to bring her back to my flat and spill my guts.

I tease her about her love of pasta. I ask her about her tattoo. I listen to her gush over *The Handmaid's Tale*.

Then I send her home in the limo. And I spend the afternoon as planned. Digging into a rival company. Finding someone else's weak spots and attacking them.

But it's not the concentration I need.

My mind keeps slipping back to her.

Her groan, her laugh, her smile.

I find the place in Little Italy she mentioned. A New York chain that's spreading around the country. I send her a pint of the non-dairy mint chip. Try to put her out of my mind.

But it doesn't work.

I keep thinking of her laughing with her sister. Digging into her ice cream, utterly at ease, perfectly content.

That same look Laura had with that arsehole.

Like she's exactly where she's supposed to be, doing exactly what she's supposed to do.

I try to tell myself I don't want that.

But it's no use.

I want Eve.

Her need, her desire, her affection, her love.

———

An hour at the gym calms me. A shower. Dinner.

I'm not like Shepard. I don't have a staff to cook my meals or clean my room.

Military training dies hard. I make my bed every morning. Put everything in its proper place.

I can't concentrate surrounded by mess.

Not in my house.

Not in my head.

Thankfully, the steps to this meal are worn into my body.

A simple roast. Meat, potatoes, peas, carrots, rosemary.

I pass the time with an old paperback. One of the novels Eve loves.

After a few pages, I lose myself in the words.

Until the buzz of my cell interrupts.

Not the timer.

A text from her.

Eve: Do I need to know anything about dinner?

Ian: It's the meal after lunch.

Eve: With your friend on Thursday? Is he secretly your brother or something? Are you secretly judging me as marriage material?

Ian: Are you waiting for a proposal?

Eve: Would you get married again?

My stomach twists at that word. *Again.*

Of course she knows. Everyone knows. But it's different on her lips.

Ian: No.

Eve: Never?

Ian: The world is a big place. Anything is possible.

Eve: That's not an answer.

Ian: It is.

Eve: So, maybe you'd get married again. But not in the foreseeable future.

Ian: Are you proposing now?

Eve: In your dreams.

Ian: My dreams of you are much dirtier than that.

Eve: Oh.

Ian: Oh?

Eve: Yeah. Oh. You must know my oh by now.

Ian: Oh, I have no response to that, because I'm too rocked with desire to think.

Eve: Basically.

Ian: Good.

Eve: Addie thinks it's strange that I never want to get married.

Ian: You're young. You might change your mind.

Eve: Would you like it if I said that to you?

Ian: I'm not young.

Eve: You're not old.

Ian: I've been married. I know what it's like.

Eve: What is it like?

The oven beeps. The timer.

I need to finish the roast. Turn off my cell. Eat dinner with a book. A movie. A friend who will distract me from the emptiness in my gut.

How does she know the exact place to press on the bruise?

Why do I want to reply so badly?

I set my cell on the leather couch. Move to the kitchen.

Like most of the new buildings in the financial district, this one is modern. Sleek. One massive den/kitchen/dining room combo. Then three bedrooms.

I use one to sleep. Use the other as an office. The third for overnight guests.

It's excessive, yes, an entire room for sex. But it's necessary too.

A thick line, drawn in black. A room completely different than mine. Louder, bolder, sleeker.

A four poster-bed, silk sheets, restraints, toys, lube, condoms. An armchair. A desk. A dresser.

Anything and everything.

My room is much simpler. A king bed. White sheets and comforter. Black dresser. Framed photographs of the city.

It's too easy to picture her there.

The white sheet at her chest. Her lips parting with a groan. Her grey-green eyes alive with passion, curiosity, affection.

I can see it now.

This conversation in my bed. Her as naked as she's asking me to be.

I've never backed away from a challenge before.

I've been a lot of things. A soldier, a spy, a business-man, a husband.

Never a coward.

But I can't answer her question. My fingers are too stiff. My head is too fuzzy.

Ian: I hate to say goodbye, but I have a meeting.

Eve: Hmm.

Ian: I'll send a car tomorrow. Meet me at the restaurant.

Eve: This is a test, isn't it?

Ian: What kind of test?

Eve: For me. Or maybe you. Or your friends. It's something.

Ian: I'm inviting you to dinner with a friend. It's dinner.

Eve: I don't think so.

Ian: Then don't think so. But that's all it is.

I don't believe it myself. Maybe she's right. Maybe it is a test.

But not for her.

For me.

Chapter Twenty-Seven

IAN

"**F**our days and you're already obsessed with her." Shepard sips his mineral water. "You're not going to make it the month."

"I will."

"What is it you normally do? Wait until day thirty to fuck the poor girl?"

"No."

"No." His blue eyes light up with realization. "It's worse. You wait until you've had your fill. Then you fuck her and send her home early."

This time, my shrug fails to sell my disinterest.

Yes, I've had my fair share of casual relationships in the last four years. A dozen, maybe.

Yes, I set a firm timeline. And I occasionally end things early.

But it's not because I'm done with a woman the second I fuck her.

It's because she's looking at me like she has ideas about unlocking my heart. It isn't happening. Better to end things before I hurt her.

"I end things when they're over," I say. "Some women want anticipation more than anything else. Once we've fucked, there's nothing left to anticipate."

He shakes his head, not buying it. "I've heard you discuss this. Bragging about how badly women were begging for your cock by day thirty. And how you managed to resist temptation until the very end."

"If you want to hear about my sex life, all you have to do is ask."

"I don't have to ask."

He's right. I talk a lot of talk. Though I don't feel that same compulsion now.

I want to keep my thoughts of Eve to myself.

I don't want him to know the sound of her groan. Or the way her head falls to one side. Or the feel of her fingers against my thighs.

"You're the one bragging about your limo," he says. "Since when do you have a limo?"

"It's a service." I hold up my gin and tonic, beckoning a toast. "Besides, I've heard stories about your limo."

He laughs. "Have you?"

"Jasmine isn't so tight-lipped."

"Are we toasting to that?"

"You don't want to toast to her?"

"To what?" He holds up his mineral water. "True love?"

"True desire."

He chuckles *sure* and taps his glass against mine. "You don't fool me, Ian. You can act as casual as you want. Ask as many questions about my sex life as you want. I can still do the math."

"You can? Damn, I didn't realize the CFO could do maths. When did you learn that?"

He shakes his head *not fooling anyone.* "You've never invited a woman to dinner with me before."

"You were unpleasant company before."

He half-smiles, accepting the claim but not the overall reasoning.

It's true. Before Jasmine, Shep was a beast. Constantly frustrated, quick to anger, free of joy. Now—

There it is.

His eyes turn to the entrance as his wife enters the room.

She looks as gorgeous as always. Subtle makeup lining her almond eyes. Dark hair in a sleek line. A strapless red frock that falls just above her knees.

Sexy yet demure.

Exactly what winds his watch.

She crosses the room to us.

He stands. Pulls her into a tight embrace. Whispers something dirty in her ear.

She blushes as she releases him.

I stand. Offer my own hug. "You look lovely."

"Thank you." She lets Shepard pull out her chair. Sits. "You too."

"Thank you. I was going for lovely," I say.

She laughs. "I can never tell which of you is teasing the other."

"Ian lives to torment me," Shep says.

"Yes. It was his idea. But why would meeting his—what do you call her?" she asks.

"Eve," I say.

She turns to Shep. "Why would meeting Ian's girlfriend torment you, baby?" Her eyes fix on her husband. "You're not going to be upset if she doesn't like you."

"No one likes me," he says. "I'm used to it."

She squeezes his hand. "I like you."

"Now."

She nods *true*. They share a look. One of those looks of pure understanding.

They know exactly what they want to communicate.

They don't know everything about each other.

She knows more about his secrets than I do, but she doesn't know everything. She's asked my help enough I can see that.

But she does know his heart. Knows every place she needs to tread carefully. Every wound she wants to mend.

It's bizarre, seeing my miserable friend this happy.

It fills me with a familiar warmth. And it twists the knife in my back.

I'm happy for him.

But it hurts to see this kind of love up close. It's gnaws at the gaping hole in my chest.

"Am I early enough?" Jasmine breaks from her husband's stare. Scans the room for a clock.

Shep holds up his left wrist, so she can check the time. It's a mindless gesture. He doesn't realize he's doing it. She doesn't realize she's following.

It's routine. Something worn into their bones.

Only three weeks of marriage and they have a routine.

They had a short engagement too.

Though… they were high school sweethearts, a million years ago. Shep never has told me what happened.

I know a lot. Mostly rumors I picked up before I met him. Or dirt I dug when I was deciding if I'd buy into his latest company.

He had quite a reputation before rehab. And after. Tied a lot of models to his bed.

"I want to see her come in. No, I want to see your face when she gets here." Jasmine's pitch rises. "I never thought I'd see Ian Hunt smitten."

The server drops off another round of drinks. Mineral water for Shep. Gin and tonics for me and Jasmine.

"What was it like? When you met? Was she how you imagined? Did you know it was true love right away?" She holds up her drink to toast.

"Princess, don't encourage him." Shep rolls his eyes, but he still holds up his glass of mineral water.

"To new beginnings." She runs her thumb over her engagement ring as she turns to me. "Spill."

True love is far beyond my understanding. I ignore that question. Focus on the other. "Exactly the same and completely different."

She motions *go on*.

There's no way to describe it without bringing up my ex-wife. "What was it like the first time you saw Shep again? Was he as you remembered him?"

"The exact same and completely different."

"It was like that. I had no idea she had green eyes. Or round hips. Or the world's most perfect laugh. But there was something about her I knew."

"You didn't know what she looked like?"

"Only her hair. And her style. Though words didn't do it justice… She's beautiful in an entirely different way. She is pretty, but it's not about her gorgeous eyes or her strong nose, or the slope of her chin. It's her."

"You are obsessed with her." She taps Shep. "You were right, baby."

"Wonderful. I was right about Ian. And now we're going to talk about his love life after dinner." He feigns irritation, but he fails to hide his smile.

Jasmine doesn't try to hide hers. "Did it feel the same? Finally seeing her in person?"

Movement at the entrance draws my eyes.

The door opens. Eve steps through.

She's wearing a long black frock. A low-neckline. A chiffon skirt with a slit up to her thigh. And at the end of those long legs—

Heeled combat boots. The same as yesterday, with one change.

Teal laces.

Jasmine shoots me a knowing smile. One I recognize. One that means *it's so sweet how much you adore your girlfriend.* She turns to the entrance. Waves to Eve.

Eve nods back to Jasmine. Then me. Despite the nerves in her eyes, she moves with steady steps.

Jasmine stands as she approaches the table. Shep follows her lead.

They let me introduce them, shake, sit.

Eve takes the seat next to mine. She looks up at me with wide eyes. Asking for reassurance.

"I've told them a lot about you," I say. "Jasmine especially."

"It really is great to meet you." Jasmine fails to contain her enthusiasm. "Ian is… I've never seen him like this."

"In the three months you've known him?" Shepard asks.

"Three months is enough time to know someone," Jasmine says. "And I know Ian. He's one of my closest friends."

I hold up my drink.

She taps her glass against mine.

"Three months?" Eve looks to Jasmine. "How did you meet Ian?"

"A dinner with Shepard. After we were engaged." She doesn't add any details about the terms of their engagement. "It was a surprise, to know Shep had such a good friend. And one so handsome too."

"Ah, she remembered she's my wing woman," I tease.

Jasmine just smiles. "Yes, I'm supposed to talk about how great you are. So why is Shep here?"

"To talk about how much he can't stand me. Make it a challenge," I say.

Shep chuckles.

Eve's laugh is more awkward. She's still outside the circle. Unclear of the dynamic.

"Really though, I want to hear about you, Eve. Who cares about Ian? A British guy with all the money in the world. Been there, done that." Jasmine waves her hand dramatically, as if she could not possibly find me less interesting. "At least tell me how you get your hair that color. It's gorgeous."

"Thank you." Eve blushes at the attention. But there's something in her eyes. A confidence. "I have it down to a science."

"Would you do mine?" Jasmine asks.

"Princess, in what universe would you dye your hair green?" Shep asks.

"Let me fantasize." She keeps her eyes on Eve, even as Shep leans in to whisper something dirty. "He is right. I'd never change my hair. But maybe something like that." She motions to the tattoo on Eve's forearm. "When did you get it?"

"A little while ago," Eve says.

"You're old enough?" Shep asks.

Jasmine shoots him an *oh my God, what are you doing* look.

"See, he's here to bring me down." I chuckle, though it is a good question. "Where did you get all these tattoos?"

"I know a guy," she says.

My stomach twists at the thought of someone else touching her.

It's ridiculous, but there's no point in fighting it.

"Well, a girl." Eve laughs. "We were good friends in

school. We still are, I guess. Just… too busy to hang out much."

"You should go. Get a tattoo with her," Jasmine says. "It's romantic."

"It's good work." I motion to Eve's tattoo. "Beautiful."

"Are we getting a couple's tattoo?" Her eyes meet mine. They light up with that curiosity. "What in the world does Ian Hunt want on his body forever?"

"Besides your hands?" I ask.

"Well, you…" She fights a blush. "You know what I mean. Lyrics to a song? A Latin quip? A lock and a key?"

"What would you want?" I ask.

"I don't know," she admits. "The lock and key maybe. But I want the key. All the power of the phallic symbol."

Is that all it is? Or does she want the power to unlock my heart?

"I can ask her to design something," Eve says. "She's great at taking a sliver of an idea and running with it."

She holds up her other arm. Turns it over to show off the tattoo on her wrist.

A EKG reading of a heartbeat.

Because of her sister's time in a hospital? Or something else?

I shouldn't know those details. I should wait until she offers them to me. It's not fair, taking them.

But I already have them.

I may as well hold them close.

Jasmine watches with interest. She turns to Shep with love in her eyes. "Would you get one with me?"

"If it was the right design," he says.

She smiles. That smile of pure, deep love. She leans in to kiss Shep.

For a moment, they're the only two people in the universe.

Then she pulls back. Turns to Eve. "Enough about us. Tell me about two things. Every step toward keeping your hair that amazing. And this." She motions to Eve's tattoo from *The Handmaid's Tale*. "The book or the show?"

"The book." Eve shakes her head with distaste. "The show is fine, but the book… it's perfect."

"It's been a long time since I've read it," Jasmine says. "What about it?"

Every last bit of tension fades from Eve's expression. Her eyes light up as she launches into a discussion of her favorite thing. She's bright, animated, moving her hands so fast she nearly knocks over my drink.

Exactly in her element.

Charming the pants off Jasmine. Impressing Shep.

Getting closer and closer to the key she needs to unlock me.

———

JASMINE AND EVE CARRY THE CONVERSATION. THEY'RE both lovers of literature, even if Jasmine is more partial to plays than novels.

They jump from one classic work to another. Then to more modern pieces. TV. Film.

Shep watches his wife with intense concentration. His blue eyes fill with love and wonder. Like she's the only thing in the universe he wants.

I don't order for Eve—I can tell she doesn't want my friends to see that—but I do point her to the dish she'll like best.

We talk through dessert. Tea. Shep promising to make use of Jasmine's extra energy.

Then goodbye.

The two of us, alone, on a warm summer night.

The air heavy with possibility.

Eve plays with her simple black purse. "I like your friends."

"Even Shep?"

She laughs. "I can tell he's a good friend. I'm glad you have that."

"Do I need it?"

She looks at me with all that curiosity in her grey-green eyes. There's something on the tip of her tongue, but she doesn't say it. "Don't you?"

It's more a statement than a question. Another brush of the key. Another look past my defenses.

I mean to dodge with a joke, but I don't.

"Yes." Lightness spreads through my chest. Then my limbs. Half freedom. Half fear.

I want her too much.

All of her.

I need something I understand. The only fucking thing I understand.

I let my voice drop to a demanding tone. "I need something else now."

She stares back at me.

"I need to make you come."

Chapter Twenty-Eight

EVE

Sleek hardwood floor. Floor-to-ceiling windows. Soft blue New York sky.

Ian's apartment fits him to a T. From the black leather couch to the flat-screen TV to the neat bookshelf.

A stack of blu-rays.

Paperbacks, old and new.

What does he read? What does he watch? Is he inhaling classic literature or modern genre fiction?

Does he sit on that couch watching restrained British dramas or thoughtless action flicks?

One or the other.

The depths of human experience.

Or easy thrills that distract.

I've never really understood the appeal of easy thrills. In theory, sure, I like thrills as much as the next girl.

An exciting mystery about detectives solving a murder? Sign me up.

But it's only exciting if I buy into the world. If the dialogue is sharp and the plot is coherent and the characters are real.

He presses his palm into my lower back, erasing all my thoughts.

TV. Movies. Books.

Him taking off my clothes.

One of these things is much more interesting than the others.

He closes the door. Clicks the lock. "A drink?" He motions to the kitchen in the massive room. All stainless steel appliances. Nothing out of place.

"Let me guess. Fever Tree and some small-batch gin that costs four hundred dollars a bottle."

"Four hundred? You're going to be disappointed by what's in the fridge."

"Two hundred?"

"Less."

I motion to the small kitchen. It's impossibly neat. Sleek. Simple. Elegant. Like everything in the apartment. Everything he wears. "Can I?"

"I don't usually ask guests to do labor."

"You're not asking."

He nods *go on*.

I step forward, breaking contact, buying a little bit of sense.

I miss his touch immediately. I don't want sense. I want to dissolve in a puddle of desire.

Only...

He asked for thirty days, yes, but did he really want all thirty?

Or was it some way to dance around what are his true intentions?

Is he going to say goodbye as soon as he punches my v-card?

The logical part of my brain tries to argue. *So what if he says goodbye? That goodbye comes with four-hundred grand. That's enough to keep warm at night.*

My heart hears none of it.

My body?

It doesn't care about tomorrow. Or next week. Or next month.

Only about touching him.

God, I need to touch him.

I move into the kitchen.

It's huge by New York City standards, but that's still pretty small. There are only so many cabinets.

I find the liquor in the one next to the fridge. The cocktail glasses on the shelf below it.

Ice in the freezer. And food too. Ingredients for meals. Not premade dinners or breakfast burritos.

Steaks, bags of shrimp, tightly packed vegetables.

The mint-chip ice cream I love. The non-dairy one.

My chest warms. My stomach gets light. It's here for me. I'm not sure how I know, but I do.

He bought me ice cream. Yes, he sent ice cream to my place, but that was different. This is taking up his space. In his life.

I fill the glasses with ice. Close the freezer. Move to the fridge.

Four packs of Fever Tree. Of course. Two original, one light, one elderflower.

I take two bottles of the original. Mix the ingredients. Cut the limes. Squeeze them into the drinks.

"A mess on your clean counter." I cross the room to Ian. Hand him his drink.

He takes a long sip. Lets out a sigh of pure pleasure. "You mix well."

"Thank you." It is good. The perfect balance of bitter,

sweet, sour, alcohol. I never favored gin. But now it tastes like him. Like the promise of everything.

"Did you follow my instructions?"

"These?" I tap my boot against the floor.

"The lingerie."

"Partially." I take a long sip. Still refreshing. Still unable to cool me. "This isn't a bra kind of dress."

"Show me." He sets his drink on the side table. Holds out his hand, asking for mine.

I place the cocktail glass in his palm. "Help me." I turn so my back is to him. Motion to the zipper at my lower back.

His fingers skim my skin. A soft line down my spine. The smooth friction of his wet skin. The coldness of the ice. Warmer and warmer, until it's only heat.

Until I'm only heat.

He traces the dress's edge then he pulls the zipper down. He traces the line back up my spine. Over my neck. All the way to the strap of the dress.

He pushes it off my right shoulder.

Then the left.

It falls at my waist. I start to turn, but he stops me.

"Take it all the way off." His voice drops to a deeper tone. Less softness. More demand.

It makes my knees shake. My hands too. They steady as I bring them to the waistband of the dress.

Slowly, I roll it off my hips.

The chiffon flutters to the ground. I lift my feet so I kick it aside. And then I'm standing in front of Ian—and half the Financial District—in only a black thong and combat boots.

"Gorgeous." His voice is heady. Needy.

I turn to face him.

He looks me up and down slowly. Like he's never seen me before. Like he's never seen a woman before.

His dark eyes fix on mine. "The knickers too." He sits in the lush leather chair. Places his hands on the armrests. Like he has all the time in the world to watch me.

Like he wants to spend all that time watching me.

My breath catches in my throat. His expression is so intense. Like he'll die if he doesn't see me naked.

And there's this ache in my core. I'll die if he doesn't see me naked.

No. He has seen me naked. I was naked in his lap. But not like this. Standing in front of him—in front of this wide, open window—posing for his viewing pleasure.

I push the panties off my hips. Kick them aside.

Take a small step backward. To give him a better view.

He lets out a groan of appreciation. His pupils dilate. His fingers curl into his slacks.

His eyes move over me. Slowly. Impossibly slowly. Taking in every single inch of my skin.

My short hair, my narrow shoulders, my small breasts, my wide hips, my thick thighs.

Down to the boots. Then back up again. Not my figure, but the details. The lyrics on my side. The cherry blossom on my forearm. The sparrow on my shoulder.

The deep berry lipstick. The charcoal line around my eyes. The teal locks falling over my cheeks.

His eyes settle on my lips. "Turn around."

I do it slowly.

My gaze shifts to the window. The sprawling view of the city. The little yellow lights in offices. There's a man working at his desk. A woman reading a book. Another building. Apartments.

Friends at a party.

A couple on the couch.

A woman watching a movie.

No one is looking, but if I can see them—

The thought makes my sex clench. It's so fucking hot, being on display for anyone who cares to glance.

And for him.

My eyes catch something else in the window.

The reflection. The soft glow of the sky falling over my pale skin and dark boots.

Casting highlights on the sleek hardwood floor.

Disappearing into Ian's navy slacks.

His fingers brush my lower back. The same line up my spine. Then down. Over the curve of my hips.

His palms flat against me, he pulls me into his lap.

His lips go to my neck.

One hand to my chest.

The other pushes my legs apart.

My legs over his, my back against his chest, my ass against his cock.

All that fabric in the way, but I can still feel him. Hard. Ready.

I need that.

And I need this.

He sucks on my neck as he runs his fingers over my inner thigh. Closer and closer and closer-

Until I'm shaking with pent-up need.

Until my breath is shallow and strained.

Until my voice is a whine.

"Please." The words fall off my lips with ease.

He responds with a deep groan. And his fingertips on my clit.

He holds me close, sucking on my neck, toying with my breasts.

Rubbing me exactly how I need him.

My gaze flits to the window for a second.

There's a hint of our reflection. His dark hand against my pale skin. His slacks below my thighs. His hand between my legs.

It's faint. Barely there.

But the knowledge the entire fucking city can see us—

It deepens the ache in my core.

I'm already so close. So desperately in need of him.

My eyelids flutter closed.

His thumb rolls over my nipple.

His teeth sink into my neck.

The soft, steady circles with just the right pleasure—

There.

My eyes burst open as I come. I groan his name. Watch him rub me through my orgasm through the reflection.

Somehow, it makes my pulses harder. It pushes the pleasure deeper. So much I can barely take it.

So much I can barely breathe.

But I can.

And as soon as I catch my breath, I need more. I need everything.

I let my head fall onto his chest. "I want to touch you."

"You will." His voice is steady. Patient.

He's still hard—I can feel him against my ass—but he's so fucking patient.

"There's a full-length mirror in my room." He pulls my hair aside to press his lips to my neck.

"Oh. So you…"

"Want you to watch as I fuck your pretty mouth."

Chapter Twenty-Nine

IAN

Eve's heels tap the floor. Her eyes go the window letting in the soft blue light.

The building across from this one. Bright yellow against dark sky. A woman working late.

The slight reflection of her light skin and teal hair. Like the moon on the water. Luminous and fleeting.

I bring my hand to her shoulder. Turn her to the mirrored closet door. An ordinary feature turned illicit.

An entire wall reflecting the blush on her cheeks, the heave of her chest, the curve of her lips.

And my hand on her shoulder, side, stomach.

Her eyes flutter closed. Her head falls to one side. Her hair goes with it.

She's already lost in anticipation. In a world of deep, pure desire.

I need to keep her there. In this place that makes sense.

And I need to lose myself in her.

To pin her to the bed and split her in half.

To claw at her soft back and come on her lush ass.

My head fills with delicious ideas.

Too many ideas. I can't afford to lose control.

She trusts me with her body.

Yes, she wants it hard and fast, but she's not ready for that.

I can't promise soft and slow, but I can show some restraint.

A fucking modicum.

I press my palm into her stomach, holding her body against mine.

She purrs as she melts into me. Her back against my chest, her arms against my sides, her ass against my cock.

I need to feel that. To feel her flesh against mine. Her soft hand wrapped around me.

"Ian…" She arches her back, rolling her ass over my crotch. Her eyes flutter open. They go to the mirror. She blushes as she takes in our reflection. "I want to, but I've never…"

"I know."

"I might not—"

"You will."

"And you'll…" She makes eye contact through the mirror. She stares into my eyes like she's staring into my soul. Maybe she is.

She's in *my* room. My space. My life.

She's in my room and I want to keep her here. I want to tie her to the fucking bed so I can fuck her senseless.

And then talk to her all goddamn night.

"Will you go hard?" Her voice is shy.

It makes my balls tighten. "Do you want me to?"

"Yes," she breathes.

Fuck, I'm already going out of my mind. "Give me your hands."

She does.

I take one and place it above her head. Against the mirror.

She leans forward enough her ass rocks against me. A groan falls off her lips.

She wants more, and she's not patient.

Still, she stays soft. Pliable.

I place her other hand on her hip.

She watches as I unknot my tie and toss it on the black sheets. As I unbutton my shirt. Do away with my belt.

"Can I?" She makes eye contact through the mirror. Motions to the shirt. My chest.

I nod. "Turn around."

She does. She looks up at me, those grey-green eyes wide with need, desire, curiosity. Slowly, she trails her fingers over my chest. Down my stomach.

She undoes the last three buttons. Pushes my shirt off my shoulders.

I toss it aside.

She runs her fingers over my collarbone. The Latin quote tattoo on my chest. The compass beneath it.

She stares up at me with those grey-green eyes. All curiosity. All tenderness.

Asking for more in every sense of the word.

There's one part I understand.

The rest—

Fuck, I want it too badly. To wrap my arms around her waist, lay her on the bed, kiss her as our bodies join.

To feel all that tenderness. To soak in all her sweetness. To promise more than sex.

But I can't.

It's not possible.

No matter how badly I want it.

I wrap my fingers around her wrist.

She gasps as I pull my hand from her chest. Surprise fills her eyes. Then that perfect need.

Fuck, she's too beautiful like this. It's irresistible.

I can't give in to how much I want her. Not yet.

I need to stay in control. To lead her. Teach her.

It's what I do. It's not normally a problem.

But Eve is something else.

I bring her hand to my belt.

She looks up at me, asking permission. When I nod, she unzips my trousers.

I push my boxers out of the way.

Her eyes go wide. She stares—flat out stares—as she wraps her hand around me.

Fuck. That feels too good. She's already testing my stamina.

But maybe that's for the best. This is her first time. Even if I'm gentle—

Who am I kidding? I'm not gentle.

I bring my hand to the back of her head. Knot my hand in her hair. Pull just enough she gasps. Just enough she knows she's mine.

Then I bring her into a deep, slow kiss.

I claim her as she runs her hand over me.

She takes her time exploring me. Her thumb. Then the pads of her fingers.

She's not hitting every spot I need, but the way she runs her fingers over me patiently, like she needs to explore every centimeter—

I tug harder at her hair. Kiss her deeper. Pull her closer.

She gasps as I pull her head back.

Her eyes meet mine. That same intense gaze. Curiosity, need, desire.

I let my voice drop to a demanding tone. "Put your hand around me."

She wraps her fingers around my cock.

"Thumb against your index finger."

She does what she's told.

I bring my hand to her wrist. "Run your hand over me. Like this."

She nods as I guide her motion.

A few strokes as she has the speed. The posture. "Harder."

"How hard?"

"Hard."

"You're really—" Her eyes go wide as she watches herself work. That same sense of wonder. Like my cock is her favorite book. Like she's got to find every deeper meaning.

It makes my balls tighten. My thighs shudder. My body whine.

I need to fuck her. Now. No patience, no teaching, no biding my time.

Me deep inside her. Her groaning my name.

Fuck.

More pressure. Enough my eyes close. Enough bliss overwhelms my senses.

More with her next stroke.

More.

"Fuck, Eve." I bring my lips to hers. Kiss her hard as she strokes me. Again and again. Until I haven't got a bit of sense left.

I tug hard at her hair.

A soft gasp falls from her lips.

Her hands go flat against my chest.

I bring my hand to her chin. Turn her head toward the mirror. "Watch."

"Everything?"

"Yes." I run my thumb along her jawline.

Her eyes flutter together. "What is everything…"

"What do you want, vixen?" I run my thumb along her jaw. Over her bottom lip. "Do you want to watch as I fuck your pretty hand?" I release her lip. Bring my hand to her chin. Tilt her so we're eye to eye. "Do you want to watch as I fuck your pretty mouth?"

Her chest heaves with her inhale.

"Or do you want me to throw you on that bed and split you in half?"

"Yes."

"Yes?"

"All of them. Yes."

"Pick one."

"I want to…" Her eyes trail down my body. Her tongue slides over my lips. "I want to taste you."

Fuck. "Say it."

Her cheeks flush. That intoxicating blush.

My cock pulses. I need that blush. "Say it, vixen." I run my thumb over her chin. Down her neck. Along her collarbone. "Say, 'I want to suck your cock.'"

Her blush deepens. She opens her mouth to speak. Lets out a gasp as I cup her breast. "Not fair."

"I don't play fair." I run my thumb over her nipple.

"Ian—" Her voice breaks to a whine. "Please."

"Please?"

She nods. "Please."

"Say it."

"I…" She presses her palm into my stomach. Then my hip. "I want to suck your cock." She lifts her chest. Looks up at me with those proud, defiant eyes.

What the fuck did I do to get this lucky? "Wait."

This room isn't set up for sex. I want to push her limits, yeah, but not because the floor is making her knees ache.

I find a pillow. Place it in front of her. "On your knees."

She practically falls onto the damn thing. Then it's all that pride and curiosity in her grey-green eyes.

"Hand around me to start." I take her hand. Bring it to the base of my cock.

She looks up at me as she wraps her fingers around me.

"Lips around your teeth."

She nods.

I knot my hand in her hair. Hold her head in place as I bring my cock to her mouth. The soft brush of her lips, then that sweet, wet warmth.

Fuck.

It's been too long. It feels too good. And knowing it's Eve—

My gaze shifts to the mirror. It's almost too much to take.

Those pretty red lips stretching to take me.

Her fingers around my cock.

Her teal hair in my hands.

"Tongue flat under me." I tug hard enough she groans against my cock.

The vibration is divine. And the sound of Eve—

I'm too far gone.

Way too fucking far.

I hold her head in place with one hand. Bring the other to her chest. Toy with her nipple as I push into her.

Slowly at first.

Those red lips stretch as she takes me.

Deeper.

Deep enough to push her.

I pull back and do it again.

Still slow. But faster. Still soft. But harder.

Then again.

Again.

Deeper.

Deep enough she coughs. Jerks away. Falls back and wipes her lips. "That's a little—"

"I won't go so hard."

"I want you to. I just—"

"We can work up to that, vixen."

She blushes. Again. It's absurd. And sexy as sin.

"Try to relax your throat."

"How?"

"Swallow."

She tries it. Pushes herself upright.

Eve looks up at me as she wraps her hand around my cock. Then it's her soft lips. Her wet tongue. All the sweet pressure of her mouth.

Her gaze shifts to the mirror.

She watches her lips stretch around me.

Watches as I push into her.

Still slowly.

Then faster. Harder.

Until I'm at the rhythm I need. Not enough to make her gag. Not enough to scare her. Only—

Fuck.

I tug at her hair. Roll her nipple between my thumb and forefinger.

It's almost too much, watching her red lips stretch around me, watching her teal hair fall over her cheeks, watching her pink nipple disappear between my fingers.

I hold her in place as I thrust into her.

That steady rhythm.

That perfect pressure.

Then deeper. Until I can feel the back of her throat.

She gags the first time. Then she swallows to take me.

I thrust into her again and again.

I take in the sight of her—a perfect angel, on her knees, in nothing but her fucking combat boots—then I let my eyes fall closed.

One more thrust and I pull back. I growl her name as I come, spilling onto her chest, tugging hard at her hair.

Her head falls back. A groan falls off her lips.

She looks up at me with fire in her eyes. Pride. Satisfaction.

Fuck, she's perfect.

It's terrifying.

I zip my trousers. Help her to her feet. Wipe her clean.

She looks up at me with all that pride. Then her eyelids flutter closed and her lips find mine.

I kiss her like I'm claiming her.

But it's not just her body. It's something else. Something more. Something that terrifies every molecule in my body.

Chapter Thirty

IAN

Eve rolls onto her side. She lets out a high-pitched yawn as she stretches her arms over her head.

Those grey-green eyes fix on me. Fill with that perfect curiosity. Like I'm a book she simply must understand.

Her lips curl into a smile. No dark makeup. Her eyes aren't lined. Her lashes aren't long. Her lips aren't raspberry.

A soft pink that's all her.

A soft pink the color of her cunt.

For a split second, the thought steals my attention. I consider tossing the white sheets aside. Finding a tie in the closet. Binding her to the bed and forcing her to take all the pleasure I want to give her.

Then my eyes flit to hers and I can only think one thing:

She belongs here.

In my bed.

In my flat.

In my life.

It's ridiculous. There's no room for anyone in my life. No matter how badly I want to cancel my meeting and cook her breakfast.

I cooked for Laura.

I don't cook for anyone else.

"Morning." Eve pushes herself up. She pulls the sheet with her. Holds it against her chest. Shy again.

Driving me out of my fucking mind again.

"Are you leaving?" Her eyes move over me slowly. That same care and curiosity. "I guess it's a stupid question. Or maybe you hang out in that suit. I still haven't seen you in casual clothes."

"You saw me without a tie."

"Without a shirt."

"I can't help that you fell asleep before me and woke up after. I was naked."

"Were you really?" Her cheeks flush.

I shake my head. "Boxers."

"Hmmm." Her eyes light up with an epiphany.

Does she realize I had to wear something to keep myself from touching her? Or is there something else going on behind her gorgeous green eyes?

"I've never slept over before. Well, not with a guy. With my friends from high school. And the one who—" She motions to the tattoo on her forearm. "She rushes me out sometimes. Or she did. It's been awhile."

"You don't see her anymore?"

"I've been busy. Though… I guess I could now." Her voice shifts to a playful tone. "Or I could make an appointment for the couple's tattoo."

"Is that a dare, Miss Miller?"

"If it is?"

"Only one way to find out."

224

"I'll consider that." She scoots a little taller. Pulls the sheet a little higher. "Do I need to—"

"No. Stay as long as you want. The door locks on the way out. But if you stay until I'm back from work, I'll make it worth your while."

"Ah."

"There's tea in the kitchen. And porridge on the stove. That's what you prefer to eat?"

She nods. "Thank you."

"Take your time. I want to imagine you naked in my bed."

Her blush deepens. She shakes it off. Looks up at me. "Good morning. And I guess... goodbye." She lets her sheet fall as she scoots to the edge of the bed. Wraps her fingers around my tie. Tugs gently.

I bend enough to wrap my arms around her. Pull her upright. Hold her against me as I kiss her goodbye.

It's sweet, gentle, domestic.

Dizzying.

"What do I say here? Have a good day?" Her smile is soft. "Have a good day."

"You too."

She falls back into bed. Wraps herself in the white sheets. Watches me leave.

I try to put her out of mind as I walk to work—it's only a dozen blocks, no reason to take the subway.

When that fails, I try to imagine her tangled in my white sheets.

Her head thrown back, her hair falling over her eyes, her hand between her legs.

I try to imagine her groaning my name as she strokes herself to orgasm.

For a minute, I do. Then my mind shifts to unfamiliar places.

Eve groaning over her tea. Donning one of my shirts. Laughing at a TV show from the couch.

Pulling out her notebook, twirling a teal lock around her finger, chewing on the cap of her pen.

Making herself at home as she spills her thoughts.

As she finds everything I try to hide.

Chapter Thirty-One

EVE

I fall back asleep. Dream of a tall, dark, handsome stranger whisking me to his massive apartment and erasing my problems. Wake to the sun bouncing off the steel and glass. Casting light all over the airy room.

Plain walls, framed photos, white sheets.

Exactly what I expect of Ian. Only lacking in a personal touch.

Sure, the framed photos are nice—greyscale shots of Manhattan—but they aren't him.

He's not a man who loves the city. His heart is in London. No matter what he claims.

There isn't anything of him in the room. Only a closet full of pressed suits. Ties in every color. Dress shoes and belts in black and brown.

The man knows style. I guess we have that in common.

We know what our attire projects. Know how we're presenting ourselves. Take care in cultivating a shield that doesn't look like a shield.

He *does* have casual clothes in his dresser. Under the drawer of boxers—all black, mostly silk, some cotton.

Those fitted running pants.

Sweat wicking tanks.

Jeans.

T-shirts.

A pair of actual shorts.

It's hard to imagine Ian in shorts. What the hell is he going to wear to this beach party?

And why is he throwing a party in the Hamptons? Maybe it's for my sake. To show me off to his friends. Or show his friends off to me.

Maybe his motives are more simple. He wants to strip me out of my bikini and fuck me in the pool.

I don't exactly object.

There's something in the bottom drawer. A leather photo-book.

I leave it where I found it. Resist the urge to peel open the worn cover and run my fingers over old images.

He's twice my age. He's already lived an entire life.

Yes, I want to know every detail. To understand why he stayed married so long and divorced so quickly. To understand why he offered me half a million dollars for thirty days.

To understand him.

But it's not a good idea. This ends in less than four weeks. That's it. I never see him again. Never feel his rough touch. Never taste his soft lips. Never hear his dirty demands.

It's going to be hard enough giving that up.

If I fall for him?

Not considering it.

I put the photo book out of mind as I fix breakfast. The oatmeal warming on the stove is still good. There are raisins in the drawer next to the fridge. Cinnamon. Almond milk.

A mug of chai sitting on the counter. I add almond milk. Warm it in the microwave.

He made me tea and breakfast.

He bought this for me. An entire tin of Masala. Or maybe he already owned it. Maybe he's a man of eclectic tastes. Just because he orders Earl Grey or English Breakfast every time we—

No, I'm getting ahead of myself. The tea I like is in his cabinet because he wants me in his apartment.

Because he wants me naked in his bed.

Those are the terms of this agreement.

And I…

Well, I can't exactly complain.

I finish my breakfast. Wash the dishes. Leave them in the drying rack.

For a rich man with the world at his fingertips, Ian is surprisingly DIY. His entire kitchen is built for effort. No processed food. No dishwasher. No crock pot.

Pots, pans, spices, raw ingredients. The highest quality. Everything, always.

His military training or a love of cooking? Both, maybe. And maybe I shouldn't contemplate that. Or anything else about his life.

But I do. I look for something to wear in his dresser. Find an over-sized t-shirt and a pair of boxers. They're soft and smooth even if they're a little tight.

He's athletic—a broad chest, a tapered torso. I'm all hips and ass.

I move to the couch. Find the remote next to the flat-screen TV. Scan the available DVDs.

Quiet dramas with all sorts of subtext and pent-up suffering.

And thoughtful thrillers. The kind with twists that make viewers go *of course*.

A shelf filled with books. All classics, loved and modern, arranged by theme. Marriage, war, dystopia.

An entire shelf of Margaret Atwood.

For me? Or the reason why he likes me?

Maybe that's his kink. Maybe he goes crazy for girls with tattoos from *The Handmaid's Tale*.

I grab the book reflexively. Run my fingers over the worn pages. Let the book fall open to the place where the spine is creased.

A highlighted passage. Notes in the margin.

His handwriting. Not something left by a former lover. Something he adorned.

It means something.

Maybe that he has an open mind—a lot of men dismiss female authors—and good taste in literature.

Maybe that the book is incredibly well-known and incredibly popular—how many Emmy's has the TV show won?

Maybe more.

Instead of contemplating more, I settle into the couch with the paperback. Flip to a chapter and read it carefully.

Yes, I trace his highlights. Check his notes. Try to figure out what the fuck he's thinking.

But that's just—

Ahem.

Then the next chapter. Another.

Until the buzz of my cell interrupts me.

Fuck, it's almost noon and I haven't checked in with Addie. Today is a workday for her. She's at her internship. But still…

I text my sister before I read the new message from Ian.

Eve: Hey! Spent the night at Ian's place. Hanging out there now. Enjoying the air-conditioning. It's very strong. Work okay? Still on for dinner? It's too hot to cook. Let's order Indian.

She texts back right away.

Addie: How was it?

Eve: No comment.

Addie: That bad?

Eve: I am not telling you about my sex life.

Addie: Better than the bassist?

Eve: Much.

Addie: What do straight girls talk about in this situation? Are you all obsessed with dick size or is that just a thing in the movies?

Eve: You did not just say dick size?

Addie: I did.

Eve: It's men who are obsessed. I've never really cared.

Addie: You can do a lot with a mouth and two hands.

Eve: OMG TOO MUCH INFORMATION.

Addie: Did you not realize that, already? That's too bad. Ian seems generous.

Eve: What about him? No. Don't answer that. I don't need to hear your take on his sexual aura.

Addie: Who's the Long Island grandma now?

She has me there.

Eve: Okay. You can comment. Just be more quiet next time you have sex upstairs. I am never getting those details out of my head.

Addie: If you'll be quiet this weekend.

Eve: Ahem.

Addie: Long Island grandma.

Eve: Pot. Kettle.

Addie: He bought you a new wardrobe just because. Well, probably because he wants to picture you naked in the dressing room. But it's kind of sexy, in a weirdly controlling way.

Eve: It is.

Addie: Is he controlling?

Eve: Are you asking if he's bossy in bed or if he's an unsafe partner?

Addie: More the latter. But the former… might be too much information.

Eve: It's weird, isn't it?

Addie: Yeah. I really don't want to know what gets your rocks off. No offense.

Eve: Me either. No offense.

Addie: Okay, Grandma. Is he treating you well?

Eve: Yeah.

Addie: And this whole thing started…

Eve: He's my new job. We met at work. It happened kind of fast. I wanted to tell you the entire truth, but I didn't think you'd approve.

Addie: That's the entire truth?

Enough of it. All I can tell her.

She isn't going to understand what I'm doing or why. I barely understand it. And I don't want her to feel responsible. After last year…

I'm not doing this for her. It's for me. Because I want her to be okay. Because I want us to be okay.

Eve: He's helping out. Financially.

Addie: So he's like a sugar daddy or something?

Eve: I guess you could say that.

Addie: Don't tell me if you call him daddy.

Eve: Please stop with the TMI.

Addie: Ew. You do! Gross! Straight people are so weird.

Eve: I do not.

Addie: Are you staying safe?

Eve: Yeah.

Addie: And you trust him?

Eve: Enough.

Addie: Do you like him? Or is it more what he can offer you?

Eve: I like him. I like him a lot. He's funny, smart, thoughtful. But take-charge too. It's not that he makes decisions for me, exactly. But he sets them up in a way that I barely have to think about it. He knows what I want before I do.

Addie: This is about sex again.

Eve: Maybe.

Addie: He is funny. And thoughtful. Did you know Lock insisted on driving me home and picking up lunch on the way?

Eve: Sounds right.

Addie: Lock is a riot too. It's kind of weird he has an assistant, but I guess that's rich people.

Eve: They are weird.

Addie: How's his apartment?

Eve: Gorgeous. Perfect view. Elegant and sparse.

Addie: Let me guess. Black sheets.

Eve: White actually.

Addie: The comforter?

Eve: It's summer.

Addie: There wasn't one?

Eve: It was black.

Addie: Of course.

Eve: Shut up.

Addie: And a teal accent. Just like you.

Eve: Not yet. But maybe soon.

Addie: Everything like that lingerie he bought you?

Eve: Kind of, yeah. But we're veering into TMI again.

Addie: Do you think it might be more?

Eve: That a divorced millionaire might want to marry me?

Addie: The heart wants what it wants.

Eve: I guess anything is possible.

Addie: That's the most romantic thing you've ever said.

Eve: I'm reading The Handmaid's Tale right now. That's why.

Addie: You brought it with you?

Eve: It's always on my Kindle. But no. He has a copy. With notes in it.

Addie: It is true love!

She's not kidding. But maybe she doesn't have to kid.

This *is* the way to my heart. Through my brain.

And he…

God, I really do like him. But I need to keep things carnal. To focus on the parts of him I can have.

To read his text and see only dirty desires.

Ian: There's something for you in the room down the hall. The second door on the left. In the top drawer of the dresser. Send me a picture once you've found it.

Eve: Why should I?

Ian: I'll make it worth your while.

Eve: How?

Ian: A picture for a picture.

He doesn't mean he'll send a picture of himself…

Does he?

Chapter Thirty-Two

IAN

S he makes me wait.
Through an hour of research.
A meeting with Shep.
A business lunch.
Most of the afternoon.
Finally, my mobile buzzes.
A text. No picture. Yet.
Eve: Is this a sex room?
Ian: Yes.
Eve: That's weird.
Ian: It's out of the ordinary, yes.
Eve: We didn't use it last night.
Ian: We didn't.
Eve: But you left a drawer for me.
Ian: Did you open it?
Eve: Yes.
Ian: And?
Eve: I haven't used it yet.
My balls tighten at the thought of her fucking herself.

I can see her in my white sheets. Turning to watch her reflection. Letting her eyes close. Throwing her head back.

I need to see it. To watch her come all fucking night. To tie her to my bed so she's powerless to resist.

Ian: Why not?

Eve: It's kind of a lot. But I guess you are too.

Fuck, she's too funny.

Ian: Oh?

Eve: Oh is my thing. Don't take it. And don't play dumb. You know what I'm getting at.

Ian: Since when do you mince words?

Eve: Mm-hmm. I'm not going to stroke your ego like this. It will make your head too big.

Ian: My head?

Eve: See. It's already happening. Men are all the same. You think your dick size means something.

Ian: I brought it up?

Eve: No. But you're thinking about it.

Ian: I'm thinking about you stroking me.

Eve: Are you really?

Ian: Yes.

Eve: I liked that.

Ian: I know.

Eve: This isn't Star Wars. You're supposed to say something about how you liked it too.

Ian: I haven't heard an Original Trilogy reference in a while.

Eve: Addie likes it. She likes the over-the-top fantasy.

Ian: What do you like?

Eve: Crime dramas. The really horrible, gritty ones where everyone dies.

Ian: American?

Eve: Sometimes. Sometimes a Swedish show about serial killers. And sometimes a British drama. They have a certain charm. Everyone is so restrained. There's more subtext.

Ian: We're known for our stiff upper lip.

Eve: See. Bringing it back to stiff already.

Ian: Am I?

Eve: Yeah.

Ian: Are you sure you're not the one who's obsessed?

Eve: It's possible.

She's quiet for a moment. I'm not sure if I want her to ask about my life. Or my cock. I want everything from her.

I want too much from her.

Eve: You have a nice collection of movies.

Ian: Also true.

Eve: You have a favorite?

Ian: I don't watch a lot of films.

Eve: Still. You must have a favorite.

Ian: Weren't we talking about you stroking me?

Eve: We were.

Ian: Seems as if we're getting off track.

Eve: I watch more TV than film. Or read. But I do like quiet dramas. The ones based on plays.

Ian: I usually watch mysteries.

Eve: Now is when you say something about how you liked it too.

Ian: Was that not clear?

Eve: You have to remember I haven't done this before.

Ian: I couldn't tell.

Eve: Really?

Ian: The way you look at me, with all this curiosity in your eyes. It's the same way you look at me when I'm dressed.

Eve: Oh.

Ian: It drives me wild.

Eve: What else?

Ian: What else?

Eve: Drives you wild?

How hard should I push her here?

Ian: You have a sweet mouth, vixen. I can't wait to fuck it again.

Eve: Oh.

Ian: Oh?

Eve: Yeah. Sticking with oh.

Ian: I did like it. Very much. And I'd very much like to make you come all night. If you stay at my flat, I will.

Eve: I'll consider that.

Ian: Mysterious.

Eve: Am I taking your thing?

Ian: Yes, but I'm not complaining.

Eve: Generous. But I'm claiming "oh."

Ian: Good. I want to hear it on your lips again. As soon as possible.

———

SHE STAYS ON MY MIND THROUGH RESEARCH, ANOTHER meeting, a trip to the gym, the ride up the lift.

My flat is silent. She isn't here, watching a depressing British drama or playing thrashing guitar music or reading on the couch.

She isn't here.

But her knickers are. The ones she was wearing last night.

The black thong is lying on my bed—on the smoothed but not made sheets—in the middle. Beneath a torn piece of paper.

Plans with Addie tonight. And tomorrow. Next time, I'll stay. I'll make a mess of your kitchen and everything.

Think of me tonight. I'll think of you.

- Eve

She *is* teasing me. She's driving me out of my fucking mind.

I fix dinner. Shower. Try to focus on a new TV show.

The crime drama is supposed to be the most exciting,

thought-provoking thing to grace the small screen all decade.

The dialogue is sharp; the characters are vibrant; the world is clear and moody.

But it fails to hold my attention. My thoughts keep slipping back to her smile, her laugh, her groan.

All the curiosity in her grey-green eyes.

She owns my thoughts until I prepare for bed. Put away my cell. See a text from her. A picture.

From this morning.

Her in the bed—my bed—in the lingerie I left for her. A sheer lace bodysuit with a delicate floral print. All of her, from her head to her toes.

I give up on thought.

On reason.

On anything besides fucking myself to her picture.

And sending one in return.

Chapter Thirty-Three

EVE

Original Sin
Friday, June 20th
Nine p.m.

Dear Diary,
 I like a boy. Does he like me? Let me find a daisy and count the petals. He likes me. He likes me not. He likes me. He likes me not.

Can you imagine?

I suppose I shouldn't make fun of infatuation. That's denial, plain and simple. And, really, it's more internalized misogyny. We make fun of women who count petals on a flower.

What about the men? Is it always women, waiting, wondering, begging men to love them back?

That's silly.

I'm not mocking this girl. Even if she's an idea, not an actual human being.

I am holding up a mirror, laughing at the difference in our experiences.

There are no petals in this story. Unless you count the ones that make up my "virtue." Or whatever antiquated term you want to use.

There's no field of daisies.

No beautiful day in the park, with the bright blue sky, and the world full of possibilities.

Only there is.

Sure, I'm not lying in the grass, counting petals. Sure, I'm in my apartment, in only a tank top and panties, sweating my ass off despite the ice water on my desk.

Sure, I'm not a blond in a pastel dress.

But I'm sitting here, trying to spin my thoughts together, failing to quiet that voice asking: Does he like me?

No, I know he likes me, but does he *like* me?

Here I am. An ordinary girl. Twirling my hair around my fingers. Planning my next trip to Sephora. Wondering what I'm going to wear when my sister and I go out for ice cream.

Thinking about the boy I like.

Only he's not a boy.

Mr. Tall, Dark, and Handsome is all man. He's twice my age. Old enough to be my father. With an entire history. An entire life lived before I learned his name.

A life I want to know.

It's not like with the cute boy from my chemistry class. It's not like with the bassist with the cold hands. Or the guy I kissed at my best friend's party.

It's not a crush.

It's deeper, stronger, infinitely more painful.

He's my new favorite book.

I want to pry apart his pages, underline his explanations, dive into every ounce of his meaning.

Does the metaphor make sense?

Am I really using this space to talk about a boy?

But then he's not a boy.

And this isn't a normal summer fling.

This time next month, I'll never see him again. That's the deal. That's what's so terrifying. Not that I'm going to lose him. That's scary, sure, but it's not what I feel in my bones.

There's this idea about ledges. People aren't afraid of falling. They're afraid of jumping. They're afraid they'll see the ground beneath them and give in to the urge to meet it.

I'm not afraid of falling.

I'm afraid of jumping into the abyss.

I don't want to say goodbye. But knowing I have to…

There's something freeing about that. Like this space. I can spill every ugly thought in my head. I can tell him about my shitty father. My fantasies of ending the asshole forever.

I can tell him about what happened with Addie and how I was so scared I'd lose her. And under that, so jealous she had the guts. So in awe of her bravery. Because I felt that way too. I wanted out too. I would have done anything to make it better too.

And I…

It was a lot of things. Impulsive, unfair, desperate, tragic. And brave. I don't want to admit it. I don't want to consider it. I don't write about it here. Or anywhere. Because I'm too scared of the ledge. I'm too scared of jumping.

I'm too scared of landing in a puddle on the floor.

That's what he's going to do to me.

He's going to undo my binding. Spread my pages on the floor. Let them blow away in the wind.

I'm mixing metaphors here. I'm not thinking straight. Because I can't think straight.

Only of his soft lips and his rough touch and that deep

tone of his voice.

And how much I want to hear him say *come for me, vixen.*

And how much I want to hear him say *I love you, all of you, the ugly parts and the beautiful ones. The girl you hide behind the makeup and the combat boots and the girl you present to the world.*

All the scars. All the secrets.

Everything.

But I can't want that. I barely know him.

Only that isn't true. Not anymore. I do know him. Not just because his hands have been inside me. Not just because I've tasted him. Not just because I've felt his name on my lips.

Because I have the book right here. I'm prying it open, peeling the pages apart, underlining all my favorite sections.

Asking *what the hell does it mean?*

Maybe it's like any great literature.

Maybe there is no right answer.

Or maybe I'm already halfway to the ground. Because I can't think of fiction without thinking of him.

Splat.

I'm a puddle on the concrete.

Pages blowing in the wind.

A mixed metaphor to end all mixed metaphors.

I guess I should state it plainly.

I'm terrified of falling in love with him.

It feels so boring, so obvious, so done. How can I be so conventional?

Maybe I'm not the rebel I think I am.

Maybe I'm a coward.

But I see that ledge and I want to jump.

To give him my body, my mind, my heart.

Can I do that?

Can I handle what he'll give me in return?

Chapter Thirty-Four

IAN

I wake to a Google alert. A new entry on Eve's site.

I haven't looked. I've been good. Practiced restraint.

He Likes Me, He Likes Me Not

Dear Diary,

I like a boy. Does he like me? Let me find a daisy and count the petals. He likes me. He likes me not. He likes me. He likes me not.

Can you imagine?

It's about me.

She's telling the fucking world about me.

I need to know what she's saying. What she's thinking. Everything inside her beautiful head.

My finger brushes the cell screen. Every molecule in my body wants to click the link. To dive into her thoughts. Take every one of them, hold them close, claim them as mine.

I fight the urge.

Put the fucking phone aside.

Dress.

I'm late for flying a fucking helicopter. I don't have the mental space for this.

She demands it anyway.

She stays in my head as I eat, fly, finish an hour at the gym, shower, fix dinner.

He Likes Me, He Likes Me Not.

The curiosity in her grey-green eyes.

The sly smile on her raspberry lips.

The proud lift of her chest.

Not just her body.

Her heart. Her mind.

I can't handle how much I want all of her.

But I can handle how much I want to fuck her.

I can give her what she needs there.

I pull out my cell.

Send exactly the text to tease her.

Chapter Thirty-Five

EVE

I sleep in late. Take Addie to brunch. Listen to her swoon over her girlfriend. *Isn't Marisol funny? And she's so smart too. I'm pretty sure she knows everything. She introduced me to this amazing new movie. It's all artsy and weird. You would love it.*

When we order refills of our drinks—coffee for her, a pot of masala chai for me—she spots a tall guy in a suit. Changes the subject to Ian.

"It's the weekend." She fixes her coffee, making sure to leave half the side of almond milk for me. "Why aren't you with him?"

"Hmm... Maybe I like spending time with my sister? Imagine that." I left his apartment yesterday. It's been less than twenty-four hours.

But I sent him that picture...

And he still hasn't replied.

Or maybe he has. My cell is still charging at my desk. I haven't checked since last night. Addie and I made a *no phones* policy for our weekend breakfasts a long time ago.

They're usually oatmeal at the kitchen table. Sometimes pancakes or toaster waffles.

This... an actual brunch out. Raspberry chocolate chip pancakes, loose leaf tea, house-made almond milk, someone bringing food to us—

It's a dream.

Or it was. Two weeks ago.

Now...

The world at my fingertips and I'm spending my time thinking about a boy.

That isn't quite true.

I'm here, with my sister. I'm writing in my journal. I'm reading. What's more important than family, self-discovery, literature?

Why does my mind keep going back to Ian?

"You want to be with him. Or at least you want to be on top of him. It's all over your face." She draws a circle around my face with her hand, as if to prove a point. "You look so... needy."

"I do not."

She nods *yeah, you do*. "Check with your pocket mirror. Trust me. It's a new look for you."

"Horny?"

Her laugh is easy. "More or less."

"I am not."

"Uh-huh."

Okay, that's not exactly true. "I... he... It's really none of your business."

"Okay, Grandma." She holds up her mug to toast. "To your... prudishness."

"I hate you."

"I love you too." She smiles. "It's nice, being the adventurous one for once."

"We're very... I thought we agreed this is TMI?"

She laughs. "The details, sure, but… it just has to be said, Evie. It's clear you're thinking about fucking him right now."

"Maybe. I just… I don't want you to think he's…" Oh my God, why do I care if my sister thinks Ian is a selfish or generous lover? "I am satisfied."

"I hate to pull this card, but I know what a satisfied woman looks like."

"You fuck one woman and you're an expert?"

She sits back, surprised. Speaks softly, "I've been with other women."

Oh. "Who?"

"A few." This time, her expression gets shy. "I thought you knew? There was a girl at the hospital… and two this year. I just… I didn't like it, when we moved fast. So I wanted to move slow with Marisol."

"That's sweet."

"I like her so much."

"She is really smart."

She lets out a dreamy sigh. Takes a long sip. Catches herself drifting into fantasies. "Uh-huh. We're talking about you and Mr. Moneybags."

"Mr. Moneybags?"

"Yeah, I have something called Google. And it's got a lot of zeroes after his net worth. I showed Marisol his picture and she… I got really jealous, actually. She's never gone that gaga over me."

"She's really into you."

"Maybe. But the way he looked at you… I've never seen that before."

My cheeks flush.

"You did have sex? At his apartment."

"Not exactly."

She raises a brow. "You realize who you're talking to?"

"Yeah. We uh… yeah."

"It has been an entire day."

"It feels like a million years." I bite my lip. "I want to go over there right now. And just… touch him. You know? I want my skin against his skin. However, I can get it."

She nods *I know*. "Why don't you tell him that?"

"I… I left the ball in his court."

"Trust me, Evie, he wants his skin on your skin too… why does that sound like something a serial killer would say?"

It does. It's easy to laugh. Easier than facing how much I want him. "I just want to touch him. And feel him touch me."

"You really like him, huh? In a forever kind of way?"

Maybe. I don't know. It doesn't matter. We have terms. I understand them. "It's not serious."

"Why not?"

I'm not explaining that. I don't want to think about it. It's so ridiculous. How can I want him this badly? It's like he owns my mind. I only want to think of him. "It's not what he wants."

"How do you know?"

"He was clear when this started."

"Well… maybe his feelings have changed. Or maybe they will. Or maybe… you only get this. And it's like *Casablanca*. And don't tell me that you can't stand that there are no strong female characters in *Casablanca*. That's true but beside the point."

"Since when do you like *Casablanca?*"

"Since always. It's romantic! The point is… it's better to have loved and lost. Which would you regret more? Going for it? Or not going for it?"

"Not having these breakfast conversations with you." I

strain my tea. Add almond milk and a little honey. Tap my glass against hers.

"That's very sweet. But also beside the point."

Maybe.

"You always go for it. That's what I admire about you." She brushes a blond strand behind her ear. "One of the many things."

"But the only one that serves your point?"

"Maybe."

"Totally."

"Okay. Hold on to your heart if you want. I get that. But go." She motions to the check sitting on the table. "Go get laid."

"Oh my God."

"Trust me. If you don't… you're going to regret it."

"He might be busy."

"I said go. Not give me excuses." She motions to my purse. "Get your cell. Then go."

"What if I want to invite him to our place?"

She laughs. "It's way too hot. But sure. I have to do some summer reading anyway. Go. I'll be out for a while. Text me when it's safe to return."

"Oh my God."

"I said go." She pushes me gently. "Less talking. More whatever straight people do…"

"Okay." I take a long sip of my mug. "Can I at least finish this?"

She shakes her head. "And you can't get the check either."

"Not even a takeout cup?"

"I said go. Now! Get your rocks off. That's an order."

Chapter Thirty-Six

EVE

I t's right there. My cell, lying on my desk, next to my
notebook and my closed laptop.

Flashing with a text from Ian.

Ian: I thought of you.

Short, simple, incredibly suggestive.

Of course, he doesn't say *I came so hard when I thought of
you* or *I fucked myself as I thought of you.*

He's waiting for me to ask.

Trying to make me earn what he'll give.

I don't care that the room is stuffy—even after I open
the window. I still want him here. Want him undressing
me.

Watching me undress.

Watching me.

Eve: Did you really?

Ian: Yes.

Eve: When?

Ian: Last night.

Eve: In your bed?

Ian: Yes. It still smells like you.

Eve: What did you think of? Exactly?

Ian: The look in your eyes when you watch yourself. Of how much you like watching and being watched. Of how much I want to watch you come.

Eve: Oh.

Ian: What are you wearing?

Eve: A dress.

Ian: Show me.

Eve: Show you?

Ian: You took a picture naked in my bed. You know what I'm asking.

Eve: You didn't say please.

Ian: I don't say please.

My sex clenches. That shouldn't be so hot. But it is.

I pull up my camera. Put it in selfie mode. Wave as I snap a photo of my outfit.

There. Send.

A normal picture. Something I might put on social media. *Hey, look at my short black dress. Perfect for summer. Why is it so hot in New York?*

Only it's not that at all.

It's inviting him to undress me.

Ian: What are you wearing under it?

Eve: Underwear.

Ian: Do I need to come over there? Make you behave?

Fuck, yes.

Eve: What if you do?

Ian: I'm not coming until you invite me.

He's making me work for it. And asking for permission. In a way that sounds like an order. He's good at that. Asking what I want. Giving it to me.

Eve: What if I do?

Ian: I'll bend you over my knee. Spank you until you behave.

Fuck.

Ian: Is that what you want, vixen? Want to be punished for being a bad girl?

Eve: Maybe.

Ian: Or do you want to be rewarded?

Eve: What's my reward?

Ian: Show me what you're wearing under your dress.

It's the only way he'll give it to me. Whatever it is he's giving.

I turn my fan on. Slip out of my dress. Turn the camera to me.

There.

I send him the photo.

Me, from my shoulders to my toes, in black lingerie. From him. A lace bra. Matching bikini underwear.

Illicit and fancy. Undeserving of my poorly put together room. But better for it.

This is my space.

The only space that's really mine.

I'm inviting him into it. Just barely. But I am.

Ian: Good girl.

It makes my sex clench. I don't want to think about the implications—what the fuck is wrong with me, wanting him to purr *good girl.*

It winds me so tight.

I'm already on edge.

Ian: Take it off.

Eve: Here?

Ian: You're in your room, aren't you?

Eve: Yes.

Ian: Do you normally fuck yourself somewhere else?

Holy shit.

Eve: No. Here.

Ian: How do you fuck yourself?

Eve: I rub my clit. With my fingers. Normally, the middle. Some-

times, the ring.

Did I just write that? My entire body flames. It's there, in text, forever.

Ian: Did you fuck yourself last night?

Eve: Yes.

Ian: You thought of me?

Eve: Yes.

Ian: What, exactly?

Eve: The feeling of your hands in my hair. And your cock in my mouth. And the way you held my body against yours. I could feel you were hard. You were so close. I wanted you inside me.

Ian: Did you want to watch?

Eve: Yes.

Ian: Did you want me to watch?

Eve: Yes.

Ian: Do you want me to watch now?

Eve: Yes.

Ian: I can come over.

Eve: It's too far.

Ian: Impatient?

Eve: Yes.

Ian: I should make you wait for that.

Eve: Please don't.

Fuck, I'm begging him. I'm not even sure what I'm begging for. Only that I want it. That he's the only one who can give it to me.

Ian: Take off the lingerie.

I slide out of my bra. Then the panties.

Ian: Show me.

I point my cell to my chest. There. Snap.

Me.

Naked.

For him.

Can I trust him with it?

I take a deep breath. Channel the logic left in my brain.

It's a risk, but that's what makes it thrilling.

I trust him.

And, fuck, I want to send this so badly. To be exposed for him. To risk someone else seeing.

There.

Ian: Fuck. Beautiful.

How do I reply? *Thank you* feels silly. Anything dirtier…

It's hard to form the words.

The cell buzzes in my hand.

Not a text.

He's calling me.

There only one reason to call…

Fuck.

I answer. "Hello." It feels strange saying *hello*, when I've just sent him a picture of my breasts, but where else do I start?

"Hello." His voice is that low, demanding tone. There's this tiny hint of impatience. He needs this too. "Are you alone?"

"Yes."

"Put the phone on speaker."

I do.

"On the bed."

I do.

"Climb into it."

I lie on the smooth sheets.

"I like to picture you there. Your head rolling back, your fingers in your cunt, your expression wracked with pleasure."

Fuck. "You picture me touching myself?"

"Constantly."

"Oh."

"Oh?"

"Yeah. Oh."

He lets out a low laugh. For a moment, it defuses the tension in the room. My shoulders relax. My breath steadies.

I'm talking to the guy I like. Not lying in my bed, waiting for his instructions. Waiting to come for his listening pleasure.

"You're adorable," he says. "It makes me wild."

"Why?"

"Knowing I'm the one who can make someone so tough and strong blush… it drives me out of my mind."

"Oh."

Again, he laughs. This time, it doesn't defuse the tension.

It winds me tighter. "What do you do? When it drives you out of your mind?"

"Wait."

"You wait?"

"Yes."

"You don't fuck yourself?"

"Sometimes. If I don't think I'll be able to control myself when I see you." Impatience drips into his voice. "If I can't take the agony of waiting anymore."

"What would happen? If you couldn't control yourself?"

"I'd pin you to the table in the restaurant. Roll your knickers to your ankles. Dive between your legs."

"You'd fuck me?"

"Taste you. Then fuck you."

"Oh."

His voice drops to something impossibly demanding. "Lie down."

"Okay." I lower myself completely onto the bed.

"Sheets out of the way."

I push them aside.

"Touch yourself. Your breasts to start."

I don't usually play with my breasts. But with him listening... there's something about knowing I'm being watched.

Fuck, I'm already on edge.

It's like he's touching me.

A gasp falls from my lips. "Will you?"

"Will I what, vixen?"

"Fuck yourself."

"Now?"

"After."

"If you ask me to." It's there again. That dare. That demand.

"Do you want to?"

"Yes."

"You're hard?"

"Very." His voice drops. "I'm in control now, vixen. You do exactly what I say. Understand?"

"Yes."

He lets out a low groan of pleasure. "Is there a mirror in your room?"

"Yes."

"Can you arrange it so you can see yourself?"

"I'll try."

"Good girl."

Fuck. I can barely move. My knees knock together as I slide out of the bed.

There's a mirror hanging from my door. Normally, I use it to check my outfit. But this...

I take it off the hook. Tilt it against the wall so it's facing the bed.

It's not perfect, but it's a start. I climb into bed. Turn

the other way. So it's easier to see my reflection. "Done."

"Show me."

I don't think. I take a picture of my reflection. Send it to him.

"Fuck." His voice is a low groan. "Perfect."

My fingers dig into the sheets.

"Now, lie back. With your head toward the mirror. Watch everything you do."

I nod. "Yes."

"I'm going to ask you to do it again. For me. In front of me."

"When?"

"After I've fucked you. I don't have the self-control to watch you fuck yourself and not touch you."

Fuck, yes. I let out a sound that's a collection of vowels.

He understands my meaning. "Now, eyes on the mirror as you play with your tits."

I watch my hand go to my chest. My fingers close around my nipple. It's not the same as watching him toy with me, but knowing he's on the line—

It's intense.

Overwhelming.

Only the sound of the fan.

My heavy exhale.

His steady breath.

He waits until I let out a groan. "What do you want, vixen?"

"You."

"How?"

"Inside me. Touching me. Tasting me. Groaning my name."

"Do you want to come?"

"Yes."

"Show me."

I slip my hand beneath my bellybutton. Let my legs fall to the sides.

For a moment, I watch my reflection. Watch as I draw circles around my clit.

It's so strange. I've never thought about how I looked. Never found thrill in masturbation.

Sure, I enjoy it. But I've never considered it sexy, really. More... effective.

Right now, with Ian's breath in my ears—

"Fuck." My eyelids flutter closed. My breath hitches.

I work those steady circles. No teasing. No toying. No drawing it out.

Exactly the pressure I need. Exactly the spot I need it.

Steady circles.

Winding me tighter and tighter.

My breaths run together. Turn to groans.

His name falls off my lips.

I'm so close. Too close.

"Watch," he orders.

My eyes blink open. Go straight to my reflection. The flush of my cheeks. The heave of my chest. The squeeze of my toes.

Slow circles.

Again and again.

"Come for me, vixen," he demands.

It pushes me over the edge. With the next brush of my fingers, the tension winds to a finger pitch. Impossibly taut. About to snap.

Then it does.

It unravels. Taking me with it. Sending a wave of pleasure through my body.

It knocks me onto my back.

My sex pulses.

My eyes close.

My fingers dig into my thighs.

His name falls from my lips again. Like he's here. Like he's watching. Like this is for him.

No. It is for him.

He is here. Listening, but still here.

He waits until my breath steadies. "Good girl."

Fuck. I'm ready to go again. But I don't want my hand. "I want you."

"Soon."

"You promise?"

"Yes."

"When?"

"Soon." He lets out a soft laugh.

My shoulders fall. But my sex keeps whining. "Tonight?"

"I can't tonight. I'll call tomorrow."

"You'll call…"

"To listen to you fuck yourself."

"Oh."

"Unless that's a problem."

No. Except that… I want him here. I want his body pressed against mine. I want his lips on my lips.

Not just because I want to fuck him.

For all the other reasons too.

"I could come over. So you can watch properly." My breath catches in my throat. I'm at the edge again, only it's a different one. I want his yes, his approval, his need.

"Tomorrow night," he says. "Seven. I'll send instructions."

Relief spreads through my limbs like wildfire.

I'm too far gone.

But I don't care.

I need to take whatever he's offering. Everything he's offering.

Chapter Thirty-Seven

IAN

She's perfect. Too perfect.

She talks literature at dinner. Why *The Hunger Games* is unappreciated in the "war is hell genre." Do I have insights, as a former member of the military? It doesn't have the realism of *All's Quiet on the Western Front* or *The Things They Carried*, sure, but it's every bit as intimate.

Or has she been as dismissive of great literature as critics are of *The Hunger Games?*

The way her eyes light up when she speaks—

The curiosity in them as she listens—

She listens with her entire body. Like my words are the most interesting thing in the entire world. Like she can't imagine a subject that fascinates her more.

It's been a long time since I've read *All's Quiet on the Western Front* or *The Things They Carried*. I can't admit I only picked up *The Hunger Games* trilogy after she discussed it on her site.

I can't match her wit, intellect, insight.

But I can share mine.

The series doesn't skimp on the brutality of war. It's

CRYSTAL KASWELL

horrible, yes, but not quite as grounded as the other books. Maybe that's what's great about it. How fantastical it is. That makes it easier to absorb.

She teases me about my third chance to impress her with a perfect dinner. Groans over the seared sea bass I order for her. Then chocolate mousse, Vietnamese black tea, hours of conversation.

After, I take her back to my apartment. Order her to undress. Watch her eyes go wide as she looks to the mirror. Watches herself come on my hand.

She's gorgeous, open, sexy as hell.

Offering her body to me.

Offering herself to me.

She melts into me, completely spent, completely at my mercy.

I bring her to the bed, help her into the sheets, hold her close.

She falls asleep in my arms.

Wakes with those same curious grey-green eyes.

"Hey." She rolls onto her back. Looks up at me with all the trust in the world. "You broke your promise."

"You were too tempting."

She beams. "Oh." Looks up at me, taking in my workout attire. "Not a suit."

"Hard to believe?"

She nods. "Almost like I'm dreaming." She gives me a long, slow once-over. Like I'm the one who exists for her viewing pleasure. "You look good. Of course. It's not fair."

"And this?" I motion to the sheet covering her soft body. "This is fair?"

She nods *mm-hmm*. Sits up, pulling the sheet with her.

Completely perfect.

Grabbing the key to my heart and burying it somewhere deep inside her.

It doesn't matter how much I focus on her soft curves or her sweet mouth—

I want more than her body.

I want her everything.

Want it enough to risk shattering the only steadiness I have left.

"Go back to bed." I brush a hair behind her ear. "It's early."

"Will you be here when I get up?"

"I'll make you breakfast."

She smiles. Bites her lip. "Okay." She sinks into the mattress. Completely at peace. Exactly where she wants to be.

It warms something inside me. Some place that's been cold for a long, long time.

I don't have a choice.

I can run or deny it, but it won't change the facts.

No matter what I do, I'm falling for her.

—

Chapter Thirty-Eight

EVE

After a long, lazy morning, we watch *Austin Powers* on the couch.

I leave just before lunch. To meet with Addie. So I won't dissolve into a being of pure need.

It helps, but not enough.

I'm brimming with need. So much I'm overflowing.

I post on Original Sin. I make a playlist. I write a fucking poem.

I barely sleep.

Then he texts me a request and I do dissolve. Tiny pieces of bliss blowing in the wind.

Ian: I can knock off work early. Wednesday. Take you to the Hamptons that evening. So we have a few days alone.

Eve: A few days alone?

Ian: So I can fuck you senseless.

How can I say no to that?

Chapter Thirty-Nine

IAN

"You're not serious." Eve's eyes go wide as she steps out of the limo. She fixes on the helicopter. Then on me. "Even for you."

"Even for me?"

"It's too showy. Even for you." She shakes her head, but she does nothing to hide her smile.

She's as radiant as she always is. Teal hair in a neat line, dark lips, grey-green eyes filled with curiosity. She's wearing a short black frock and those combat boots. My eyes should be on her long legs. But they refuse to budge from her eyes.

I need that look. All of it. Forever.

"You're making it too obvious." She runs her fingers over my suit-jacket. My wrist. My thumb. Her fingers intertwine with mine. "Showing off your skills. It's blowing your cover."

"You're worried about my cover?"

She squeezes my hand. "Player to player."

"You admit your true identity?"

"Theoretically. If I were a spy—"

"An assassin."

"I'd offer professional courtesy."

"How honorable."

"Thank you." She turns back to the helicopter. Shakes her head *ridiculous*. "Or maybe I'm saying that to lull you into a false sense of security."

"Kill me the second we land."

"In the air."

"Ambitious."

She nods. "Easier to throw your body in the Hudson."

"How are you going to weigh it down?"

"Are you telling me how to do my job?"

My laugh is low. Hearty. "How patronizing of me."

"I count on men underestimating me."

"It's not working then." I motion for her to follow. "I know you're capable of anything. That's why I'm taking precautions."

"Oh?"

I nod *oh*. Lead her to the helipad. Help her into her seat.

She shakes her head *this is fucking ridiculous*, but that doesn't hide the glee in her expression. Those eyes filled with wonder.

"I have to keep you restrained." I pull the belt over her chest. A standard harness. Not enough.

She realizes. Looks at me curiously. Unsure of my next move.

I undo the knot of my tie. Bring her hands together.

She stares up at me as I bind her wrists. "I could object."

"You could." I stare back, daring her.

She just barely blushes. "I will. Later. If this isn't…"

"If I don't keep you restrained when I make you come?"

"If you don't make it worth my while."

"Are you questioning my honor?"

She nods.

"I'll have to get you back for that."

Chapter Forty

EVE

Holy fucking shitballs, helicopters are insane.

And Ian piloting one?

With my wrists bound?

My chest stays light. My limbs stay airy. My body stays in free fall.

Off the ledge. No ground in sight.

Metaphorically speaking.

The ground is very much in sight. Close enough for details. Far enough I'm floating.

The tops of skyscrapers. The lush green of the park. The wrought iron of the Williamsburg Bridge.

Then the azure of the Long Island Sound, the soft waves of the Atlantic, the rows and rows of houses, the lines of freeways, the bright blue sky.

We move fast. Descend slowly. Land on the roof of an equally nondescript helipad.

Ian helps me out of my seatbelt. Into a car. A rental, I guess. He buckles my seatbelt. Gets into the driver's seat.

Says nothing as he pulls out of the parking garage. Drives through the scenic streets.

It's not crowded yet—it's still early on a weekday—but getting there. People in linen and pastel walking along boulevards, licking ice cream cones, laughing in convertibles.

He turns off a main drag. Onto a quieter street. One with houses the size of a Duane Reade. Then another, with houses the size of a city block.

He parks in a driveway of a massive modern house—all glass and columns and white paint and picket fencing. An actual bridge to the beach. A huge backyard. A deep pool.

The sand beyond that.

The ocean.

The sunny sky.

Like a greeting card, an advertisement, a fantasy of another life.

A million times nicer than Marisol's parents' place. And a billion times more illicit.

He smiles as he helps me out of the car, lifts me into his arms, carries me to his bed.

He lays me down on the teal sheets, rolls my dress to my waist, hooks his thumbs around my panties. A pair he bought for me.

"Good girl," he murmurs as he peels them off my feet.

He releases the binding on my wrists for long enough to pull my hands over my head. Re-tie them.

So I have to take whatever he gives me.

My body aches. I'm pure need. And there's so fucking much of it.

Ian pries my legs apart. Pins my thighs to the bed.

Then his lips are on my calf. Just above my boot. Higher and higher. Until he's kissing the inside of my knee.

"You're going to come on my face, vixen," he murmurs

into my thigh. That deep tone. Still demanding. Dripping with desire.

Fuck.

His fingers curl into my thighs. Enough pressure I feel it. Enough pressure I know I'm his.

I want to be his. Here. And everywhere. It's scary how much I want it.

Then he drags his lips up and to my thigh and I forget everything outside this moment. I want him here, now, between my legs.

I want to come on his face.

I want everything.

He teases me with soft slow kisses. Up my thigh. Then down the other. All the way to my calf.

Back up.

His nails scrape my skin. He pushes harder. Hard enough I sink into the soft sheets.

He looks up at me for a second. Then his eyes move down my body. Over my chest and stomach—still covered by my dress—to my pelvis.

My thighs.

My sex.

"Fucking beautiful." His voice is low and breathy. Like he needs this as much as I do.

It's such a strange compliment. But my body knows how to take it.

My chest heaves, my lips part, my fingers curl into the sheets.

He brings his lips to my thigh. Then his soft mouth is on me. A brush of his lips. The strange sensation of his tongue. Soft. Up and down. Exploring every part of me.

It's different than his hand. Warmer. Wetter. Softer.

More.

So much more.

I try to reach for him. Find the tie binding me. Groan as it tugs at my wrists.

My head falls to one side. The window. The beautiful, blinding light of the beach. The barest hint of our reflection.

Then the other side. The mirrored closet door. Every detail. Every scrape of his nails. Every heave of my chest. Every shift of his shoulders.

His dark hands against my pale thighs.

His navy jacket under my calves.

My black boots against his back.

It's too much to take, watching him between my legs. It pushes me too far to the edge. Overwhelms me with sensation.

The soft, wet pressure of his mouth. The tension winding tighter and tighter. The need racing through my hips.

To watch him. To watch us.

Fuck.

I have to close my eyes. To focus on the new sensations. The soft pressure of his tongue. Everywhere. Then in one place. Firmer and faster. Up and down. Left and right. Circles and zigzags.

Then the soft suction of his mouth around my clit.

More and more. Until I can barely take it.

I have to groan. I have to reach for the sheets. I have to dig my heels into his back.

All the fabric in the way—he's always in his fucking suit —but I can still feel the pressure of his skin.

And, fuck, seeing myself halfway out of my clothes, still in my boots—

His motions change. Back to soft flicks of his tongue. Pressure and pleasure everywhere. Then more. Higher. Left.

There.

"Fuck, Ian." I reach for him. Find the tie binding me. Keeping my arms over my head. Keeping me at his mercy.

He focuses on that perfect spot. Again and again. Until I'm brimming with sensation. Pleasure and pressure and deep, pure need.

He pushes me to the edge.

I let my eyes open. Let my gaze shift to the reflection. Focus on the hard scrape of his fingernails. The sound of his groan dissolving into my flesh. The smell of his skin.

Every sense, all at once.

Too much.

Not enough.

How can it be both?

How can I want more when I can barely take this?

My thoughts disappear with the next flick of his tongue.

He winds me tighter and tighter. Until it's too much to take.

But I do take it.

More and more tension.

More and more pleasure.

More and more.

With the next flick of his tongue, I unravel. Pleasure spills through my limbs as I come.

I groan his name, bucking my hips, desperate for every bit of him I can get.

He works me through my orgasm, but he doesn't release me. He keeps that same perfect pressure. So much it aches. It's too much. More pain than pleasure. But I need that too.

Then it's all pressure. So much I ache. So much I'm desperate for release.

I come fast this time. And hard. So hard I see white.

The room disappears. Only the sound of my groan and his breath and his name on my lips.

He releases me. Places a kiss on my thigh. Pulls my dress down my legs.

No underwear.

And no bra either—I don't need one in this.

I'm naked under here. Still his, to claim, whenever he wants, however he wants.

How can I feel so desperate and satisfied at the same time? My body is humming with bliss. With relief. With an ache for more of him.

Him inside of me.

I want that so badly. To touch him, taste him, feel his cock stretching my walls.

My eyes blink open. The window this time. Too bright for our reflection. That perfect white light.

The sun bouncing off the water. The sand. The ocean. The wide open sky.

Paradise.

One idea of it.

I'm a New Yorker, through and through. I'll take the city any day. But here, in his bed, his hands on my wrists, his lips on my neck—

Fuck.

"Ian." I dig my nails into his neck. "Please." I don't know what I'm asking. I never know what I'm asking him. Only that I need it right now.

He undoes the knot. Tosses away the tie. Brings my wrists to his lips. Plants a kiss on each. "After I feed you."

"What if I'm not hungry?"

He lowers my hands to my sides. Wraps his arms around me. "You're going to need your strength. Trust me, vixen. I'm going to drain every drop of your energy."

Chapter Forty-One

IAN

Eve places her feet on the footrest of a kitchen stool. Presses her knees together. Smooths her frock.

"This is insane." She takes in the wide, open room. The windows looking out on the beach. The others looking out on the garden.

The barest hint of sunset. A soft glow. A faint orange hue.

I'm not sure how long we've been here. Only that it's something out of a dream.

Eve in my bed. Lazing on the couch with her Kindle. Scribbling in that notebook she brings everywhere.

In my space, my house, my life.

Though it's not my space. It's not my house.

And it's not my life.

This is a vacation, a daydream, a fantasy.

Maybe that's better. Maybe that's where she belongs. Some fantasy of a life where I'm capable of loving her fully, letting her in, catching her when she falls.

She's there too. In a daydream. Looking at the house like it's something out of a film.

It is.

Marble countertops, glossy tile floor, turquoise stools around the kitchen island.

The entire place is shades of blue and green. Aquatic colors. Subtle beach imagery.

Cerulean towels, soft blue leather couch, tile in a shade of sand.

I didn't think hard about this rental. A place on the beach for the summer. One close enough for a day trip or a weekend holiday. It's only forty minutes in a helicopter. A few hours in a car or on the train. Close enough for an evening.

And it's blue and green everywhere. The colors I associate with her. One of the only things I knew about her when I signed the check for this rental.

It's an obvious choice. The colors of the ocean for a place by the beach.

The colors of my obsession for a place to fuck her.

Which is it?

The beach? Her body? Her heart?

I don't know.

I want to fuck her. I want to fuck her senseless. To bring her back to the bed, spread her thighs, drive into her until she's groaning in equal parts bliss and agony.

And I want to hold her, cook for her, feed her, listen to every thought in her head.

"Aren't you supposed to mock American excess?" She swings her stool so she's facing me. Drops her voice an octave. Attempts to put on a British accent. "Ah, you Yanks just love your big houses." She drops the impression. "Or something."

"Is that how I sound?"

She nods. Smiles that sly smile that lights up her gorgeous eyes. "It is ridiculous. Have you seen the size of houses in Iowa? The bedrooms are bigger than my apartment. Some of them are bigger than your apartment. Well, maybe not your apartment."

She slides off the stool. Looks to the dining room. A wide-open space with a long oak table, matching chairs, simple shell decorations.

"This room is bigger than your apartment," she says.

"Almost."

"And that's not excessive?"

"Why come to the States if not to enjoy excess?"

"Uh-huh." She turns to me. "When did you rent it?"

"This spring. Places in the Hamptons go fast."

"What do you... do with it?" Her eyes flit to the beach, then they're on me. "I just can't see it. You're still wearing your suit."

"I'm not wearing a tie."

Her cheeks flush at the memory. "It's still a suit."

I shake my head.

She nods. Moves closer. Until she's close enough to run her fingers over my suit-jacket. Up my arm then down the neckline. She undoes the button. Looks up at me *can I?*

I nod *yes.*

She peels the jacket off my shoulders then drapes it over hers.

Her eyes meet mine as she strikes a pose. "How do I look?"

"Fetching."

"I was going for dapper."

"You need trousers for that."

She smiles as she removes the jacket. "Should I put this somewhere?"

I motion to the stool.

"It won't mess up your… what does this cost?"

"What it's worth."

"Three figures or four?"

"I don't keep track."

"Uh-huh."

"How much did your frock cost?"

"A hundred-something dollars. A lot for me. But nothing compared to some of the things you've sent me."

My eyes trace a line over her body. She looks gorgeous draped in black chiffon. And she looks like Eve. "A bargain then."

Her teeth sink into her lip. Her eyes pass over me. Taking me in. Picturing me naked. "You stare the most when I'm naked."

"Do I?"

She nods. "Does that make the lingerie a waste?"

Not in a million years. "No."

"What do you like about it?"

"What do I like about knowing you're wearing the lingerie I bought you under your clothes? Is that actually a question?"

"Yes."

I motion for her to *come here*.

She sets the suit-jacket on a chair. Takes three steps toward me.

I wrap my arm around her waist. Bring my hand to the crook of her neck. "I like picturing you in it. Knowing something from me is on your body. On the most delicate parts of your body." I run my fingertips along her neck until she purrs. "It's our secret."

She nods.

"But if you'd like to wear nothing under your clothes. I'm not sure I can object to that."

Her eyes flutter closed. Her head falls to her right. Her hair goes with it.

That beautiful haze of pleasure.

I want to fuck her. Here. Now.

And I want to whisper promises in her ears all fucking night.

I bring my hand to my side.

She blinks her eyes open. Looks up at me with all that curiosity. Brings her hands to my button-up shirt. "Do you usually cook like this?"

"Of course not."

"Of course not?"

"Naked. Except for my apron."

Her laugh lights up her eyes. "Can I make that happen?"

I take her hands, bring them to my right sleeve. She rolls it to my elbow. Does the same with the left.

"This is not naked." Her fingers linger on the tattoo on my forearm. A geometric rose, shaded black. "But I like it. And this—" She traces the lines with her index finger. "A secret for me to unwrap."

"Oh?"

She nods. "When did you get it?"

"A long time ago."

"Is there a story?"

"My brother Ty. The day he turned eighteen. I told him we could do whatever we wanted for his birthday. He already had this picked out."

"He wanted you to get a tattoo?"

"Us. Matching ones. He'd worked with the artist on the design. His is the same. Only crimson."

She traces the lines with her fingertip. "Why a rose?"

"Our mother's favorite flower."

"Is she still… around?"

I nod. "And still tough. Your mother?"

Her lips press together. "She was around when I was really young. But one day… she started getting high. And it was all she did. She did whatever it took to find her next high. Or whoever. She overdosed when I was thirteen. But I didn't know for a while."

"I'm sorry."

"Don't be. I'm glad she's not in my life."

"Even so. It's hard, not having someone there to take care of you."

She nods. "Your dad?"

"He was in the military. He wasn't around often."

"Now?"

"He had a heart attack. Died before he got to the hospital."

"I'm sorry."

"Thank you."

Her fingers wrap around my forearm. "Did you ever get time with him?"

"Time, yes, but not enough. He was always deployed. When he was on leave, he made an effort. But I was young. Angry he abandoned me. My mother tried to explain it. The sense of duty. Not just to his country, but to us. He was taking care of the family. He had to leave, to make what we needed to live. All parents did. It was just a matter of how much. He was sacrificing for us. So we could live in a safe place. Afford new clothes and books. I understood the reasoning, but—"

"He still wasn't there when you needed him."

"Yes."

"Why did you join?"

"Trying to make him proud. He was. It was the only time I understood him. And when I served… I understood why he did. Why he wasn't able to give up that life."

"What about it?" she asks.

I step back, breaking her touch. Heat floods my body, but I still move to the fridge. Pull the door open. "I'm supposed to cook you lunch."

"Are you?"

I nod. "Something you'll like. A surprise."

"Can I help?"

"You do take instruction well."

"Only in that one context." Her cheeks flush. "I'm an okay cook. I usually do what's cheap and fast, but I know the basics."

"Perfect." I gather the ingredients. Basil, Roma tomatoes, courgettes, fresh pasta, Parmesan. Then garlic, olive oil, lemon. "Put a pot on to boil. Then chop the courgettes. Thick. Or they'll get soggy."

"There's a double meaning in there somewhere."

"What is it?"

"I'm not sure. But I'm going to figure it out." She fills a pot with water. Sets it on the stove. Finds a chopping board. "What was it that kept you in the military?"

"My ex-wife called me an adrenaline junkie."

"Hmm." Her eyes flit to me for a second. "I can see that."

"There is a thrill to it. The danger. And the sense of duty. You need to be ready to die for your country. For the man standing next to you. To know he's willing to die for you. It's…"

"That sounds scary."

"It is. But it's comforting too."

"Why did you stop?"

"I was recruited for British intelligence."

"You really were a spy?" Her eyes go wide.

"I wasn't a field operative for long. I was considered more valuable in another position."

"A digital spy?"

"More or less," I say.

"So you're just a giant nerd?"

"Did it take you this long to realize that?"

Her laugh is soft. Easy. "You hide it well."

"It was dangerous at times. It still is. But my ex-wife... when I met Laura, I didn't want to stay away any longer. I wasn't willing to die for my country any longer. I wasn't willing to fight for some greater purpose."

"Because you loved her?"

I swallow hard. "Because I wanted to fall asleep next to her every night. Wake up next to her. To live a long life with her."

My chest tenses. I haven't considered Laura in a long time. I certainly haven't thought about falling in love with her.

The years we were good together.

There were so many of them. But how many? When did she start looking for someone else?

When did she start fucking him?

When did she stop loving me?

I swallow my frustration. "That was when I stopped understanding my father. How he could still risk his life when he had a wife. Two sons. Not everyone sees it that way. A lot of men I served with were husbands and fathers. They were making the world safer for the people they loved. They were taking care of their families."

"I've never thought about it like that. I don't know anyone who went into the military. But one of my friends from school wanted to be a police officer. That made more sense to me. Keeping the city safe. New Yorkers... we're our own universe. But I can understand it through that lens. Or thinking about Addie. If there was some threat to her... even if it was a threat to the country too—"

"You'd enlist?"

"I don't know. I don't *usually* like following orders."

"You think I do?"

"No. It's hard to imagine." Her eyes find mine. "How did you survive it?"

"A different way of thinking."

"You got used to it?"

"I was a pilot. Usually on my own. I'm not sure I could charge into battle on the ground."

"Is that part of why you left?"

I nod.

"I guess, it sounds obvious that way. Follow orders and sleep on a cot? Or don't follow orders and sleep next to your wife." She frowns at the word *wife*. She doesn't like the sound of it.

I know why I tense at the word.

But Eve is young. Without the baggage of a failed marriage.

Is she afraid of commitment? Against the patriarchal notion of marriage? Jealous?

I want her jealousy. I want her to hate that I loved anyone else, had anyone else, promised myself to anyone else.

But that's ridiculous.

I'm ridiculous. I need to focus on sautéing garlic. Not on silly fantasies.

She continues, "Your brother? Did he serve?"

I shake my head. "No. He's worse than I am. Can't stand being told what to do. And after our father died and I married… someone had to be there for our mother."

"She's still in London?"

I nod.

"How old is he?"

"Thirty."

"A lot younger."

"Hey."

She laughs. "You are older."

"You like that I'm older."

"Maybe."

"You do."

She pulls an imaginary zipper over her lips. Turns to her chopping.

I focus on cooking. Stirring the garlic, adding onions, boiling pasta.

She finishes, sets the knife on the counter, turns to me. "I am sorry. About your dad. Was it hard to lose him?"

"It was. Not so much because I missed him, though I did. Because I lost the chance of ever really knowing him. I always told myself things would be different when he was older. When he retired. When the two of us had time. But that never happens. No one ever finds time. They make it or they don't. And he made his choice. His job over us."

"Do you think he saw it that way?"

"Probably not. But it was that way. You must understand. Your mother—"

She nods. "She made her choice."

"And your father?"

"My daddy issues?" She laughs, though it's more sad than anything. "He tried. For a while. He was never sober, really, but he held it together for a long time. He wasn't *there*. I couldn't count on him to make dinner or walk me to school or hug me when I cried. But he did work enough to keep us afloat. Addie and I figured out the rest. But after… I guess you already know, that she overdosed on her anxiety medication. That she was in the psych ward."

"Not the details."

"She has an anxiety disorder. She wasn't taking care of it. And Dad disappearing for weeks… showing up at school wasted. It didn't help. So when he disappeared that time, I didn't ask if he was coming back. I changed the locks. I forged his signature. I did what it took to survive without him. He sent cash every so often, but otherwise we were on our own."

"I'm sorry."

"She… I still worry about her. So much. I don't care if I never see my father again. But if I lost Addie… I don't know if I'd survive that."

I move closer. Pull her into a soft embrace.

She wraps her arms around my waist. Melts into me like a drop in the ocean.

Like the two of us are destined to float together until the end of time.

I don't know what to say. Where to move. How to handle the need in my veins.

There are too many things I want to say. Too many things I want to ask. Too many bridges I want to cross.

I'm lost in the fucking ocean when a sound interrupts me.

The doorbell.

Then a familiar voice.

"Put your clothes on. You have company."

Eve jumps backward. Looks up at me with surprise in her eyes. Asking me to explain.

"My brother," I say. "He's supposed to arrive Friday."

Which means negotiations in London aren't going well.

Which means the three thousand miles between me and my past are going to melt.

I can't avoid this forever.

I can't avoid it at all.

He's here and he's going to tell her. He's going to tell her things I don't want her knowing.

And there's nothing I can do to stop him.

Chapter Forty-Two

EVE

"Tyler. Though I go by Ty." Ian's brother offers his hand. "You must be Ian's current obsession."

I make my grip as strong as I can. But it's not as strong as his.

He has an overwhelming presence. Like Ian's, but different. Less burdened. More dangerous.

He's wearing jeans—actual jeans—and a t-shirt. His tattoos are visible. His dark eyes are filled with fire.

Somehow, he's more open and more closed at once. Or maybe I've learned how to read Ian.

That doesn't seem possible. There's so much about Ian I don't know. So much I want to know.

I release Ty's hand. Focus on this moment. And not how much I want to unlock Ian's heart. "Everyone says that."

"Everyone?" Ty raises a brow. Flashes Ian a brotherly look. One where he communicates *everything* in a glance.

"Jasmine has to look for romance somewhere now that she's married to Shep," Ian says.

Ty doesn't even begin to buy that. He shakes his head. Turns to me with a smile. "It's nice to meet you, Eve."

"You too, Ty." I don't add *do you go by Ty because you like to tie women up? That would be silly. But it sure would be interesting if that ran in the family. Is it a genetic thing? Or something to do with your upbringing? Can you tell I want you to leave so I can fuck your brother senseless?*

Ahem.

That same knowing nod. "Ian's actually rolled up his sleeves. How metaphorical. Fitting for what we have to discuss."

"I thought you were arriving Friday," Ian says.

"Nice to see you too. My flight was fine. Thanks for asking," he says.

How did he get here so fast? It's a couple hours from JFK in a car. We took a helicopter. Or maybe he flies helicopters too.

Honestly, it wouldn't surprise me. I'm not sure there's anything either one of them could say that would surprise me.

"How was your flight?" I ask.

"A woman with manners. I appreciate that." His laugh is easy. So much like Ian's laugh. A little higher pitched. A little more playful. "A charter. Quiet. Time to work. Not too much turbulence."

"Oh, so you're also super rich?" My cheeks flush. "Oh, did I say that out loud?"

"Not as rich as Ian." He shoots his brother a look. "But I'm gaining on him."

"I've only flown coach before. And only once out of the country. To Toronto," I say.

Ian chuckles. "Of course."

"What?" My blush deepens. There are two of them now. Two smooth, sexy as sin British men. They speak the same language. But there's a subtext I don't begin to understand.

Ian wraps his arms around my waist. Pulls my body into his. Shoots his brother some look that makes him react with an aborted eye roll.

It is possessive. Possessive in a way I really, really like.

This time, Ian's hand goes to my tattoo. He traces the lines of Latin. "Your obsession."

"I'm not obsessed." Okay, I am obsessed.

And I…

Can't think. At all.

This is too intense.

Ian holding me in a way that says *fuck off, she's mine*.

His brother staring *please, why would I want to take her?* But still looking at me like he's picking me apart.

And something else between them. This history I don't share. This subtext I don't know.

For the first time, I understand why some women fantasize about two men at once. I wouldn't want Ian's brother to join us. But I get the appeal. All that intensity and possession and heat.

"A scholar this time?" Ty interrupts my dirty thoughts. "That's a refreshing change for you."

"That's his idea of a compliment," Ian says.

I want to ask more. What types of woman does Ian usually date? Why does he want me so much? Ty knows something.

But now isn't the time. Now is…

I should give them some space. It's what I would want, if it was me and Addie. "We're actually cooking dinner. Are you hungry? I can finish up if you need to talk."

Ian shakes his head. "Ty's a good cook."

"Putting me to work already?" Ty asks.

Ian nods *of course*. "We're almost finished. You can set the table."

Ty chuckles. "The honor." He looks to me. "For you, Eve, I'll set the table. Ian can fuck off."

"Only if Eve's going to watch," Ian says.

Once again, I turn red.

Once again, Ty barely avoids rolling his eyes. "You've been in the States too long. You've lost your sense of subtlety."

"Since when do you appreciate subtlety?" Ian asks.

"It has its uses." Again, a knowing look.

Again, I have no fucking idea what he means.

But something tells me I shouldn't ask. Or maybe I'm scared to ask. Scared to hear something that will rain on my parade.

Ty does set the table.

Ian pulls me into a tight embrace. Runs his lips up my neck. Along my earlobe. "Sit with him."

"Who with what?"

He chuckles. "He's heard a lot about you."

"You talk about me?"

"All the time."

"You talk to your brother often?" He's only mentioned him in passing.

"He runs the London office of one of our companies."

"Oh." So many questions. Too many. "You work together?"

"Not directly. Not most of the time. If he's here... I imagine it's because of a negotiation in London."

"Oh."

"Oh?"

"Yep. Oh."

"This party was supposed to celebrate... a few things. It's nearly his birthday."

"You threw a party in the Hamptons to celebrate your brother's birthday?"

"It's more complicated than that."

"How?"

He releases me. Looks to his brother, who's now pouring generous helpings of gin over ice. "We have a tradition. One-upping each other. Last year, he rented a villa in the Caribbean."

"It sounds like he won." My laugh is awkward. There's something I'm missing here. But I think he's inviting me to find it. Maybe. "Villa in the Caribbean is way better than house in the Hamptons."

"Last minute. I had something booked for him and his fiancée, but she ended things," he says.

"Oh."

"It's a sore subject. Don't bring it up."

"What happened?"

"He hasn't said. I'm not sure he wants to."

"You're worried about him?"

"Always. He's my baby brother."

"I get that."

"I know." He leans down to press his lips to mine.

Need floods my senses. The softness of his lips. The smell of his soap. The perfect white light.

When I blink my eyes open, I'm dizzy. I want to stare into his dark eyes forever. I want to understand every single thing in them.

"What do you drink, Eve?" Ty calls from the table.

I force myself to step backward. "What are you having?"

Ty shoots Ian a look. When Ian waves him away, Ty turns his attention to me. "Is there anything besides gin here?" He motions to the top-shelf bottle on the table.

Ian chuckles. "Plenty. But it's for the party."

"He's cruel." Ty motions to a cocktail glass of ice. "I imagine there's plenty of Fever Tree in the fridge if you prefer that."

"You don't like gin?" I ask.

"They kick you out of London if you admit you don't like gin." He fills my glass then offers it to me.

"So it's a secret?" I take the glass. Hold it up to toast.

He laughs. "No, I like it. But when in Rome… what do they drink in the Hamptons?"

"White wine, probably. Or hard seltzer," I say.

His face screws with distaste. "Hard seltzer?" He shakes his head. "If you can't handle the taste of alcohol, don't drink it. Maybe if you're a teenager. No offense, Eve."

"Eve works as a bartender," Ian calls. "Careful challenging her."

"I agree. Hard seltzer is a waste. The wine coolers for my generation. I want to taste what I'm drinking." I take a sip. Mmm, smooth, sweet, botanical. And, most of all, it takes like Ian. My thoughts are already in the gutter. "But it's an easy order. So I don't mind."

"I tried my hand at tending bar for a few weeks," he says. "I didn't have the smile for it."

"Ah, but that's why the manager hired me." I laugh. "He said he didn't have enough 'punk bitches.' I guess some men prefer women who ignore them."

"Some, yes." His eyes flit to Ian for a second. Then they're on me. "What about you, Eve? Do you still tend bar?"

"I'm between jobs at the moment," I say.

"Of course. Ian always takes care of his… friends," he says.

"Does he have a lot?" I ask.

"He did. After his divorce finalized. No, it was worse

then. He fucked every woman in London. That's why he had to leave. Too many awkward run-ins." Ty winks at Ian.

"Is that why you're here?" I ask.

Ty chuckles. "To flee all the women who can't get enough?"

"I imagine you have plenty calling to ask for more," I say.

"It's happened." Ty pulls out a chair for me. Motions for me to sit. When I do, he sits across from me. "I've seen one of Ian run-ins. He handled it well."

"Go on…"

"He'll kill me."

"You can take him," I say.

He chuckles. Holds up his glass. "I like her. She's bad news."

"I know." Ian smiles. "There's no way you can take me."

"Not if I want to fight honorably." Ty turns his attention to me. "We were at a coffee shop. Ian was complaining the place had shit tea. The woman at the counter looked our way. Her eyes lit up. She blushed. She could barely ask our order. Kept calling him Mr. Hunt in a way that said *Daddy*."

"Jesus, Ty." Ian chuckles. "He's exaggerating."

Ty shakes his head. "No. She looked at him the way a starving man looks at food. She was going to die if she didn't have him immediately. He was calm. Friendly. Wished her well. Left twenty pounds in the tip jar. She stared at us the entire time we were there. Heartbroken. Nursing a pain she'd forgotten until she saw him again. Irritated he thought a tip would buy her off."

"Oh." That's not a pretty picture.

"I already have Shep coming. I don't need another

anti-wingman." Ian laughs, but it's not as easy as it was. There's something else there. A tension.

Another thing I don't understand.

But maybe it's just his brother.

If Ty was just dumped… well, he's not likely to view run-ins with an ex—even an ex-fuck buddy—positively. Maybe he's the one nursing a broken heart he's trying to forget.

Or maybe I'm going to be the girl at the coffee shop this time next year.

I'm not sure what's scarier. The thought of him breaking my heart and leaving. Or the thought of him unlocking my heart and staying.

Both.

All.

Everything.

"I hate to admit it, but he's right." Ty takes a long sip of his drink. "Ian fights dirty. If I want to keep my honor, I won't be able to beat him."

"Who needs honor?" I ask.

He laughs. "You more of a results girl?"

"Honor is a privilege. I haven't always had it."

He nods with understanding. "Sharp observation."

"Via *The Handmaid's Tale*. Most of my observations are. But it works well with men. Most haven't read it," I say. "Even with the show so popular."

He chuckles. "Interesting." It's knowing again. Over my head again. Some secret. Some circle that doesn't involve me.

But I don't mind. I'm the same with Addie.

I'm glad Ian has family members who love him. Who know him. Who fly across the Atlantic early for him.

I don't know why Ty is here.

But he is here. And he has stories to tell. So I ask for one that will embarrass Ian.

He goes off. Spins the tale of a school dance where Ian was caught making out in the closet.

He didn't mind, of course, but their mother practically locked him up for the next year. She lectured him about safe sex nonstop. Said she'd kill him if he made her a grandmother before she turned forty-five.

Then another. His first breakup. The mixtape he made to try to win her back. The truly horrible Phil Collins song he sang as he moped around the flat.

The bachelor party where he got 'so pissed he couldn't walk straight' and started offering details about his sex life. Far too many for Ty's taste.

Who wants to know their brother's predilection for rope?

Besides, who hasn't tied up their partner once or twice? It's nothing to brag about. Any good fuck is game for anything.

Of course, he doesn't want to embarrass me by bringing up Ian's tastes.

Even though it's obvious I'm ready to pounce. Maybe he's been in the States too long if he's forgetting his manners.

But there's no reason to play coy either.

Everyone knows Ian's MO So everyone knows exactly what we're doing.

And how badly both of us want to do it all night.

———

DINNER IS PERFECT. FRESH PASTA. SWEET BASIL. SOFT tomatoes. Lemon and garlic and oregano.

Flavors melting together in a delicious mix of sweet and savory, strong and subtle, soft and firm.

Ty pours stiff drinks. I match his pace for a few rounds. Until the room spins and my head blurs.

Ian scoops me into his arms. Carries me—actually carries me—to the bed. Lays me on my back. Brings a glass of water.

He helps me out of my dress carefully. But he doesn't slide his hand between my legs. Or tie my wrists together. Or order me onto my knees.

He pulls a t-shirt over my head. One of his.

It smells like him. The same soap. That scent that's uniquely Ian.

He leans over the bed. Brushes my hair behind my ear. Presses his lips to my forehead.

I reach for him. Pull him into a deep, slow kiss. "Do you have to go?"

"Yes."

"Why?"

"I'm going to fuck you if I stay."

"I want you to," I say.

"I know."

"So…" My nerves are fuzzy. Far away. "Why not?"

"You're drunk."

"I wanted you to when I was sober."

"I know. I want you to be sober. I want you to remember every second. Not a haze of pain and pleasure." He leans down. Kisses me again. "I'll be a few hours with Ty. Call me if you need anything."

"Will you fuck me tonight?"

He chuckles. "In the morning."

"Is that a promise?"

"Let's see if you're hungover first, vixen."

"If I'm not?"

"Then yes. It's a promise." He squeezes my hand. "Get some rest."

"Will you leave?"

"Now?"

"After you fuck me? Will that be it?" The words spill from my lips. Stupid gin erasing my inhibitions. "Will you be tired of me. Like with the other women?"

"No."

"You promise?"

"No."

"Oh."

"It's happened before. But... that isn't how I feel about you, Eve. There are too many things I want to learn about you. Too many things I want to teach you."

"Oh."

"Oh?"

"It sounds like a promise."

His voice softens. "Get some rest, vixen. You'll feel better."

"I feel fine."

"Then get up. Shower. Watch TV. But no swimming alone."

"I'm a strong swimmer."

"I don't care. You're pissed. You're not swimming alone." His voice drops to a firm tone. Worried. Angry even. "I wouldn't forgive myself if something happened to you."

"You wouldn't?"

"Never. It would break my heart." He kisses me one more time.

Then he leaves.

He presses the door into the frame softly. His footsteps move down the stairs.

It means something.

Maybe it means everything.

But I can't put the pieces together at the moment. He's right. I'm drunk. Everything is a blur of pain and pleasure.

God, what a way to describe existence.

One big blur of pain and pleasure.

All this desire. For everything he's willing to give me. And everything he isn't willing to give too.

Chapter Forty-Three

IAN

"Jesus, Ian, did you at least wait until her eighteenth birthday?" Ty shakes his head. He laughs *sounds like you*. "I thought I was the depraved pervert."

"Based on what?"

He chuckles *fair enough*. Motions to the cocktail glasses on the table. *Another round?*

Was I this bad when Laura left?

No, I was worse. Much worse. Pissed for weeks straight.

When I finally sobered up, I ran three thousand miles away.

He's doing both at once. But then he's always been smarter.

"One more," I say.

"Getting old?" he asks.

"You'll be there soon."

He chuckles as he pours two more glasses. "What's there to see around here?"

I motion to the beach in front of us. Through the sliding glass doors.

It's beautiful. Like something from an American TV show. No flaws in sight.

"You're going out in that?" he asks.

"You sound like Eve."

He shakes his head *I don't know what the hell to do with you*. "Fuck, she's so young I can't even mock you for it. If she was twenty-two, it would be borderline. Worth discussing. But she's starting college in what…"

"Next month."

He chuckles *fuck, you're ridiculous*. It's easy. The easiest he's been all night.

But then it's always easier focusing on other people's problems.

I can handle the inquisition if it's what he needs.

Ty continues, "You asked about my schedule three weeks ago."

"So?"

He moves through the living room. Motions for me to follow.

I do away with my shoes and socks. Follow him into the sand.

It's dark now. The sky is a deep shade of blue. The stars are shining bright.

Between the quiet roar of the waves, the smell of salt, and the soft breeze, this place is a picture-perfect beach.

"You started reading Atwood books five months ago," he says.

"I didn't realize you kept tabs."

"You couldn't stop talking about them."

"Great literature."

"Since when do you read great literature?" He takes a long sip. "And don't say Lee Child is literature."

"It's not my fault you don't appreciate a good mystery."

He rolls his eyes. Not in a dismissive way. In that

playful Ty way of his. The way that says *you're so full of shit you're covered in it. Don't expect me to buy it.* "You kept talking about the woman who recommended them. Her... obsession. Her intellect. Her wit. You were talking about her, weren't you?"

"If I was?"

"Are you going to tell me you only met her a few weeks ago?"

I say nothing.

He laughs. "You think the poker face works on me? I was there every minute of your divorce. You may have convinced Mum you're okay, but you've never fooled me."

"I am okay."

He shakes his head *still not buying it.* "You don't look okay. You look... Happy."

"Jesus, the indignity. I look happy? Thank fuck you've told me so I can correct this immediately."

"You're in love with her."

"Don't be ridiculous."

"I'm the ridiculous one?"

"Yes."

"Not you?" he asks. "Lying to yourself. Trying to sell me this story about how you met three weeks ago and you only want her sweet pussy."

"Don't say pussy."

He chuckles. "You sound like an American. I shouldn't use—"

"A fifteen-year-old American, maybe."

"Ah, so more appropriate for your girlfriend."

"She's not—"

He shakes his head. "Isn't she?"

Eve is young, yes, but she's lived an entire life. She'd be bored to tears by a nineteen-year-old, much less a fifteen-year-old. "It's complicated."

"Uh-huh."

"She has a website. Anonymous. I only read her posts. I only knew she was smart as a whip. Then that she dyed her hair teal. Then that she wore combat boots."

"And that was it? Lust for combat boots? Something you need to tell me about your time in the military?"

I flip him off.

He chuckles. Motions *go on*.

"It's hard to explain without showing you her site. And I'm not showing you."

"It's not public?"

"It is. But…" I have no excuse. If I can read it, anyone can. If it's wrong for him to read it, it's wrong for me to read it.

But I *am* avoiding it. I haven't looked. I want to look. I want it in my bones. But I haven't.

I don't bother justifying my desire for secrecy. "She's sharp. Insightful. Writes all sorts of brilliant things about films, TV, books, society. Then there's the other half of her site. Her feelings. Almost a journal. Raw. Beautiful. Her heart, laid bare for me. It's—"

"Of course."

What the fuck? "What do you mean 'of course.'"

"It doesn't take a shrink, Ian. Laura was fucking someone else. Lying to you. Hiding that secret. Hiding everything she wanted. Every feeling that had changed. So now you have this girl willing to—what was it you said? Lay her heart bare? Of course, you're obsessed."

Fuck him for being so perceptive. "I wasn't going to look her up."

"But you did"

"There was a man at her work. Trying to pay for her virginity."

He laughs *of course*. "Fuck, you are trying to take my crown. I'm the dirty pervert here."

"Since when?"

"Ask Rory."

"Is that what happened?"

"Part of it." His gaze shifts to the sky. Still the pale shade of twilight. "She mentioned this guy on her site?"

"Yes."

"And that was when you looked her up?"

"Yes."

His expression gets incredulous. "You didn't know what she looked like?"

I shake my head.

He nods *hmmm*. "It's not like you. To choose a woman for her heart and mind."

"She's different."

"You're different with her."

"Yes, I'm happy. It's terrible. I need to correct this problem right away. We've covered that."

He shakes his head *you're not fooling me*. "You're softer with her."

"Maybe."

"Like you were with Laura. At first."

"Don't—"

"Do you have a list of topics you'd like me to cover? You know why I'm here early. We can dance around it if you want, but we need to get there eventually."

"I know," I admit.

"So…"

"What does she want?"

"A meeting."

My stomach drops. "Why?"

"I'm not the one who was married to her." His gaze

shifts to the ocean. He takes another sip. Shakes his drink so ice clinks against glass. Taps his fingers against the chair.

Stalling.

It's his tell.

"What?" I take the seat next to him. "There's something."

"I don't want to ruin your holiday."

"You won't."

He shoots me a look. *Trust me on this.* "Lie to yourself if you want. Don't lie to me. Are you ready to hear why Laura's ready to dissolve?"

I want to say yes, but I'm not sure.

"Maybe if you love this new girl... fuck, Ian. I'm not sure which of us is worse at this." Hurt drips into his voice. It's there. All that pain of Rory leaving. Pain I know. Pain I understand. Pain I can't erase.

"Was there someone else?" I ask.

"No. I wish there was. That would be easier to understand than *I'm sorry, but I'm not in love with you anymore.* She'd already bought a fucking dress. She was planning the honeymoon." His voice breaks for a split second. He stops. Steels himself. "I'm not pissed enough for this conversation."

I can't really talk there. "I'm sorry."

"It isn't a bad thing. If you're happy. I hope you are. It's been a long time since I've seen you like this. Since—"

"Don't say—"

"I won't. But I... I'm tired of being the bearer of bad news." His gaze shifts to the sand. "I don't mind the duty. I just wish... I wish there was good news for once."

"It can't be that bad."

"Maybe not." He looks to the sky. "They got married. You knew that?"

I nod.

"And now… she's pregnant."

"Oh."

"Maybe it doesn't matter to you anymore. Maybe you're over it. Maybe this is the last time you ever want to see her."

"It is."

"Then I'll schedule a meeting. Have our lawyer finish the contract. She wants to sign. I imagine that's why."

Now that she's having a child with her new husband, she wants to dissolve our final tie.

She owns part of our information company. Part of the divorce agreement. She wouldn't let me buy her out then.

I thought it was one more way she wanted to fuck me. But maybe it was something else.

A way to stay in my life.

To pretend we can be friends.

She's been collecting profits for years. It's tied us together for years. Meetings every fucking quarter.

Her lying smile every fucking quarter.

My stomach twisting every fucking quarter.

Now, she wants out. She wants closure. She wants me to forgive her.

I should. For my own sake. For Eve.

But what does that matter? This ends next month.

Eve will move on. Go to school. Find a guy her age. Some literature major who understands the same things she does.

Who doesn't cart a truck full of baggage.

She'll think of me sometimes, sure. As the guy who took her firsts. Who made her come. Who taught her to pick out good gin.

She won't care if I worked through my inability to trust. She won't care if I forgave my ex-wife. She won't care if I moved on.

I gave up on moving on a long time ago.

I don't love Laura anymore. I don't want Laura anymore.

She's nothing but a painful memory. An emptiness where my heart used to be.

It's impossible to fill. I've tried.

So why do I feel this ache in my chest?

There's not supposed to be anything there.

No hope, no love, no wish for more.

"We need another round," Ty says.

This time, I agree.

———

FOR A WHILE, WE TRADE OLD STORIES. DANCE AROUND THE elephant in the room.

Then he hits that point—where he can barely sit, much less stand—and he starts spilling his guts.

The break in her voice as she pressed the ring into his hand. The hurt in her eyes. The ache in his heart.

He wants to hate her for breaking his heart. But how can he hate her for falling out of love? For needing space to find herself? For realizing she wants something else?

I wish I had advice. Wisdom. Some way to help.

It should be easy for me to hate Laura—she was coming in another man's bed—but I don't.

It's easier to focus on the sex. The betrayal. The red I see when I picture that arsehole's face.

But focus always fades. I start asking why.

She didn't fuck him to hurt me. I won't forgive her for it. Or excuse her.

But I want to understand it.

How could the woman I knew do that? She's never

been selfless, sure, but she's never had malicious intentions either.

How could she turn into someone I barely recognized? Someone who spent a year dodging rough patches, spinning lies, sneaking around.

Was she the one who changed?

Or was it me? Was I the one who failed her?

I must have.

Why else would she fall out of love? Stop offering me her head, her heart, her body?

Yes, we fucked that last year. But it was different. She wasn't there. She was off someplace. Thinking of him.

I insist Ty spends the night in an extra bedroom. He's in no state to drive.

He complains a bit, but he still stumbles to the room.

I undress. Shower. Join Eve in the bedroom.

She stirs as I slide into bed. Blinks her eyes open. Looks up at me with a soft smile. Then her eyes flutter together.

She reaches for me. Slides her hand over the sheets.

I take it.

Her eyes still closed, she closes the distance between us. Wraps her arms around me. Melts into me.

She doesn't say anything. She's asleep. It's her subconscious.

It means something.

And it means something that I hold her close. Feel her heartbeat against my chest. Fall asleep with her in my arms.

Chapter Forty-Four

EVE

For the first time, I wake before Ian.

Watch the sun cast highlights over his body.

He's not wearing a shirt. Or pants. Only boxers.

It's the most naked I've seen him.

Or maybe that's arguable. I mean, I've had him in my mouth, so—

Ahem.

He's handsome, not beautiful, but with the morning sun surrounding him in a soft glow—

This is beautiful.

The steady rise and fall of his chest. The softness in his brow. The ease in his shoulders.

No secrets, no subtext, no heartbreak.

Not his. Not mine. Not the pain of parting.

Only peace.

And those lines of ink. They're more obvious in the light of day. Without all those clothes in the way.

An in memoriam for his father.

A Latin quote.

Veritas lux mea.

Truth is my light. I'm not sure that's the translation, but I recognize enough.

When did he get it? Before his marriage? After it fell apart?

And the tree with roots reaching into the ground—

My fingers itch to trace the art. To feel his skin. To soak up every ounce of meaning.

I want to know him. In a way I've never wanted to know anyone.

It's hard to explain. Overwhelming. As overwhelming as my desire.

Somehow, I keep my hands to myself.

I slip out of the bed. Into the bathroom. Move through my morning routine.

I run a brush through my hair. Then quick makeup. Moisturizer, concealer, eyeshadow, eyeliner, brows, mascara, blush.

Enough I see a badass in the mirror. Enough I have a shield.

I love my look. It feels like me. But it feels like too much today.

I don't want a shield. I want to strip away everything between me and Ian. So I can feel all of him and he can feel all of me.

Am I ready for that?

I don't know. I certainly look better without the dark circles. Less tired. Less hungover.

My head isn't throbbing, but it's a little achy. And the light is too bright. And my stomach is… ugh.

Alcohol. So many charms. Why is it people adore it so much? Besides the loss of inhibitions?

Or maybe that's everything. What makes it terrifying. What makes it appealing.

I want that now. To climb into bed with him. Spill every thought in my head. Every feeling in my heart.

Listen and stay. Have me and stay. Please, whatever you do, stay.

Ahem.

I move into the bedroom. Ian is still asleep, peaceful.

There's a sound downstairs. Footsteps. His brother.

I change into the first thing I find. A chiffon dress I bought for the trip. A gorgeous floor-length black number. With thin straps, a low neckline, a breezy skirt.

Too sexy for the circumstance.

Or maybe not sexy enough. Ian did promise…

I try to put the thought out of mind. Try to find a solid *I'm not thinking about fucking your brother* face. Then I move into the hallway. Down the stairs.

The house is even more beautiful in the morning.

No sign of last night's dinner. Or drinks. No empty bottle of gin on the counter. No water stain on the table. No agony in Ty's expression.

He nods *hello*. Offers an easy smile. Motions to the coffee maker. "How do you take it?"

Mmm, the java smells good. It always does. Rich and robust. I drink coffee in the mornings when I don't have other options. But I always feel off. Like I started my day on the wrong foot. "Tea."

He nods *of course*. "Are you like Ian?"

"Handsome and tall? I try."

He chuckles. "Can't stand coffee?"

"I can stand it."

His laugh gets easier. His expression gets knowing. "I see why he likes you."

"That means something."

"You know you're funny."

"I do."

"And quick. Smart." He looks at me carefully for a

moment. Then he turns to the neat row of appliances. He fills the electric kettle. Returns it to its stand. Hits the number for boil. "He's rather boring. Drinks English Breakfast."

"Are you allowed to call that boring?"

"Isn't your country based on the superiority of coffee," he teases.

"I think it was more an overreaction to taxation. But, kind of. Especially in New York. They say we have the best coffee in the world, but—"

"You don't." His laugh is easy. "Better than London. But nothing on the Pacific Northwest."

"Don't say that in the city."

"I wouldn't dare." He checks the cabinet. Scans several tins of tea. "What will you have?"

"Chai. I can do it."

"Nonsense." He motions to the table. *Sit.* "Tell me how you take it."

"If you'll let me fix breakfast."

"You negotiate?"

"Of course."

"Of course," he says it with a different inflection. One that means *of course he likes you*. Which… is a compliment. I guess?

I move past the dining table. Into the kitchen. "Double strength. Two teaspoons for one cup of water. Brew for five minutes. Then strain. Combine with a cup of warm almond milk. I usually warm it in the microwave after I pour the hot water."

"Specific."

My cheeks flush. "I know what I like."

"You two have that in common."

My blush deepens. "Do you have a preference? With breakfast?" I check the fridge. Full of fresh food, of course.

How long does Ian plan to keep me here? Not that I'm complaining.

"Don't care for porridge."

"My heart. You're breaking it."

He chuckles. "Eggs?"

"Eggs work. Scrambled okay?"

"I suppose you wouldn't know how to make a full English?"

"Not a clue."

"Then yes. Scrambled is perfect." He fixes a cup of coffee. Leans against the counter as he nurses it.

His shoulders ease. His exhale deepens. The poker face fades to some mix of exhaustion and frustration.

Maybe he is hungover. Or heartbroken. Or both.

I want to ask. I want to say something to comfort him. I don't really know Ty, but he seems like a good guy. If he's renting out villas for Ian's birthday—

Or flying across the Atlantic to deliver news of some kind—

He can't be too bad.

"Drink too much?" I ask.

"Is it that obvious?"

I motion *a little*.

Again, he laughs. It's more tense. Less easy. "You're very American."

"Thank you?"

"Blunt. I'm not used to it."

"Why beat around the bush?"

His laugh is knowing. "You are perfect for him."

"How is that?"

"Ian… how much has he told you about his ex-wife?"

I make that same *a little* motion.

"She was a performer. An actor and a singer. Always expressive. Bright and vibrant. At first."

"At first?"

He nods, as if that explains everything. "She was forthcoming. Or maybe she only wanted to seem that way."

Okay...

"She shared everything with him. He got used to that. Counted on that. Shared everything with her too. Until, one day, he didn't. And she didn't. And it all spiraled from there, until she was six months into an affair with her singing instructor."

"Oh."

"I probably shouldn't tell you this."

"Okay." I pull the eggs from the fridge. Find a bowl. Crack. Stir.

"Ian doesn't know."

"Okay."

"I don't want him to know."

Is he still drunk? Why in the world would Ty ask me to keep a secret? He barely knows me. "What don't you want him to know?"

He laughs that same pained laugh. "I suppose I should spell it out."

"Probably." I focus on finding a pan. Warming it on the stove.

"I'd like to tell you this, because I think you should know. I think it will be best for him if you know. But I need you to promise you won't share the information."

"Oh."

"If you can't promise... I understand. Secrets are a burden."

"They are." I add oil. Tilt the pain until it's coated.

I shouldn't promise I'll keep a secret. Secrets *are* a burden. And I have my own burdens. But I want to know. Everything inside me is itching to know.

"You really think it's best for him?" I ask. "If you tell me?"

"I do."

I nod *go on*.

"His ex. Laura. I saw her at a pub one night. With the singing instructor. They were close. Not close enough I could be sure, but close enough I was suspicious. When I confronted her, she confessed. Begged me not to share with Ian. Promised she was getting ready to tell him. Swore it would be better if she did."

"Oh."

"She was desperate to tell me. To tell someone. All that guilt… I guess it wears on you. I believed her. That it would be better if he heard it from her. That it was theirs to figure out."

"What happened?"

"Nothing. For a while. Until some party. She got drunk. Pulled me aside. Spilled more details. The explicit ones. And others too. How it happened. The first time… it was a drunk mistake. A kiss. Only one kiss. One moment. One mistake. She thought… it was better not to share. That it would be selfish to share. That was her reasoning. If it really was one time, and it never would happen again… was it fair to ask him to carry that burden?"

It's a good question. My instinct is *bullshit*. A secret is a secret. But Ty is right. Secrets have a weight to them. "I would want to know. He would want to know."

"I thought so too. But what if it was one time? What if it really was a drunk mistake and it really didn't matter? You don't know what you don't know."

"I guess that's true."

"Still bollocks. An excuse. But they could have overcome that… Only, it caused this ripple. She was carrying the guilt. She didn't look at him the same way. Didn't feel able to spill her guts. Wasn't able to ask for what she wanted anymore. She didn't always share Ian's tastes."

"Oh."

"They… compromised. I'm sure he would have taken less. Offered more. If she asked. He loved her with his entire heart."

My stomach twists. I don't like this story. I don't like thinking about him loving someone else. Or having his heart broken. "Oh."

"I won't make excuses for her. Laura was like a sister to me, but she was a smart, capable woman. She knew what she was doing. I'm not saying this to excuse her. Only to—"

"Explain?"

He nods *yes.* "Ian wasn't there. He was obsessed with a work project. He was traveling all the time. Guilty about acting like our father. Unable to admit it. Unable to face himself. I'm sure… he was responsible for the distance as much as she was. But he loved her. She loved him. They both had good intentions."

It's hard to imagine Ian in love with someone else. Someone who hurt him. I don't like it.

"One thing. One secret. After one tear in the canvas, it was easy to rip the entire thing. It was easy to find the weak spots. There are always weak spots."

Is that true? I don't know. I've never been in a real relationship before. Addie is the only person I trust.

There are things we avoid. Subjects we don't touch.

They do cause a rift.

Even with us.

I nod *go on.*

He does. "The other man was there. He was listening. He was open to her." He shakes his head. "It was one thing. Then two. Three. A dozen. Until there was a gulf between them the size of the Atlantic."

Okay... I understand that. Sort of. I add eggs to the pan to buy myself time. They sizzle, but they fail to illuminate. "Why are you telling me this?"

"She was right. The secret was a burden. I felt it for months. After that night, I demanded she confess. But what did that help? He was more miserable than ever."

"You can't run from pain."

"No. You can't." He finishes my mug of tea. Places it on the counter behind me. "Though that's easier said than done."

"What happened with your girlfriend?"

"She fell out of love. I don't know why. Or how to explain it. I don't want to. I want to get pissed and forget her existence."

"I'm sorry."

"And Ian... I'm not trying to burden you, Eve. I want you to understand where he is. Why he's so unable to open his heart. He cares about you. He doesn't want to admit it, but he does. And he's going to... he's going to ask for a lot. More than is fair. But it's what he needs. And the heart doesn't care about fair."

"What are you asking?" Seriously, is vagueness something they teach in London? Or is it the people Ian knows?

"Consider it. Consider him. Do what you need to do. To protect yourself. But don't write him off because he's ridiculous."

"Okay." I think I know less than when this conversation started.

Is Ty still drunk? Or just distracted?

I guess it's sweet; him trying to put in a word for his brother. But I have no idea what that word is. Maybe hazy. Unclear. Confusing. Something like that.

I do want to give Ian a chance. If he asks for it. But, so far, he hasn't. So far, he's been incredibly clear about our terms. Thirty days. Then it's over. Forever. "I care about him too. I wouldn't hurt him on purpose."

"I know."

"How?"

"I have a sense about you."

Okay... I focus on stirring the eggs. Adding leftover basil, tomato, mozzarella. "Do you think he still loves her?"

"No."

"But he's not over her?"

"Not over the damage."

That makes more sense. "And you... want him to get over it?"

"I want him to be happy. Whatever that means. Whatever it looks like to him."

"You try not to judge?"

"No." His expression eases. "I judge. But I want him to be happy, no matter my opinion."

"Oh." I stir the eggs. "I guess that's sweet."

"Maybe. He's a pain in the arse when he's miserable."

"So, it's really a selfish motivation?"

"Absolutely." This time, his laugh is easy too. "Now, let's talk about something more interesting. How in the world did you meet Ian?"

"He didn't tell you?"

"I'd rather hear your side of it."

I nod *okay*. Finish the eggs. Launch into the story of a strange meeting, a strange offer, a strange dinner.

I tell Ty the particulars. But I keep the important details to myself.

The sweet taste of Ian's lips. The rough feel of his hands. The deep sound of his groan.

I'm in the middle of describing dinner with Shep and Jasmine, and asking Ty for any dirt he has, when footsteps move down the stairs.

Ian. And he isn't wearing a suit. He's in a black robe. It's open enough I can see his chest.

Mmm... yes.

He shoots his brother a look. "Jesus, who are you? Hugh Hefner?"

"Only if you're going to put on a bunny costume." He winks at me.

Ty shakes his head *how disgusting*. He turns to me. "This might be the end of our gossip."

"Oh?" I ask.

He nods. "Something tells me Ian has other plans for your morning."

Ahem.

"Yes." His voice stays deep and steady. "I did promise."

Chapter Forty-Five

EVE

Ty heads for the door the second he finishes breakfast. Ian walks him out. They linger at Ty's rental car, whispering secrets. Business or pleasure?

I don't know.

I can't begin to contemplate it.

He promised.

Last night, he promised.

And he just said—

And we're going to—

Fuck. I finish my last sip of chai. Chase it with half a glass of water.

Enough to wet my throat. Not enough to calm my nerves.

My pulse is racing.

My body is buzzing.

Every molecule inside me is screaming the same thing: *Need. Ian. Now.*

I thought I knew want before. The torture of sweltering summers. The discomfort of wet socks. The ache of a broken heater in December.

I knew the agony of too hot, too cold, too tired, too hungry, too thirsty, too worn.

This is different.

A painful, blissful, all-encompassing need.

I finish my glass. Stand. Shift my weight between my legs.

The door opens and shuts. Footsteps move closer.

Ian stops at the table with a smile. "You're on edge, vixen."

I shake my head.

He nods *yes*. Takes another step toward me. Then another. Another. Until he's close enough to touch. Until he does touch.

One hand around my neck.

The other at my hip.

He pulls me into a slow, deep kiss.

He floods my senses.

The taste of cinnamon on his lips. The soft pressure of his lips. The soft light of bliss.

He's impossibly patient. Slowly, pulling my body into his, slipping his tongue into my mouth, claiming me.

I want that so badly. I shouldn't. I should hate the idea of him possessing me.

But I don't.

I love it.

I need it.

I need it so badly.

He pulls back with a heady sigh. Slips his hand into my hair. Cups the back of my head, equal parts gentle and demanding. "Are you ready?"

My nod is much too enthusiastic.

His laugh is low and easy. "No hangover?"

"Better now."

"You sure?"

"Very."

His smile spreads a little wider. God, it's such a beautiful smile. It lights up his dark eyes. "Enthusiastic."

"You're evil."

"I know." His fingers curl into my scalp. His eyes fix on mine. They stay bright. Teasing. Utterly in control. "You're killing me with that dress."

"I know."

"Good girl." He pulls me into another kiss. He's not patient this time.

He slips his tongue into my mouth, swirling it around mine, claiming my mouth as he knots his hand in my hair.

When our kiss breaks, his eyes find mine. They're not playful anymore. They're entirely demanding.

"Go upstairs. Close the door. Wait on the bed."

I nod. Take a step backward. Hold his gaze for as long as I can.

The need in his eyes sets me on fire. Fuck, he's so hot. I can't stand it.

I force myself to turn. To move to the stairs. Then up them. Down the hallway. Into the bedroom.

The same white light. Only brighter. Closer to afternoon.

It casts highlights over the sleek sheets, the hardwood floor, the dark fabric of my dress.

My eyes go to the mirror. My reflection. A girl I recognize—messy teal hair, raspberry lips, dramatic black dress. And one I don't—

A sex goddess. A vixen. A woman who knows how to command the room.

That's how he sees me. And knowing he's making me wait—

I'm nervous, but that's such a distant concern. Overwhelmed by desire. By the bliss making my veins buzz.

Even that voice, the one in the back of my head, asking *what if this is the end*—

It's far away. Quiet. Aware it's less important.

Maybe it is the end. The last time I have him. But, fuck, I need to have him.

Whatever that means.

He's driving me out of my fucking mind. I need to do the same to him.

I find my boots in the closet. Slip them on.

There. I have my way to tease him.

With the thought of me in his bed, in only my boots.

It's so—

Fuck. I can barely see straight.

I force myself to sit on the bed. Press my knees together. Let my gaze drift around the empty room.

It's so much like Ian's apartment. Wide open space. Sparse details. Sleek design.

Lighter colors. But the same bold choices. Teal and white, not teal and black. Teal and—

God, what if that's it? What if my hair is the only reason why he likes me? If my color fades in the surf—it always does—and the magic is gone.

I know it's not true. It's silly. But it's there, somewhere deep in my thoughts, that question.

Why is he here? Why does he want me? Why in the world did he pay me half a million dollars for thirty days?

I would have said yes if he asked.

And, now, if he asked me to choose—the rest of the money or him—I'd choose him. Even if it was one time. One night.

My libido is running my brain.

Do I even have a brain? Or am I a being of pure want?

I close my eyes. Let my thoughts drift to memories of him.

His hand between my legs. His tie around my wrists. His lips on my neck.

Eventually, my eyes blink open. My gaze drifts to my reflection. The thin black straps of my dress. The dramatic line the fabric draws between my breasts. The hint of cleavage.

Footsteps move closer.

Then a knock on the door.

"Come in." I press my knees together.

The door slides open. He steps inside. Presses it closed.

He's still in that silk robe. My fingers itch for the smooth fabric. The warm skin beneath it.

I need to touch him more, see him more, feel him more.

Everything, right now.

Everything, all the time.

"Stand up so I can look at you." His voice is firm, deep, demanding.

It makes my thighs shake.

I take a deep breath. Push myself off the bed. Onto my feet. Well, my heels.

I pull my dress a few inches. So he can see my shoes.

He smiles, almost breaking character. "Are you teasing me, vixen?"

"Following orders."

He looks at me in a way that screams *you're still teasing and I'll make you pay for that*. "Is that right?"

"You want me in your bed. In only my boots."

"True." His eyes move over my body slowly. From the top of my head to my combat boots, then back up, all the way to my eyes. "You're gorgeous."

"Thank you."

"Turn around."

I do.

He lets out a low sigh of pleasure. "You test my patience, Eve. You know that?"

I shake my head.

"I go out of my mind, thinking about what I want to do to you."

I turn so I'm facing him. "What do you want to do?"

"Fuck you so hard you see stars."

I swallow hard.

"I want to tie you to my bed and split you in half." His voice stays firm. "And I want to hold you close. Kiss you as I drive into you slowly. As I savor every second."

I don't know what to say to that. So I nod.

"I want to make you beg, vixen. But I don't have the patience."

"No?"

"No. I want you too much." He motions *come here*.

I turn. Then take four steps to him.

He takes my hands. Places one on his chest. The other on his stomach. Nods something that means *touch me as much as you want*.

I'm not sure that's possible. My want is infinite. Even with all the time in the universe, I won't touch him enough. I'll need more. I do need more.

But, fuck, the feel of his skin against my palm—

The warmth of his body. Soft skin over hard muscles. And those raised lines of ink. I want to trace every one. To understand all of him.

I run my fingers over his chest. Down his stomach. To the waistband of his boxers.

A groan falls from his lips.

He presses his palm into my lower back. Pulls me into another deep, slow kiss.

He's right. It's not as patient as before. It's not patient at all.

The same need that's inside me.

It pours from his lips. Vibrates down my throat, chest, stomach, thighs. All the way to my fingers and toes.

To the parts that need him most.

His tongue dances with mine.

His fingers curl into my dress.

He pulls back. Shifts his position. Behind me. So I can see our reflection in the mirror.

Ian tosses his robe aside. The smooth fabric shifts against my skin. Sleek and cool and expensive.

Then the warmth of his body. Of his skin against mine.

His chest against my bare back. His hands on my upper arms. His lips on my neck.

His gaze shifts to our reflection. "Watch."

I nod. Not that I need to be told. Watch. How could I not?

He brings his hand to my chin. Turns my head so I'm looking at him. So I have to take in the intensity in his expression.

My knees buckle.

My thighs shake.

My body whines *more, more, more*.

Another deep kiss. Hard and hungry. He's claiming me. And, fuck, I want to be claimed.

He releases me with a sigh. Brings his lips to my ear. His hands to my chest.

One moves higher, curling around my throat. Hard enough to hold me in place. To remind me he's in control. To remind me I'm his.

The other pushes my dress aside.

I watch as my breast spills from the sheer black fabric. As he cups me. Runs his thumb over my nipple.

Fuck. It's too much. Too intense. I'm already wound so tight. I'm already so desperately in need of him.

He moves his hand to my other strap. Pushes it off my shoulder. So my dress falls to my waist. So I'm exposed.

The window opens to the beach. The ocean.

No one is there. No one can see. Only the two of us.

Somehow, I feel more exposed. Knowing he's watching. Knowing I'm watching. Knowing he's watching me watch.

"Ian." I don't know what I'm asking. Only that I want it. Need it. Immediately.

In response, his grip around my throat tightens.

My sex clenches. "Fuck." My breath is a struggle. Because I'm wracked with desire. Because he's gripping tightly. But I don't want him to let up. I want more.

His gaze shifts to the mirror. For a long moment, he watches me watch. Watches my eyes widen, my chest heave, my cheeks flush.

He teases my nipple with his thumb. Slow, but not patient. Rough enough it hurts in the best possible way. Rough enough, I know he needs me as much as I need him.

He presses his lips into my skin.

Then it's the soft scrape of his teeth. Harder and harder. Until it hurts as much as it feels good. Until I have to let out a deep groan.

He toys with me until I'm panting. Then he moves to my other breast and teases it just as mercilessly.

My breath catches in my throat. My toes curl into my shoes. My hands reach for him. Get his side. The warmth of his skin against my palms—

It's enough to make me dizzy.

This is already so much. Too much.

The sight of his body behind mine, the feel of his teeth on my neck, the sound of his breath on my skin, the pleasure building inside me—

I have to close my eyes. To suck a breath through my nose. To dig my nails into his skin.

He groans against my neck. Brings his hand to my stomach. Over my dress.

He pulls my body into his. So I feel his chest against my back. His cock against my ass.

There's too much fabric in the way—this skirt has too many layers. I need that. Now.

No more teasing. No more patience. No more waiting.

I rock my hips, grinding my ass against him.

He lets out a low groan. Brings his hands to my hips. Holds me in place. "Not yet, vixen." He drags his teeth over my neck. "I need to ease you into this."

I shake my head.

"What makes you think you get a say?"

It shouldn't make my sex clench, but it does. "Please."

"Please?"

"Fuck me." My cheeks flush—did I really say that?—but I move forward. I'm too in need for inhibitions. "Please, Ian. Fuck me."

He groans against my neck.

"Please."

His hand goes to my back. Finds the zipper of my dress. There. The garment catches on my hips. "Off."

I nod. Shimmy out of the dress. Kick it aside.

There. I'm standing in his bedroom in only my boots and panties.

In front of him.

His body behind mine.

Both of us almost entirely exposed.

Ian brings his hands to my hips. In one swift motion, he pushes my panties to my knees.

I do away with them.

He brings his hand to my stomach. Holds my body against his. Looks to the mirror, taking in the sight of us.

It's like we're paused. A still photo for later. This moment on the precipice. I'm standing, yes, but I'm still splayed out for him. Naked except for my boots.

Even though he's only in his boxers, he's standing with that firm posture. Lost in desire and utterly in control at once.

Dark against light.

Skin against skin.

His hands. At my stomach. My hip. My chest. My throat.

Then between my legs.

He wraps his hand around my throat as he brings his thumb to my clit. Holds me in place as he rubs me.

Fuck, that's intense. A soft touch that feels like so much. I'm already wound tight. On the edge.

Watching my chest rise and fall, his arm between my breasts, his hand around my throat, his thumb working my clit with steady strokes—

He winds me tighter and tighter.

The pleasure inside me builds and builds.

Until I'm there. At the edge.

Then his teeth scrape my neck and I tumble over the edge. My sex pulses as I come.

I rock my hips, groaning his name as I reach for him.

His side. The warmth of his skin. His hip. The smooth fabric of his boxers.

The steady pressure of his thumb.

He rubs me through my orgasm. Releases my neck. Makes eye contact through the mirror. "Fucking beautiful."

I nod. It's all I can do.

"The best thing I've ever seen." He presses his lips to my cheek. Brings his hands to my hips. "I want to watch you come all day."

"Okay."

"Fuck." His groan gets low. Breathy. "But I need to be inside you. Come here." He guides me to the bed. Lays me on my back.

He places his body between my legs. Then it's his hand on my inner thigh. The brush of his palm.

One finger teasing me.

Two.

Three.

"Fuck." I reach for something. Get the smooth sheets.

He watches my expression as he pushes two fingers inside me. It's hard and fast. It's too much. It hurts. But I want more.

"Please," I groan.

He holds his position for a moment, then he pushes deeper. Pulls back. Drives his fingers into me again.

My eyes close.

He does it again. Again. Again.

God, that feels so good. So close to what I need. But not close enough. I need him inside me. His cock inside me.

Our bodies pressed together. All the weight of him sinking into me.

"Please," I say it again. "Do you want me to beg? I will. Please, Ian. Please, fuck me."

He drives his fingers into me again.

"Fuck."

Then again.

I reach for him.

He grabs my wrist. Pulls it over my head.

I keep it there as he drives his fingers into me again.

Two.

Then three.

I close my eyes. Soak in the feeling of his rough touch.

One more push of his fingers. Then he pulls his hand away.

He shifts off the bed. Stands as he does away with his boxers.

Then it's just him. Naked. Nothing in the way.

He climbs onto the bed. Between my legs. Up my body.

His lips find mine.

He kisses me hard as he guides my legs around his waist.

Then his hand is around my wrist. He pulls my hand over my head. Then the other. Then it's the soft pressure of his palm against my wrists.

He's in control.

I'm his plaything.

Fuck.

He kisses me hard and deep. Then he pulls back. Enough to look me in the eyes. To study my expression. "Breathe."

It's a good reminder. I'm not sure I am breathing. I'm too lost in sensation. The weight of his body. The warmth of his skin. The pressure of his palm.

His cock against my sex.

A hint of a touch. I barely feel it. But, fuck, what I feel.

"Breathe," he says it again.

Inhale. Exhale.

His cock brushes my sex again. The same hint of a touch. Enough my entire body aches. Enough, I scream with emptiness. With that impossible need to be full.

Inhale. Exhale.

He presses his palm into my wrist. Digs his fingers into the flesh of my ass.

He holds me in place as he pushes into me.

Pressure. More than I can take.

My eyes close. My teeth sink into my lip. My nails dig into my palm.

"Breathe, vixen." His voice is steady. Reassuring.

It shouldn't be so hard to remember.

I take another deep breath. Let out another steady exhale.

His eyes fix on mine for a moment. Then his lids flutter closed. His lips find mine.

He kisses me as he shifts into me. Slow and patient.

Stretching me.

Pushing farther and farther. Until it's all I can take.

I pull back with a gasp.

He holds his position. Brings his lips to my neck. Releases his grip on my wrist.

My hands go to his skin immediately. His shoulders. His back.

I pull him closer. All that weight of his body against mine. Pressing me into the bed. Keeping me safe. It's over-whelming, how safe that feels.

Another deep breath.

And he pushes farther.

Stretching me farther.

Then he pulls back and drives into me with another slow, steady thrust.

Pain fades to pressure. So much it overwhelms me. It's all I feel. This unbearable pressure.

Then a bearable one.

A pressure that feels good.

Right.

Like the weight of his body over mine. The feel of his

lips against mine. The sensation of his fingers digging into my skin.

I don't have a better word than good. But good isn't enough.

Great, amazing, fantastic.

Really fucking fantastic.

Really fucking right.

His lips brush my neck. My chin. My cheek.

He kisses me as he pulls back and drives into me again.

It's a slow, steady motion, but it's still overwhelming.

I turn my head. Let a groan fall from my lips.

He shifts enough to look at me. He studies me as he pulls back and thrusts into me again.

Fuck.

My eyes close. My nails dig into his skin.

"Breathe, vixen." His voice is patient. And needy. How can he be both at once?

It's so much, too much, but I'm still desperate for more. This sense of fullness.

Not just physically.

Emotionally too.

Our bodies are joined.

He's inside of me.

"Breathe," he says it again.

I suck an inhale through my teeth. Push an exhale through my nose.

He watches me as he pulls back and drives into me again.

Again.

He cups my cheek with his palm. A different way of telling me he's in control. He looks down at me, asking if I'm ready.

I nod.

For a moment, he stares into my eyes. Takes in everything in my expression. Then his eyes flutter closed.

His lips find mine.

He kisses me as he drives into me.

It's slow. Steady.

Almost too much to take. Right at the edge. Not over it.

My lips part. His tongue slides into my mouth. Dances with mine.

Another slow, steady thrust. It doesn't hurt this time. It's not too much. It's a lot. But just right.

I kiss him harder.

He drives into me again.

I rake my nails over his back.

He shifts his hips, driving into me with another slow, steady thrust.

Discomfort fades to pressure. This overwhelming sense of fullness.

Rightness.

With every thrust, I ease a little more. Until it's exactly what I want to take. Until I need more.

So much more.

He kisses me as he drives into me with those slow, steady thrusts.

I soak in every ounce of sensation. The softness of his lips. The low roar of his groan. The sharp scrape of his nails.

That sweet, perfect pressure of his cock inside me.

Stretching me.

Winding that sweet, perfect tension inside me.

Fuck.

I'm so full. So right. So his.

And he's so mine.

That's more overwhelming than anything.

He wraps his arm around me as he moves faster.

Deeper.

Harder.

Until he hits his pace. Until it's just right.

Fuck.

I have to pull back. To groan. To dig my nails into his back.

Those steady thrusts wind me tighter and tighter.

That perfect pressure again and again.

Until I'm so, so close.

So, so ready for release.

So impossibly taut.

Then he brings his hand to my throat and I go over the edge.

I groan his name as I come. Pleasure spills through my senses. My torso, chest, legs, arms, fingers, toes.

Everything spent and satisfied and somehow still in need of him.

I need to feel him come.

I need it in a way I've never needed anything.

I run my nails over his back.

He drives into me with that steady pace.

His touch gets rougher. Harder.

Until he's there, groaning my name, pulsing inside me as he spills every drop.

Mine.

In this moment, he's mine. I'm his. The entire universe makes sense.

It's a beautiful, bright place, brimming with bliss.

Slowly, he untangles our bodies, lies next to me, pulls me into his arms. My back against his chest, my head against his shoulder, my ass against his crotch.

His lips on my neck.

His arm around my waist.

His body still one with mine. In a completely different way. A way I want just as badly.

Chapter Forty-Six

EVE

I'm not a virgin.

I fucked Ian.

No, Ian fucked me.

It dances in my head all night. As we make dinner. Eat on the patio. Watch a restrained British drama based on a play.

I'm not a virgin.

Ian fucked me.

And even though I'm tired and sore and overwhelmed, I need him to fuck me again.

He knows without asking. Or maybe he feels the same. This need to intertwine his body with mine. To have his hands on my skin, his lips on my lips, his cock inside of me.

He takes me to his bed. Strips me out of my clothes. Orders me to come for his viewing pleasure.

Orders me onto all fours.

Strips out of his clothes. Brings his hands to my hips. Teases me again and again.

Finally, he drives into me.

Fuck, it's a lot. Pressure and pain and pleasure all wrapped together. Still everything, but not so overwhelming.

I turn to the mirror. Watch him drive into me. His hands on my hips. The arch of my back. My tits shaking with each thrust.

His cock filling my body.

It's too intense. I come too fast.

He works me through my orgasm. Brings his hand to my clit. Rubs me until I'm coming on his cock again.

And he's there too. Rocking his hips, groaning my name as he comes inside me.

Fuck, there's something about the pulsing of his cock. I need it. That feeling of him inside me, him filling me, him coming for me.

I want more.

I want it again and again.

Constantly.

———

I WAKE UP SORE AND HAPPY AND INCREDIBLY IMPATIENT.

He knows. Enjoys it. Spends breakfast in only his boxers. Shooting me smoking hot looks that scream *I'm going to have my way with you*.

I barely finish my oatmeal.

I drink my chai in a flash.

Finally, he brings me to the armchair in front of the beach. No one is here. But someone could walk by.

Just like the armchair in his apartment.

Again, he asks me to strip.

Again, he holds me close as I come on his hand.

But this time, he doesn't stop there. He pushes his boxers aside and pulls my body into his.

I'm on top of him. My hands are on his shoulders. My body is above his.

I kiss him hard. Grind against him. Try every angle.

Fuck, that back-and-forth motion—he hits me exactly where I need him. The pressure inside me builds quickly. Almost too quickly.

I come fast. Hard. Groan his name as I grind again and again.

It feels fucking good, looking down at him, watching him watch me. But it's not what I want.

I want him in control. His body over mine. His hand on my throat. All that presence and power aimed at a singular goal: having his way with me.

———

WE MAKE OUT ON EVERY CONCEIVABLE SURFACE. LIKE we're horny sophomores too scared to go all the way.

Like he knows exactly how to tease me.

He kisses me at the kitchen table.

He spoons me on the couch.

He lays me on a patio chair and orders me to come on his face.

He brings me to the shower. Pins me to the slick tile. Tugs at my hair as he fucks me from behind.

Holds me close as he comes inside me.

Then he kisses me so sweetly I forget about our arrangement. About our expiration date. About anything except the softness of his lips.

And how much I want to kiss him all night. All day. Forever.

I want everything. All night. All day. Forever.

I only get so much…

Two weeks left with him.

Two weeks to fuck him senseless, to learn his favorites, to unlock his heart.

Chapter Forty-Seven

IAN

Eve holds her hand over her eyes, blocking the glare from the sun. She traces a line down my body. Slowly. Taking in everything. "You're naked."

"I am."

"I feel like… it's kind of an invitation."

"Is it?" I tease her.

She nods. Her eyes light up with need. She wants more. Wants to come on my hands, face, cock.

Wants me to claim every part of her.

Again.

I will.

But this first—"You should take it then."

"Hmm." Her eyes flit to my cock. "Soon."

"Soon?"

She nods.

"What is it you say—that's my thing?"

"Is it?"

"Yes."

She smiles. Says it again anyway. "Soon. I'm a little

sore. Well… I've been sore. But I think it's finally too much."

"It's possible?"

"Maybe. Right now, it's just a theory."

She closes the distance between us. Places her palm on my chest. Rises to her tiptoes to press her lips to mine.

Fuck, she tastes good. Like sugar and need.

We're cleaned up, fed, caffeinated. An entire afternoon spent in a haze of ease and pleasure.

Our last night together before Ty's party. Before reality intrudes.

And it's nearly over.

The sun is already sinking into the horizon. It's nearly time to fix dinner. To bring her back to my bed. Hold her close as I drive into her.

Or tie her to the frame and fuck her mercilessly.

I want both. It scares me. Terrifies me how much I want to be slow and gentle with her. Not because she's still new to this. Not because I'm careful with her.

Because I want the sweetness.

Because I want the intimacy.

Because I want to make fucking love.

I pull Eve closer. Her lips part. My tongue slips into her mouth. She melts into me as I claim her.

"Vixen." I release her with a sigh. "You do that again, and I'm fucking you right here."

"Is that a promise?"

"Yes."

"Oh." Her teeth sink into her lip. Somehow, she does it with a smile. The lightest hint of a blush. Fucking adorable.

She drives me out of my mind.

"Soon." Her blush deepens. "Very soon." She turns to

the massive pool. Pulls her—well, my—t-shirt over her head. Looks to me as she does away with her knickers.

She dives into the bright blue water. Surfaces with a gasp.

She looks at me, a dare in her gorgeous eyes, then she dives under the water. Swims halfway across the pool.

When does she practice her swimming? She lives in Brooklyn. She's never mentioned days at a public pool, laps at the gym, a season on the school swim team.

There are things about her I don't know. There's so much about her I don't know.

I want all of it. I want to understand every part of her.

She surfaces at the other end of the pool. Shakes her head *are you coming?*

I push my thoughts aside. Dive in after her. Meet her at the other end of the pool.

She laughs as she hooks her arms around my neck. Looks up at me with wonder in her eyes.

"I still can't believe you're naked." Her fingers brush my neck.

"We spent the last two days fucking."

"Still… it's different here." She stares into my eyes. "Like you really have your guard down."

"And this?" I brush her hair behind her ear. Run my thumb over her lower lip. No makeup. She's just as beautiful without it. Different. The Eve no one else sees.

She nods. "You don't like it?"

"It's the same for you, isn't it?"

Her eyelids flutter together as she leans into the gesture. "It is."

It took two days of fucking her senseless.

No, we've been here. Dancing around how much we want forever.

"I am."

She digs her fingers into my skin. Not the *this is the only way I can take the intensity* of earlier. A gentle gesture. Like she's trying to explore me.

Her chest heaves with her inhale. I can feel the rise and fall against my chest. Her skin against mine.

The water makes her slick. Cool. The contact is too brief.

I pull her closer.

She lets her head fall into the crook of my shoulder. "It scares me. Thinking about our expiration date."

I nod.

"And it scares me… thinking about going past that. I guess… I don't let people see weakness. I don't know what they'll do. If they'll run or stay. I don't know which is scarier."

I don't either.

"I haven't let anyone get close in a long time. Only Addie. And even then… there's so much she doesn't know."

"Like this?"

She nods. "She has some idea… but not the extent."

"Everyone tries to protect their family."

"Maybe." Under the water, she slides her arm around my waist. "But there's something else too. I want to protect myself. I don't want her to see me differently. Think I'm a whore. Or a sellout."

"Would she?"

"I don't know. I don't think so. But she… she wouldn't like how much I've kept things from her. How much I've tried to shield her. I don't like it either. I'm treating her like a child when she's four minutes younger. I'm not her mom. I don't want to be anyone's mom."

"Now or ever?"

"Ever." She laughs, but it's not easy. "Is that a deal breaker? For the next two weeks?"

"I won't say that you might change your mind—"

"But I might change my mind?"

"Maybe not that. I never did. Laura either." Her name makes my chest tense. "But I guess that changed."

Her eyes stay on me.

"That's part of what Ty had to tell me. She… she still owns part of one of our companies. Marital property. She wouldn't let me buy her out in the divorce. She's changed her mind."

"Because she's having a…"

"Yes."

"Oh." Sympathy fills her expression. "That's a lot. I'm sorry."

"I'm happy for her."

"Really?"

"No. But I want to be."

"I don't know… if someone cheated on me… I don't know if I'd ever want the best for them. That's very mature."

"I'm very old."

Her laugh is easy. "It's better for you. To forgive. That's what Addie always tells me about our father. But I can't. He's done so much to hurt us. To hurt her. It's not the same, but… I understand the hesitation."

She does. She's not just saying that. The way people do.

Not that I give anyone the chance.

I only talk to Ty.

She looks up at me, vulnerability in her eyes. She wants to offer her trust. To ask for mine. "How long was it going on?"

"A year and a half. Maybe two."

"Fuck." Her eyes soften. Not the pity that makes me sick. This need to know more. To understand. "How long were you married?"

"Almost nine years."

"Fuck. I just said that, didn't I?"

I nod. "It went fast."

"That's a really long time."

"It is."

"She must… no wonder you… your brother said something to me. About how I needed to give you a chance even though you'd ask for too much. Even though it wouldn't sound fair. I didn't really get what he meant. I'm not sure I do now. Maybe you understand it."

No, but I can guess. Either he's talking about Laura or Eve's site. Trying to explain why—"I don't trust easily."

"It's hard for me. And I…" Her fingers curl into my back. "That's a long time to love someone. To wake up next to them. To lose that… not the betrayal or the rejection. Just that… it would kill me if I couldn't wake up in the same apartment as Addie anymore."

"You won't always."

"I know. I hate it. I hate that she'll eventually move in with her girlfriend. Or go to grad school across the country. Or decide she wants to be on her own. But, even then, I'll still have her. I'll still be able to call her and visit her and hug her and tease her about ordering channa masala again… Fuck. I know I just said that. But fuck." She moves closer. "I'm sorry."

"Thank you."

"If she'd betrayed me… rejected me… if I found out she'd been lying to me for two fucking years. It's not the same, I know, but… fuck."

My laugh feels strange. Wrong and right at the same time.

"I'm sorry. I can't imagine how much that would hurt... the one person who loved me, understood me, knew all my scars... for them to do that..." Her eyes meet mine. "You try to hide it. But it's there."

"I don't hide it."

"Do you really believe that?"

"No."

Her eyes flutter closed. Her lips find mine. It's different than the way she normally kisses me. Still soft and slow, but less yielding.

She's the one claiming me.

She's the one looking for something deep inside me.

I want to give it to her.

All of it.

So I kiss her back with everything I have. I guide her out of the pool, lift her into my arms, carry her to the couch.

And right there, still sopping wet and sticky, I pull her body onto mine.

It's soft, sweet, slow.

Terrifying.

Exhilarating.

Chapter Forty-Eight

EVE

We make dinner together. Fresh pasta. With shrimp, olive oil, oregano. Then chocolate covered strawberries for dessert.

It's agony waiting for the chocolate to set—even when we put it in the fridge—but it's worth it for the perfect mix of rich and sweet.

A quiet night. We're both in our pajamas—Ian in actual, honest to goodness pajamas—tangled on the couch, watching a classic film. *Roman Holiday*. Because I need a European education, he teases.

Or maybe it's because the movie is about two people who experience one perfect day together.

One adventure, then they part, him to his job, her to her duty.

Is that what he wants? What I want?

Or does he just like the fucking movie?

Really. It's just a movie.

But I still think about it as I move through my evening routine. As I climb into bed next to him. Fall asleep in his arms.

Is this it?

One perfect month then we part?

Or is it really possible there's more?

———

Addie tosses her overnight bag on the bed. Notes the teal walls, the turquoise sheets, the white dresser. "Hmm."

"Hmm…"

"It's like… your hair. In a room. Well, your normal hair. I'm guessing you want to touch it up."

"Of course." It doesn't look as bad as I expected—more like mint ice cream, less like puke—but still in need of dye.

"Did it fade that fast?"

"I haven't touched it up yet. I'm scared of staining the perfect counter." And I haven't cared. I don't care about anything except talking to him, touching him, fucking him. Even now, when I haven't seen my sister in days, and I'm desperate to catch up with her—

I want him.

His lips. His hands. His cock.

His eyes. His smile. His laugh.

She makes that *hmm* noise again. "You let him see you like this?"

I bite my lip. "That doesn't mean anything."

"You're not wearing makeup yet."

"It's early."

She looks at me with that *uh-huh, yeah, you're not full of shit* look. "You really like him?"

"A lot." There's no sense in denying it. It's everywhere.

She nods *hmmm*. Moves into the bathroom. Runs her fingers over the clean white counters.

"Do you want help?"

"Help?"

"With your hair." She pushes herself up. Onto the counter. "Or with admitting you're in love with him?"

"What?"

"You are." Her eyes light up. "It's all over your face. Oh my God, Eve!" She jumps. Pulls me into a hug. "This is so exciting. I'm so happy for you."

Am I? I don't know. I've never been in love with anyone before.

I really like Ian.

I want to spend the weekend with him. I want to watch him smile. I want to tease him about Austin Powers. And American excess. And his obsession with gin.

God… there are so many things I want. Too many to count.

She releases me. Shoots me a knowing look. Like she's singing *Eve and Ian, sitting in a tree, f-u-c-k-i-n-g.*

How would that go?

First comes a fucked-up arrangement.

Then comes sex.

Then…

It's still up in the air.

"This is amazing. We need to celebrate. With coffee." She presses her finger to her chin. Thinking. "Is there good coffee here?"

"I think so. Ian's brother drinks coffee. But he isn't here yet, so…"

"We have time? Before the party?"

"A few hours." It's early.

"We'll go out. But first…" She motions to my hair.

It's true. She can see me like this. Ian too. Other people… no way.

"Everything is under the counter," I say.

She nods *no problem*. Moves into the bathroom. Bends to gather the supplies.

A mixing bowl, a brush, plastic gloves, two bottles of Special Effects.

"Where's Marisol?" I ask.

"You're not distracting me."

"It's a question."

"We got in a fight and I don't want to talk about it. I want to talk about you. Being in lurrrrrrrrrve."

"You're ruining it."

"You admit it?"

"Maybe." I really don't know. I like him so much… but I want to hold on to that too. To keep it close, where no one else can take it.

I sit on the bed. Give her a minute to fix the dye. Or maybe five. It's quiet here. Peaceful.

And my thoughts *are* all tuned to him. Is that love? Or lust? Infatuation?

There's no denying my lust. Even now…

I'm insatiable.

Addie finishes. "Ready." She motions for me to sit on the edge of the shower.

I move into the bathroom. Pull the teal curtain aside. Sit.

She's careful about applying Vaseline to my hairline and ears. "It's okay, you know."

"Huh?"

"If you're in love with him… if you want everything that comes with it."

What?

She runs a comb through my hair. Slowly. Gently. Waiting to explain. "Spending the weekend with him. It's okay. I don't need you watching me all the time."

"I know."

"Or if... I know it won't happen yet. But one day. Maybe it won't be Ian. But it will be someone. One day, you're going to want to move in with your boyfriend. Get married. Live your own life."

"I don't want to get married." It doesn't feel true. If I close my eyes, I can see it. Ian in one of his dashing suits. Me in some fantastic dress—mostly white, with a little teal. Or maybe black. Why not? It's my fucking wedding.

"Okay." Despite the incredulity in her eyes, Addie doesn't argue. "You don't want to get married. But you want him. You want to be with him. Maybe not forever. But right now."

"I do." I really do.

"You want to spend the next two weeks with him?"

"Not every day. I want to see you too." Only it is every day. As much as I'll miss her, I want to spend every fucking minute with Ian.

"I'm not going to talk you into facing your feelings." She takes the brush. Applies teal dye to a chunk of hair. "They'll hit you soon. And when they do... it's thrilling falling for someone. But it's scary too."

It is.

"I just want to say... you don't have to worry about me anymore, Evie. I'm okay. I've been okay."

"Yeah?"

"Yeah."

"And I..." Her voice steadies. It's practiced. She knows exactly what she wants to say. "I know things can't be like this forever."

I swallow hard. "How are they going to be different?"

"You're really going to Hunter next year?"

"It's a good school."

She shakes her head. "Maybe. But you got into better

ones. And if… I'm not stupid. I know there's more going on with Ian than you say."

"Yeah."

"You don't have to tell me."

"Okay."

"But you… you could afford to go to a better school now. If you wanted."

"Maybe." Tuition is expensive. It will swallow that money fast.

"You can go somewhere better than Hunter. If you don't want to, fine. If you want to stay in Brooklyn and not challenge yourself, fine. I love the city too."

"I do."

"Don't do it for me."

"But—"

"Please, Evie. Please, don't do it for me."

"It's for me. Because I want to hang out with you. You're my best friend."

"I know. You're mine too. But… you have to live your life."

"I do."

She nods. "Since you met him, yeah. If that's just the money, fine. If it's him, all the better."

It's both. The money gives me space to breathe. But Ian… he makes me feel alive. Like every part of my body is buzzing.

"If you kept seeing him, if he asked, would you want to live with him?"

"He won't ask."

"If he did?"

"Yeah." God, the thought of waking up next to Ian every morning… I like it way too much.

"Or if he wanted to take you to Europe for three months?"

358

"Three months is a long time." Longer than we have. Too long to be away from Addie.

"You're hiding from my point."

"I know."

She sets the mixing bowl and brush down. Sits next to me on the edge of the tub. "I love you, Eve. You're my best friend. You're my favorite person in the world. I know you're trying. That you don't mean to look at me like I can't handle myself. But you do." She pushes through her next breath. "I'm so sorry for what happened last year."

"Me too."

"I still don't know if I... I didn't think about things ending. I wasn't trying to die. My head was just so full. There was too much pressure. It was everywhere. I needed it to stop. Any way I could. I didn't think... I wasn't trying to—"

"I know."

"Do you? I know it was scary for you. It was scary for me too. And I hate that I put you through that... but do you know that I'm okay now?"

"Now, but..."

"I might slip?"

"It happens."

"I know." She folds her hands in her lap. "It scares me too. I'm vigilant about my anxiety now, but... it's not something that goes away. It's going to be there. Forever. I have to manage it forever."

I nod.

"But *I* have to manage it, Eve. I won't tell you to not worry. Or not be scared. Or not... I don't know. Want to protect me. I want to protect you too. But I need you to put yourself first, for once."

"I..." Don't. I can't say I do. Addie is always first. "I don't want something to happen to you."

"Yeah, but what about me? Do you think I want to see you shouldering the entire world alone?"

I shake my head.

"Worry. I worry too. Just… trust me. That I'll tell you if I'm not okay. I will. I promise. I know how to do that now."

"Yeah?"

"Yeah."

"Are you sure?" I blink back a tear. "Because I… Addie, I was so scared. In the ER. And after. When you were in the hospital. I thought I might lose you. I… it was like someone tore out my soul. I didn't think I'd ever breathe again."

"I'm sorry." She rests her head on my shoulder.

"You don't have to be sorry."

"I know. But I am. Let me have that. Let me apologize for putting you through that."

"Okay."

She steadies. Her voice. Her posture. "I can't promise I'll always be here. No one can."

"Life is a bitch."

"Sometimes, yeah. But I… I promise I'll tell you if I need help. If I'm slipping. Okay?"

"Okay."

She turns enough to look me in the eyes. "I need you to promise to trust me. Unless I give you a reason not to."

"Okay."

"Okay?"

"I'll try."

"I appreciate it so much, Eve. That you're willing to sacrifice for me. That you want to make sure I don't take on too much. But I know my limits now. I can tell you if it's too much now."

"Okay."

"I need you to treat me like an adult. If we're going to

live together, I need us to be partners. Even if we're not going to live together, if you're going to move in with him... I want it to be me and you against the world. Not you protecting me from the world."

I wipe a tear from my eye. "You're okay?"

"Yeah."

"You're sure?"

"Yeah."

I wrap my arms around her. "I won't stop worrying."

"I know."

"But I... I'll try. I will."

"Yeah?"

"Yeah." I release her. Wipe my eyes. "I... you have to do this today?"

She nods. "When you'll remember why you need to put yourself first."

"He's not... We're not..."

"Maybe not. But what if you are?"

I take a deep breath. Push out a shallow exhale. It's a good way of putting it. *What if we are?* So many ways to fill in the blanks.

"I just... I want you to go for it. If you're ready. I've kept you from a lot. I can't keep you from this too."

"You haven't... I was glad to, Addie."

"I know."

"It's not a sacrifice. I want to keep you safe."

"I am safe. I have a scholarship. I'm studying STEM." She laughs. "I'm going to figure it out. In a few years, I'll be the one with everything together."

"I'll sleep on your couch while I get my PhD."

She smiles. "I'll save the spot for you. Or... maybe you'll be with him. I don't know what will happen. Only that you'll always be my best friend."

I nod.

"And that… I need you to go for it."

"Huh?"

"With Ian. Do me that favor. Please."

"You're blackmailing me?"

She nods *I am*. "Please, Eve. I've kept you from too much. Maybe he's not the one. Maybe it's just a fling. But if he is… I can't keep you from that." She wipes a tear. "So promise me. Promise me you'll go for it. Promise you'll jump and trust him to catch you. If he doesn't, I'll be there. To pick up the pieces. But promise you'll give it a chance."

"Okay." I nod. "I promise."

Chapter Forty-Nine

IAN

"Hey." Eve knocks on my office door. "Addie and I are going out for coffee. We'll be a little while."

I turn off the monitor. "Come in."

She turns the handle. Steps inside.

Gorgeous in a simple black top and shorts. Her hair is touched up. A deep vibrant teal. As dramatic as her eye makeup, her lipstick, her combat boots.

She catches me looking at her shoes. Smiles. "You're obsessed."

"You wear them to torture me."

"Maybe." She motions to my suit. "And this? You're working in your office. At home."

"I'm working."

"By yourself. You can wear pajamas."

"I can't concentrate in pajamas."

She presses the door closed. Moves closer. To the desk.

I stand. Motion for her to *come here*.

She does.

I wrap my arms around her. Pull her into a soft, slow kiss.

Fuck, she tastes good. Like Eve.

She breaks our kiss with a sigh. "You're distracting me."

"I came in here showing off my gorgeous legs?"

Her eyes flit to my trousers. "Mmm... it's true. Not a lot of leg. But what about this?" Her fingers trace the line of my lapel. Then my fuchsia tie. "It's a lot."

"To complement your hair." I lean in to whisper. "The next time I tie you up."

Her fingers curl into my chest. Over my shirt. It's not enough. I need her hand on my bare skin. "You're the one teasing now."

"You started it."

"Mature." She looks up at me with a smile. Pure affection. But there's something in her eyes. Something she isn't saying.

I bring my hand to her cheek. "Are you okay?"

She nods. "Just a talk with Addie... it's good though. We're good."

"Are you sure?"

"Yeah. Good. Just... a lot."

Whatever it is, she doesn't want to tell me. It's fair. There are plenty of things I haven't told her.

I'm not about to spill Ty's secrets.

I can't ask for her sister's. I don't need to. Not right now.

I trust her. To tell me when she's ready.

"And she... uh, she had a fight with her girlfriend. The ex showed up. She got jealous..." Eve takes a step backward. "They'll be okay. But there's a lot to discuss."

No place for my advice. "There's nothing close. I'll call a car."

"Fifteen-minute walk. It's a nice day." She taps her heels together. "I have comfortable shoes."

"You don't need anything?"

"Hmm… well, if I had time, I'd ask for all sorts of things." She smiles. "But they'll have to wait. Do you?" Her eyes meet mine. "Need anything?"

"Just this done." I motion to my computer.

She nods. "I can bring something back. From the coffee shop."

"Tea from an American coffee shop?"

She laughs. "We're pretty good with iced tea."

"No thanks."

"So polite as you insult my country." Her fingers skim my tie.

"You'll see. If we go to London."

"I hope I do." She smiles. "Are you sure?"

My face twists.

Her laugh gets louder. "Give it a chance. You might like it."

I lean down to kiss her. "Go. Before I have my way with you."

"Will you really?"

"You have sixty seconds."

She smiles. Makes a show of counting *one, two, three*. Rises to her tiptoes for one more kiss. Then she releases me, steps backward, turns to the door. "Until then." She disappears into the hallway.

I sit at my desk. Let the quiet flood my ears. Let the room fill.

Already, I miss her. Want her here. Want her to claim a place in my home, my space, my life.

———

Eve's frock flutters as she steps out of the house. The wind catches the chiffon. Blows it over her long legs.

She looks like a model. An alternative model, maybe, but still beautiful, poised, statuesque.

She nods something to her sister. Approaches the bar. Stands next to Ty.

He's living by his *when in Rome* credo in linen pants and a blue t-shirt.

Eve laughs at something he says.

He whispers in her ear.

She laughs again. A little louder. She leans over the bar, ordering drinks for both of them.

Two cans of hard seltzer.

She's teasing me. Teasing him.

She's here. With me.

Here.

Mine.

I want it just as badly with her dressed.

No. I want it more. More than I've wanted anything in a long, long time.

"Ian, I have to be honest. Most of your conquests… are rather dull. But Eve… I think I want her for my birthday." He holds up his drink. "What do you say? Cheers?"

"You'd like me to toast to you—"

"I don't want to fuck her. No offense, Eve," he says.

"None taken," she says.

"None?" I ask.

"I don't want to fuck you either, Ty," she says.

He presses his hand to his heart. "Eve… that hurts."

"Sorry… but I'm just not feeling it," she says.

He laughs. "It's not you. It's that I can't be Ian's sloppy seconds."

"And I'm the kind of girl who would sleep with my ex's brother?" She raises a brow.

He chuckles. "If only things were different…"

"Our cross to bear." She taps her can of seltzer against his. Laughs as she turns to me. "This is truly awful." She takes another sip of mango seltzer. "Despicable."

"Is it?" I ask.

Eve nods. Turns to me. Crosses the space between us.

"Would it be wrong? To threaten to tear this off?" Her fingers brush my shirt. "I thought you'd be less sexy out of a suit… but. Nope." She looks up at me with a smile. "It is strange. To see you in casual clothes."

"Still?" I ask.

She nods *still*. "Mostly it's the suit. Or nothing."

"Please, spare me these horrible details," Ty says.

"He sleeps naked." She smiles, enjoying Ty's pain.

"Boxers, sometimes." I wrap my arm around her waist. Her dress is backless. I can feel her skin against my palm. The warmth of it. The softness. "Otherwise I can't control myself."

She rises to her tiptoes. Presses her lips to mine.

She tastes like heaven. Even with the mango seltzer on her lips.

Eve pulls back with a sigh. "Mmm, gin is so much better than this."

"Take it somewhere else." Ty shakes his head in mock disgust, but he's smiling. He is happy for me. Even with his broken heart.

Eve mouths *sorry*. "You must know what it's like, Ty, being so irresistible."

He nods. "It is a burden."

"But you carry it so well," she says.

"She's dangerous," he says. "Be careful with her."

"I know." I offer her my gin. "We can trade."

"I can't ask you to do that." She stares at her can of seltzer. "This is…"

"Rubbish," Ty offers.

"It really is." She nods.

"Even so." My smile is easy. This is easy. I nearly forget why my brother is here.

"If you insist." She trades drinks. Takes a long sip of gin and tonic. Lets out a low sigh of pleasure.

"Jesus, what have I done?" Ty shakes his head. "I've seen Ian… interested in women before. But never like this."

"Oh?" She just barely blushes. "How is this different?"

He looks to me. Raises a brow *do you really want me to tell it?*

I nod. I'm not sure what he's going to say, but I don't need him sugar coating anything.

"Well, he doesn't usually bring his *dates* to events. And when he does… he doesn't seem as interested in conversation," he says.

"Straight to sex?" she asks.

He laughs. "More or less."

"When it's more? Or wait, would it be less?" She takes another sip. "Does he ever seem to have a mental connection?"

"Every so often. But never an emotional one. He's always… removed," Ty says.

"But not now?" she asks.

He nods. "Since his divorce."

"Oh. Right." She takes another sip. Sucks on an ice cube. Bites it in half. Chews. Swallows. "I guess we shouldn't bring it up. Is cocktail party etiquette the same in the UK? No religion, no politics, no exes?"

"I've never heard the no-exes bit," he says. "Intuitive."

She nods.

"You actually follow this?" His gaze drifts to her tattoo. "It's too bad you weren't in London last summer. One of our chain bookstores went all out for the release of *Testaments*."

Her eyes go wide.

He laughs. "You would have liked it."

"What did they do?" She reaches over. Squeezes my arm. That mindless gesture. One to steady her? Or let her excitement flow into me?

Ty's laugh gets louder. He shoots me a look that can only mean *you're so obviously in love with her*, then he turns all his attention to Eve, and he details the displays.

She hangs on every word.

Then he asks her about the book and she launches into a discussion of the plot, characters, themes, motifs.

I watch her light up. Watch her beam. Watch her soar.

It's so fucking beautiful.

I want it so fucking badly. Whatever it means for me.

I let Ty introduce her to everyone. Tease her. Flirt shamelessly.

Every few minutes, she looks in my direction. Shoots me a knowing glance. One that screams *I need to fuck you*.

And others. Ones that whisper *I need to hold you*.

For once, I listen to both. Let both fill my soul. Figure out the best way to give her exactly what she needs.

I make her wait. Let her anticipation build.

I give her time to grab lunch, refill her drink, dip her feet in the pool.

Then I find her inside. In the downstairs hallway. Just outside the bathroom.

I surprise her. Pull her into my office.

Pin her to the wall. Pull her wrists behind her back. Use the fuchsia tie to bind her wrists.

She groans as she turns her head to the side. "Fuck." Her hair falls in front of her eyes. "Someone might see."

"Do you care?"

Her response is a groan.

"Or do you like it? Do you want someone to watch as I split you in half, vixen?"

Chapter Fifty

IAN

Her gaze flits to the wide window. It's not in direct view of the party. A little to the side. Only visible from the perfect angle.

Only visible through the sheer curtains.

But it is visible.

And that's making her pant.

She rests her forehead against the wall. Sucks a breath through her teeth. "Yes."

"Yes?"

"I do." Her voice is heady. Already lost. "I want someone to watch. I want this... to know we might get caught. To know someone might see."

I tug at the tie to test her restraints.

She groans. "Ian." Her fingers curl into her palms. "Please."

"Please?"

"Yes... please. Fuck me."

"You have to earn that, vixen."

She responds with a groan.

I run my hand over the backline of her dress. From her shoulder blade to the small of her lower back.

Then back up.

Back down.

"You wore this to torture me?" I pull the zipper a centimeter.

She nods into the wall. "Yes."

"You think of me when you dress?"

"Yes."

"You think of how much I'll want to tear off your clothes?"

"Always."

"Always?"

She softens. Melting into me. Into the wall. "Even when you aren't around. I wonder what you'd think. How you'd look at me. I love the way you look at me like you want to consume me."

"I do." I pull her zipper a little lower.

She whimpers.

Pain, pleasure, anticipation?

I'm not sure.

She's thoroughly pinned. No space between the two of us. No space for her to breathe.

It's necessary.

For her to feel I'm in control.

For the intimacy I crave.

For her to believe I might hurt her.

Is that what she wants?

I *can* pull her into my lap, roll her dress to her waist, spank her until she promises to behave.

But she is behaving.

She doesn't want punishment. She wants reward.

And I want to give it to her.

I pull the fabric over her arse. Push one strap off her shoulder.

She shudders as the fabric falls over her chest. "Ian… Please…"

This is what I need. Eve buzzing with anticipation, every molecule in her body tuned to me and me alone.

I need to be her universe.

Everywhere.

If this is the place I get it—

I tug at the tie again.

She lets out a groan. "Please…"

"Please?" I shift my hips so she can feel my hard-on. "Please pull harder?" I tug again. This time enough she arches over me.

She groans as her arse glides over my hard-on.

"Throw you on the bed?" I run my fingers over her shoulder. The strap of her frock.

She groans as I push the strap off her shoulder. As the fabric spills over her chest.

I bring my hand to her breast. Run my thumb over her nipple. "Fuck you right here? Against the wall. So hard your forehead bruises."

"Yes," she breathes.

"Ask for it."

"Ian…"

I tug at the tie. "Ask for it." I shift my hips, pinning her harder.

So much she can barely breathe.

But she does. She sucks a breath through her nose. Pushes one through her teeth.

"Please." She shifts her hips. Just barely. She hasn't got any room.

But it's enough to drive me insane.

I need to be inside her. Now. No teasing, no patience, no games.

I need to stay in control.

To stay her entire universe.

"Please?" I draw circles around her nipple. Harder and harder. Until her groan is pain as much as pleasure.

"Fuck me. Please."

"Fuck you?"

"On the bed. In front of the mirror."

"You want to watch?"

"Yes."

Fuck. I can't say no to that.

"Please." She just barely shifts her hips.

Yes. But not yet. I need to feel her this close. To feel every part of her body pressed against mine.

I push her dress off her hips.

Then her knickers.

She lets them fall to her feet.

"Not yet." I hold her in place as I do away with my clothes.

Then I bring my hands to her hips. Hold her body against mine.

Soak in all her warmth, her softness, her need.

She needs to be mine.

But it's not—

I don't know what's possible anymore. Only that I need her.

I press my lips to her neck. A soft kiss. Then harder.

Hard enough she groans.

Hard enough she whines.

I keep one hand on the tie binding her wrists. Bring the other to her hip. Tilt her just enough.

"Fuck." Her voice is pure need.

It's there. Everything I feel.

The bliss of my body joining hers.

The sweet softness of her cunt stretching to take me.

Slowly, I push inside her.

I hold her close. Inhale everything about the moment. The smell of her shampoo. The taste of her skin.

Then I pull back and push into her again.

She groans as her forehead presses into the wall.

Again.

Slow at first.

Then harder.

Hard enough her groans run together.

Hard enough she yelps. Turns her head. Reaches for release.

Part of the scene?

Or an actual request?

I promised to push her. I did. I have.

But right now—

My thoughts aren't straight enough. I don't trust myself enough.

I bring my hand to her throat.

She groans as I take a half-step back. Pull her with me.

Her eyes go to the floor. The wall. The mirror across from the bed.

Perpendicular to us.

She can't see our reflection.

She's reaching for it.

I hold her body against mine. Bring her to the bed. Push her onto it.

She lets her head roll to one side. Then the other. Her gaze shifts to the mirror.

She's desperate to watch.

And I—

Need more first.

I turn her over. Drop to my knees in front of her. Push her legs apart.

"Watch." I press my lips to her thigh. "Watch as you come on my face, vixen."

She responds with a groan. For a moment, her eyes fix on me. She stares at me like I'm the only thing she wants.

Then her gaze shifts to the mirror.

She watches as I pin her thighs to the bed. As I drag my lips up her leg.

Bring my mouth to her cunt.

She tastes like heaven.

And the way she shakes as I lick her—

I take one moment for myself. To taste every fucking part of her.

Then I bring my mouth to her clit. To the spot she likes.

She gasps as I flick my tongue against her. "Fuck." Her breath hitches.

I dig my nails into her skin as I flick my tongue against her.

Again and again.

Until she's writhing against my hands.

Until she's there.

I pull back to take in our reflection. The pleasure spreading over her expression. The arch of her back. The bind of her wrists.

My hands on her thighs.

I keep her on the edge for one perfect moment.

Then I bring my mouth to her clit. Give her exactly what she needs.

She groans as I flick my tongue against her.

Again and again.

Until she's there, groaning my name as she comes on my lips.

I work her through her orgasm. Then I rise. Flip her onto her back. Redo her binding.

Through the mirror, she makes eye contact. Stares at me with all the need and trust in the world.

She trusts me with her body. Trusts me to tease her. To give her exactly what she craves.

I push her legs apart.

She watches as I lift her hips and slide inside her.

Her eyes close for a moment. Bliss spreads over her expression. It's too much for her to take.

But she is going to take it.

"Watch." I run my nails over her arse.

She just barely nods. Slowly, her eyes flutter open. Slowly, her gaze fixes on our reflection.

She watches as I drive into her again.

And again.

Fuck.

She's soft and wet and mine.

Mine.

Maybe not forever.

But right now.

I drive into her again and again.

Until she's so wracked with pleasure she has to close her eyes.

Until I'm the only thing in her fucking universe.

Then I bring my hand to her throat. Grip her tight enough to push her over the edge.

This time, she comes fast.

Her cunt pulses around me. Pulling me closer. Consuming every thought in my brain.

A few more thrusts and I'm there.

I groan her name as I come.

As I spill every fucking drop.

Then I release her. Undo the tie binding her wrists. Hold her close.

She curls into my chest.

Dissolves between my arms.

Still mine.

Maybe not forever.

Or for long enough.

But for now.

———

I WAKE TO NEWS FROM TY.

The meeting is set.

The date is fixed.

In a week, I sign the papers that sever the last tie between me and Laura.

In two weeks, I send Eve on her way.

In two weeks, I return to my usual state. Alone. No attachments threatening to tear my heart in pieces.

I need every single day with her.

So when Eve wakes and moves into the kitchen, I pull her into my arms.

Whisper in her ear, "I have to go to London. Next week."

"For how long?"

"A few days."

"You're going to London for Fourth of July?"

Of course. "I didn't consider that." I press my lips to her neck. "Come with me."

"Go to London for Fourth of July?"

"I'll take you to see Hamilton in the West End."

"Huh." She pulls back enough to look me in the eyes. "I'm not sure where that lands on the patriotism scale."

"What about that dancer?"

"With the Union Jack?"

I nod. "I'll buy you American flag knickers."

She laughs. "That's… something. I… I'll have to consider it."

"Or you could skip the knickers."

She rests her head on my chest. Melts into me. "Are you sure? I've never been to London. I'll be an annoying tourist. You'll be an expert."

"I'll see the city through your eyes."

"Yeah?"

"Yeah." I press my lips to hers.

"Plus the underwear?"

"Of course." I kiss her again. "What could be better than a vixen in red, white, and blue?"

Chapter Fifty-One

EVE

Tragically, we fly to London with Ty. Don't get me wrong. I like Ty a lot. And this is probably the last time I'm going to see him. Or one of the last.

Only it's the end of my time with Ian.

I don't want to talk to his brother.

I want to climb into Ian's lap and follow his every command.

I want to fall asleep in his arms. Wake up in his bed. Tell him all my secrets.

One of those things is possible.

The others…

I don't know anymore.

———

THE CITY IS PERFECT.

Somehow bigger and smaller than New York. More space, more history, more politeness. The giant bookstore Ty mentioned. All over the central part of the city.

The more I see, the more I want to see. Prisons and

crown jewels at The Tower of London, the Houses of Parliament, Big Ben, Borough Market.

High tea at an iconic department store.

A gin tasting—six gins, on their own, and with tonic water.

It's exactly like Ian said. Fever Tree is everywhere. A dozen varieties.

Sure enough, he goes all out on Fourth of July. An "American Barbecue" restaurant in the outskirts of the city. Balcony seats at *Hamilton*. An "American Bar" that serves mostly Coke and bourbon.

And when we get back to his apartment…

He's wearing American Flag boxers.

It's absurd.

And too sexy for words.

But I guess that's Ian Hunt.

Chapter Fifty-Two

IAN

A perfect week in London.

Leading to this.

I sign the papers tomorrow.

Face my past tomorrow.

Lose my fucking shit tomorrow.

Sleep is impossible.

Around three a.m., I give up.

For a moment, I watch Eve. She's wearing one of my t-shirts, her teal hair messy, her face free of makeup, her expression serene.

I can wake her up. Talk to her. Ask her to reassure me. Promise she isn't hiding anything that matters.

Promise she isn't falling for some other man.

Fucking him.

Thinking of him as she fucks me.

It's ridiculous. I trust her. She trusts me. She's offered me so much.

And it's completely illogical. Impossible. When would she have met another man, much less fallen for him?

My head refuses to accept my reasoning.

My heart refuses to accept her open smile.

The idea stays in my head.

My thoughts scatter.

My chest tenses.

My sky clouds.

Less than twelve hours until I face my ex-wife. Until I listen to her bollocks excuse.

Or maybe an apology.

A snub.

Nothing.

Which is worse? I don't know.

I let Eve sleep. Slide into my office. Try to find a distraction. A game. A TV show.

Work.

Email.

Pictures she's sent me.

Pictures of us.

Nothing steals my attention.

It's there. This ticking clock.

Five hours.

Less.

And there's the one thing I want.

It's right there. On my fucking monitor. The RSS feed for Eve's site.

Three new entries.

She asks for time to herself. To read, write, think. Post thoughts of me for the entire world.

It's right there.

Her head, her heart, her secrets.

Her secrets.

Not mine.

I can't take them.

There's no justifying it.

I can't take her thoughts.

But I do.
I read every word. Every new post. Every old one.
Every single thing in her head.
Every feeling.
Every thought.
I take them. Hold them close. Claim them as mine.

Chapter Fifty-Three

EVE

here's a brush of lips on my cheek. Fingers on my neck. A soft goodbye.

He's already leaving.

He's already dressed. Black suit, fuchsia tie, black dress shoes.

The tie he uses to bind me.

The Ian I met a month ago. And the Ian I know now.

There's so much tension in his dark eyes.

"Go back to bed, vixen." He pulls the covers up my chest. "No reason we should both suffer."

"Are you sure?" I reach for him, but he's too far away. "I can come with you. Hold your hand."

"No." He presses his lips to my forehead. "I have to do this alone."

———

I TRY, BUT SLEEP ELUDES ME.

I get up. Pee, wash my hands, brush my teeth, dress. Then it's breakfast, tea, makeup, extra makeup.

Anything to occupy my hands and my mind.

After my fourth round of eyeliner, I give up on typical distractions. Find the ultimate distraction in my suitcase.

Ian's copy of *The Handmaid's Tale*.

My favorite book. His notes.

My obsession.

His thoughts.

The perfect marriage of everything I want.

I start from the beginning.

Chapter Fifty-Four

IAN

The office is the same as always. So much like my office in New York. Only missing the most important element: The western coast of the Atlantic.

The same wide windows, ergonomic chairs, open spaces.

The all glass conference room. So everyone can see exactly what's happening. So everyone can watch Laura twist the knife in my back.

No. This is a good thing. The tearing of the plaster.

It has to hurt now.

I can take it.

The office is bustling, as always. Quiet conversations, typing, the steam of the electric kettle. My brother.

"You look terrible." He offers me a mug of tea. "Should I put a little rum in this?"

I wave it away.

"Honestly, Ian. Especially for a man who spent the last week getting laid—"

"Don't—"

He chuckles. "You're defensive about her."

I nod. Of course, I'm defensive about Eve. How else would I be?

"You like her."

"We've been over this."

"I like her too."

"You certainly talked enough."

There's a hint of tension in his laugh. He's trying to hide it. To keep me from hurling the nearest object at one of these ridiculous glass walls.

I should thank him for the effort. But my mouth is sticky. My limbs are stiff.

I take the tea. English Breakfast with extra milk and honey. The way our mother drinks it.

Almost familiar enough to comfort.

"I'm sorry." His voice stays teasing. "Was it that painful, going six hours without getting her naked?"

I almost laugh. "It was."

"I can imagine."

"You better not."

"If I do?" he asks.

"I'm ready to hit someone."

"Yes, but do you know which woman is causing this stir in your chest?"

"This is not the time, Ty."

He nods *of course not, but when is it the time?* "You're usually more restrained."

"I'm restrained."

He makes that *hmmm* noise that means *like hell*. "Are you ready to set up now?"

"Not yet."

His gaze flits to his watch. A gift from me. Not the one he usually wears, the one he bought with his ex-girlfriend. "You have a few minutes."

I have no concept of time. Has it been minutes or hours? It's too bright in here. Too hot. Too suffocating.

"I'll set up. Compose yourself." He takes my tea. Motions to the loo down the hall.

It's fair advice. I watch him move into the conference room. Watch as eyes turn to Ty.

He's in the office most days.

Maybe this is what everyone does when there's a meeting. Maybe it's got nothing to do with the upcoming train wreck.

I suck a breath through my nose. Push an exhale through my teeth. It's not enough.

I move down the hall. Into the quiet room.

Cool water fails to help.

I wash my hands three times. Dry them on a paper towel. Try to find some greater sense of calm. How do I normally do it? What do I normally think?

The last time I was this ready to burst—was when I read the offer on Eve's site. But it was different. A primal need to protect her, hold her, claim her.

To run toward what I wanted.

Not away from a great source of pain.

Who runs toward a fire?

After another deep breath, I move into the hallway. Around the corner. All the way to the conference room.

She's there.

All fair skin, brown eyes, dark hair. Like Snow White. Or maybe the Evil Queen who poisons Snow White.

She laughs at something Ty says. Not a full laugh. Not the no-holds-barred joy she's capable of. That she was capable of.

I don't know what the fuck she's capable of now.

Her smile gets wider. Softer. More honest.

Her hand goes to her stomach. She's not showing, but it's obvious from her posture.

I want to be happy for her. I do.

Some part of me is.

She looks the same. Still tall and curvy. Still impossibly poised and more stylish than anyone else in the room.

Trendy red frock. Black pumps. Long hair hanging loose over her shoulders. And whatever she's done with her jewelry and makeup—

She looks like Laura. There's no other way to explain it.

She follows Ty's gaze as he looks to me.

Her eyes catch mine. They fill with all sorts of things I don't want to place. Regret. Pity. Affection. Relief.

I'm not throwing anything. Not yet.

I take a deep breath and move into the conference room.

"Ian." She takes a step toward me. Offers her hand. "It's good to see you."

Ty looks at me like I'm a bomb with ten seconds on the clock. "We're a little pushed for time. We should get started."

"It's fine." I'm fine. I am over her. She has no power over me. I'm going to forgive her, wish her the best, move on.

This is it. The end of a fifteen-year saga. Not the happy ending I expected, but it's not as if I want that any longer.

"You are glowing." It's three steps toward her.

She shakes with a firm grip. "Is it that obvious?"

"Yes."

"I…" She releases my hand. "Thank you."

I pull out her chair for her. After she sits, I take the seat across from her.

We have the width of the table between us, not the length.

Two meters maybe.

It's not enough space.

She folds one leg over the other. Smooths her dress. Folds her hands in her lap.

Ty motions to the folders on the table. "It's simple. The two of you sign. I act as your witness. That's all."

Laura's voice is soft. "That's all?"

He nods. "Ian buys your share. The money in escrow transfers to your account. That's all."

She turns to Ty. "Could we have a minute?"

He shoots me that same look. No, it's worse. As if the bomb is flashing *one second* and he doesn't know which wire to pull.

"Why don't you bring us something to drink. To celebrate. It won't be champagne, but we must have some sparkling cider." Somehow, my voice stays even. Calm. One meeting and it's over. She's completely out of my life. I'm completely out of hers.

"It almost sounds as if you think I'm your assistant." Ty's voice is equal parts playful and threatening. "I'll tell you the same thing I told Eve. For Laura, of course. But you can fuck off, Ian."

"Eve?" Laura's eyes flare with interest. "You're seeing someone?"

Ty nods *you're welcome* and moves to the door. "I'll give you a few minutes."

I wait until he's down the hall. "Yes."

"Is it serious?"

My gaze flits to her wedding ring. "We're taking it day by day."

"Oh." She wraps her hand around her mug. Coffee,

I'm sure. Decaf maybe, but undoubtedly something with a lot of milk and sugar. "For how long?"

"It's new."

She nods *right*. Takes a small sip. Places her cup on the table.

The soft thunk echoes around the room.

The air-conditioning hums.

Her heels clack.

"Are you happy?" She places her palm on the table.

"What does that matter?"

"I know you don't understand it, but I do love you, Ian. I'll always love you. I want to know you're okay."

I see red. Only bright, blinding, vicious light. "You love me?"

"Yes."

"Was that what you were thinking when you were fucking David?"

"Ian—"

"Ten months. That I know about. How long was it really?"

She holds her position.

"A year? Two? Our entire fucking marriage? Is that why you went to bed so early in Paris? Because you needed to get up in time to call him and talk him off?"

"Of course not."

"Of course?"

She shrinks back, hurt. But she knows it's fair. Presses on anyway. "It went on longer than it should have. I'm sorry. I don't need you to accept that. I don't need you to forgive me. But I am sorry."

"Why are you here, Laura?"

She's quiet for a long moment. "Don't you want closure?"

I swallow hard.

"I still loved you, Ian. It wasn't that. I just… it was one little thing. One thing I couldn't tell you. I can't even remember what it was now. Something about work. Something I knew you'd dismiss. I knew you'd tell me you could find me something else. That I didn't need to stay at the job I hated. That you had plenty."

"You're here because you don't want my money?" That's rich. She's walking away from this deal with seven figures in her bank account. "Should we rewrite the terms? You relinquish everything?"

Her inhale is sharp. "If you don't want to listen, fine. I'll sign the papers, leave, never contact you again. You're right. I'm the one who slept with someone else. I'm the one who pulled the plug. I'm the one at fault."

I don't want her apology or her non-apology. I've heard it before. I've heard it enough I'm numb. It's fucking *Wonderwall*. I never need to hear it again.

"I'll say it once. I'm sorry. Really, Ian. I'm sorry I lied to you. I'm sorry I didn't wait until we were through. I'm sorry I put that burden on you. I was a coward. I was weak. I was wrong."

What am I supposed to say—thank you?

"I just… I want you to understand. For both our sakes."

"For my sake?"

"Yes." Her voice stays soft. Careful. Like I'm a child she's trying not to scare. "Don't you want to understand what happened? Why we grew apart? Why I'd wake up in the morning next to you and feel like I'd slept with a stranger?"

"You were with someone else."

"Before that. For a long time before that. I… you were gone, Ian. You weren't there with me anymore. I know that doesn't excuse anything, but I… I don't want to be absolved. I don't want to hurt you more. I just… I want to shake your hand and know that we'll both be okay."

"You've done fine."

"And you haven't?"

"No." It echoes around the room. Fills the air until the entire place is suffocating.

"I wish things had been different. I really do."

"You were—"

"Yes, I was fucking someone else. That was my fault. If you want to keep repeating it, fine, I'll go. But let me say this first. Please."

"Fine."

Her gaze flits to the floor. She stares at it for a long moment, like she's expecting some sort of solace. "I still don't know what happened. Not exactly. One day, you were my rock. I understood you perfectly. I knew what you wanted for breakfast. I knew what you'd say to my friends. I knew how you'd handle a bad day. And I knew I'd be okay if I woke up next to you."

Her eyes meet mine for a moment. They search for something. Some sympathy she's not going to find.

She continues. "Then… it started so long ago. After that trip you took to Madrid. You came back distant. You wouldn't share the same way. You wouldn't ask the same questions. When I talked, you were off someplace. Sometimes, at first. Then all the time. I should have said something then. It was still so small, but it kept getting bigger. I kept telling myself it was fine. That I'd handle it later, when work was easier, after the holidays, after I finished these doctor's appointments. Then my mother got sick—"

And she was already pulling away from me.

I saw it then. I didn't stop her.

That doesn't excuse anything.

But—

I do know how that hurts. How much it hurt her, losing her mother.

How much it killed me, that she wouldn't let me share that burden.

"I am sorry about Beth," I say.

She nods a *thank you*. "By the time I was dealing with it, you were on another planet. I didn't know how to bridge the distance. And David was there. He listened. He cared. He still looked at me like I was new and exciting."

"I cared."

"I know. I knew then. I just... I needed to feel it." She presses her hands together. "It's not an excuse. I should have done something to make you listen. I should have tried harder. But... I didn't know what else to do. You weren't there. I needed you and you weren't there."

No. That's ridiculous.

I was—

I don't know anymore. Her voice is honest, raw, vulnerable.

The Laura I knew. The Laura I loved.

So close. And different in some impossible to place way.

It explains everything.

And nothing.

It just happened.

What the fuck does that explain?

Where's the godforsaken closure?

"Is that all?" I pick up the pen.

She presses her lips together. "I don't know... I thought you'd have a response."

"Why?"

"I just told you—"

"Why didn't you try? Why didn't you give me a chance? Why did you break my trust like that?"

She swallows hard. "Because it was easier. And I wasn't strong enough."

That's the best explanation I'm ever going to get.

It's not enough.

To erase this.

To forgive her.

To unlock the safe hiding my heart.

I have to find that somewhere else.

I sign the paper. Push it to her. "I understand."

She nods. Accepting my response. Finding no solace in it.

I suppose that makes two of us.

Chapter Fifty-Five

EVE

I t's there. On the page.

The brilliant words of Margaret Atwood.

And Ian's writing in blue ink.

Is this the place where she falls in love? Or is it later?

It doesn't make any sense. Not as a comment on the book. It's not a scene about Offred's husband Luke. Or her would-be lover Nick. She's not remembering her family. Or asking if her husband is dead, wounded, free?

The comment makes no sense.

Unless...

No.

A few months ago, I did a full re-read on my site, Original Sin. I went through the book, section by section, diving into my favorite scenes, trying to find meaning in every word.

I devoted a lot of text to this one.

Called it the place I really fell in love, on my first read.

I've talked about the book a lot. To anyone who will listen. And I do have this very obvious tattoo on my arm.

But I've never discussed this scene with Ian.

Or have I?

I talk about this book so much. It's easy to forget. Like my tea every morning. I don't remember any specific chai latte. Just the taste of cinnamon and cardamom.

I turn the page. Skim his writing. Comments about the book. The scene. The place in society.

Then another one.

From experience or imagination?

A scene at a brothel.

I talk about my job. At Devil's Point. I don't say the club, but I'm not shy about the details. The men who think twenty dollars buys them free rein. The assholes who treat me like a challenge—*maybe I can get her to show me her tits, at least*. The jerks who rate dancers' bodies on a one to ten scale.

Yes, working at that place put this book in a new light. It opened my eyes to all sorts of things I tried to ignore.

But Ian…

He knows I worked there.

But when would he have written this?

And how did he know I like chai? That I've never been to London? That I love my sister more than anything?

That I needed money desperately?

Why did he come into Devil's Point that night?

He knew… he already knew what he was doing.

There's only one explanation that makes sense.

But he would have told me by now. He would have told me he read Original Sin. That he saw my post about the doctor and—

Fuck.

Why would he offer me half a million dollars?

Unless he knew.

He read my site.

He found me there.

He came in looking for me.
Not because I was a virgin in search of a benefactor.
Because it was me.
He knew and he—
All this time.
And he didn't tell me.
How could he not tell me?

Chapter Fifty-Six

IAN

There's noise in the apartment. Not a quiet drama. Or prestige TV show. Or the thrashing guitar music Eve adores.

Her footsteps.

Loud and harried.

They stop as the door swings shut.

Then they start again.

She's in the bedroom. And she's rushing.

"Eve?" I move through the main room.

My heart rises in my throat as I turn the corner.

She's in the bedroom, in jeans and a tank top, pushing clothes into her bright pink suitcase. She catches the shadow moving over the room. Turns to me.

Her eyes meet mine for a split second. The same curiosity, but entirely different. *How could you?*

She—

Fuck.

"Where are you going?" I move into the room. Stand in front of the door. It's not fair to block her exit, but I don't give a fuck.

"Anywhere."

"Don't."

She shakes her head, sending stray locks over her eyes.

"You don't know the city, Eve. It's not safe."

"You lost the right to offer paternalistic advice." She shoves a black sandal in her suitcase. Looks around the room. Scanning it for what's left. She doesn't find anything on the floor. Turns to the door instead. "Could you please move?"

"No."

"Do I need to ask less nicely?"

"No."

She moves to the door. Stands in front of me, all fire and anger and defiance.

"You can go. But let me book you a hotel. Or call someone."

"I'm a grown-up."

"Please."

Her eyes fix on mine. "You already know why I'm leaving?"

"Does it matter?"

She takes a half-step toward me. Challenging me to push her back or pull her closer. One of the two. "That's not an answer."

"Yes, I know."

"Are you going to try to stop me?"

"If I can. If I can't, at least let me arrange for your transport. Please."

"Was it this whole time?" She holds her position. "Have you been reading everything I've written this entire time?"

"No."

"No? Only when you needed to laugh to yourself *ah, how stupid is this little girl, she'll never realize I hold all the fucking cards?*"

"No." I reach for her arm.

She slips sideways. Moves past me. Through the hallway. To the bathroom. Hurries through collecting her makeup. "Then when?"

"It's how I found you, yes."

"Didn't think to mention that?"

"What would I have said?"

"That's not the point."

"I couldn't let someone else…"

She shakes her head. "Oh no, couldn't let someone else touch me. God forbid."

"Eve—"

"That *is* what it was about."

"Yes. It still makes me sick. Thinking of someone else touching you, kissing you, fucking you. Some other man making you come, holding you tight, waking up next to you."

Her cheeks flame red. Not adorable blush. All fury.

She scoops makeup into her patent leather case. Her gestures are messy. She's too angry to move.

"You should have told me." Her breath is heavy. "You found me through Original Sin, fine. It's a public site. You didn't know me. You didn't owe me anything. But Ian, you… you touched me. You fucked me. You came inside me. How could you not tell me?"

What the fuck can I say? I've spent the last four years hating Laura for holding her tongue. I know *I'm sorry* is insufficient. But I don't have anything better. "I'm sorry."

"Why?" She shakes her head. Holds her bag to her chest. "You know what, it doesn't matter. I don't care that you're sorry. I don't care if you had good intentions. You should have told me before you fucked me."

"Eve—"

"No. You can't arrange my transport. You can't book me a hotel room. You can't call me a car."

"Please."

"No. I want you to worry. I want you to stay up all night wondering if I'm fucking someone else."

My stomach turns.

"You don't get to sleep safe and sound. Not when I have to spend the entire night wondering what the fuck you were pulling with me."

"I wasn't pulling anything."

"Bullshit." She stares at me. Seething. Shaking with anger. "Move."

I can't let her go. Not like this. "Our arrangement isn't over."

She scoffs.

"You have to be where I say."

"Fuck you."

"I won't ask you to stay here."

"Seriously, Ian. Fuck you."

It's pushing her further away. Maybe forever. But I have to take that risk. I'm not letting her run around the city alone and angry. I've been there. It's not a pretty place.

She's scrappy yes, but she can't hold her own against a man who wants to hurt her. I'm not giving anyone the chance.

"I'm calling Ty," I say. "To pick you up. I'll leave. Give you the chance to pack in peace. I won't ask anything else from you. Do what you want with the next five days. After I make sure you get home okay."

Her eyes narrow. "You're not doing a noble thing."

"Even so."

She turns, putting her back to me. "Fine." Her voice just barely steadies. "If you leave right now."

"Okay."

"Not soon. This instant."

Fuck, this might be the last time I see her. It swallows me whole. The fear of losing her. A need to hold her close. To inhale every detail. "Goodbye, Eve."

She says nothing.

"Take care. Please." I give her a moment to respond, but she doesn't.

Chapter Fifty-Seven

EVE

Ty arrives quickly. Fixes two drinks—gin, on the rocks, of course—brings my things to a cab, whisks me into the back seat.

He doesn't try to reason with me. Or ask what's wrong. Or offer some explanation for his brother.

He doesn't remind me of the promise I made in New York.

Or how I don't really have a say in where I go. If Ian wanted, he could demand I stay in his apartment until the end of day thirty.

He doesn't suggest that this—Ian only insisting on arranging safe transportation—is generous.

I don't have to say it's bullshit. I'm an adult. I've taken care of myself, in New York City, for a long time. I can find my way around London. I can get to the airport.

I can.

But it's different being here. Unfamiliar. In an exciting way. And an unnerving one. I don't know the subway map. I don't know the best way to the airport. I don't know the places with the best tea.

Ian does.

This is still his city.

And I…

Ugh.

The cab stops at a quiet street. Mostly apartments, a nearby park, a pub. It's still early, but I know where I want to go.

Ty helps me out of the car. After he pays the driver, he grabs my suitcase and leads me to a new apartment building.

Through a lux lounge. Up the elevator to the penthouse. It's beautiful—all white tile and hardwood and wide windows.

Clean. Modern. Sparse.

No. Not sparse exactly. It isn't like Ian's place in New York. It isn't free of the things that make a house a home. It's just the touches are subtle. Small. Framed photos of family. Packed bookshelf. Pots of flowers.

And missing spaces where framed photos used to be. Has he already started to erase his ex from his life? Or does he need time to process?

Is it better to forget someone who hurt you? It can't be better to forget.

"I'll put you in the spare bedroom." He looks to me for permission. When I nod, he carries my suitcase to a room down the hall. Leaves it there. Returns. "Rory left some toiletries." He pushes through the hurt in his voice. "If you need anything else."

"It's only for today."

"You're not going to shower today?"

Right. He's not the one who lied to me. I shouldn't let my resting bitch face escalate to active bitch face. "Thanks, Ty."

He nods *of course*. "Are you hungry?"

I shake my head.

"Thirsty?"

"What do you drink here?"

His laugh is soft. Easy. "Anything you like."

"What if I like hard seltzer?"

He offers me a sad smile. It hurts him too, filling this role. Because he likes me? Or because he doesn't want his brother to get hurt? "Anything a reasonable person would like."

"Were you really a bartender?"

He nods.

"How's your Manhattan?"

"Homesick?"

"Maybe..." I don't usually drink bourbon. And I certainly didn't have many Manhattans at Devil's Point. There's no way our bitters were worthy of any bourbon. "I thought... I don't know. Whatever you're having."

He nods. Fills two glasses with filtered water from the fridge door. Looks to me. "The couch or the counter?" He motions to the kitchen island.

"Couch."

He brings the glasses to the couch. Motions for me to sit.

I hug the pastel purple blanket as I sit. It's not enough to comfort, but it's something. It's all I have.

Ty watches me for a moment, then he moves into the kitchen. And, well, he still keeps one eye on me—it's all one, big room—but the other stays on drinks.

He really does have everything. Bitters, orange peel, maraschino cherry, Vermouth, shaker, cocktail glass.

He finishes the drinks. Brings them to the table. Hands one to me. "Cheers." He holds his glass to toast.

"Cheers." I tap my glass against his. Take a long sip. It's been awhile since I've had a Manhattan. It's sweeter than I remember. And stronger. My head is already spinning.

But that must be my imagination. Alcohol doesn't absorb this quickly.

And I…

Maybe that's it. I need to get drunk, cry to Addie, go home… cry to Addie more. Not think about how I'm three thousand miles from home in a near-stranger's apartment.

All right, that isn't fair. I know Ty well. Well enough, I trust him.

He rests his back on the couch. Takes a long sip. Lets out an easy sigh.

He's wearing a suit, but he still looks at home. But then isn't today… a Wednesday? I'm not sure. I lost track a few days ago.

If Ian and Ty went into the office—it must be a work-day. He's supposed to be at work. But he's here.

"You're taking time off to babysit me?" I ask.

"None of my babysitters fixed me Manhattans."

"No? Only straight gin on the rocks?"

He laughs. It's an easy laugh. It lights up his eyes.

He really is handsome. He looks so much like Ian but so different too.

He's confident, rich, sexy.

But I don't want him. Not even a little.

He's just… not Ian.

Ugh.

I take another sip. Let it warm my lips, tongue, throat. "I need to find that babysitter."

"What am I?"

"Loyal to your brother."

He nods *fair*. "But I mix a good cocktail."

"Cheers to that." I raise my glass to toast.

"Cheers." He takes a long sip. Studies me. His eyes look

so much like Ian's, but the way he studies me is completely different. All concern, no fascination.

"Are you trying to loosen my tongue?"

"Why would I do that?"

I take another sip. Mmm, it really is good. Rich and sweet. Expensive. "To learn Ian's secrets."

"No offense, Eve, but I don't have any interest in what my brother does when he ties you up."

"Jesus."

"I've heard enough for one lifetime."

"I meant more…" Fuck, I can't think. Damn Ian's sex appeal. Distracting me even when he isn't here. "Other types of secrets."

"You have some?"

I nod. "And you?" It hits me with my next sip. The promise he asked me to make in New York. "You knew, didn't you?"

"Knew?"

"Don't play dumb. You're obviously quick. You knew he was reading my site."

He nods. "He told me in New York."

"You didn't know before?"

"I had my suspicions." His eyes flit to the bookshelf in the corner. "Ian doesn't read a lot of literature."

"Oh."

"Six months ago… it was all he could talk about. This brilliant woman who had all these insights. How he never appreciated *The Handmaid's Tale* or the appeal of intellectual women. His ex-wife is more…"

"A singer, right?"

He nods. "Smart, but not cerebral. Interested in things she sees and hears. Not abstract ideas. Or the themes in literature."

"Music?"

"Yes, but not the lyrics or the theory. The experience of it. The melody, the rhythm, the feel of dancing. It was good for him being with someone like that. He was too much in his head. Especially after Dad died. But… no relationship is perfect."

"If you're trying to convince me to give him another chance, you can save your breath."

"I know better than to try to convince you of anything."

Uh-huh. "How's that?"

"You're stubborn."

"Oh, it's because I'm stubborn? Not because he's full of shit?"

"Is he?"

Whatever. I finish my drink. Set it on the coffee table. Pull the blanket a little tighter.

Ty lets the silence fall. He finishes his drink slowly. Stands. Brings both glasses to the kitchen.

He's methodical about fixing another round and bringing it to the coffee table.

He waits until he's on the couch to speak. "Do you want to know what I think?"

"Do I have a choice?"

He laughs. "I really do like you, Eve."

"Thanks." I guess.

"When Ian told me you'd be at the party, I didn't know what to think. He doesn't invite women into his life. And his arrangements… you're not on even ground. I suppose his parting gifts make that easier, but…"

"It's not for you?"

"No. I'm not sure it's for him, really. He wasn't happy with a new woman every few months. He enjoyed it, sure, but there was something missing. He didn't admit it. He didn't see it… but I did. I know what he looks like happy."

"Oh."

"You make him happy. You're good for him." He takes a long sip. "We've just met. I can't say if he's good for you. But you did seem happy around him."

"Because I didn't know he was…" How could he not tell me? I take a long sip. It's too much. So much I cough. But I push through it. I need to relax my thoughts. Make everything fuzzy. "I should probably tell you to fuck off. Since you knew."

"Probably."

"Would you have told me?"

"No. Like you said. My loyalty is to him."

"So this… I can't really trust a thing you say?"

"Probably. But that won't stop me from arranging your flight. Or taking you to the airport."

"I can find my own way."

"I'm sure you can. But a promise is a promise."

I guess that's true. And I'm sure there's no sense in arguing with him. And even though he is an awful traitor —even if he did have no reason to pledge loyalty to me—I appreciate the familiarity.

I can't collapse in my bed and cry to my sister.

This is the best I can do.

It's not enough.

But it's still the best I can do.

Chapter Fifty-Eight

EVE

After my third Manhattan, my thoughts blur.

Ty keeps me entertained with British TV and takeaway. We order Indian food.

Ian was right. It's fucking amazing. Better than anything I've had in New York. Or maybe that's the Manhattans talking.

After a few hours of Agatha Christie adaptations, Ty cuts me off. He gives me space.

I change, shower, put myself to bed.

Wake up at three a.m. with a splitting headache and a painfully dry mouth. Sleep returns in fits. An hour here. Twenty minutes of *what the fuck* there.

I can't explain why I feel so betrayed. Ian had every right to read my site when he didn't know me. It's out there. It's a public site.

In theory…

I invited the entire world to read it.

But it's mine. My space to spill my ugly thoughts.

He knew that. He knew it was mine. He knew he was taking something that wasn't his.

Why was it okay when he didn't know me and wrong when he did?

Why didn't he tell me?

If he'd just told me…

I don't know. What would I have done if he told me?

———

Fuck. It's bright in here. Too bright.

And loud.

The air-conditioning is screaming.

I push myself out of bed. Shower. Brush my teeth twice. Fail to wipe away that fuzzy feeling. Manhattan, how could you fuck me like this?

I'm trying to get home to you. Okay, to Brooklyn, but close enough.

What's so great about alcohol anyway?

It's fun for a few hours. For a few drinks. But the second I cross that line—

It's nonstop misery.

Whose brilliant idea was it to fly across the Atlantic with a hangover?

Ugh.

Ty is in the main room. Awake and dressed in casual clothes. He looks at home in jeans and a t-shirt. But then he looks at home in his suit too.

"You look different without makeup," he says.

"You know you're not supposed to say that."

"I didn't say better."

"You didn't say worse."

His laugh is easy. "More vulnerable."

Is it that obvious?

"Prettier. But less yourself."

"Should I say thank you or fuck you?"

"Up to you."

"Maybe slap you. Just in case."

"Maybe." He half-smiles. "How did you sleep?"

I shake my head.

"There's a painkiller on the counter. Porridge on the stove. Ian says that's what you prefer."

"Yeah, thanks."

"He dropped something off."

My stomach seizes. My heart thuds against my chest. "He did?"

Ty nods. Rises from his spot on the couch. Moves to the kitchen island. A thermos—a tacky touristy one with a picture of Big Ben—filled with chai. And a small, leather-bound notebook.

"What is it?"

"He didn't tell me. Forbade me from reading it."

"Oh." My fingers brush the cover. It's faded. Worn. Like it's been through hell and back. Or been loved to death. Is there a difference?

"We have to leave in two hours. If that isn't enough time to pack—"

"No. I'm mostly packed. I just… Can you turn down the sun?"

He laughs. "I'll ring up God and get on that."

"Thanks. I appreciate it." Ugh. I find the sunglasses in my purse. Change into something presentable enough for the airport, apply a little lipstick, enough concealer I don't look like death. And while I'm at it, how about some thick eyeliner? And maybe blush too.

There. I still look tired, but in a *fuck off* way. Not a *notice I'm heartbroken and offer to help* way.

I linger in the quiet room. I need the space to myself. The distance from everything.

When I can't take the lack of caffeine anymore, I move into the main room.

The chai is still warm. And it's perfectly mixed too. A hint of honey, a lot of cardamom, enough almond milk it's rich and creamy.

I pick at my oatmeal. British style oatmeal is mushier than I like. And my stomach is not in the mood for food.

I know it will help, so I force myself to eat a few bites. Chase them with another ibuprofen and a tall glass of water.

The notebook is right there. Waiting for me. Begging me to peel it apart.

My fingers skim the edges. The leather tie holding them together. The papers inside. Thick. Like they're bursting from the pressure of the thoughts they contain.

I pick it up.

A sheet of paper falls to the counter.

A note. From Ian.

Eve,

You're right. I should have told you. I should have stayed away from your site after we met. I tried. But I wanted into your head too much.

It wasn't fair. I should have asked your permission.

I was a coward. I was weak. I have no excuse. I don't offer this as an excuse. Or even a fair exchange. I took your thoughts. I offer this freely. It's not equal or fair, but it's the best I can do.

I hope this explains things.

If you can't forgive me, I understand. If you're not willing to give me another chance, I understand. But I am going to ask you to try. Even though it's not fair. Even though I haven't earned your trust.

I'm not willing to let you go.

I care about you too much.

Love,

Ian

MY EYES FIX ON THE FOUR-LETTER WORD.

How he signs all his letters to friends?

Or just for me?

It must mean something. But I can't let myself believe it.

This already hurts too much.

If he loves me—

I can't deal with that possibility.

I read the card again and again. Until Ty taps on the table. Tells me we need to leave for the airport.

It stays in my head the entire ride. Does he love me? Can I forgive him? What the hell do the pages in the notebook say?

Chapter Fifty-Nine

EVE

irst class is no private plane, but it's still the second nicest flight I've ever experienced. I don a blindfold. Play The Ramones. Try to sleep.

It comes and goes.

Eventually, I give up. Request a tea. Eat the caprese sandwich Ty packed for me.

The lunch is good—fresh and simple—but the tea is terrible. Weak. Cold. Unable to comfort.

I read the note again and again.

Eventually, I peel open the first page.

Ian's writing. A loose cursive script. A date on the right corner.

Years ago.

The year he divorced.

This is a ridiculous exercise. Am I really paying someone to tell me to write my thoughts? I'm perfectly capable of doing it for free.

Living well is insufficient revenge. But it's a lot better than "self-reflection." Who's ever said "it's fine my wife fucked another man for the last six months. It's fine she groaned his name as she came.

Thought of him when I fucked her. Swallowed his cum. It's fine, because I've taken the time to sort out my feelings"?

Someone maybe.

Someone lying to themselves.

If only I'd learned that from her.

I guess that answers the *did Ian really keep a journal* question.

But the ones it raises...

I close the book. Slip it into my purse. Grab his marked copy of *The Handmaid's Tale* in exchange. I shouldn't appreciate it—he read it to get into my head—but I do.

Maybe some part of him had good intentions.

Maybe most of him.

But it hurts to consider that.

Chapter Sixty

EVE

There's a car waiting for me at JFK. A chauffeur with my name written on a piece of paper. I want to say *no, fuck you Ian, you don't get a say in how I arrive home, you don't get to pat yourself on the back.*

But I want to spend the next hour in a cab less.

So I greet the driver, let him open a limo door for me, close my eyes, try to fall asleep.

Instead, my head fills with images of our afternoon in a limo. His lips on my neck. His hands on my ass. My shorts around my knees.

Fuck.

I give up on picturing anything else. Until the car stops in front of my apartment and the driver opens the door for me.

Addie runs down the stairs. Throws her arms around me. "I'm sorry."

But I didn't tell her. I didn't say anything. Only that I'm arriving home soon. I guess that was enough. Or —"Did he?"

"His brother."

"Oh." I'm not sure if I'm relieved or disappointed. "I have to, uh… jet lag."

"Tea first?"

"Yeah. But inside."

She nods, grabs my suitcase, carries it upstairs, sits me at the table. "I got ice cream."

"Mint chip?"

"Of course. That first? Or tea first?"

"Ice cream."

"It's that bad?"

"Worse."

———

I TELL HER EVERYTHING. EVEN THE THINGS SHE DOESN'T know. The money. My website. The days left on the clock.

The way I felt whole when he held me.

The hurt in his eyes when I walked away.

And the words I'm desperate to consume.

I tell her everything. Then I climb into bed and I sleep.

A few hours here. A few entries there.

At some point, I shower, I eat, I change into clean pajamas. Then I climb back into bed and read more.

Pages and pages of raw pain. And not the pretty kind. Anger and violence that should scare me. That does scare me. But most of it isn't directed at his ex-wife.

It's at himself.

It's like I can see him self-destructing in real time. Blowing up his entire life. Burning down every bridge. So he has no choice but to move to New York.

It's as ugly as anything I've written.

Only for himself. And he's offering it to me.

Because he really wants me to know?

Or because it's the only play he can make?

My thoughts jumble. A mess of pain. An impossible lock. The only key in existence.

I finally sleep through the night.

Wake to an alert on my phone.

Six figures deposited in my account. It's early. He has a few more days. But this…

This is it. Our deal is over. I never have to see him again.

I drag myself out of bed. Shower. Dress in actual clothes. Fix chai and leftover jalfrezi.

Then I read through his journal again. Everything, from start to finish. A few days after his ex served him with divorce papers, his move to New York, failed attempts to distract himself with alcohol, work, sex.

I hate reading about him with someone else. I hate feeling his pain. But having access to it, to his ugliest thoughts, all these things he doesn't want anyone to know—

I want to read forever. If I had the chance… would I keep reading?

I fix more tea. Don a comfortable black dress. Pore over the pages until Addie interrupts me.

"Eve." Her voice is nervous. Uncertain. "You have company."

My heart leaps into my throat.

"Do you want me to tell him to leave?" she asks. "He did bring chai. He can leave the chai."

"I can," he says.

There's his voice. He's here. In my apartment. In my space, my world, my life.

I want it so badly. Too badly.

But he… I don't know. I don't know how to forgive him. If I already have. If I ever will.

I suck in a deep breath. Push out a heavy exhale.

Addie moves closer. Whispers through the door, "It's okay. If you want him to leave, I'll ask him to leave. I'll let go of my dreams of you marrying Prince Charming."

I just barely laugh. It feels so strange. Like shoes that don't quite fit.

"What do you think, Eve?" she asks. "Do you want him to go? Or do you want him to stay?"

Chapter Sixty-One

EVE

"**H**e can stay." My words are a whisper. As foreign as my laugh. As traitorous as the flutter in my stomach. I want him to stay. I want him to hold me. I want him to love me.

"Really?" There's surprise in her voice. Excitement too. "Are you sure?"

"Yeah."

"You want me to leave?"

"No. Not yet. Maybe…" If somehow everything works out. And I need his body over mine. No, I do need it.

Even though it's so fucking hot in here.

Even though he hurt me.

"Okay." She taps the door three times. Our secret knock. "I'll stay out here. Until you need me to go." She says it loudly. For both our benefits. Then a whisper for me. "Take your time."

Doing what?

All the makeup and hair dye in the world can't help me now. What's it matter if my dress is cute or my shoes are right?

I guess, if this is the end…

I need an easy getaway. I put on my boots. Pack my purse. Wallet, cell, ID, journal. His and mine. All his secret thoughts, next to mine. It means something. It has to.

Deep breath. Steady exhale.

I move into the main room.

He's standing in front of the door, hands in the pockets of his jeans, navy t-shirt falling over his shoulders.

Fuck, he looks just as good in casual attire. Still handsome, but less put-together. More vulnerable.

Like he really is showing me his scars.

I guess he is. He has. I just…

Can't think with him this close.

"You own jeans." My voice is strained. My throat is still raw. From crying. Screaming. Wanting to scream.

He nods *I do*. Stays exactly where he is. In front of the door. Waiting for permission to move closer.

"You look good in them." I pull my bedroom door closed. This is the first time he's really been in my space. It should feel like an intrusion, but it doesn't.

I want to pull him into my bedroom. Drag him to my tiny bed.

He's so tall. He won't even fit on it.

"Thank you." He stays in front of the door.

"It makes it hard to think. With you this close. With you so sexy." I remember our afternoon in the limo. His hands on my skin. My body buzzing with desires. "Can you try being less sexy?"

"I can try." He takes a half step toward me. Motions to the tea on the table. "Would you like it now?"

"You call that trying?"

"What would you like me to do?" He picks up the tea, offering it to me.

It's three steps to him. My fingers brush his as I take it. "I guess we should start with your face."

"My face?"

"It's far too handsome. Maybe if you wear some dorky glasses…"

"Do you have some?"

I shake my head. "It won't work anyway. You'll look all smart *and* sexy. I can't handle that."

He half-smiles. "Sunglasses?"

"Only if they look ridiculous. I have some star-shaped frames. With pink glitter. I can get them for you. But… you'll probably pull it off."

"There must be something."

"I think… The face is a lost cause. But this—" I draw a line in the air, around his torso. "Have you considered baggy clothes? Maybe a huge sweatshirt? Something to hide your physique?"

"It's the middle of summer."

"Sometimes you have to make sacrifices. For the people you love." The word falls off my lips. It's easier than it should be. Too easy. I want to hear it. Say it. Demand he say it.

"I do." His voice is quiet. "I do love you."

Fuck.

"It doesn't excuse anything. It might not change anything. I'm not sure that you want to hear it. But I do. I love you, Eve."

Addie's eyes go wide. For a second, she swoons. Then she remembers she's pissed. Folds her arms. Tries to look angry.

She looks to me. Mouths *should I go?*

I nod *okay*. I want her here. I want her to keep me safe. But I need to jump. Whatever that means.

She pulls me aside. Hugs me tightly. "I love you. Be careful, okay?"

"Okay."

She releases me. Shoots Ian the world's least intimidating stare. "Don't hurt her."

"I'll do my best," he says.

"I've seen your best. It's not good enough. Do better." She moves through the door. Slams it shut.

"That's the angriest I've ever seen her." I almost laugh. It does nothing to ease the tension in the air.

He loves me.

He. Loves. Me.

I…

He…

Fuck.

Ian takes a half-step toward me. "She wants to protect you."

"She let you in," I say.

"If you want me to go, I will."

I shake my head. Look for something to steady me. Find only the thermos in my hands. But it doesn't help. Even the familiar taste of Masala isn't enough. I drink half the mug. Set it on the counter. Rest my ass against the surface.

"The payment cleared?"

I nod.

"So I don't have to talk you into accepting it?"

"Why wouldn't I accept it?"

This time, his laugh is full. "Pragmatic."

"What? Am I supposed to reject four-hundred grand because I like you? Get real."

His laugh gets louder.

"Even if you hadn't hurt me… It's a lot of money. Money I need."

"I'm glad you have it."

"Is that all?"

His eyes meet mine. He doesn't say it again. He doesn't tell me the ball is in my court. After all, he just said he loves me and I…

My head swims.

"I'm sorry, Eve." His voice is soft. Honest. "I don't have anything better than I'm sorry. I have explanations. I have reasons. I can tell you all sorts of things, maybe things you've already read, about my fucked-up marriage. And how much it killed my ability to trust. How it filled me with this desperate need for honesty. But those are excuses."

"Okay."

He takes another step toward me. "I knew what I was doing. I was wrong. I'm sorry."

"Is that it?"

"Is what it, vixen?"

The pet name makes my knees weak. Fucking body. It's ready to relent. No, it's desperate to relent. Whatever gets his hands on my skin faster. "Is that why you kept reading it? Because you needed honesty?"

"I stopped after we met. No, after I realized I had asked for your trust. I knew I shouldn't cross that line. But eventually… I thought I was strong enough to resist the temptation to take your secrets. But I wasn't. I had to know everything in your head. I had to know you. Whatever it meant."

It almost sounds sweet like that.

"I should have told you."

I nod.

"I should have stopped."

I nod.

"I can't promise I'll do better next time. I can't promise I'll resist the urge to understand you. But I will try. I'll try to earn your trust every day." He takes another half-step toward me. "And I'll try to give as much as I take."

"What does that mean?"

"You offered me your heart. Your honesty. Not just on your site… Here. With me."

Yes. Without thinking. I just… had to.

"I want to do the same. I can't promise I'll do it well. I'm not good at this. I haven't tried for a long time. But—"

"You gave me your journal?"

"Yes," he says.

"Because you wanted me to know? Or because you didn't have any choice?"

"Both." His fingers skim my collarbone. "You read it?"

"Yes."

"And?"

"You were a mess."

He half-smiles. "It was ugly."

"Very ugly."

His hand curls around my neck. "I'm shaking. Can you feel it?"

"No."

"It terrifies me, showing you my past, being here, asking you to love me. I haven't done it in a long time. I never thought I'd do it again." His fingers curl into my skin. His eyes find mine. "But I am doing it. I am asking you to love me."

"Oh."

"I love you, Eve. I love you so much it scares me." His eyes stay on mine. "If that's not enough, if I've crossed a line that can't be crossed—"

I rise to my tiptoes and bring my lips to his.

He kisses me like the ship is going down.

"I can forgive you. Not all at once, not all the way. But

I can." My forehead finds his chin. "I want to. I love you too."

This time, he's the one that pulls me into a kiss.

It's deep and slow, like I'm the only thing in the world he wants.

Then it's faster. And harder. And I'm tugging at his t-shirt. Leading him into my bedroom.

Asking for all of him.

Offering him all of me.

Epilogue

EVE

Original Sin

It's been awhile. Maybe too long.

It didn't *really* occur to me that anyone could find my site. That it was easy. Trivial. Not until Mr. Tall, Dark, and Handsome told me.

No, there's no reason to use a pseudonym. Not anymore.

I didn't really consider how vulnerable I was. Not until Ian told me how he stumbled on this site. How he found my real name, my workplace, my address in a matter of minutes.

Of course Ian isn't your average reader. He's an actual, factual former spy. Digging dirt is his specialty.

Mine is laying my heart bare.

That's what I wanted to believe. For a long time.

It's true. I'm good at sitting at my computer, spilling my thoughts, sweeping them into something beautiful.

I'm good at vulnerability. When I'm anonymous and in control.

When the incredibly handsome, impossibly wounded man I love is looking at me like I have his heart in my hands—

It's a lot harder. Doing this with another human being. Learning to show him my scars. To trust he'll accept them. To trust he won't try to claim them. Or make them his.

To trust he'll bare himself to me.

I still spin my thoughts into words. But, now, I do it with a pen and paper. In a place that really is mine and mine alone.

The rest—

I save most of them for him.

My raw honesty, my scars, my wounds, my bruises. I've shown him all I can. And he's shown me his too.

It was slow at first. Painful.

His journal. All those pages of hurt, anger, self-destruction. A snapshot of a place and time. A place where his entire life exploded, rearranged, refused to come together.

He shared his past with me.

The journal at first. Then his words. The hurt in his eyes. The tension of his chest.

The softness that came after.

So many nights in his bed, his body curled around mine, his voice in my ears, his deepest thoughts filling the room.

And mornings, on the couch, my hands around a mug of chai, my eyes on the clean hardwood floor, my secrets filling the space.

We spent the entire summer tangled in each other.

Okay, it wasn't exactly a festival of secrets. There were lots of secrets, sure. And lots of long walks, breakfasts, tea breaks, lunches at the park, afternoons reading together, dinners, evenings in his bed.

Or on the couch.

Against the kitchen counter.

In my bed.

In the back of a limo.

On his desk. In his office. The one at home.

The one at work.

Every surface in our hotel room in Hawaii. And a quiet beach where we absolutely, positively should have been caught.

The coat check at his favorite restaurant.

The balcony at my favorite rooftop bar...

An entire summer filled with every kind of intimacy that exists.

Matching tattoos. Like he teased.

An ornate key on my forearm.

A locked heart on his chest. Right below the Latin quote that defines him. *Truth is my light.*

That obsessive need for honesty.

Well, I hope he's as ready as he thinks he is.

I keep burying the lead. It's a bad habit, I know, but there's so much I want to say. I can fill pages with my feelings about Ian.

His beautiful eyes, his charming smile, his sweet laugh.

And that low, deep groan—

He's too sexy for words. Which is a real problem for me. Now that I'm turning him into words.

It's not just that I *can* fill pages with my feelings about Ian. I *am* filling pages with my feelings for Ian.

It started as a project for my creative nonfiction class. (It's supposed to be a senior class, but I begged the professor until she felt enough pity she let me in. Or maybe it was my amazing talent. Either way, I aced the class).

It was supposed to be a simple, one-semester project. A collection of entries. Memories to fill in the gaps.

Every detail—the ones I share and the ones I hold close.

The ones that are mine and the ones that are his.

I spent my Fall semester working on the project. *Original Sin.* Of course.

At Hunter. It has the second-best literature program in the city, despite what some snobbish sisters think. (We can't all get into Columbia).

And it's close. To our place in Brooklyn. To his penthouse in the Financial District.

Only, it's not our place anymore. Addie rented out the spare room for a while. Then invited her girlfriend to move in with her.

This isn't his place anymore.

In October, I moved in with Ian. I took his beautiful, clean, sparse apartment and made a mess of it. I made a home of it.

His sheets are still the perfect shade of white. His comforter is still a deep black.

But the rest—

It's bursting with love, affection, tenderness. Framed posters of the films we've seen together, an extra bookshelf filled with first editions, all *The Handmaid's Tale* paraphernalia in existence.

Little touches of color. Purple, pink, teal, turquoise.

Like my hair. It's still blue-green. I can't bring myself to change it. Not when I see the girl he fell in love with every time I look in the mirror.

(And, okay, yes, not when I see him fucking me senseless every time I look in the mirror).

I turned his house into a home.

He loves it. And hates it. The way I never make the

bed, the way I leave dishes in the sink, the cinnamon that collects on his table.

The man is a neat freak. I don't care what he says. He makes the bed EVERY SINGLE DAY.

Even the days when he leaves before me. When he climbs into the soft sheets to kiss me goodbye and whisper *I love you*.

He lets me sleep in, yes. But he makes the bed the second he arrives home. Even if it's midnight. Even if we're about to go to bed.

Okay, not when we're about to go to *bed*. Then, well… he has other uses for the sheets.

Some days, I wake before him. I lie there, on my side, watching his chest rise and fall with his breath.

Watching the light fall over his skin.

Watching him exist in the same space I do.

It's so lucky that the universe exists. That, somehow, the two of us are alive at the same time, in the same city, with the same raw, fractured hearts.

It's so lucky I needed him when I did. That he was there to catch me when I fell. That he was willing to jump with me.

Some days, I wake before him. I lay there, watching him sleep, counting my blessing.

Some days, I wake before him. I lift his arm, settle against his chest, soak up the warmth of his skin.

Mine.

It's the biggest thought in my head. And it dances there again and again.

Mine, mine, mine.

I guess, I'm still burying the lead. This isn't for my site anymore. It's not even for a school project.

This is for me. For him. Everyone else, I'm not sure. But I know I needed to write this. To write our story.

This note is supposed to go at the end of the book. Or maybe the beginning. Somewhere to explain exactly how I feel about him. Exactly what he meant to me.

Exactly what happened to the two of us.

The truth is, I can't explain it. Not exactly. I have metaphors and similes and analogies, but none of them do him justice.

I love him so much it hurts.

And he loves me even more. It's in his dark eyes every time he looks at me. In his soft lips every time he smiles. In his steady voice every time he says my name.

He. Loves. Me.

It's as exciting as it was the first time he said those three words. I still feel warm, safe, alive.

And I love him.

I love him so fucking much.

How else do I explain it?

He offered me his heart, and I took it.

I offered him my heart, and he took it.

And kept it safe.

For two years, I've lived here, with him, in our apartment.

I've joined him on his quarterly business trips to London. And others to Madrid, Tokyo, Rome, Paris, Los Angeles.

He's shown me the world in so many ways.

Sometimes, he goes alone. I have school. I have friends. I have a sister a subway ride away.

I miss him so badly. When he's away. Even if it's only a few days.

And he misses me too. He worries. His head—there's this voice that always wants to whisper *what is she doing, where is she going, can you trust her alone?*

He's never going to get past it, not completely. I understand that. I respect it. Even when it frustrates me.

He only promised that he'd try.

And he does. Every day. So when he calls at three a.m. just to say hello, with that harried tone—the one that means *I know it's ridiculous, but I kept picturing you with that guy in your British Literature class*—I stop, listen, reassure him.

His voice steadies. He asks about my day. Asks me to keep the phone on speaker until I fall asleep.

Well, when it's so late I can't think. Other times, when I have the energy, he orders me to take off my knickers and come for his listening pleasure.

And, well…

I'm not a fool. My sexy as sin boyfriend wants to listen to me touch myself. I'm not saying no to that.

Other times, I'm the one calling at three a.m. Or waking him up in the middle of the night. Worried he's keeping something from me. Worried he's pulling away. Worried he's going to run into his ex-wife in London and freak the fuck out.

It's just as ridiculous. London is enormous, and besides, he doesn't love her anymore. He doesn't hate her anymore. They're not friends. They're just not… the fucked-up mess they used to be.

Ty is in touch with her. More or less. He passes along well wishes. And that's really all anyone wants.

Even though it's absurd, I'm worried and jealous and scared, Ian talks to me, and reassures me, and promises to split me in half.

And, okay, usually those phone calls end the same way as the others.

I'm still completely insatiable.

I'm still completely over the moon.

For two years, my life has been full of love, school, friendship, art, writing, reading, reflection.

For two years, I've been happy. Ian has made me happy. It's not always easy. Some days, it's really fucking hard. Some days, he shuts down, locks me out, demands more than I'm willing to give.

Some days, I get scared or hurt or angry. I run away. Close myself off. Push him away.

But we get through it. Bit by bit. Together.

And now…

Two more years of school. Then we talk about the rest. I never thought he'd want to marry again, but he gets this look in his eyes every time we pass a jewelry shop.

He teases me about how I'd never want a diamond, but a couture dress that shows off my perfect ass…

He gets this look… like he knows I'm picturing this big, beautiful future we're going to have together. Like he wants to make it official, that he's mine forever, and I'm his forever.

One day. Soon. After I finish school.

Two years to go.

Then…

An entire life.

I don't know what I'm doing with it. I don't even know what I'm doing with this book. Am I ready for the entire world to see into my soul?

To see into his?

Am I ready to show Ian all these scars he doesn't notice?

Yes.

There, I know. I'm ready to drop one more wall. To let him a little bit closer.

I don't know what the future holds. I don't know where

I'll be or what I'll do. Only that I'll be beside him the entire time.

And he'll be beside me.

Mine.

Forever.

––––––

Want More?

Sign up for <u>my mailing list for an exclusive Dirty Desires bonus scene</u>. What are Ian and Eve up to a few years after the end of Dirty Desires? Find out!

Ty's book is coming soon. In the meantime, get to know Shepard and Jasmine with <u>*Dirty Husband,*</u> an arranged marriage romance inspired by *Beauty and the Beast*. Turn the page for a sample.

Already read Dirty Husband? Check out <u>*Dirty Deal,*</u> a steamy Cinderella story with a demanding hero and an inexperienced yet strong heroine.

All caught up on Dirty Rich and still need your older man/ forbidden virgin fix? Check out <u>*Tempting*</u>. Brooding tattoo artist Brendon is obsessed with his little sister's best friend. He wants to have the bookish virgin every way he can—especially tied to his bed.

Dirty Husband - Special Preview

JASMINE

Get *Dirty Husband* Now

I *shouldn't be here.*

This chapter of my life is over. Done. No matter what he thinks.

Sure, we've only spoken ten words in the last five years, but I still know how Shepard Marlowe operates.

It emanates through the building. Bounces off the shiny silver sign. The clean grey carpet. The glass walls.

The one thing that inspires him: money.

The receptionist taps her headset, putting her conversation on hold. "Right this way, Ms. Lee."

She stands and leads me through a busy hallway. Straight to the corner office.

"Can I get you anything?" She rattles off a list of espresso drinks.

I nod a yes to something. I don't need the caffeine—I'm already shaking—and I'd prefer tea. But I do need something to occupy my hands.

Something to keep me from touching him.

It's been so long since I've seen him in person. Longer since I've heard his voice, smelled his soap, felt the softness of his lips.

But then there isn't a softness to his lips. Not anymore.

I sit in the expensive leather chair. Cross my legs. Smooth my skirt.

It's wrong. Too tight. Too normal. Too unsophisticated.

Most days my business attire—button-up shirt, pencil skirt, practical pumps—feels like a shield.

Today, knowing he's on his way?

My heart thuds against my chest.

My head screams *leave now, before it's too late*.

But my body?

It shares none of my caution.

I cross my legs the other way. Uncross them. Try to shift my thoughts to practical places.

It doesn't work. My head fills with memories.

His lips on my neck. His hands on my waist. His voice in my ears.

You feel so good.

The opening door draws my attention.

I turn, expecting the assistant or a lawyer.

But it's him.

"Jasmine." His voice is as cold as his clear blue eyes. He looks down at me with vague familiarity. Like I'm a colleague he hasn't seen in a few years. A colleague who irritates him. "I'm glad you made it."

I bite my tongue so I won't snap.

He moves into the room, but he doesn't take a seat. He stands next to the big leather chair beside mine. "I wasn't sure you'd come."

His eyes meet mine. It's a different stare than the one

he had when we were kids. That boy was sweet, loving, soft.

This man—

He's cold, angry, hurt.

God, his eyes are still so blue. So beautiful. But that coldness—

It makes my heart ache.

I try to hold his gaze. Try to think up something to say. Some small talk to convince him I'm ready for this. Whatever it is.

Nothing comes.

His gaze is too intense. I have to look away. To the clean carpet. The supple fabric of the chair. The shiny patent of his shoes.

Eventually, the door opens. The assistant—she has a name, but I can barely remember mine at the moment—steps inside. Holds up two tiny espresso cups.

"Ms. Blackstone will be here shortly." She sets both cups on the expensive oak desk. Nods *enjoy*. Disappears.

She's everywhere and nowhere at the same time. Never imposing, always friendly, always smiling. Skills I recognize. Skills I mastered a long time ago.

Skills I need right now.

I take a small sip. Bright espresso. Creamy milk. A hint of softness. But not enough to dull the bitterness.

Shepard looks down at me, the tiniest hint of curiosity in his eyes.

He wants something.

I shouldn't be here. It echoes through my head again, but it's too late. My body is already buzzing. It's already screaming for him, remembering every kiss, every touch, every fuck.

I uncross and recross my legs. It does nothing to ease the ache below my belly button, but it does draw his gaze.

449

His eyes flit to my tan skin.

He swallows hard. Steels himself.

"I'm on my lunch." I'm not sure what he wants. Only that he's confident he'll get it. Which is ridiculous. He's the one who hurt me. Why does he think I want anything to do with him? "I don't have a lot of time."

I know why. It's money. It's always money.

All the men I work with think the world revolves around them. Because it does.

Shep's family was well-off when we were kids. But now?

Now he owns half of Manhattan.

He can destroy me with the snap of his fingers.

Of course, I'm here.

Shepard takes a seat across from me. He folds one leg over the other, making a four with his limbs. Then he leans just a little closer. Just close enough I smell his soap.

Rich. Earthy. Money.

He's every part the distinguished professional. Navy suit, turquoise tie, brown dress shoes.

But there's a tiny hint of the boy I loved in his clear blue eyes.

"I have a proposition for you." His voice stays even.

I pretend as if I'm more interested in my drink. "Yes?"

His voice just barely softens. "I need a wife."

"A wife?" My heart thuds against my chest, drowning every thought in my brain. "You need a wife?" I repeat the words. They make even less sense this time.

He's twenty-five. He owns the hottest tech company on the market. He screams of power, money, control.

Filthy rich and incredibly handsome.

The body of an Olympic swimmer. The face of Prince Charming. There are ugly parts to Shepard, yes, but those scars are hidden beneath the surface.

They're—

"I need you, Jasmine," he says. "I need you to be my wife."

Get *Dirty Husband* Now

Author's Note

Most of my readers know me as "the queen of broken bad boys." I wear the crown proudly). Bad boys are where I feel at home. Not so much because of their dirty-mouths or devil-may-care attitude or even their tattooed arms. Because they're outsiders. Because they reject normal social conventions.

When I returned to the Dirty series (after a four year hiatus) to write *Dirty Husband*, I did it because I *had* to tell Shepard and Jasmine's story. When I met Ian in *Dirty Husband*, I felt the same way. I needed to get in his head! Only, Ian didn't want to let me into his head. He acted all cool and aloof, but he was guarded as hell. That was my way into the story. I knew exactly what Ian needed and exactly what would tempt him: an idea I'd been considering for a long time.

When I was in high school and college, I kept an online diary. It was the thing to do at the time. Xanga, Diaryland, Diary-X, Live Journal--they were huge and I had sites on all of them. I suppose you could say it was the original blogging, though my thoughts were much messier. They were for my sake. So I could sort through things. So I could strip out of my defenses and show off my naked pain and find someone who would call it beautiful.

When I thought about Ian--about his trust issues, his desire to completely understand someone while staying in control--I knew he was the perfect fit. And, as I started writing, I thought... well, I used to be in Eve's place, why couldn't Eve be someone like me?

Not me--it's hard to write characters who are too much like you, there's no perspective--but someone who identified with my values. Who fit into the roles I wear.

An outsider. A woman who doesn't buy into social conventions. Who dyes her hair unusual colors even when it's not *the* thing to do. Who wears whatever the fuck she likes. Who reads and criticizes unapologetically. Who sees media as something to understand and dissect. Who has no time for men who fail to respect her intellect.

The billionaire books I'd read--and the ones I'd written too--featured a variety of heroines. But never girls with purple hair and combat boots and an unapologetic love of feminist literature *and* thinkpieces about said literature. Never outsiders who rejected status symbols, who saw through commercialism, who didn't want marriage or kids or a white picket fence. Never women like me.

I didn't see myself in those books. I didn't consider someone like me fitting into one of those books. But why not? If alternative girls can fall for tattoo artists and rock stars, why not handsome business men?

With this book, I wanted to bring a little Crystal Kaswell energy into the billionaire space. Readers know me for my bad boys. They talk about my tattoo artists. They talk about my rock stars. They do not talk about my business men. Blake and Nick don't get a lot of attention. It's frustrating sometimes--like when I was trying to promote *Dirty Husband* and *Dirty Desires*--but I understand. *Dirty Deal* and *Dirty Boss* have a different energy than my other books. I love them for what they are, but they aren't as "Crystal Kaswell."

Dirty Desires is my attempt to change that. To write a billionaire book that's me that still appeals to readers of the niche. Hopefully, I achieved that. Hopefully, you're dying for Ty's story and reading my entire catalog in the meantime.

If not, that's okay too. I am an outsider, after all. I want to make you feel something. Whether or not you like it-- that's a secondary concern.

I don't hope you liked *Dirty Desires*. I hope you loved it, obsessed over it, need all of it, all the time.

If not, that's okay too. There are lots of books and authors out there. I can only be me. And you can only be you. Let's be the best versions of ourselves we can.

Love,

Crystal

Acknowledgements

My first thanks goes to my husband, for his support when I'm lost in bookland and for generally being the sun in my sky. Sweetheart, you're better than all the broken bad boys in the world.

The second goes to my father, for insisting I go to the best film school in the country, everything else be damned. I wouldn't love movies, writing, or storytelling half as much if not for all our afternoon trips to the bookstore and weekends at the movies. You've always been supportive of my goals, and that means the world to me.

Thanks so much to my amazing audio narrators, Shane East and Vanessa Edwin. You've done a wonderful job bringing my characters to life.

A big shout out to all my beta readers. And also to my ARC readers for helping spread the word to everyone else in the world.

To all my writer friends who talk me down from the ledge, hold my hand, and tell me when my ideas are terrible and when they're brilliant, thank you.

Acknowledgements

Thanks so much to my editor Marla, my assistant Gemma, and my cover designer Hang Le.

As always, my biggest thanks goes to my readers. Thank you for picking up *Dirty Desires*. Check out Shep in *Dirty Husband*, Nick in *Dirty Boss*, and Blake in *Dirty Deal* to keep your steamy billionaire fix going.

Stay In Touch

Sign up for <u>my mailing list</u>. (You'll get first notice on cover reveals, teasers, and new releases, and a bunch of awesome bonus content like the extended epilogue to *Dirty Desires)*.

You can also <u>like my page on Facebook</u>, <u>join my fangroup</u>, <u>follow me on Instagram</u>, <u>follow me on Twitter</u>, or <u>friend me on Facebook</u>.

Also by Crystal Kaswell

Hooking Up - Walker

Pretend You're Mine - Ryan

Hating You, Loving You - Dean

Breaking the Rules - Hunter

Losing It - Wes

Accidental Husband - Griffin

The Baby Bargain - Chase

Inked Love

The Best Friend Bargain - Forest

The First Taste - Holden - coming 2020

Standalones

Broken - Trent & Delilah

Come Undone Trilogy

Come Undone

Come Apart

Come To Me

Sign up for the Crystal Kaswell mailing list

Made in the USA
Las Vegas, NV
07 September 2022

54883695R00273